9|0

ANTONIA LIVELY BREAKS THE SILENCE

Antonia Lively

Breaks the Silence

—————

A NOVEL

DAVID SAMUEL LEVINSON

ALGONQUIN BOOKS OF CHAPEL HILL   2013

Published by
Algonquin Books of Chapel Hill
Post Office Box 2225
Chapel Hill, North Carolina 27515-2225

a division of
Workman Publishing
225 Varick Street
New York, New York 10014

This is a work of fiction. While, as in all fiction, the literary perceptions and insights are based on experience, all names, characters, places, and incidents either are products of the author's imagination or are used fictitiously.

LIBRARY OF CONGRESS CATALOGING-IN-PUBLICATION DATA
Levinson, David.
Antonia Lively breaks the silence :
a novel / by David Samuel Levinson — First edition.
page cm
ISBN 978-1-56512-918-4
1. Widows — Fiction.   2. Women authors — Fiction.
3. Triangles (Interpersonal relations) — Fiction.   4. Upstate New
York (N.Y.) — Fiction.   I. Title.
PS3612.E9285 2013
813'.6 — dc23   2013001893

10 9 8 7 6 5 4 3 2 1
First Edition

To my family,
especially to my grandparents,
Stephen and Mimi Fürth—
Ich vermisse euch.

Innocence always calls mutely for protection, when we would be so much wiser to guard ourselves against it; innocence is like a dumb leper who has lost his bell, wandering the world, meaning no harm.
—*The Quiet American,* Graham Greene

To publish, and not only to publish, but to succeed, to excel, without shaking the right hands or attending the right parties, to publish without osculating the right derrieres, or browning one's nose—here is how a writer ought to go about his business, if his business is writing and not arriving.
—*Words Travel Fast,* Henry Swallow

In Medias Res

———

We thought ourselves good people who lived good lives. Some of us had lived in the town for generations and had never considered leaving. Many of us, though, had relocated there from the city, in the process learning what it was like to desert the place we loved, longed for, and hated. Winslow wasn't a big town and couldn't offer the charms of Manhattan, nothing as remarkable as the rooftops at twilight or Central Park in the rain. While many of us had grown sick of the city's neon signs and glass towers, many others of us put up photos to remind ourselves daily of what we missed.

No one came to Winslow looking for variety: we had one museum, the Finch; a community theater, the Vortex; and only a handful of restaurants, outstanding though they were. Two blocks long, Broad Street consisted of Page Turners, the local bookstore; Mayfair Cinema; Custard's Last Stand; a barbershop; a launderette; and Einstein's Video & Arcade. Not far from there — nothing was that far — was Breedlove Hardware; College Breads; Maddox Cafe; and Tint, the bar and restaurant connected to the historic Tweed & Twining Arms hotel. Then there was the heart of the town, Winslow College, giving reason to the place, the lure that had drawn many of us there, to teach and to study.

Some who came were either running from combative or cheating spouses, while others were just running. Some ended up staying; others gave it six months or less before the moving trucks arrived and took them away. We saw the trucks and shook our heads. "You haven't given it enough time," we said. "One more day!" One more day, though, might become one more year, and those who fled already had grown tired of the things they'd initially come for, the quiet, the cordial hellos in the morning and the good-evenings at night. Those who didn't last wanted what we didn't have and could never offer — invisibility.

I knew this only because, once, I had been one of them. I, too, had come there from the city but not to escape the barrage of sirens and chattering crowds — things I'd cherished, at least in memory. I came to Winslow out of love; I followed my heart.

That was years ago now. For the first year, I hated our house and the town and my heart for luring me there. Yes, my life in the city might have been stressful and chaotic, but it had also been blessed. There was spontaneity, and there were friends and dancing and cocktail parties. I liked parties back then, when I was younger. It was an exciting time. I thought about myself as a writer, filled with promise. Promise, though, has a way of never happening, and much of what followed was painful, though not nearly as painful as this story I'm about to tell.

"The action of any good story," Wyatt used to say, "always begins in the middle."

This story, my story, however, began long before the events in Winslow, before I met Antonia Lively. It began long before Henry Swallow moved to town. Although it's my story, it began in 1968, set in motion by two brothers in a cabin in the woods. I didn't know any of this until later, though. I didn't know any of this until I'd read Antonia's novel and gradually wove each individual story together — the brothers Linwood and Royal's, Henry's, Antonia's, Wyatt's, Catherine's, mine — into this one, ours.

Wyatt also used to say there weren't any fixed rules in writing. I know now, though, that you have to learn the rules first before you can break them. Learn about voice, plot, and point of view. Learn about imagery, setting, and character. Learn all of these things — then let the story dictate how it wants to be told, and never get in the way, because it's not about you, the writer. It's about the relationship between the story and the reader. Give the reader a good story, and he'll forgive just about everything else.

I spent years reading through Henry's criticism and Wyatt's lectures, absorbing and learning these rules of theirs. This story is the result. If I am a writer, it is because I had no other choice. If I tell this story well, if it rings true, it's because all of our voices that summer and, over time, became one. The reader, though, will be the judge. For now, this story's as close to the truth as I can get, and that, I'm afraid, will simply have to do.

PART ONE

The King and Queen of Letters

Red Wine, Black Coffee

The best place to begin is right in the middle, on that hot June afternoon, as Catherine struggled through her yard. In one hand, she lugged a bag of groceries; in the other, a heavy bag of books. Exhausted and grumpy from another long shift at the bookstore, on her feet all day, she couldn't wait to set the bags down; the runny French cheese and her favorite wine were calling her name as usual. More than this, she couldn't wait to get out of her heels, put on her bathing suit, and swim some laps in the pool. The sun blazed through the trees, the air as miasmic as ever. Another summer in Winslow, she thought glumly. Blow, winds, blow. But there weren't any winds, only the monstrous heat and an absolute stagnation, as if the entire world had stopped turning. Everything sparkled with dust and crackled in earnest. Every step she took through the brittle grass reminded her of how long they'd gone without rain. Revelation is at hand, people said, though Catherine didn't believe in omens or doomsayers, even less in the meteorologists, whose predictions for a break in the weather had dried up along with the town's hope. They were living through the longest, most abject heat wave on record.

As sweat dripped down her arms, the house shimmered before her, and for a moment Wyatt was back at the door, already hurrying to help with the bags. There was Wyatt, her husband, her love, rising out of the dust and heat. She'd heard that it was possible for the heat to play such nasty tricks on people, and when she realized that she'd called out his name, she cursed herself. Deflating, she became who she was again — Catherine Strayed, his thirty-nine-year-old widow. Again, she felt Wyatt's absence acutely, as sure as the weight of the bags in her hands. Books, cheese, wine — the precious cargo that carried her through.

Inside the sanctuary of the shuttered house, the idea of fall settled around her. Fall, months away — when the quality of light shifted from an incessant, blaring yellow to a muted, lustrous gold, when the students returned and with them a kind of liveliness, an energizing optimism that floated in the cooler air, when life resumed, and with it came the possibility of love — fresh, unmarried faculty faces, divorcés, widowers. It was like this every fall; she took another deep gulping breath, inhaling hope. While most people she knew looked forward to spring, Catherine looked forward to fall, the drops in temperature, the change in the light and leaves.

In the house, she set the bag of books down, collected the flurry of mail scattered across the hardwood floor, then slid out of her heels and damp sundress, comfortably naked except for her bra and underwear. A narrow hallway connected the sitting room with the kitchen, and she hurried through it, cradling the groceries in her arms, the mail pressed under her arm. In the kitchen, she placed the mail on the table, the wine in the cupboard, then removed the cheese and opened the refrigerator, leaning into the cold. She shut her pale green eyes, and let the frosted air creep over her, the sweat drying gradually. She was happy to be home.

On the counter at her back, the answering machine flashed red, noting a single message. She was in no rush to check the machine, knowing the caller was Jane. Jane, one of her best friends. Jane, who felt compelled to remind her of tonight's dinner at Maddox Cafe, even though they'd been meeting there every Wednesday night for years. Catherine knew these calls were well intentioned, yet she resented them anyway, as she had the calls and visits those first few weeks after Wyatt's death, when Jane showed up at the house unannounced. Then, she'd brought food, movies, playing cards, and more concern than Catherine knew what to do with. Sweet, yes, but wholly unnecessary. You can't be alone, Jane had said. Can't, or won't, be? Catherine had asked. She never turned Jane away, because they were friends and because she understood her welfare was more important to Jane than it was to herself.

A year and a half ago, that's when it happened. She'd been standing in almost the same spot, gazing disappointedly into the empty refrigerator, wondering where Wyatt was — he'd been gone all day — and why he hadn't bothered to buy the groceries. After all, it was his turn, she'd thought. She'd seen him drive off that morning, the sky leaden and threatening snow. The snow had come — that time, just as they'd predicted — and it was snowing still as she slammed the refrigerator shut, going for her boots, parka, and purse in the other room. She was putting on the boots, when there were heavy footfalls on the porch, and the irritation she had felt evaporated. She went to the door, expecting Wyatt, his arms loaded down with everything on the list she'd made — milk, cheese, wine, fish, tampons, toilet paper — these things they'd needed.

It wasn't Wyatt but an officer of the law, and Catherine suddenly understood, without having to be told, that moments like these — a missing husband, a blizzard, a policeman — were sometimes as unavoidable and unaccountable as love itself.

Since then, there'd been winter in its dread and dreariness, and the spring had passed and the summer and the fall, followed by another winter, another spring; and here it was summer again, all spent without him.

Now Catherine sipped a glass of wine and nibbled at a plate of cheese and crackers while she riffled through the mail. There were the usual bills, and the odd letter to Wyatt, the occasional piece of fan mail. It still surprised and, yes, infuriated her, that he continued to get these letters, because it seemed to her a real fan would have kept better track of him, would have heard about his death. The letters were always sweet, and said the same things, the writers mostly young women, who praised Wyatt's novel, even as they went on to ask the inevitable — Are you single? Had he been there, he and Catherine would have had a great laugh. He wasn't there, though, and God, how she missed him.

With a steak knife, Catherine sliced open the bills and set them aside before picking up the powder pink envelope. She turned it over in her fingers, noting the return address in Des Moines, Iowa. She pictured the lonely young woman holding Wyatt's novel, her excitement as she flipped the pages, never wanting to put it down. It was that kind of book, a page-turner, something to fall in love with, and it cheered her to know Wyatt had found his way to this stranger. Wasn't that the true test of success? For most people maybe, but not for Wyatt, who couldn't help comparing the minor strides he'd made with the larger and, as he often declared, less-deserving strides of others. The disparity tormented him.

And it also tormented me, she thought, just as the silence was broken, and she heard a series of insistent knocks accompanied by a loud hello. It was the kind of thing that happened on occasion: the random Jehovah's Witness, a Girl Scout in pigtails, friends showing up to check on her. At one time, there'd also been a troop of reporters from as far away as Buffalo, all of them trying to piece out the story of Wyatt's death. She didn't speak to any of them. Yet even as she slammed the door in their faces, she'd wanted to say, "You vultures. Where were you when he was alive?"

Catherine sat still, hoping the woman at the door would take the hint and go away. Instead, she knocked again, louder, harder, her hellos echoing through the house again, filling the silent rooms. Still, Catherine did not move, did not breathe, clutching the letter in one hand, the wineglass in the other. Go away, she thought. Please just go away.

Yes, there'd been reporters at one time, and photographers, even a news van stationed in front of the house. There'd been the click of cameras when she left for work in the morning and again when she returned at night. What right did they have to intrude? For what — to pry the details of Wyatt's last days out of her? For weeks they came, until the story, like any other, finally faded, and the journalists, reporters, and news teams turned to fresher, more grisly tales. Even after they'd forgotten the story, however, their awful, ugly rumors and insinuations lingered, for a time making even leaving the house to go to work unbearable.

As the intruder called out another hello, Catherine concentrated on the letter, the perfumed pink paper and the slanted blue words, the curlicues, the misspellings, all of it blurring the longer she focused, the longer she held her breath. What did this stranger want? What had any of them wanted but the story of their lives, Catherine's life with Wyatt, and then the story of a life that continued without him?

Go away, she thought again, but then realized this time she'd said it out loud — shouted it — and she dropped the letter and took a gulp of wine. The knocking stopped, and then the afternoon again fell into silence, as it had the afternoon a year and a half ago when she'd opened the door and the world changed. Today Catherine didn't have time for an unexpected visitor, whoever she might be; she had the girls in less than an hour.

Since the woman had obviously heard her, and she herself couldn't stomach rudeness of any kind, Catherine rose grudgingly and passed through the late afternoon sunlight that flooded the room, highlighting the streaks and scuffs Wyatt's life and hers had left over the years. He was there, in the finely knifed crosshatches on the counter, the concentrically ringed stains on the blond-wood kitchen table, the fanned, spidery cracks in the kitchen window he'd slammed shut the day before he disappeared. He wasn't just there, of course: he was everywhere. As she made her way to the door, through the dim, hushed hallway that led to the sitting room, still full of what they used to joke was their starter furniture, she smelled the cigarette smoke in the air and all at once felt more alone than she had in months.

She'd been a heavy smoker from junior high well into graduate school. It was how she'd crammed for midterms and handled twenty-page essays, and it was how she'd met Wyatt that wintry day in Penn Station back in 1981, when you could still smoke everywhere. If she'd been paying more attention, they might never have met, but she hadn't been paying attention: while rummaging through her purse, she'd brushed Wyatt's sleeve with the tip of her cigarette. She apologized and wiped away the smudge with her finger. "Attractive women shouldn't smoke," he'd said, waving away a gray plume. Am I attractive? she'd wanted to ask.

Both her mother and father had been career smokers, and if it hadn't been for Wyatt, who refused to see her if she didn't quit, she suspected she would have been a career smoker, too, until her death.

Now, as she went into her bedroom and slid into a sundress, then made her way to the front door, which was open as usual on these hot summer days, she wanted nothing more than to finish her glass of wine and take a drag on a cigarette, specifically the cigarette that hung casually from the glossy lips of the girl who was peering through the screen door. Though Catherine recognized her instantly, she'd never met Antonia Lively — this young woman who'd written the celebrated short story, "Vitreous China," this young woman whose much trumpeted debut novel was coming out in early July.

For the last couple of weeks, Catherine had caught glimpses of her about town, sometimes on a bench in the park, her head in a book, sometimes just idling outside one of the shops on Broad Street. She came into Page Turners once, last week, rummaged the used-book bin, picked up a frayed copy of Wyatt's novel, *The Last Cigarette,* read the first page, replaced it, and left the store without a word. Whenever Catherine saw her, wherever she saw her, Antonia was usually dressed in loose-fitting halter tops and thigh-high shorts, and was never without a cigarette, somehow pulling it all off gracefully, as only the young can.

That liquid-hot afternoon, Antonia was less made up than she'd been in the photograph accompanying the brief interview in last month's *Modern Scrivener,* but traces of that girl were still apparent in the pink-smudged cheekbones and metallic green eye shadow. She was tall, thin-limbed and seemed so young that, for a moment, Catherine was taken back to her own youth, when she, too, had had the courage to go around in skimpy shorts and tight blouses. There was something else, though, something garish, even sad about Antonia's getup — it was too self-conscious. She was trying too hard to be provocative and alluring, which merely called attention to one simple fact: she wasn't beautiful. No, she wasn't beautiful; striking, maybe even exotic, but not beautiful. The cigarette only made her less so.

Had Catherine known her, she might have scolded her, saying, "Cigarettes kill, or haven't you heard?" It had always been her experience that girls like this, who thought smoking made them seem more mysterious and adult, would go on smoking because that's what they did whether you worried about them or not. For a moment, it looked as if Antonia were about to fling her cigarette to the curb (a natural inclination in the city, a revolting one in Winslow), but then she thought better of it and asked Catherine if she had an ashtray. She pointed to a barren terra-cotta flowerpot, which, until recently, had housed a pink begonia, another casualty to the summer's abominable heat. Antonia took one final drag, then planted the cigarette in the loose, dry earth.

Although the habit was disgusting, smoking seemed to suit her, Catherine thought, and was a part of an idea she had of herself— the lonely writer in the lonely world. Catherine couldn't help but notice, however, the awkward way she'd held the cigarette, as if she couldn't quite understand how it had gotten in her fingers. This should not have surprised her, since the girl's entire manner was awkward.

"I've seen you before. You work in the bookstore, right?" she asked. Nodding, Catherine introduced herself. "I'm Antonia," the girl said in response. She smiled, her lips pulled tight over her small, gray teeth. Catherine let her into the house without another word but felt as if it were Antonia inviting her inside and not the other way around. Antonia apologized for disturbing her and took great care to compliment the house, a polite yet needless gesture, Catherine thought, knowing the house's shortcomings. Once inside, Antonia removed her sandals, a winning gesture that left Catherine wondering how the girl knew she didn't allow shoes in the house. (This, too, went back to Wyatt and his need for absolute silence whenever he was working. Although she hated the sight of her big feet, Catherine had gone barefoot in the house anyway, just something else she did out of love and respect for him.) "I'd like to see the whole place, if that's all right," Antonia said.

"The whole place?" she asked, having no idea what she was talking about, or why she was there.

The girl's blue eyes swept the room back and forth and fell on Catherine, her freckled skin and tan face, the faded sundress threaded with colorful posies, a dress she'd had since college.

"Aren't you renting the house?" she inquired. "I mean, Henry told me that you were." She sounded exasperated and winded, and Catherine wanted to ask her to sit down but didn't, because at the mention of Henry's name she flinched and went silent. "Everything I've seen is either too far out of town or just isn't right. I loved this little house on the east side, but I'm not sure."

At one time, the east side of the town had been Winslow's wealthiest, most tended neighborhood, but it had fallen into disrepair, the Victorian homes going to ruin in the current economic climate. With good reason, those on the west side tried to forget about the east, as everything unpleasant in Winslow seemed to originate from there. Catherine had already seen enough of Antonia to know she wouldn't be happy across the railroad tracks.

"It isn't safe there," she said, thinking about Henry, who'd sent the girl. She didn't need to ask which Henry it was; she'd seen them together more than once. "But there's been a mistake. I'm not renting my house," she told her, all the while thinking, *Why did Henry send you here?*

As Antonia slid on her sandals, and they moved back to the

porch, Catherine said, "He must have meant the house on the corner," and pointed to a small green house with a wraparound veranda at the far end of the block.

At this, the girl brightened and said, "I'll check it out. Thanks," and off she went, lighting a cigarette the moment she crossed the yard.

Catherine remained on the porch, growing concerned by this unexpected visit. She wasn't a suspicious person by nature yet wondered if something else weren't at work this afternoon. Henry, she thought, even as she plucked the half-smoked cigarette out of the flowerpot.

In the house, she poured another glass of wine and took it with her on the deck out back. Out there were the aboveground pool and an ancient sycamore that shaded the cottage, Wyatt's cottage, which glowed blue in the fading sun. There, on the deck, Catherine drank the wine and smoked the rest of the cigarette, taking great pleasure in the mixture of tastes. She stayed until there was no time left, all the while thinking only about Henry Swallow, the man who had helped to kill her husband.

Dinner with the Girls

———

Instead of taking the unreliable, old Corolla, Catherine walked to the cafe, which sat across from Danvers Park, the town square, and was a good ten minutes from her house. Louise, Jane, and Catherine met there most Wednesday evenings. The park was empty, save for a gang of teenagers who laughed and smoke cigarettes in the white gazebo. During the school year, when the weather was good, the college's theater and music departments frequently put on plays and concerts in the park, many of which Wyatt and she had attended. As it had done every year since they'd come to Winslow nine years ago, in 1982, the local arts council hosted a couple of summer festivals, hiring local bands for entertainment. She remembered those evenings with Wyatt, when they had sat on a blanket leisurely listening to the music or watching a play, eating pâté and crackers and drinking rosé.

This evening, every one of the cafe's thirteen tables was taken, filled by many unfamiliar faces, those urban vacationers who came to Winslow in droves and made the town their own, however temporarily. (Wyatt used to call them tanned rats in Range Rovers.) They sought the cooler climes of upstate New York, the chance to take in the area's natural splendor — the town sat at the base of the Mohawk Mountains — and enjoy the secluded quiet. The tourists and the students, their coming and going, lent the town a sense of restless impermanence. Still, even after Wyatt's death, Catherine never thought about selling the house or leaving. She loved her house and her job and had made some good, lasting friends, like Jane and Louise, who were seated at their usual table in back.

Louise, the matriarch of the trio, was fifty-four years old and still a handsome woman, her hair the color of autumn grain. In 1985, she'd struggled through a battle with breast cancer and ultimately had to have a mastectomy. This happened around the time that Wyatt's novel was being published. Yet, even through the nausea and pain and shame, she'd come to his reading at the bookstore, her support of him as ferocious as Catherine's support of her.

Jane, at thirty-five, was the youngest of the friends. She was Catherine's height and coloring, and had the same thick, untamable blond hair. When they were together, people often mistook them for sisters. Whereas Catherine had put on a few extra pounds over the years, Jane hadn't gained an ounce. Tonight, she was wearing a lemon yellow blouse and a short pleated skirt, which showed off her athletic legs.

As Catherine sat down, Jane said, "And baby makes three," and smiled.

Catherine settled in her seat and was about to launch into an account of the events of that afternoon, when she turned and spotted Antonia Lively at a table near the window. To the bewilderment of her friends, Catherine laughed; she found the coincidence more than amusing. Sometimes life was like this: we meet someone new and then run into them again, right away. Catherine was pleasantly surprised to see that Antonia was alone, without Henry, her face in a book.

Louise caught Catherine staring and said quietly, "I hear she's been looking at some places in your neighborhood, like the Turner house." Louise, a native of Winslow, was the gatherer and dispeller of information, true or otherwise. "I mean, do Sandra and Jerome really believe they'll find someone to rent at the price they're asking?" she added. "It's such a dark, cheerless house, don't you think? All those shaggy willows and overgrown rosebushes. A total eyesore. I'd be depressed after a single night in it."

"Maybe there's nothing else available," Catherine said, feeling protective of the girl. Unnecessarily, she reminded her friends about the girl's celebrated short story, "Vitreous China." "It's set in Georgia. It's about a young woman who cleans toilets for a living and finds a diamond engagement ring in one of them. You read it, Louise, remember?"

Louise did remember and crinkled her nose. "I've read better. After finishing it, I felt like I needed a bath. That poor girl and what those nasty soldiers did to her! It was just too gruesome for words. I wonder what compelled her to write such a ghoulish story."

Catherine ignored the comment. She hadn't said as much, but she knew Louise disapproved of the ghoulishness in Wyatt's novel, too.

"She showed up at my door this afternoon," Catherine said, with a certain pride. "Apparently, she thought I was renting my house." She omitted Henry's involvement completely.

"You're leaving us? Where are you going?" Jane asked, horrified. "Not back to the city, because I won't let you." Originally from Queens, Jane missed New York City more than anyone Catherine knew, herself included.

"I'm not renting my house, and I'm not going anywhere," she said. "Besides, I couldn't, even if I wanted to."

She gazed at Antonia, who'd finished her meal and was now heading for the door. Part of Catherine wanted to join her, to go after her — just as she should have gone after Wyatt. All at once, she was transported back to another night in this very cafe: her last meal with Wyatt before he vanished. They'd taken a window table, perhaps the same one as Antonia had taken, she couldn't quite remember. Wyatt had just ordered an expensive bottle of champagne — a luxury they couldn't afford. She didn't deny him or say a word, though; they were celebrating. It was his night. He'd just completed the penultimate chapter of his second novel, a book he'd been laboring on for a couple of years. Catherine had learned not to ask him of his progress or what the novel was about — "You know how much I hate that question. Ask about the characters. Ask about the setting. Just don't ever ask me what it's about!" — and he never gave her any clues. The one time she did ask, he said that it was his big revenge book. So that's what she took to calling it — Wyatt's Big Revenge Book.

As Catherine thought over that evening, she felt her face flush and all at once she had trouble breathing. She reached for her wine, but it seemed miles away, the table stretching into a streak of candlelight and cream-colored linen. Dizzy, she stood up, and stumbled toward the door, past the table and that night so long ago, when their faces still smiled with love and hope, and Wyatt still promised her that everything was going to turn out all right. It hadn't turned out all right, she thought, reaching the street and collapsing on the first available park bench. She looked around, her thoughts a scrambled blur. There was the gazebo, empty now; the soft sputter of the electric-flamed gas lamps; the tree where she and Wyatt had kissed, drunkenly, for the last time. Her heart was racing, and she glowed with sweat, when, moments later, Jane and Louise appeared, concerned and anxious.

"Are you all right?" Jane asked.

"She's fine," Louise said, her voice soothing and maternal. Then, "I love you, you know that, but you have to stop this. You have to stop blaming yourself."

"Louise!" Jane said. "Catherine doesn't blame herself. She didn't do anything wrong!"

She had, though. They knew she had. Only they didn't know all of it. How could she ever tell them, her dear friends, that complicated and unflattering story? How could she ever tell them about Henry Swallow?

"If you want, I can stay with you tonight," Jane offered.

"That isn't necessary," Catherine said, but even as she said it, she realized she dreaded going home alone. She wished for Wyatt at the door of the house, the comfort of his forgiveness. The loneliness came down hard then; cold, she began to shiver.

"Let me take you home," Louise said, more of a command than an offer.

"No," she said, "please," thinking, What is going on here? Yet she knew exactly what was going on — another bad reaction to the regret and guilt she continued to carry with her. Even though they had other responsibilities to tend to — Jane had a new puppy, and Louise a demanding husband and son — her friends didn't leave her side. She loved them for it and hated them for it, but mostly she hated herself, for letting Wyatt leave, for letting him take their bright and golden futures with him.

They sat in silence, Jane to her right, Louise to her left, and after a while, the moon broke through the clouds and her friends were saying that they wanted a drink, and something — anything — to eat. "How about Tint?" one of them suggested, but Catherine wasn't listening. The air was full of insects and a faint music and too many shadows, and finally she pushed off the bench and said good-bye, heading home alone despite her friends' objections. Walking often slowed her thoughts, and made her feel better. Tonight, instead of going directly home, she walked up one street and down another, gradually breathing more easily, the spell of despair passing and taking with it those awful, indecent feelings that had brought it on. Yet how could she not blame herself? How could she get beyond the inexplicable?

A couple of days after Wyatt's accident, Louise showed up at the house with an envelope — a ticket to Paris and a thousand dollars in travelers' checks. "Wyatt promised you Paris. See Paris. Everything's been taken care of," she said. Louise might have respected Wyatt, but she hadn't liked him, his pontificating and extravagant ego. When Catherine got to John F. Kennedy Airport, however, she watched her plane board, then depart without her, because she realized she would be alone in Paris just as she was alone in Winslow. It didn't matter where she went, because wherever it was she'd be without Wyatt. At the time, she didn't think there was any place her sadness wouldn't follow, not even in Paris, so she returned to town and she worked and she gardened and she slept. She slept and she smoked and she drank red wine. She drank red wine and she took long walks and she talked to Wyatt. She talked to Wyatt, avoiding the places they'd frequented. She avoided certain foods and songs, anything that brought back memories, and if she had to get from one side of town to another, she skirted the perimeter of the college, never once driving through it.

A place isn't your own until you walk the heart of it, Wyatt used to say, and the heart of the town, the real heart, was Winslow College, where he had been an assistant professor of creative writing. Founded in 1862, the college sat like a huge, stationary wagon wheel with six streets radiating from its center. A modest-sized liberal arts college, with about fifty-five hundred undergrad and grad students combined, it came with rolling lawns and ivy-clad brick buildings. This evening, despite having no intention of going there, she found herself crossing the flat plane of Shaddock Green, coming to the empty parking lot that opened onto Mead Hall. The building's gothic facade was dark and foreboding, even with a couple of the windows lit. She hadn't been back here for a year and a half, not since she'd packed up Wyatt's things: his literary journals, his books, his students' essays, the manuscript he'd been working on, an old windbreaker, a chipped coffee mug, all of which sat in the house, boxed up. She still hadn't mustered the courage to go through any of it.

As Catherine stood, gazing at what had been Wyatt's office window on the third floor, she realized she wasn't alone; someone was gazing down at her. She thought she caught the glimmer of something — glasses, binoculars? — as the light brushed them. She blinked, and for a moment she put Wyatt in the window again, she put Wyatt in the world again, all of this creating an unbearable sadness. She dropped her eyes, and when she looked up, the figure was no longer there. Had it been a maintenance person or maybe the current occupant of Wyatt's office?

Had it been Henry Swallow?

Once home, she grabbed Wyatt's novel off the shelf. "Why did Henry send her, Wyatt?" she asked, sitting down on the sofa, the book in her lap open to the back flap. Her husband's handsome face stared up at her with the same enigmatic smile that he'd worn the day he'd driven away. Even now, Catherine wondered what that smile meant. There were so many possibilities. Smiling, he'd climbed into his car, and smiling, he'd backed out of the driveway. Who was that smile for, and where was it taking him? Was it for someone else, a potential rendezvous? Or — and in the days and weeks and months after his death, she thought about this often — was it for Henry? Had he finally decided to deal with that at last?

Sometimes while working, Catherine let her mind wander, putting Henry in the car instead of Wyatt, putting Henry on the bridge. She again remembered that blustery summer night three years ago, when Henry had shown up at the house unexpectedly. "What are you doing here?" she'd asked. Her heart had pounded at the sight of him on the porch, the wind pushing against him, whipping at his eyes. He blinked back tears and took a step toward her, even as Catherine kept her grip tightly on the door, feeling that if she were to let go of it, she'd fall. She had repeated her question, and thought, Now that would be something if they were real tears.

"I've come to talk to Wyatt," he'd said.

"Wyatt isn't home," she'd said.

"Tell him I'm here, Catherine," he'd said.

"I will do no such thing," she'd said, slamming the door and extinguishing the porch light.

Just as she'd closed the door, Wyatt had emerged from his study and asked Catherine whom she had been talking to. Pressed up against the wood of the door, she felt heavy and weak. "It was Henry," she said. "He wanted to talk to you. Why would he want to talk to you, Wyatt?" Even as she said this, her husband was already pushing past her. She followed him onto the porch.

Henry was walking slowly through the yard as Wyatt caught up to him. They spoke quietly for a moment, and then they were both heading back toward the house. Catherine retreated into the bedroom without protest, even though she found the idea of Henry in the house unpleasant. She did not come out again that night, and Wyatt did not come to bed.

The next morning, she found him on the sofa. She didn't want to fight. She merely asked, "What was Henry doing here?"

Wyatt said nothing for many minutes, just sat staring into the empty fireplace. Then he finally said, "The college — my department — hired Swallow. He starts in the fall." As if overpowered by the ugly weight of his words, Wyatt sank back into the sofa.

Catherine froze, her eyes fixed on Wyatt. Her chest tightened as the coil of her despair wound tighter and tighter around her heart. "How is that even remotely possible?" she asked, but Wyatt, already passed out, didn't answer her.

Over those next few days, Catherine had wanted to ask him about his encounter with Henry, but she knew that pressing him would do no good, just as she had known that nothing positive could have come from a meeting between the two men. Like so many other discussions that should have happened and didn't, the right moment to ask Wyatt about his conversation with Henry had never come along. Time passed, yet the moment had never left her completely alone, or at peace. Though it had taken her some years to adjust to life in Winslow, she'd always found comfort in the distance that had separated Wyatt and her from Henry. Shouldn't leaving the city, she thought, have guaranteed that at least?

Once, a few weeks after she'd learned about Henry's relocation to Winslow, Catherine had brought up the idea of Wyatt's looking for a new position at a different college. "Um, go where, and with what exactly?" he'd asked. "Oh, you mean with my best-selling novel that everyone's reading? No, Catherine, I don't think so. This is our life. We might as well get used to it."

Sometimes as Catherine crossed the bridge and drove past Henry's house on her way into the mountains, she liked to imagine what might have been rather than what was — that Henry had never taken her on as his advisee, that she had never brushed up against Wyatt in Penn Station. That she had never known what it felt like to hate a man as much as she hated Henry Swallow. Sometimes she liked to believe in a kinder, more benevolent spirit who had never tangled her fate up with Wyatt's or Henry's, a spirit that had worked through her and had cautioned the girl she'd been about the path she'd set for herself. Sometimes, like tonight, she imagined that she had listened to this spirit and that it had worked through her and that she was more prepared to meet her future — whatever it might be. A future where she and Wyatt were on their way to Henry's house for dinner at that moment. Once there, they'd laugh and reminisce about their days in New York, when they were younger and their potential seemed like something real. She pictured his stately old house on the hill, the rolling, manicured lawns, the mountains in the near distance. Like so many nights since Wyatt's death, she imagined Henry's house filled with light and music, the table done up with china and candles, the savory, delicious smells of a lavish meal. At the door, Henry, in an apron, would welcome them with a big hello as Wyatt handed him the bottle of wine and Catherine let go of his hand to take Henry's. Then she'd toss her arms around him, hugging him like the confidant and good friend he'd been, while Wyatt poured the wine into three perfect glasses, and they toasted one another, and friendship everlasting.

The Envelope

— — — —

It was a wildly hot, bright afternoon in 1988 when Henry Swallow stepped off the train in Winslow for the first time. He was fifty-six, years removed from the younger man who'd taught and mentored Catherine Strayed. Still, even as he headed to his meeting at the college, he couldn't help but look for her in the faces of every woman he passed. What would she make of his appearance in the town? Winslow was the last place on earth he ever imagined himself, yet when the position as director of the college's writing program became available, Henry's name was at the top of the list of candidates. He was suddenly free, with oceans of time before him: after several years of teaching at Columbia, he had resigned his position before the university could bring him up on charges of sexual misconduct — just as NYU had done years earlier. Perhaps love was more important than teaching, he reasoned, and he left quietly and without a hint of fuss or regret. But a man had to eat and to pay his bills and to live his life, and so to the utter bafflement of his friends and colleagues, and certainly to Wyatt and Catherine, Henry Swallow, the consummate New Yorker and renowned Pulitzer Prize–winning critic, abandoned his Upper West Side apartment and the city he loved, saying good-bye to an ex-wife, Joyce, and his only son, Ezra, for a new beginning in rural upstate New York. He bought an old yellow Italianate house out on Old Devil Moon Road, a place that came with ten acres of land and a glorious view of the mountains. He had chosen the house out of so many others, yet today as he stood gazing at Deadwood Library from his office window, he realized the house had chosen him. Once a beautiful house, half of it now lay in ruins.

In the weeks since the fire, he'd only been back once to pack up some clothes and collect his typewriter, all of which sat in his small hotel room. He hadn't had the stomach to check the workers' slow, laborious progress or repairs. They told him it would take months, though he was sure it would stretch on and on, not because he didn't trust them but because everything in Winslow moved at its own leisurely pace. He had grown used to the town's glacial slowness but not to its overzealous neighborliness, the hellos in the morning and good-evenings at night, the door-holding, the well-wishing, the pleases, and the pardon-me's. For the first year, he made frequent trips to Manhattan, hating himself for how quietly he'd given in and left. His life and all that he loved was still there, going on without him, and the realization overwhelmed and saddened him. More than once, he wrote a letter of resignation, but then something happened — a family of deer in his yard on a snowy morning, a minor flirtation with a talented young writer, a good meal at the cafe — and he was renewed, vowing to fall in love with Winslow.

Henry turned from his office window toward his desk, where the novel, his latest review assignment, sat open and calling. While the writing was adequate, the story was less so, the plot empty of heart, the characters empty of life. He thought about Wyatt Strayed, the poor review he'd given *The Last Cigarette,* because that's what it had deserved, because that's what most contemporary novels that he read deserved. He thought, however egotistically, that he'd been doing Wyatt a favor. Though the guy had real talent, it just wasn't apparent in this incarnation. At least, that's what he maintained as he'd written the review and confirmed later as he saw it in print. His reviews were nothing if not fastidious and candid and, above all, true. Over time, they had achieved a certain pitch and majesty; he wasn't Henry Swallow for nothing. He had hoped, as always, that the writer understood this and that after the initial shock and disappointment wore off he'd find something in the review that was helpful, something that enabled him to see the flaws, the novel that should have been written rather than the novel that was. They never learned, though, did they? They just kept writing one awful book after another, he thought. Not Wyatt, however. No. Not Wyatt.

Sitting down at the desk, Henry picked up the novel and here, beneath it, was the envelope, still unaddressed. He sighed, glowering at it. He never addressed them, not until he arrived at the post office, and even then, after all these years, he found that his hand still shook whenever he wrote the address across it.

It was an early Thursday afternoon, the sun pinned high over his head, when Henry strolled out of Mead Hall. Even in shorts and T-shirt, he was drenched with perspiration by the time he got to the post office, a squat rectangular building on the edge of Broad Street. He waited his turn in line, asked for a stamp, then went off to write the dreaded address. Before dropping the envelope into the chute, however, where it would be sorted and, later, would make its way out to Osprey Point, Long Island, Henry stared at it, as though in shock. He was thinking about the girl, as he always did at these moments. Yes, there was also this, the sudden, inevitable arrival of memory and the weightless envelope in his fingers, this ongoing, despicable reminder of the last six years of his life.

How Happy I Was Last Night

———

In the years between knowing him the first and second times, Catherine had heard various stories about Henry Swallow. She never sought out these stories — Wyatt offered them up to her without prompting. Since the review of his novel, he'd turned Henry into an unhealthy obsession and took great joy at any news of failure. While this pastime of his appalled Catherine, she knew she was powerless against it.

"He went to bed with a student. He's just so predictable," Wyatt had said, disgusted. "Tell me something, Catherine: what girl in her right mind would sleep with that fusty parasite?"

His reaction upset her, yet she said nothing, her fear of discovery keeping her silent. Of course she knew what kind of girl bedded Henry Swallow, since at one time she had been one of his students and had learned everything there was to learn about him. This was ages ago, before she'd caught the tip of her cigarette on Wyatt's sleeve, before she'd married him, and moved to Winslow.

When they'd met in Penn Station, Catherine was on her way to visit her father in New Jersey, Wyatt to visit his parents in

Connecticut. She was younger then and more likely to speak to a handsome young man with floppy blond hair and a fleshy mouth, a frayed copy of *The Sun Also Rises* under his arm. He was reading it, he said, because he had to.

"My instructor met Hemingway once. It changed her life. Can you imagine being in the company of someone like that?" He told her then that he was in his last semester at NYU and was at work on a novel, which was also his MFA thesis. "My adviser loves it, but I still have a long way to go," he said morosely. "She has this theory: that if I'm patient, the novel will tell me what it wants to be." Your novel, Catherine said. What does it want to be? "It wants to be the death of me, I think," he replied, laughing. Whom did he like to read? Who were his inspirations? "The Russians," he said. "Tolstoy, Turgenev, Dostoyevsky, Bulgakov, Gogol." He spoke about them with deference. "I've read *Poor Folk* a dozen times," he said, quoting the first line: *My dearest Barbara Alexievna — How happy I was last night — how immeasurably, how impossibly happy!*

In the twenty minutes she'd been with him that first day in Penn Station, Catherine began to imagine Wyatt as being as talented as any of his literary heroes.

"I see the Pulitzer at thirty," she said. "I see the National Book Award at thirty-five."

"Why stop there?" he said. "How about the Nobel Prize at forty?"

Then her train was announced and Catherine had to say goodbye, even as Wyatt scribbled down his number and offered it to her. She took it without hesitation, although she was already involved with someone else. That day in Penn Station, she couldn't have known she'd just met her future husband; she wasn't one of those lucky women who bumped up against a man and said, "Oh, yes, you'll do." As Wyatt often reminded her later, it took a great deal to get her involved.

At the gate to her train, she turned around — she thought she'd heard her name — and caught a glimpse of the back of him, the slouchy brown corduroy jacket with the beige elbow patches. He already looked like a professor, though he wasn't, not yet. He was just a man of twenty-five who worked as a proofreader at a law firm to put himself through grad school, while Catherine was a woman of twenty-nine, who was also at NYU getting a PhD in comparative literature, and wholly unskilled at romance.

That was before I met you, Wyatt, she now thought, leaving the bookstore this late Thursday afternoon and wandering into the relentless heat. By the time she got into her car, she dripped with sweat and sagged with exhaustion. Everything shimmered in the sun, and when she blinked, her eyes stung. Having been unable to sleep, she'd read away much of the previous night. While rummaging through a stack of old magazines, she'd come across Antonia's short story and reread it and thought again just how wrong Louise had been. She believed that while it did have dark and disturbing elements, a good reader, a sharp reader, would have been able to see beneath this distraction to the story's beating heart, the redemption flowing through it. The writing, Catherine believed, was a triumph.

She'd been surprised, of course, even irritated the previous afternoon to have found the girl at the door, smoking, the easy way she'd breezed into the house, as if it were already hers. Then the way Antonia had glanced around the room, judging, thought Catherine, the shabby furniture, the disheveled bookshelves, even as she gaily complimented it all. Had her show of friendliness simply been an act? Catherine wasn't sure, but she was sure about Antonia's irrefragable talent, which, she had to admit, was exciting to her. Wyatt, she knew, would have hated the story, not because it was terrible but, on the contrary, because it wasn't. When

Catherine read it again, like before, it had moved her to tears, further proof of the girl's daring gift.

She had many questions she wanted to ask the writer — about the mother and the father, the town (Galesburg, Vermont), and the era in which it was set (the late sixties) — and wished she'd had the nerve to ask when she'd had the chance. There was one, though, that lingered: was it a story Antonia had heard, or was it something she had lived through? The story had so much heart, and this heart, it seemed to Catherine, did not belong to Antonia's narrator but to Antonia herself.

If so, then the poor girl, she thought as she pulled up to the house. Had Antonia written the story as a way out? Was it about her own mother and father, her own tempestuous childhood? The story had touched Catherine in ways she couldn't begin to explain, at least not to her friends. If Wyatt had been here, she would have been able to explain it to him, because he knew her. Now sitting in the car, the broken air-conditioner pushing around the hot, stale air, Catherine felt again what she'd felt last night — that Antonia had reached down into her own life and, with surgical precision, carefully sliced back the skin to get at the dark matter of her girlhood. Not that Catherine had lived through anything as brutal as Antonia's narrator had, but the sentiment, the themes — of ownership, betrayal, and abuse — were just as clear. She sat in the car and looked at the cottage that sat a few feet behind the carport, in the far corner of the lot, imagining it filled up with light, the industry that had once been Wyatt's. She gazed at the opal blue wood, the navy blue trim and the opal blue door, these colors that she'd fought so hard for (Wyatt had no eye for aesthetics and had wanted the whole of it painted a dismal beige), willing the door to open and for Wyatt to step out. It was his cottage; she'd given it to him out of love. Now it was hers and she still had the unpleasant task of figuring out what to do with it. Finally, turning off the car's engine, she stepped out and thought, What if . . . ? In that moment, in all that silence, as the loneliness settled around her, Catherine thought again, What if . . . ? Then she climbed back into the car and headed out of the drive, the destination clear in her mind.

In the remaining daylight, the bony edifice of Mead Hall seemed to her less gloomy, the ivy a brighter shade of green against the stark red brick. Parking the car, she wondered if what she was doing was crazy, would seem impulsive. As she had no way of finding Antonia — clearly, thought Catherine, she's come to town to teach — she realized she'd have to start at the college. So here she was again, on campus, a place she'd sworn off, yet a place that also kept calling her back.

Glancing up at Wyatt's office now, she couldn't see a thing, because the sun's glare washed the window in orange. Still, she wondered if Henry had been at the window last night, and if so, why? The idea that it had been Henry left her feeling numb, and she thought twice about what she was about to do. Could she stand to be so near him again, to breathe the same air?

Though she hadn't spoken to Henry since the night he'd come to the house three years earlier, she had the misfortune of having to see him around town. Whenever she did happen to catch a glimpse of him, he was usually on his bike, or walking apace. He still had that sharp, clipped stride, which, she thought, was more appropriate for big cities than small towns. As she'd expected, he hadn't shown up at Wyatt's funeral, though a few days later he'd sent flowers and a condolence card. Then a few days after that she'd discovered a stack of books — advance-reader copies — on the porch. *Fiction is the only solace,* his note said. He'd always known what she liked to read, and she consumed the books in a matter of days. Yet it seemed to her that the real story lay beyond those pages, in the shadowy world she and Henry had shared for a time.

Through the steamy heat, she made her way into Mead Hall, up the stairs, past the bulletin board with its array of flyers — poetry readings, fiction and screenplay contests, grants — and headed straight to the writing program offices.

The administrative assistant, a graduate student named Bertrand, sat behind the desk, exactly where she'd last seen him a year and a half before.

"Hello, Madame Strayed," he said in a still-thick French accent.

"Hello," she said, and smiled. "Is he — is Henry in?"

Bertrand shook his head, saying, "He is in, he is out. I cannot keep track."

"I was really looking for Antonia Lively," she said. "Have you seen her? She came by my house yesterday looking for a place to rent and I didn't think about it at the time, but I have — "

"Yes, I know that she has been on the lookout," he said, glancing up, his brow furrowed. "We all know she is looking, because, *entre nous,* that is all I hear about since she arrives."

"I see," she said, wanting to press him yet resisting. "Do you have any idea where I can find her?"

"Honestly, I do not know or care to know," he said, excusing himself to answer the phone.

The sunlight pushed at the windows, shining across the door and the polished brass placard — HENRY SWALLOW, DIRECTOR. As Catherine, defeated, turned to go, the door to Henry's office swung open and there he was, his hazel eyes glittering behind his glasses, then dimming just as quickly. He blinked back the sunlight, against the sight of her, it seemed, and she wondered, as they stood there, if he'd been expecting someone else. A hush settled over them as she peered into his office, seeing a heavy wooden desk, a small stained-glass lamp (the same one, she remembered, that had sat in his office at NYU), a leather chair, and books, oceans of them lining the shelves and stacked about the floor. There was something else that caught her eye, something that shimmered pale and green on the surface of the desk, though before she could get a good look at what it was, Henry pulled the door shut. She felt the curious, inquisitive girl she'd once been awaken for a moment, wanting to ask him what she'd just seen. Then she took a hard look at where she was, and the girl's curiosity vanished, even as she shifted her gaze to him. His handsome, scholarly face hadn't changed all that much. At fifty-nine, he was still thin and well kept, his thick black hair bushy and peppered with gray.

"Catherine," he said, "what a pleasant surprise."

Is it pleasant? I'm not so sure, she thought. And how can it be a surprise when you just overheard Bertrand and me talking? Still, upon seeing him again, thousands of feelings swept through her, the least of which was anger.

"Yes, it's good to see you, too," she said, her heart clenching at the lie. All at once, she wanted to flee but just as suddenly realized there was no point. Wyatt was gone; she had no ties to or allegiances left at the college. Even so, she didn't want her name associated with Henry Swallow's.

"I came here to talk to Antonia," she said. "Is she in her office?" For a moment, Henry looked baffled, as if she'd spoken in tongues. "You sent her to me and told her my house was for rent," she added. "Why would you do that?"

"I don't remember doing that, but if I did, then it must have been a mistake," he said. "Plain and simple. She should have gone to the house down the block."

She said nothing, and the silence between them grew, as if

someone had come along and vacuumed up the sound. "It's so quiet," she said at last.

"Amazing, isn't it? The moment I get used to the students, the term's over and they're gone. I almost miss them," he said. "Luckily, the dead months don't last forever."

The dead months — a term Wyatt had also used to describe summer, when the halls emptied of people and the campus went still. "I'll be blunt," Catherine said, shivering, unaccountably frightened by Henry. Even more frightening than Henry, though, was the thought that he sensed the fear coming off her. She remembered how light and untrammeled she had once been around him, and how heavy and self-conscious she was now. It took every ounce of her forbearance to get through this moment with him, to take what she'd come for, and go. "I'd like to show Antonia the cottage. I didn't think about it yesterday. It's close to campus, and she can roll out of bed and get to her classes in minutes."

"Her classes?" he asked, nonplussed. "She's not a student." And there it was, that upsetting, all-too-familiar hubris in his voice, a defensive, insulting scoff.

"I know that," she said, too sharply. "She'll be teaching. She came here to teach, right?" She came here for you, too, she wanted to say.

"She might teach a class for us in the fall, but she's here to work on a novel," he said. "As far as the cottage goes, though, she just signed a lease on the Turner house down the block from you."

"Oh," she said, oddly dejected. "It's a lovely house. She should be happy there."

"If you're really serious about renting the cottage," he said, "I know of someone who might be interested." He grinned, stuffing his hands deep in his pockets, which he always did when nervous. "As you no doubt have heard, I've been displaced," he said. "I'm

homeless, at least for the moment. There's just nothing to rent."
She knew he meant that there was nothing to rent that met his
standards. "I've been searching for weeks." She tried to smooth
down her wrinkled skirt in an attempt at some self-possession, but
it was useless. The curiosity she had felt when she was a girl was
stirring again in the deepest part of herself, wanting to ask about
the fire at his house and, beyond this, about Henry himself. She
looked down and away in another failed attempt to regain her fortitude. She hadn't come to hear Henry's complaints; she'd come
merely to find out about Antonia. Now that she had, she had no
reason to linger. Yet there she was, lingering. Leave, she thought.
Leave him to his troubles. They have nothing to do with you. "I
don't need to tell you that summer is hardly the best time to make a
home at the Tweed & Twining Arms. I'd love to find the architect
who designed it. The walls! They're made of newsprint! I haven't
had a good night's sleep in ages. Your cottage — "

"Henry," she said, biting her lip, his name in her mouth tasting
metallic. She had not known about Henry's living situation, although she should have. She'd read the two or three articles about
the fire at his house in the paper; she knew the police still hadn't
ruled out arson. She sighed. "Henry," she said again, feeling dim
and woozy all of a sudden, her vision narrowing, the ceiling and
walls caving in upon her.

She made a move to go. Though she could feel her legs, she
could not feel her feet or the floor. She couldn't catch her breath
fast enough before she needed another one and her fingers tingled
and her thoughts broke apart. She was in Mead Hall, but she was
also at her father's house, fingering the folded slip of paper with
Wyatt's name on it. Memories both dead and alive swirled inside
her, as if she were a snow globe, her thoughts the bits of confetti.
"Catherine," Henry said, and his voice was miles away, though his

breath was in her face, "you're breathing too quickly. Slow down." She tried, and couldn't. "I'll be right back," he added, and rushed away.

Then Catherine slid to the floor and shut her eyes. She struggled against the fierce, ever-tightening pressure in her chest and unbuttoned the top of her sweat-soaked blouse. All at once, she felt cooler, as her wildly arrhythmic pulse began to slow, and she opened her eyes to find Henry kneeling beside her.

"Drink this," he said, and handed her a glass of water. He ran a cold, wet paper towel over her face and neck, and the fright passed away as quickly as it had come, leaving a black, empty space behind, a space which Catherine filled by saying, "It's the heat. I'm probably just dehydrated. I'll be fine. Really," though she knew it would take hours, even days before she was fine again. Something unwholesome and unwanted had been released in her that no amount of rationalizing could contain.

"I'm going to call an ambulance," he said, but Catherine shook her head.

"I'll be fine. Really," she repeated, rising, leaning all of her weight against the wall.

"Let me at least walk you to your car," Henry said. "Here, take my arm." And she did, if for no other reason than out of the fear of falling; she still felt weak-kneed. They walked unhurriedly down the hall, passing one closed office door after another. When they came to Wyatt's office door, Catherine stopped almost involuntarily. She remembered last night, the figure at the window, and wanted to ask Henry if it had been him. She thought about all the times she'd sat across from Wyatt in that office and waited for him to finish up something before they went to dinner or to a movie. Her pulse quickened at these memories, that today filled her with dread more than anything, reminding her that Wyatt was

not behind his office door, that he was not waiting for her anywhere. More than this, that he had left her to go on wondering
forever about who or what had taken him from her the morning
he'd driven away.

"What's wrong, Catherine?" Henry asked, startling her out of
her reverie.

Her eyes traveled from the door of Wyatt's office to the empty
hall, then settled on Henry. "I was outside this building last night.
Someone was standing at the window of Wyatt's office," she said.
"It startled me, because I had heard it was still empty."

"That's strange," he said. "No one's using it. Not officially. And
all of these doors are locked. I'm the only one with a key besides the
janitor. Are you positive you saw somebody?"

"Don't patronize me," she said. "Of course I saw someone." She
wanted to add, I saw you!

"If someone's lurking about, I should contact campus security,"
he said. "The last thing this department needs is another scandal."

Catherine knew he meant Wyatt and the accident, and withered against his unthinking, unkind declaration. Without another
word, she walked away from him, down the stairs and into the
twilit heat. Then Henry was at her back, saying her name, but she
headed for her car, not bothering to turn around. When she finally
got to her car and eventually turned around, Henry wasn't there.

As she drove off, she pictured the cottage, which she had not
thought to show Antonia, this cottage that she'd never wanted
to have renovated. It had come with the property and had sat dilapidated and unusable, until one afternoon Wyatt suddenly announced that he wanted — no, needed, he'd said — his own space
in which to write. He needed a place away, he said, where he could
drift and listen. Catherine had given in begrudgingly, yet over time
she had grown to love the cottage as much as Wyatt did, even if

she still hated how easily she'd given in to the renovation. Tonight, however, as she rolled into her driveway, the headlights flashing across the cottage's shuttered windows, she detested the sight of it again, this reminder of a more promising time. She wanted it all back, Wyatt, their life together, every last argument and disappointment, every last word uttered in the dark of their bedroom. She wanted to fill both the house and cottage with him again, with his hard work and faith.

Twenty-five feet wide by fifty-five feet long, the cottage had been completely gutted and remodeled to Wyatt's taste. They'd had it painted the same oyster-blue as the house, and because it matched the house so well, most people mistook it for an extension, rather than what it was, a freestanding unit. Solidly built, it came with thick, double-insulated windows that kept out both noise and heat.

After climbing out of the car, Catherine went into the house, and in one long movement she stepped out of her flats and poured a glass of wine, then slumped down on the sofa. Shutting her eyes, she imagined the cottage as it once was, full of Wyatt, his incessant typing, and then as it might have been if only she'd gotten to Antonia sooner.

Until this afternoon, she'd never thought about renting the cottage to anyone, even after Wyatt's death, when she could have used the money most. It had been his space, hallowed and holy.

After she took a couple of sips of wine, she got up and flipped on the radio, the room filling instantly with the voice of an actor reading a story. With Wyatt, she'd often enjoyed "Selected Shorts," curling up beside him on the sofa, drinks in hand. She came to this evening's story in the middle and, tucking her legs under her, let it carry her away. After it was done, it was hard not to think about Wyatt's novel, how wonderful she still found it despite Henry's ludicrous, malicious review. Still rattled from today's brief meeting with him, she nonetheless allowed herself to imagine Henry in the cottage. It was, she knew, a perverse indulgence. What would it be like to see him coming and going every day? What would it be like to have him so close? Even the momentary idea of it nauseated her, and she abandoned the idea.

Still, she couldn't abandon the memories that seeing him again had revived: that he'd been awarded the Pulitzer Prize at thirty, that he was the one man in the world most able to launch or cripple a literary career, that he'd once written a novel that had never gotten published (and that he'd let her once read; one of the only people in the world, he'd told her). His collected essays still sold out at the bookstore, and his reviews, from what she remembered — she'd stopped reading them ages ago — were well written and graceful, his impassioned critiques almost never wrong. Almost.

Later, as she went around the house readying it for sleep, she recalled a different Henry, a man who'd promised her a long, fruitful life of publishing. She found it difficult to reconcile the younger Henry, the one who'd supported her dreams, with the other Henry, the one who'd damned her husband into obscurity. Yet she knew she had to set these uneasy feelings about him aside to focus on more practical, urgent matters: her overdue mortgage, the dying car, the money pit of a house — the ongoing financial strain that Wyatt's death had left behind.

Rather than fortifying the house, paying off his troublesome credit-card debt, and securing their bright, golden future, Wyatt had talked Catherine into spending tens of thousands of dollars on the cottage instead. As she propped herself up in bed to read, she thought about the empty space and how it would remain that way. No, the thought of Henry Swallow as a tenant was something she simply couldn't abide. Still, she did feel the tiniest bit sorry for him. How could she not, when it was partly her own fault that he'd wound up in Winslow?

"Wyatt," she asked, "what am I supposed to do?"

But Wyatt didn't answer.

He rarely if ever did.

A Look Never Hurts

─────

The next morning, Catherine awoke on Wyatt's side of the bed and lingered there, as she sometimes still did. Mornings were the toughest on her, and always had been, with Wyatt flying out of bed to get to his writing and her hurrying away to work, still half asleep, still half dreaming of a time when he would hit it big, and they'd have a more leisurely life. For nine years, she kept those dreams to herself, and for nine years she watched him toil — all for nought, she thought as the sun forced its way into the room, the heat already dampening her skin, darkening her mood. She'd slept poorly again, though, in the end, it was her encounter with Henry that had kept her from sleep. Try as she might, she couldn't shake him from her thoughts any more than she could shake the part she'd played in his unfortunate relocation to the town. Yes, this is partly my fault, she thought as she smoothed out the sheets.

Over coffee, she perused the real-estate ads, wanting to prove Henry wrong. Contrary to his complaints that nothing was available for rent, there were a dozen places to be had. Like always, she knew the houses couldn't possibly meet his standards, that he was being far too fussy. For as long as she'd known him, this had always been the case. Yet how could she hold this against him? The man has good taste, she thought, recalling the first time she'd stepped into his office at NYU — the sumptuous space of dark-wood paneling, the Oriental rug, the leather recliner, the real Tiffany lamp. She, too, knew beauty, which was why she'd begged Wyatt to put down part of his advance money on the 1920s Craftsman bungalow she now lived in alone.

Currently, the house was in need of both a new roof and new paint, but she thought it was still the most attractive house on the block, with its brick columns and whitewashed steps. The patchy yard could have used some landscaping, and some of the aged leaded-glass windows could have used repairing, but she had no money for such extravagances. Besides the house's upkeep, she also had to deal with the gas, electric, and water bills; the phone; property and school taxes; health insurance; and the car, the transmission of which she knew could go at any time. Though she loved the house, the history it contained, she had no idea how she could go on living in it, especially on what she made at the bookstore.

Another Friday morning and Catherine pinned on her name tag and slid behind the register while Jane was in the storeroom. The sunlight fell through the display windows, touching the green carpet, umber-colored walls, and the backs of the few people rummaging the books. Almost every college town in America had a version of Page Turners, which was one of two bookstores in Winslow and catered to locals and students alike, though the students also had their own store on campus. Such a magical space, Catherine thought, and it was, with its handcrafted mahogany bookshelves and an atmosphere that invited hours of browsing and lounging in the large, comfy chairs. Catherine had pushed Harold, the owner, into the revamp and was more than glad she had. Not only was

the store a reflection of her good taste, she believed the renovation
would help business, which it had, at least for a while.

Many, many years ago, when she'd first started working at Page
Turners, Catherine had suggested that they do what other bookstores in the country did and hold literary events. "Look around
you, Catherine," Harold had said, laughing. "You aren't in Manhattan anymore. Hell, you aren't even in Manhattan, Kansas."

Every couple of years, she'd bring it up again at one of the
staff meetings, and every year without fail Harold vetoed it. His
aversion to change astounded her, especially since he knew that
she lived with a writer and that this writer, her husband, was acquainted with some very influential people. It would not have been
impossible that he could have talked some of them into coming to
Winslow to give a reading.

Now here we are, nine years later, she thought as Jane returned
from the storeroom, took one look at her, and said, "What are you
doing here?"

"Um, I work here," Catherine said, confused.

"Oh, Lord, it figures," she said. "Harold forgot to call you, didn't he?"

"Call me about what?" she asked, although she had a sense of
what was coming, not just because of the look on Jane's face but
also because it stood to reason: it wouldn't be the car's transmission that finally did her in but Harold and his financial hysteria.
Harold who liked to show up unexpectedly from time to time just
to complain about their performances, shaking the monthly sales
reports in their faces. Sometimes he stopped in to get the small
handgun — a Raven P-25 — from under the register because, as he
said, "I have to do some target practice just in case I go bankrupt
and have to fend for myself in the wilderness."

"He shaved everybody's hours back," Jane was saying. "You
know how he gets in the summer. The big drama queen."

"Yes," Catherine said, reminding herself to breathe.

"I'm sure it's only temporary. You know what an alarmist he can be. So if worst comes to worst, I'll give you one of my shifts. You can have my Fridays," she said, smiling.

Jane didn't need the job. She'd inherited some money from her grandmother and lived in a big prairie house, drove new cars, and took fancy vacations to places like Paris and Tokyo. Yet in all the years Catherine had known her, she'd never taken a personal day, unless she was truly sick, her devotion to the store as fierce as her devotion to her friends. It's not about the money, she once told Catherine, it's about the books, and the people who buy them. For her, the job's real currency was time, the hours she spent in the store readjusting the shelves, ordering books, speaking to the customers. This job, she said, was an extension of herself, and gave meaning to her day. It gave Catherine's day meaning as well, though the job was indispensable to her. She couldn't possibly go on without it.

"I couldn't take your Fridays, but thank you anyway," she said.

She'd been working every day except Sunday for the last year and a half, earning roughly five hundred dollars a week after taxes. She was also receiving Wyatt's Social Security checks and was grateful for this extra money, although it wasn't much. It was embarrassing for her to think she'd come in this morning all prepared to ask Harold for a raise. During this time of economic hardship, with the country going through a terrible recession, Catherine understood Harold's position. Still, she couldn't help feeling that he was punishing her for talking him into the revamp. According to Jane, though, this wasn't it at all.

"Does it make cents?" she asked. "That's his big catchphrase right now. 'Does it make cents?' I think his therapist is probably having a field day with that one."

Though it made perfect sense to her that Harold might want

out of the book business — "I should turn this place into a bar. Liquor's quicker," he liked to say — she knew deep down he cherished Page Turners as much they all did but perhaps not as much as Catherine herself. She'd taken the job to give Wyatt some quiet; he often complained about the least little noise she made. That was Wyatt. He found distraction in everything — from the birds out his window to the dogs in the street. Finally, it was his typing and tantrums — his creative constipation, she secretly called it — that drove Catherine from the house. What kept her away was something else, however, a sense of desperation whenever she passed his study door.

Even as another customer wandered in and Jane went to help him, Catherine felt herself deflating, wondering how she would make ends meet. Was she doomed to live out the rest of her days working part-time in a poorly managed bookstore in upstate New York? How had she let herself come to this? She suspected that things might have been different had she just finished her PhD. Yet that was almost a decade ago, and there was just no way she could return to the university now.

She thought about Henry, who'd built his career on tearing apart the novels of others. Though Wyatt had assured her otherwise, she knew that he'd never quite recovered from Henry's ridicule. Yet more than Henry's ridicule, Catherine wondered again if it was his having to work under Henry and interact with him every day that had really done her husband in. While there was nothing she could do to bring Wyatt back, she understood now, as she wandered into the storeroom and shut the door, that to get through she'd simply have to swallow her own indignity. Did she care where the money came from as long as it came? Did it matter if Henry were in the cottage for a couple of months, just until she could find someone else?

Of course, it mattered, it mattered deeply, but Catherine knew this might be the only way. As she picked up the phone to call him, shaking as she dialed, she imagined the thrill in her fingers as they folded his rent checks. Yet the second she heard his voice, she faltered and hung up. I can't do this, she thought, the receiver still pressed to her ear. Do it, she thought, but this was her younger self whispering at her. Do it, she thought again. Ask an unreasonable price. Take him for everything you can. You deserve it.

So she rang Henry again and hung up again, picturing him at the large desk, hunched over a book, as always, so many years older than the man she remembered. Later, she thought. I'll call him later and went out to help a customer because it was Friday, she was already there, and she didn't know what else to do with herself.

CATHERINE WANTED TO tell Jane about her plan, but if she told Jane she'd also have to tell Louise, who would instantly scold her. "You can't be serious, Catherine. The things I hear, well, and after what he did . . . He's just not suitable," she'd say. Catherine knew she'd come home one day to find an envelope on the floor among her other mail, Louise's generous check inside it. Nope, no choice, she thought as the sun vanished behind a cloud, taking the last of her resolve with it. Just call him, she thought, and get it over with. Maybe he'll say no and that will be that.

While Jane was with a customer, Catherine went back into the storeroom and shut the door. After she picked up the phone, she dialed Henry, and when she heard his voice this time, she finally understood there was no turning back.

They said their hellos, then fell silent.

"Look," she finally said, "this is going to sound strange, but I was wondering if you want to come have a look at the cottage."

"You mean the same cottage you were so keen to show Antonia

but not me," he said, as the cottage rose up in her mind, empty of Wyatt but not his cherrywood desk on which he wrote his beautiful stories. In that moment, she filled the cottage with him again, the hum of his typewriter, the squeal of his red chair. How could she possibly do this to him? How could she possibly not do this for herself?

"Do you want to have a look at the cottage or not?" she asked, repeating herself, trying desperately not to sound desperate.

"I guess it couldn't hurt," he said.

"A look never hurts," she said. "Let's say nine thirty tonight."

"Nine thirty it is," he said. "Though I have to ask: are you sure about this, Catherine?"

"No, I'm not, but being sure is a luxury, isn't it," she said, hanging up before she said something else she'd regret.

CATHERINE FINISHED UP her last Friday shift, though during it her mind was elsewhere. It was in the house, straightening up, at the door, waiting for Henry. Every time she was about to tell Jane about what she'd done, the bell on the door jangled, and another customer wandered in.

At five o'clock, she said good-bye to Jane and drove home. Once there, she spent the rest of the afternoon in the pool, drifting in listless circles and reading a memoir titled *The Hunger Maiden,* all about the struggles and heroics of a young nurse during the Second World War. According to the nurse's account, she'd had sex with dozens and dozens of Nazi doctors in exchange for handguns and grenades. After smuggling the weapons past the guards and into the camps—she often got herself reassigned—she then distributed them to the Jewish prisoners, who launched a revolt. The book had been translated from the German into English and had come out in May. Even though it was still selling exceptionally well, as most Holocaust memoirs did, it had recently been debunked as a fraud, the author unmasked as a middle-aged Texas man.

Unsurprisingly, Henry had given it a deplorable review, not only calling it a filthy display of sensationalism but also calling for the publisher to pull it from the shelves, which they eventually did. Though Catherine sympathized with Henry and understood that the Texas man had violated a serious trust between writer and reader, she had bought it to find out what all the fuss was about. Rather than sensational, she found the memoir both gripping and heartrending, and couldn't put it down. She liked reading a good, moving story, even if it meant having to quiet that part of her that raged against the story's improper origins.

After dinner, Catherine poured a glass of wine, and took it out to the deck where she returned to the memoir. The night was full of distractions, though, and she found it hard to concentrate. There were fireflies and a warm wind that shook the branches of the sycamore, scraping them against the cottage. A pack of dogs trotted through the nearby alley, chasing what she couldn't see. There was music and shouting from the house next door, where a trio of blond girls was hosting their first party of the summer. She stayed on the deck for some time, taking in the smells and sounds, but when the laughter and shouts became too much, she went back into the house.

This June night, feeling more restless than usual, Catherine wanted nothing more than to sit in a bar somewhere in Manhattan, to drink and to laugh, to smoke and to forget. At times like these, she wanted to flee the house and the town and never look back. Though she liked her life in Winslow — the relatively empty summers, the simpler way of life, the friendly faces — she would have given anything for an invitation to a dinner party in the city, to feel again that sense of countless variety and endless possibility. Even now, especially now, she hated Wyatt for stranding them in Winslow, this beautiful yet luckless place. Drowsy, Catherine stretched out on the sofa and shut her eyes, imagining Antonia in the house down the block. Henry had said she'd come to work on a novel, but of all the places in the world, why here? Had she really come for love, as Catherine had, or to escape it? Was she only in the town for the summer or for good?

SOMETIME LATER, CATHERINE awoke with a start and sat up, the party still raging beyond the windows. It was well past nine thirty, so where was Henry? Had she slept through his knocks? Had he stood her up? It would be just like him, she thought. For a second, she imagined herself at the party; because they were neighbors, she'd been invited. It wasn't her normal kind of thing, yet it was a party, and it was still fairly early and she didn't have to be at work tomorrow until eleven. She checked her face, brushed her hair, then grabbed a bottle of wine. Sliding into her flats, she opened the door on Henry, who was making his way up the porch. For an uncomfortable moment, she was unsure of what to do, and she paused just as he paused, a questioning look on his face. "Three years and I still can't find my way around," he said.

Then he was through the door and in the house. His eyes were red, his cheeks glistening, and she wondered if he'd been crying. She didn't notice the book he was holding until he handed it to her — an advance copy of his forthcoming essay collection, *Words Travel Fast.* Though she'd had hours to ready herself for this moment, she realized nothing could have prepared her for how she now felt — excited, angry, nervous, disgusted — at having him in the house.

After thanking him for the book, she said, "Let me show you

the cottage," and quickly headed for the back door and the deck beyond. At the top of the stairs leading down into the backyard, Catherine slowed as Henry drew up beside her, and for one single second she imagined pushing him down the steps.

"Is it always so loud?" he asked, descending the stairs.

"Oh, that," she said, following. "The girls are usually very quiet."

"Are you sure you're up for this?" he asked. "You seem . . . distracted."

"I'm not," she said, but of course she was, because she kept expecting him to mention Wyatt, to say something, anything, about him. He didn't. Instead, he pushed through the gate, the bell tinkling as he went, and she followed again until they were standing at the cottage door. Opening it, Henry entered and took careful steps across the floor, his rubber-soled shoes squeaking. As she switched on the track lighting, he inspected the space, studying the walls. Then he climbed the ladder into the sleeping loft.

Stooping, he stared out the small window, and said, "I can see straight into your neighbor's house," then climbed back down.

Catherine took her place at the study door while Henry perused the bathroom, flushed the toilet, and fiddled with the faucets. Though it hardly mattered to her what he thought about the cottage, she still hoped she'd closed the bathroom window; during summer, the feral cats used the area outside as their litter box, and the air became acrid with the stench of urine.

When he returned, he said, "Excellent water pressure," as if he were ticking things off a list.

"We had the plumbing completely redone," she said. Turning, she gingerly twisted the knob and walked into the study. In the dim light, everything was just as Wyatt had left it: his slip-covered Olivetti typewriter was still on the cherrywood desk, which sat under the southernmost window; the overcrowded bookshelves leaned against the easternmost wall; a beaten-up filing cabinet, which held his dot-matrix printer, next to the desk. A club chair took up one corner, while the fern she and Wyatt had bought together took up another. Brown and brittle now, it reminded her of time and how quickly it was passing.

"I haven't seen one of these in ages," he said, lifting the typewriter's cover, his eyes as wide and innocent as the boy, she thought, he'd once been. She saw this boy in him, and wondered fleetingly if this boy had ever sensed the kind of man he would become.

For a moment, she wanted to shout, Don't you touch it, but instead she stood there, wincing as he struck the keys.

She realized too late the horrified look on her face, because he said, "I'm sorry. I didn't mean to — "

"No need to apologize," she said, already leaving the room, eager to be outside, away from this clumsy, thoughtless man.

Once under the open sky, she started to relax, and finally gave in to the moment — Henry in the cottage, in the study. Then he was at her side, asking, "How much?" At first the question confused her, but then it made her laugh. How much? How much rage did she still have? How much sadness? The amounts were unquantifiable. "What's the rent?" he asked.

She knew that if she quoted him an unfair price that she'd look greedy, that if she asked too little she'd look desperate. "Fourteen hundred a month," she said, at last. "I'd like the first month's rent and a security deposit up front. It is very convenient to campus, Henry. A ten-minute walk," she said, to sweeten what, to her, already seemed a sweet deal. He squirreled his hands into the pockets of his khakis and rocked on his heels. It looked to her as if he wanted to clarify something, but he didn't say a word, which gave her room to add, "We could consider it temporary. Until you find something else, or work on your house is finished, whichever comes first."

Thankfully, the throb of music filled the uncomfortable silence, because she wasn't sure how to continue. There she was with Henry, who'd shown up late for their meeting, and who, as she now realized, must have just come from having sex—he hadn't been crying, as she'd presumed; he'd merely been flush with the afterglow.

They walked through the wet heat into the front yard while the moths tapped at the windows and the fireflies lit up in orbits around them.

"Fourteen hundred a month? I'm not even sure my desk will fit through the door," he said.

"You can use the one that's already in there," she said, despairing at her own offer. "You'd have complete privacy, and, well, now Antonia lives right down the block." She knew she was reaching, overstepping her bounds, that to mention Antonia this way was brazen, but it seemed to her that if he were going to take the cottage, she had to be as clear and open with him as possible. She had to let him know that this secret of his wasn't as well kept as he'd intended.

"Yes, she does," he said, staring at her. "I don't know. What happens if after a couple of weeks I don't like it? What happens if your neighbors decide to throw another party? Then where would I be? I cannot bear noise of any kind these days. I guess that's how you know you're getting old: the things you used to tolerate become intolerable."

Drunk girls never bothered you before, she thought, but said, "The walls are doubly insulated, so you shouldn't hear a thing," remembering Wyatt's delight at the remarkable quiet once inside. Henry looked at her through the darkness, his eyes seeming to ask, Will I be happy here? She saw this in the sparkle of his iris but also in the dark flash of something else, wondering if he were thinking about that night three years ago when she'd slammed the door in his face. When he finally turned to her, his eyes had emptied of light and purpose and he spoke as if from a great distance.

"I guess that's it," he said. Even then, as he took one last look around, she wished she'd had the wherewithal to have mentioned the cottage to Antonia. Yet she hadn't been thinking about the cottage at the time; instead, she'd been thinking about Henry. "I'll be in touch," he added.

"I have someone else who's very interested," she said, surprised at the swiftness and boldness of her lie.

She waited for him to react, but he didn't. Instead, he searched the darkness again, his eyes looking across at the neighbors' house and their party.

"Do you need a ride back to the hotel, or did you drive?" she asked, though when she said it, she recalled hearing a rumor that he no longer drove.

"No, thanks," he said, removing his glasses and wiping the smudged lenses on his shirt. He glanced toward the end of the block, toward Antonia's house, a faint, unseemly smile on his face. Then he said good night and bounced away, whistling. Catherine didn't need him to tell her where his sudden buoyancy came from — a young woman waited for him a few houses away. She almost wanted to follow him, just to see him enter the house, remove his shoes and socks and leave them by the door, go into the bedroom. Just to hear what he might or might not say, what might or might not go on between them, this man thirty-odd years the girl's senior.

How had they met, and where? Had he seduced her or the other way around? What was she doing with him? More important, though, Catherine thought, why do I care as much as I do? With that, she went back into the house, determined to forget about all this, wishing she'd never mentioned the cottage to Henry, wishing Antonia had never come to her door.

The Weight of It
in Her Arms

————

The more Catherine tried to forget about Antonia and Henry, the more they haunted her. The next day, she thought about them whenever the door of the bookstore opened and she looked up to see a father and daughter, whenever she glanced out the windows and caught a glimpse of a girl with blond hair, whenever Catherine passed the front table — the new arrivals — and saw Henry's book. Thoughts of them came to her as Wyatt still came to her, and she found herself angry at the indulgence. Stop, she thought, just stop. But she couldn't. She imagined the previous night differently, that it was Antonia who'd been late because she'd been writing, that Antonia had fallen in love with the cottage and had taken it on the spot. She imagined coming home to find Antonia on the patio, smoking, the cottage lit up behind her, sharing an inaugural glass of wine with her, asking all the questions she'd been burning to ask.

Yet as the day wore on and the store grew busy, Catherine did finally end up forgetting about them, recommending books to customers, ringing up their purchases, chatting with them about the endless heat. By the early afternoon, she'd completely forgotten about Henry and Antonia until there was a decided lull and Jane said, "So I hear Mr. Pulitzer Prize is moving in."

"I'm sorry?" Catherine said. "What?"

"Louise told me. She was up at the hardware store this morning," she said. "Apparently, Henry was with his daughter picking out a window shade and talking about your cottage."

The news took Catherine aback. She hadn't had time to tell anyone about Henry and the cottage.

"He doesn't have a daughter," she said.

"You aren't seriously going through with this, are you? Not after what — "

"Yes, Jane, I am," she said. "So, please, just drop it."

"If you really want to rent it out, put an ad in the *Winslow Gazette,*" she said.

She thought fleetingly about all the kooks and weirdos the ad might attract. At least Henry isn't a complete stranger, she thought.

"I can always just set the cottage on fire, then walk into it," Catherine said.

"Not amusing," Jane replied.

"No, but here's something that is," she said, suddenly angry. "I'm almost forty and I still eat my meals over the sink and wash them down with red wine. It's fortunate that Wyatt and I never had children because what if we had? Then I'd be one of those sad women you see at the grocery store, a kid on her hip, digging crazily through her purse for her last dollar . . . "

"Deep breaths," Jane said. "We've talked about this before. Let me lend you some money."

"You know how I feel about that," she said. "Besides, Henry might say yes, but even if he does, it's only temporary."

"You know how temporary likes to become forever," Jane said, referring, Catherine assumed, to Jane's own move to Winslow. Winslow was supposed to have been a minor stop along the way, though along the way to what, she no longer knew. She only knew that what should have been a year had turned into a decade. "If you change your mind, I'll write a check and bring it tonight," she said, adding that Louise didn't have to know.

Louise would know, though, Catherine thought, and a quick fix would not resolve anything. "Thanks, Jane, but no," she said as a customer entered the store, and she went to help him, eager to leave the conversation behind.

FOR THE REST of the day, it was impossible for Catherine to think about anything else. Every time the phone rang, she jumped, anticipating Henry on the line. Every time the door opened, she expected him to walk through it. Yet every time it was someone else. The afternoon dragged on in a steady stream of customers, many of them leaving with Henry's new book. Catherine rang them up, a phony smile pulled tight on her face. Every time she slid another bookmark into the book and another book into another bag, she was reminded again of the previous night, and wondered what he had decided. What she never allowed herself to be curious about was why she cared so very much. By six o'clock, she had dropped the smile, and anticipation had turned to dread. She knew his decision — his silence told her everything.

There was no joy of anticipation now, only this, tidying up the store, rearranging the shelves, and cashing out her drawer, another day's end. Once at home, she took a quick swim, then heated up the last of the lasagna. She'd just poured a glass of wine when there was a knock at the door. Startled at first, she quickly calmed herself and remained in the kitchen, taking slow sips of the wine. The person knocked again. He can just wait, she thought, assuming

it must be Henry. But the knocking grew insistent, so she headed
into the sitting room, and opened the door.

"Catherine," Antonia said, gazing at her, a cigarette burning
brightly in her fingers.

She almost didn't recognize the girl, dressed in a black strapless
dress, black pearls and high heels, her hair pulled tightly in a chi-
gnon. She looked much older and, strangely, even more awkward
than the girl who'd come to the door a couple of days earlier. She
apologized for the persistent knocking, and told Catherine she
was late to a dinner party in Saratoga Springs. "Henry's meeting
me there," she said. "He had business in the city and left early this
morning." Then she reached into her clutch to pull out a check.

Lover and amanuensis, Catherine thought, but said, "I wasn't
sure he was interested."

"You know how men are. They just need a little push every now
and again," she said, rolling her eyes and drawing deeply on the
cigarette. "Do you think I can get the key?" she asked, the smoke
hanging like a veil between them.

Catherine headed for the small desk while Antonia remained
on the porch, the night full of her smoke and perfume and an uncontainable intensity. After she handed the key to Antonia, who
dropped it in her clutch, Catherine said, "I just opened a bottle of
wine. Would you like a glass?"

"I'd love to, but I'm late as it is," she said. "Another time?"

"Of course. Come by whenever you want," she said as Antonia
moved down the steps.

Pausing, the girl turned to say, "I'm sure Henry will make an
exceptional tenant, Catherine."

"Can I get that in writing?" she asked, and laughed nervously.

As her car's taillights faded, Catherine pictured the manicured
streets of Saratoga Springs, a stately old house and a gleaming table

full of china, crystal, and silver. She wondered if Lacey Blount, Henry's editor, then, later, Wyatt's editor as well, were throwing the dinner, imagining the New York literati who might be there, these writers whose careers Lacey had christened — Henry's, now Antonia's, but not Wyatt's. No, not his, and she remembered the time of his novel's publication, when the enthusiasm faded, and Lacey abruptly stopped returning his calls. While the novel had received some praise, which lifted Wyatt's spirits for a while, his good cheer — their good cheer — didn't last because there was also Henry and his review, a brutal, mean-spirited assessment that ended any hope for the novel's success. Catherine thought about this as she went into the cottage and directly into the study, where she removed the dead fern, then grabbed the typewriter. The weight of it in her arms was like Wyatt himself, all of him, and for a moment she wasn't unhappy thinking about their love — until she realized what the empty desk in the emptier study meant. Even after she set the typewriter in the house among the boxes, even after she poured another glass of wine and waited for Louise, Catherine still felt him in her arms, an unbearable reminder of his absence.

"I'm sorry, my love," she said. "I had no other choice." Even as she said it, she knew she was lying to him and, worse, to herself. There were always other choices, but tonight, as Louise honked and Catherine grabbed her purse, she was already mentally depositing Henry's check, already spending his money, because he owed it to her. Owed her that, and so much more.

If Names Are Destinies

————

On Sunday, as the temperature climbed near one hundred, Catherine took shelter at the movies, going from one theater in the multiplex to the next. She didn't care what was playing on the screen, only that the theater was dark and cool, her seat comfortable. She munched on her popcorn and drank her diet soda and tried to make sense of the plot as best she could. When she at last left the theater, it was evening, the temperature still in the nineties, the air wet and livid. The car, which stalled twice on the way home, had developed an odd squeal, and by the time she rolled into the driveway, she understood where the bulk of Henry's money had to go. If Wyatt were around, she would have asked him to look at the car — he had been good with all things mechanical. She thought about asking Henry, but what could he tell her? He didn't even own a car.

Letting the thought go, she got out and gazed at the silent, unlit cottage. The lease was still exactly where she'd left it this morning, on the small mosaic table, a large citronella candle pinning it down. She had things about the lease to discuss with Henry — mainly to emphasize that no one smoked in the cottage — but all that could wait until later.

Yet later turned into Monday and the lease still lay on the table. She knocked on the cottage door a few times, yet Henry never responded. She knew Antonia had been there, though, because one of her half-smoked cigarettes was in an ashtray beside the candle. On her way to the trash can to empty the ashtray, Catherine recalled how much pleasure she used to find in her first morning cigarette, the first taste, the first burn and pull, the smoke in her lungs, as she readied herself for another day of classes. She missed that first cigarette as much as she missed the last, the postprandial smoke, the smoke after sex. It was Wyatt who had come between this pleasure and her, who had given her an ultimatum — "Either you quit or I leave. It's your choice," he'd said. And so she had quit, allowing herself only the occasional indulgence, like the half-smoked cigarette Antonia had left behind that first afternoon.

At the trash can, as she tossed the cigarette away, only to rescue it a moment later, Catherine thought again about Wyatt, about how much he hated the habit, a reason, in part, for the title he had given his novel. She thought also about how she finally realized that smoking, which she'd picked up from her father, had always been her way of communing with him, a man she otherwise did not understand or like. Ultimately, of course, she did break the habit. For Wyatt.

Now, climbing into the car, she set the cigarette in the glove box for safekeeping, to smoke later on the deck, with her wine. All around her, the heat gained, falling through the glass and broiling the air. When she put the car in drive, it squealed, then shuddered and stalled, as if it were refusing to leave the shaded sanctuary of the carport. She tried the ignition again, but there was nothing. And by the time Catherine walked into Page Turners, she was sopping wet, her hair untidy and clothes damp. On her way to the bathroom to neaten up, she looked for Harold, who sometimes liked to surprise them on Monday mornings. To her relief, there was no sign of him.

In the bathroom, she fixed her hair, smoothed out her clothes, and touched up her face, thinking about Henry. The check in her purse lifted her spirits, even as the idea of Henry in the cottage threatened to depress them. For the moment she wasn't unhappy, though, as she grabbed her name tag and took her place at the register, counting down the minutes until the bank opened and she could dash across the park to deposit the check. Yet an atypical morning rush kept her in the store dealing with customers and deliveries. Things didn't slow down until close to noon, when, saying good-bye to Jane, she went to the bank at last.

After depositing the check, she strolled through the park, passing the occasional sunbathers and shirtless boys playing Frisbee. On cooler days, she liked to buy a sandwich from the cafe and eat her lunch in the park. Sometimes, before Wyatt moved into the cottage and threw himself into his new novel, he showed up at the store unexpectedly and surprised her with a picnic. They would drive into the mountains, to a spot they knew well, a clearing of smooth, flat stones and giant, fragrant evergreens that overlooked the town. They always ate quickly, because she had to get back to work and he back to his novel, but there was always a moment, right before they packed up to go, when she found herself beside him, brushing her hand through his thick head of brown hair, unbuttoning his shirt, his jeans, their kissing the only sound amid all that quiet. Their sex then was clean and bright, and she loved it. She adored him, the smell of grass and earth in her nose, their coupling on the blanket, his handsome face above her. She carried these sights and smells with her into the afternoon, thinking it wonderful to wander back into the store with the scent of their lovemaking all over her.

At other times, it was she who surprised Wyatt, sneaking home during her lunch break to drop a sandwich outside the study door. She always included a note: *I love you. You're brilliant. Can't wait to see you tonight.*

Today she had an hour to kill, and the heat was just too much and there was no Wyatt, no picnic in the mountains. She thought about having lunch at the cafe, but the idea of eating alone in a crowded room depressed her, so she wandered home. It had been ages since she'd been home on a weekday afternoon and the house felt different, museum-like. She felt different as well, oddly afraid, knowing that everything was changing again and that soon she would finally have to take a long, careful look inside those boxes in the study. But not this afternoon, she thought as she made a sandwich. After cleaning up from her meal, she headed for the back door and the cottage, to see if Henry had signed the lease. She had just stepped onto the deck when, to her surprise, she found Antonia in a string bikini, napping on one of the chaise lounges, an *Interview* magazine in her lap. Even in sleep, Catherine thought, when to all appearances she was at rest, the girl still pulsed with an awkward, uncontainable energy. She didn't want to disturb her, but then she didn't have to: Antonia opened her eyes and yawned, showing off her small mouth with its cramped teeth.

After sitting up, she shook off sleep and said urgently, "I was going to call you, but here you are."

"You were going to call?" Catherine asked.

"It's the cottage," she said, agitated now, and shivering, as if she were suddenly cold. Over her bikini, she quickly slid on a wrinkled, button-down shirt — obviously one of Henry's — and a pair of running shorts, which showed off her lissome legs, oily and dark.

"It's awful, Catherine," she said, and shot down the steps, the bell on the gate clanging.

Oh, Lord, Catherine thought, following her, wondering what had gone wrong, because clearly something had. Was the cottage flooded? Had it been egged again as it had a few months before? Was the toilet stopped up? Had the louver doors jumped their tracks? Renting to Henry will prove to be an ordeal, she thought, again regretting the impulsive decision.

Hip canted, Antonia stood on the small patio, lighting one of her long, thin cigarettes. She inhaled deeply, tapped away the ash, and blew out a straight line of smoke, averting her eyes from the cottage, which Catherine now looked at. It was awful, just as Antonia had said, and Catherine stood trembling as she took in the crude lettering. How had she missed seeing this earlier? "What in the world?" she said. The words scrawled on the wall were meaningless: *Wren Was Here.* Antonia stepped beside her, the sun punctuating the severity of her face.

The red paint looked so much like blood that Catherine turned away in horror. It ran down the face of the cottage, still wet, and splattered on the patio, the windows, the mosaic table, the sun baking it all into place. "It's terrible, just terrible," Antonia said.

A lawn mower grumbled, a car honked, a telephone rang. A dog barked. A bird sang. A boy rode past on his bike and paused, then tore away, ringing his little bell. Then there was Catherine's voice through the afternoon quiet, saying, "I just can't believe this. You don't know who did this, do you?" Enraged, the whole of her shook, as if she and not the cottage had been vandalized.

"I have no idea," Antonia said, and tears were in her eyes.

"Where is Henry?" she demanded, already heading back through the gate to phone the police while Antonia said, "I don't know," following her, only to pause on the deck to light another cigarette.

Before going into the house, Catherine paused as well, glancing at the cottage and the words: *Wren Was Here.*

Ten minutes later, a police officer arrived, to take down Catherine's statement. Then he handed her his card and said, with a nonchalance that rankled her, that it was probably just one of the college students. "You do live in west campus, Mrs. Strayed," he said, as if the blame were hers, that she should have been used to such behavior. "This isn't all that unusual," he added.

"Not unusual?" Catherine said angrily. "Someone came onto my property and defaced my home. I want to know who and why." She took a breath, but it did nothing to calm her.

"We'll definitely look into the matter, Mrs. Strayed," the policeman said, and then he was gone. She knew even then that they wouldn't look into the matter at all, that they'd let it drop.

In the house, Catherine called the bookstore to tell Jane there'd been an emergency. Then she phoned Breedlove Hardware to speak to Louise's husband, who owned it. Within minutes, Louise was at the house with a team of men carrying ladders and brushes.

"I wasn't going to say a word, but now I have to," Louise said, whispering. "You never should have rented the cottage to that man. Why didn't you talk to me first? We could have figured out something. Just look at what has already happened." She paused. "Her," she said of Antonia whom they could see lounging on the deck. "I don't like her. There's something not right about her. What was she doing here in the middle of the day anyway? I mean, really, it's the height of audacity."

"It doesn't matter," Catherine replied.

"If you invited her, that's one thing, but if you didn't, that's something else," she said.

"Louise," she said. "Please."

"This is his fault. It has to be. He can't stay, not after — "

"He just moved in," she said.

"Let me help you find someone else," she said as the men scrubbed the cottage, washing away the words, the red running in pink tendrils down the walls.

"Will they be able to get rid of it all?" she asked.

"If they don't, we'll have it repainted," Louise said. "We'll do whatever you want."

Then Catherine was crying, silent tears that slipped down her face. She cried, thinking about these words that had no meaning, hoping the men really could wash them away.

YET THE WORDS remained. They remained with Catherine while she slept on the sofa, where she'd collapsed after Antonia finally left and Louise finally left and the men finally left. In her dreams, though, Wyatt hadn't left. He was back in his study, and there was the rustle of paper and the click of his typewriter. The light was burning under the door, which meant the last year and a half hadn't happened. Wyatt was back. Then she sat up, blinking, and the typing stopped, the light under the door went out, and she was again in the dark house, alone. She went out to the car to grab the half-smoked cigarette. More than anything, she wanted to smoke the rest of this cigarette and forget about the day, the horror of those words. As she turned to go back into the house, she ran into Henry on his way to the cottage. He was walking so swiftly that he nearly knocked her down.

"Henry, we have to talk," she said. "Now."

He wore a suit and tie, neither of which she expected to see on him, given his usual casual, shabby style. As he swatted a flurry of gnats away from his face, he said, out of breath, "Do me a favor and take a look behind me." Confused, Catherine looked behind him. "Is he gone?" he asked.

"Is who gone?" she asked. "Nobody's there."

After dropping his shoulders, he let out a heavy sigh, saying, "Have you seen Antonia?"

"Yes, this afternoon," she said. "She was here when — "

Then all at once Antonia appeared in the blue twilit air and the couple fell into each other's arms and walked through the cottage door without a word. Alone again, Catherine wandered back to the house, where she poured the wine and lit the cigarette. The more she thought about the name, Wren, the more familiar the name became, until she couldn't help wondering where she'd heard it before. Whereas Catherine forgot names almost instantly after she heard them, Wyatt had always been wonderful about remembering them, sometimes long after he'd met someone, however briefly. Names are destinies, like character, he used to tell her. If this was the case, if names were destinies, Catherine thought sadly, then what did this say about his character, and what did this say about her own?

Drift and Listen

———

Wyatt used to say the writer's job is to drift and listen, to live inside his characters and record their innermost thoughts and desires. If he listens well enough, hard enough, his readers will live with these characters, will breathe their air, will see the world as they see it. They don't have to appreciate all their traits, share all their weaknesses, like all their dreams, but they do have to understand them, and then they can truly, fully participate in the gruesome crimes or the heroic acts, can take part in the events that shape the characters' lives. Breathing life, real life, into the characters is only one part of being a successful writer, for without a narrative that moves, that confounds, that compels, that excites, then the life will go out of these characters and they will die.

That Henry did not connect with Wyatt's novel from the start was one thing, but that he found no merit at all in the parts that made the whole — the exquisite writing, the intelligence of the plot, the originality of the structure — was something else. "An author must be very careful," Henry wrote, "not to sensational-ize murder or beatify the murderer, especially when the murderer is one's own flesh and blood. (What a coincidence, then, that the father of Mr. Strayed's protagonist was also serving out a life sentence for rape and murder in a U.S. penitentiary in Lompoc, California.) Mr. Strayed's 'novel' epitomizes the root problem of contemporary fiction, which all too often asks the reader to contend with long-winded passages of gratuitous violence, merely for the sake of racking up pages. (The more the pages, the higher the price!) Dostoevsky needed his pages in *Crime and Punishment* . . . I'm afraid that Mr. Strayed did not, and his efforts will not go on unpunished."

"It's just a review," Wyatt said after he'd read it, his reaction surprising Catherine.

She knew differently. It wasn't just a review, it was revenge, and it hurt her as severely as if Henry had written a letter directly to her. He might as well have begun the review, Dear Catherine. . . . During the weeks that followed, she would sometimes awaken, startled out of a dream in which Henry whispered in her ear, "I told you he was a hack, and the proof is in my review." In the morning, after Wyatt disappeared into his study, she'd read the review again, not to indulge this phantom Henry but to get rid of his whispering, sinister voice in her head. Yet the more times she read it, the more she sensed the rage that lay beneath it. The rage was misdirected, she knew, and personal, made so by her own past involvement with him: a brief affair they'd had when she was his student. Oh, Wyatt, she thought, you didn't deserve this. There had been plenty of time to tell Wyatt about Henry, about their relationship. Then why didn't I? Catherine asked herself during that dark period, when Wyatt's editor stopped returning his calls and she watched as their golden future grew tarnished.

Outwardly, Wyatt seemed to take the criticism quite well and went on as if nothing had changed. Everything, though, had changed, and Catherine knew his disappointment would eventually catch up to him. Still, he pushed on, remaining steadfast and optimistic, which both surprised and dismayed her, mainly because it was just so out of character. She expected rants and rages. What she got were smiles and bromides.

"One day at a time," he said. "This, too, shall pass," he said. "Hi ho, hi ho, it's off to class I go," and he whistled, really whistled, as he grabbed his briefcase and headed off.

Yet whenever she passed his study, it was not the sound of his typewriter she heard but just the creak of his chair and the occasional heavy sigh. What was he doing if he wasn't writing? She didn't ask, for fear of pressuring him, of sounding too earnest. If he needed this time to regroup, then she did not intend on intruding. So she went about her days as if he were busy at work, although it was more than evident he wasn't.

The semester finally ended and the days lengthened, the nights shortened, and summer finally found them again. A week after commencement, Wyatt left to go to a writers' retreat a couple of hours drive south of Winslow. He'd gone to the retreat once before, and back then, the days and nights without him were long and brutal for her. In June of 1985, however, she couldn't wait for him to depart. A pall had slowly settled over the house, over their marriage, too. They bickered about everything and nothing. She blamed him for never replenishing the groceries. He blamed her for stomping around the house. She accused him of ignoring her. He accused her of being needy. Then the weeks of fighting faded, replaced with an even more uncomfortable entente cordiale. They had sex again, inevitably, but it was quick and passionless, their kisses flat and cool whereas they'd once been warm and tumid. She felt a part of Wyatt had been burned away, the most important part, the thing that got him up at five every morning to write. The part that made him a writer. Though she still sensed a drive in him, she caught only the faintest glimmers of it. A month away, she hoped, from Winslow, from the college, even from her, might return Wyatt to himself, might bring him back to her.

Less than a week later, however, Catherine came home from work and found him on the sofa, as if he'd never left.

"They asked me to leave," he said. Though the room was in shadow, she could still make out the hurt and disappointment in his eyes. "If I'd known he was going to be there, I never would have gone."

"Who was there?" she asked. "You mean Henry?"

"Yes," he said. "Not until the fifth day. They stuck him in the room right next to mine. We shared a bathroom. I couldn't believe it." Neither could she. The idea of the two of them under the same roof hadn't occurred to her. Yet it should have. When she'd known Henry, he was often running off to some writing colony to spend much of his summer. "Yesterday, at dinner," Wyatt said, "I walked right up to him and I . . . I shouldn't have done it, but I spit in his face."

The night of his return, Catherine suggested they have dinner at the cafe. On the way, they didn't discuss the incident with Henry, or even talk about his colleagues in the English department and their woeful, negligible support of him. At the table, over gin-and-tonics, they didn't talk about the scant turnout at his readings in Manhattan, Albany, Buffalo. It wasn't until they were on their way home that Wyatt finally exploded.

"Why did he expect to identify with my narrator?" he asked, referring to the review. " 'Beatify the murderer?' What in God's name is he talking about? I mean, I know how he feels about writers basing characters on real people, but I'll be damned if he can point to a single one of my characters and say, 'So here's where you've been hiding, Mr. Strayed.' I mean, does he really believe that characters invent themselves? I would have had some respect for him, if he'd just come right out and said he hated my book. He didn't hate it, but he certainly didn't like it, either, which makes it worse. A tepid review is like telling the world, 'Hey, this book I just reviewed, it really wasn't even worth my forming an opinion about it, which means it's really not worth your time to form an opinion of your own about it, either.' "

Catherine wanted to stop him from going on, but she knew it was easier, better, simply to let him vent, which he did. He blustered on, blaming his novel's poor reception on the reading public's poor taste, on the death of the intellect, on the critics themselves. "Henry Swallow," he hissed, "is what's wrong with publishing today, not me. What does he even know about writing a novel? Has he ever published one?" He paused. "Every critic is a failed writer, Catherine. Don't ever forget it." Mainly, though, Wyatt blamed himself for writing the kind of novel he had, a novel full of big ideas. "I know we all write for our own reasons," he said. "Really, though, if it's not to illuminate the human spirit, why do it? If it's not to shine some light through the dark, why bother?"

Catherine had no other answer for him than this: "I think people write to clear their consciences."

Wyatt scoffed, then fell into a silent rumination. They walked the rest of the way without saying a word and, once home, went their separate ways, she to the bedroom to read and Wyatt to his study, where he remained until sunrise.

THIS EVENING, AS Catherine made her way to the cafe, she couldn't help thinking about Henry. You cannot trust him, she thought, pushing through the restaurant's door. She was winding her way toward her friends, when she heard her name and paused to find Antonia at the end of the bar, a burning cigarette in the ashtray, blue serpents of smoke around her head. As usual, the whole place was smoky and packed and loud — recently, it had been named the best place to dine in Mohawk County — and Catherine could barely hear Antonia above the vivid chatter.

"We keep running into each other," she said.

"Small towns," Catherine said.

"Have a drink with me," she said, patting the stool beside her. Catherine found her suggestion more demanding than friendly. "I'm meeting Henry," she said, and his name hung in the air between them. "You should join us." Catherine detected a tremor in her voice. Then she saw Henry through the big windows as he made his way into the cafe.

Before he could find them, Catherine said, "My friends, another time," and offered a good-bye, feeling, as she had the afternoon Antonia first showed up at the house, a strange, unaccountable pressure in her chest. Just as then, she'd felt as if she were being studied, maybe even judged.

As the three women ordered, they talked about the concert they were all attending this evening, the endless heat, Louise's son, Chase. When Louise mentioned the cottage and asked how Catherine was holding up, she told her that she was fine, even though they all knew she wasn't. She buttered a roll, she drank her wine, trying her best not to stare at Henry and Antonia, not to watch as he fed her olives and she moved her chair closer and closer to his. As she sipped her wine, she tasted the tannins and hints of cherry and beyond this, the sour crush of her own jealousy. Yes, jealousy, she thought, hating herself for it. That was the truth of it.

Later, an expensive bottle of wine appeared at the table. "Compliments of Mr. Swallow," the waiter said.

"Appalling," Louise said curtly, glaring at Henry, covering her empty glass with a hand.

"Take it away," Jane said, and did the same.

"Please," Catherine said, holding out her glass as the waiter uncorked the bottle. The wine was Chilean, with the tenor of leather and black cherries, tangy and nutty at once. After she tasted it, she nodded, the waiter pouring, the other women no longer demurring. At one point, Catherine raised her glass and said, drunkenly and loudly, "To Wren," and flashed her eyes on Henry. She'd been thinking a lot about this person, this Wren, a woman no doubt, and had ultimately decided that she must be one of Henry's spurned writers or, even more likely, one of his spurned lovers. Like so many, she thought morosely. Then she smiled and raised her glass again. "You are the most amazing friends a girl could have," she said, and took another gulp.

"I think it's time we found another place to have dinner," Louise said, her eyes on the couple.

"There's nowhere else to go," Jane said.

"Then we'll just have to explore new options," Louise said. "What about that little French bistro in Mohawk? We haven't been to it in ages."

"It went under," Catherine said. "Wyatt and I tried going there last week," and the moment she said it, she set her glass down, wilting. "I mean a couple of years ago," but she'd already freed the words, and the pain lingered.

When their meals arrived, they ate them in relative silence. Catherine picked at her braised quail and chive mashed potatoes, glancing out the windows at the crowd on the street spilling over from the park. Among the crowd, she spotted a modestly tall, scruffy man with thick, dark hair who had pushed his way to the restaurant window, pressing against it with a sense of urgency.

Even from where she was, she had a decent view of him — the high, creased forehead, the linear jaw, the long nose. He wore an earring in his left ear. He wasn't exactly handsome, but she found his face arresting, even extraordinary. It wasn't every day that she noticed a man, and now that she had, she couldn't turn away. He peered into the room, cupping his big hands over his brow. His lashes were long and his eyes green, with the hint of the familiar in them, which made her sad, for they reminded her of Wyatt's.

As she reached for her glass of wine, Catherine glanced down at the table for just a second, then back up at the window, but the man had disappeared. Yet the next thing she knew, he was inside the cramped restaurant. Suddenly, her attention was drawn to Antonia who dropped her fork. Her face, when she saw the strange man, lost its smile, and her eyes clouded up with fear. From across the room, Catherine heard Henry say, "Is something the matter, darling?" Then turning his head to follow Antonia's gaze, he added, with a start, "Is that — "

"Yes," Antonia said, rising and grabbing her purse. No one else seemed to notice the stranger or what was happening. Jane went on about the high price of gas while no less than ten feet away, Antonia stood trembling. She was almost at the door when the stranger stepped in front of her. Henry was behind her, his hands on her shoulders, steeling her against this menacing force, this stranger with the cold, hard eyes. Still, no one else seemed to notice. The host kept seating diners and the waiters kept serving and everyone kept eating. Catherine might have been oblivious as well had it not been for the profound fright in Antonia's eyes, the corrosive smile on the stranger's face, and the way Henry finally slid between them.

There were words exchanged, though it was impossible for Catherine to hear them over the rumble of conversation, the clatter of knives and forks. Then she did hear something, and it was Antonia's name, and it flew out of the stranger's mouth with arrow-like precision. When Antonia heard her name, she froze, the last blush of color in her face fading. Clearly, she wanted to leave, but the strange man would not allow it. "Get out of my way, please," she heard him say to Henry. When Henry refused to move, the man laughed joylessly, and said, "Do you have any idea what you've done?" Then he spit at Henry as Catherine clutched the table and flinched.

Henry wiped at his eyes, but he still did not move. There was a look of both pride and loathing in Antonia's face, and it seemed to Catherine as if she were deciding between the two men — to listen to what the man had come to say or to leave with Henry. Yet when the stranger finally took a step closer and grabbed Antonia about the shoulders, she reached for Henry's hand and ran out the door, the man rushing after them. Catherine wanted to go after them, too, but instead smoothed out the napkin in her lap and took a bite of her quail, her fingers tightly clamped around the fork and knife. She wanted to tell her friends what she'd just witnessed, but then the waiter was taking away her plate and setting down her coffee and a fresh pear tart, which she hadn't remembered order-ing. A few minutes later, she glanced up to find the stranger back at the window. When he caught her staring, he drew his full lips into a smile, showing teeth small and cramped, like a barracuda's, she thought. Like Antonia's, she thought. Then he was gone and Louise was paying the check — she always paid the check — and they were leaving, but not before Catherine said, "I'll meet you outside," and went to use the bathroom.

Once she'd finished, she wound her way toward the door, think-ing again about Antonia and Henry but mostly about the stranger. She wondered who he was and what he had wanted from Antonia and why he had spit in Henry's face, like Wyatt had, she thought, with a tiny joy. Was he another writer felled by one of Henry's reviews, or was he one of Antonia's jealous, jilted lovers? The cloud of intrigue surrounding the couple filled her with both a deepening sense of curiosity and a growing unrest, because it seemed to Catherine that whatever had taken place among the three of them was scarcely finished, and maybe was only just beginning.

Be careful, she cautioned herself, as she wandered into the twilit heat. Don't let yourself get carried away. Even as she joined her friends at the entrance to the park and the lamps flickered on and they passed the gazebo, cigarette butts and empty beer bottles littering the floor — "A travesty," Louise said — and made their way down the cement paths that led to the concert hall, she thought about him. She wondered again who he was and why he'd worn that look on his face when he'd said Antonia's name, and what he was doing in the town if only to harass the couple. Of course what Catherine didn't understand then, and what many of us don't understand until it's too late, was that she had already let herself get carried away. As she took a seat between her friends, the auditorium darkened and the crowd stopped shifting and went still.

Then a spotlight fell on the stage, and the string quartet began to play, though Catherine didn't listen, her mind elsewhere, remembering Antonia and Henry as they'd dashed away from the cafe, the stranger in pursuit. The music crescendoed around her, yet all she heard was the stranger, who whispered Antonia's name into her ear with an awful ferocity — like someone who still cared for her intensely and had come to win her back.

Yes, that must be it. He's come to win her back, she thought, sitting with the idea, the unbridled romance of it. Just like that she turned the stranger from a spiteful writer seeking revenge on Henry into a lover with inexhaustible courage, who would stop at nothing to take Antonia away from him. She liked this version of the story, and so she went on imagining it, imagining again the stranger's green eyes, Wyatt's eyes, and how they'd flashed at her through the cafe window. How could Antonia have taken the look in his eyes as hostile, and not as the painful passion Catherine had seen? She replayed the moment when the man spit in Henry's face, and again she trusted the stranger. How delicious it had been to watch Henry get exactly what he deserved! It was to Catherine like being there with Wyatt when he, too, had spit in Henry's face. Now, as the recital ended and the auditorium filled with clapping, Catherine applauded the musicians even as she also applauded the stranger, his tenacity and his fearlessness, two qualities that had lived in Wyatt's work, and which she wished had been more a part of his love for her.

The Longest Day
of the Year

———

Every year, in honor of the summer solstice, the businesses along Broad Street organized a free concert in Danvers Park. Catherine usually looked forward to the event, though Wyatt did not. He whined and complained, reminding her, in case she'd forgotten, that it often rained, that the bands were no good. Yet in the end he always relented. Later, at home, she'd remind him that he liked to put her through the same exasperating routine every summer. "You always have a ball in spite of yourself," she'd say.

"To spite you," he'd correct, laughing, which made her laugh as well.

This summer, because of the intense heat, the event had been postponed, which was fine by Catherine, who had skipped last year's. Without Wyatt — well, there had been no going without him. Still, when she saw Henry, whom she ran into slinking back from Antonia's as she was fetching the morning paper, the concert was all he could talk about, which she found odd, since there were far more important things to discuss, like the incident at the cafe. When she told him the concert was canceled, Henry's face reflected his disappointment, and he said, "Oh, that's a shame. Antonia was looking forward to it."

"Speaking of Antonia," she said. "How is she?"

"How should she be?" he asked, the words clipped, as if Catherine had no business caring. "I'm sorry," he added, softening. "She's fine, considering. You were there. You must have seen everything."

She thought again about the fracas in the cafe, about the stranger with the green eyes. She wondered if he weren't looking for Antonia at this very moment, and her heart expanded at the thought. She had seen the love in the stranger's face, the fierce sorrow, and the memory vibrated through her. Her skin tingled with the idea that Henry had a rival in the town and that this rival was more handsome and younger than he was. She was thrilled to see Henry on the verge of defeat and only wished she could have been there when Antonia had told him about the man, how much she had loved him, how much she still did. "I never loved you the way I love him, Henry," Antonia might have said. "You've been wonderful, but what we have isn't real. It never was."

"Yes," Catherine said. "I did. I saw it all."

"Then I guess you saw him spit at me," he said. "It's the second time in my life." She waited for him to invoke Wyatt's name, but he didn't. "I'd take an angry, embittered writer over an angry, estranged father any day of the week," he said. "My God, but Linwood Lively's a menace."

"Her father? I thought . . ." she said, deflating. This news of Henry's changed the valence of everything. "What kind of person makes such a scene?"

"I don't think I need to answer that," he said. "It's probably the same kind of person who paints on walls." He glanced back at the cottage. "I don't know how he found Antonia here, but now that he has, we'll just have be a lot more cautious. You saw what he was capable of last night. I'm not unconvinced that he didn't do that terrible thing to your cottage."

"Do you really believe it could have been her father? The world is chock-full of mean people," she said pointedly. The barbed reference seemed to have missed Henry completely, for he simply rolled his shoulders, shrugging. Yes, the world is full of mean people, Catherine thought, casting her eyes past him to the cottage. Though the words had been washed away, Catherine still saw them whenever she shut her eyes. "Who is she, Henry? Who is Wren? Why would Linwood Lively have written her name on my cottage?" she asked slowly, gauging his face for a reaction.

He simply rolled his shoulders again, his expression blank. "I have no idea," he said.

She allowed him to keep up his little charade and didn't press him, although it was all too clear that he'd registered the name; she'd caught the flicker of surprise in his sleepy eyes. As she stood in her yard with him on this longest day of the year, she remembered being in Wyatt's study in the cottage — she'd gone there to ask him about dinner that night — and glancing at his typewriter and the manuscript page, still spooled in it. Wyatt had become quite secretive about his work, telling her that he didn't like talking about it because it took the power out of the story. But Wyatt had gone to use the bathroom and there was the typewriter, so inviting. She took a step closer to the desk, letting her eyes skim the page, and suddenly, now, she remembered one word, one word that stood out: *Wren*. At least, this is the word Catherine thought she remembered. But how could she be sure she'd seen the name when she couldn't even tell the difference between an angry father and a valiant lover?

"If that's everything," Henry said, "I'm sort of in a hurry."

"Yes," she said. "I mean no. If you have just another minute, I'd like to go over the lease."

"I don't have a minute right now," he said, "but why don't you bring it with you tonight? Antonia is making dinner. Join us."

"That's very kind, but I already have plans," she said.

"Then I'll see you later," he said, already heading for the cottage.

"Henry," she said, somewhat hesitantly, "I don't have to remind you, do I, that I'm doing you a favor? The least you can do is sign your copy of the lease. I think it's best for both of us, just in case there are any misunderstandings." She thought about the fire at his house and all the things that could go wrong. And probably would, she thought.

"No, you don't have to remind me," he said sharply. Then, "Leases are merely formalities between two parties who don't trust each other. You trust me, don't you, Catherine?"

"I trust you to keep the cottage clean. I trust you to treat it with respect," she said. "I trust you to take the trash out on time, but mostly I trust you not to smoke in it. That goes for Antonia as well."

"I see," he said. "Well, I'm glad we understand each other." And with that, he walked through the cottage door and shut it.

Catherine went back into the house and began getting out of her shorts and T-shirt, then took a shower and dressed for work. As she did, she thought about the night before, the scene at the cafe, the look of pure terror on Antonia's face. She pictured the way Henry had just rolled his shoulders moments ago; his non-chalance infuriated her. "I have no idea," he'd said. He did have an idea, though, she thought; she'd seen the flicker of it in his eyes. How could he not understand the significance of someone, perhaps Antonia's father, sneaking onto her property and van-dalizing the cottage? How could he not see that this led back to Henry himself?

Her anger continued to build as she dressed. She was already more than sick of Henry, of the way he expected the world to turn for him, thought that everything had to be done on his schedule, at his leisure. How hard was it to sign a lease? At the door, she turned and snatched her copy of the lease off the counter, then went to the cottage. She knocked on the door, then knocked again, calling out his name. As she'd anticipated, he didn't come to the door. She noticed that his bicycle that usually rested against the fence was gone. This isn't over, she thought, heading back into the house to phone him at the college. Yet as the phone rang, she realized she wanted to have this conversation with him face-to-face. This arrangement isn't working, she thought, hanging up. I'm sorry, Henry, but you either have to sign the lease today or get out.

To her utter chagrin, Catherine found herself again driving up to the campus to speak to Henry in person.

THE COLLEGE OFFERED two summer sessions, which meant there were always some students in the town, and Catherine could spot them by their cars and by the speed at which they drove — far too fast. "Be careful with Daddy's money," Wyatt liked to jeer as they raced through the town, running stop signs and red lights, always in a hurry. They came to Winslow College from all over the country, and all corners of the world, though Catherine never fully understood the attraction. The college boasted a few major luminaries in math and creative writing, along with a prohibitively high tuition. Still, the students came, flooding the town in fall, hurling themselves into studying and partying.

Across the swell of Shaddock Green this late morning, clumps of students roamed and grazed, and through this mix of sunbathers and studiers, Catherine looked for Antonia, scanning the blue-eyed, blond-haired girls scattered on the lawns. Not that she expected to find Antonia among them, yet she looked for the girl anyway.

The air-conditioning in Mead Hall was a cool, welcome relief to the oppressive heat and humidity, but Catherine didn't slow her pace. She traveled quickly through the halls, aware of being an alien in a world in which she no longer belonged. As she neared the offices on the third floor, the corridors stirred, as a couple of Wyatt's former colleagues jutted their heads out of their offices by way of greeting. She nodded as she walked past them and into the writing program offices, where Bertrand, seemingly more slender and paler than the last time she'd seen him, stood hunched and glowering over the gray, institutional desk. In his trembling fingers, he held a Styrofoam cup, the coffee in it having spilled down his wrist.

"He got past me," he said, almost tearfully. "This place — it's just too much."

"Who got past you?" Catherine asked, mirroring the boy's own alarm. He shook his head, indicating that he had no idea.

"He did not give to me his name," he said, "but I will never forget the face. A face like — how do you say? — a bullfrog."

"Go wash up," Catherine said, gently taking his shoulder. Through the plaid, short-sleeve shirt, his fragile bones jutted and poked. When he reached for her, she let him fold his thinness around her, and she hugged him close.

"I am sorry," he said, pulling back, wiping his eyes.

Then, all at once she thought about why she was there, to see Henry. "He got past you," she said, "and into Henry's office? Was Henry in? Is he all right?"

"There was some shouting," he said. "Then the man, he was gone. I did not see where Monsieur Swallow went."

Hesitantly, Bertrand approached the hall and peered up and down. "I am not meant for such drama," he murmured, stepping out into the empty hallway.

After he left, Catherine found some napkins near the coffee-maker and wiped up the spill on the floor and the desk, dabbing at the computer. She thought about who the man might have been and knew, almost instantaneously, that it had to have been Linwood Lively. Who else could it have been? She headed for Henry's door, which was shut. With a tentative knock, she called out Henry's name and, receiving no response, she went inside. The blinds were drawn against the sun, giving the usually bright corner office a close, submerged feeling, as if it belonged in a dank, dark basement. It smelled unaired and musty, and she threw open the blinds and cracked the windows, the heated air rushing in and tussling some loose manuscript pages. Were these Henry's own pages, from something he was working on, she wondered, or was he editing them for someone else? As she gathered up the loose pages, she thought to read a few lines but then saw a spot of blood on one of the pages. Oh, Henry, she thought as Bertrand reappeared.

"Security," he said. "I have just called them, but what fools! Since I do not know the man, I am not allowed to lodge a formal complaint? I do not think I will ever understand this place or this country. Everyone here is such an idiot." And with that, he collapsed at his desk, face in his hands.

"Where is Henry?" Catherine asked urgently.

"I do not know," he said. "He left after the argument. Forgive me, I am not feeling too good. I think I shall give myself the rest of the day off." He stood up and left the room, while Catherine returned to Henry's office.

She replaced the spilled pens and pencils in the Mason jar and set the jar in the exact spot where it had been, on a dusty ring at the edge of the desk. She stacked and replaced the loose manuscript pages, all the while thinking about the last time she'd been to Mead Hall. She gazed at the desk, remembering the way it had shimmered a pale green. She knew the color could have been a trick of the light, but somehow she doubted it. If I'm right and I saw what I saw, she thought, then what exactly was Henry doing with all of that money? Why did he have it spread out across his desk?

A Sad Way
to End the Evening

————

Catherine understood there were only so many places to look for a man in Winslow. In the past, when she wanted to find Wyatt, she used to check for him in his study. If he wasn't there, she called him at the college. If she didn't find him in either place, she went to Tint, the bar next to the Tweed & Twining Arms hotel. If he wasn't at his typewriter, in his office, or drinking, then she figured he simply didn't want to be found. She knew her husband. Henry, however, she no longer knew, so looking for him would not be so easy. Still, she had to do it. It was no longer just a matter of the lease or even the way he treated her. No, something unfortunate had taken place, and though she continued to dislike and distrust him she was alarmed at the thought of violence.

As she wandered across the campus, searching for signs of him, she again pictured what she thought had been a spot of blood, his office in disarray. She thought about Antonia, then, and when she did, she was shocked to feel herself angry with the girl. She wanted to tell her that if she'd just spoken to her father, then none of this might have happened. The hot sun streaked through the trees, pummeling the air and the earth. She passed a boy holding a burning cigarette and pictured him tossing it absently into the dry grass, the campus going up in flames. After the college had hired Henry, she'd often imagined such scenarios — a terrible fire, an awful flood, an earthquake — the ruination of Winslow College and everyone associated with it. Perhaps she was crazy to care anything at all about what might or might not have happened to Henry, or to this place, she thought. Perhaps it was better to leave it all behind, as she had after Wyatt's death.

As the bell in the clock tower sounded, Catherine rushed across the campus and jumped in her car; she didn't want to be late for work, just in case Harold was already there, waiting. Instead of going straight to the bookstore, she found herself heading back to Rhapsody Drive, though she wasn't sure why until she pulled up to the green house at the end of the block, Antonia's house. She stayed in the car, peering through the open windows to see if Henry were inside. Of course, this is where he'd go, to his girlfriend's, she thought. Well, let her take care of him. He's her problem, not mine. Just as she put the car into drive, it lurched and died. As she pumped the gas, just like Wyatt had taught her to do, the car finally coming back to life, Catherine understood that complaints about the lease, and everything else she wanted to say to Henry, would once again have to wait until a more opportune time.

AS IT TURNED out, Catherine was only fifteen minutes late to work, yet as she walked into the store, Jane was already on her, saying, "You're never late. Is everything all right?"

"Car trouble," she said, which was only half a lie. She didn't want to go into the morning's business with Henry and the lease, and his likely mishap. There were certain things Catherine couldn't share with Jane, not because she didn't want to share them or because Jane couldn't be trusted to keep a secret, but because everything, somehow, eventually got back to Louise. The last thing I need, she thought, is any more of Louise's advice, or pity. I'm a grown, single woman and grown, single women are not like grown, married women. It was the first time since Wyatt's death that she referred to herself as single, and the shock of the thought startled her. Single. Unmarried. Alone. The last word was worse than the others, enough to bring tears to her eyes. She thought she'd gotten past the worst of it, but the worst of it kept returning, one nauseating wave after another, until she turned away from Jane, saying, "Much to do," and went around the store, alphabetizing the shelves.

When a shipment of boxes came in, she took care of them, unloading the books in the storeroom, while Jane worked the floor. No, there were certain things she could no longer share with anyone, the enormity of her grief being one of them. So she let her mind roam, hoping to think about any and everything other than Wyatt. She replayed the scene at Mead Hall, thinking about Bertrand, who she hoped was all right. After unpacking the last of the books, she called him at the college to see how he was faring, remembering only on the fourth ring that he'd gone home. Yet, even as she hung up without leaving a message, she realized that besides wanting to find out how he was, she'd also just wanted to hear his voice, a voice that had spoken some of the kindest, most flattering words at Wyatt's funeral. Then she was back to thoughts about Wyatt, always back to him, apologizing again for defiling the cottage by allowing Henry into it. She spent the better part of the afternoon justifying this breach of trust, though she knew, without having to be told, that her only real justification was no justification at all.

BY THREE O'CLOCK, she was hungry and tired, so she went to the deli for snacks and drinks. When she returned, Antonia Lively was at the counter, chatting with Jane. After handing Jane the soda and candy bar she'd asked for, Catherine said, "I guess you two have met."

"We were just talking about her novel," Jane said.

"Our novels," Antonia said, smiling. "Who knew there were so many writers living in this little town?"

"More than you think and less than you'd ever want to know," Jane said, grinning. "No, really. You think New York City is full of writers until you come here. I can rattle off a dozen Winslow 'writers' on the spot, young, old, and everything in between."

"Everyone thinks he's a writer," Catherine said flatly. "Everyone thinks he has something important to say." Of course, she was only quoting Wyatt, who often taught summer fiction workshops and private instruction to would-be writers.

"Everyone does have something to say," Jane said, frowning. "Don't you think so, too, Antonia?"

Antonia paused thoughtfully before answering: "I think there's something to that, yes. I also think it's important to see that as writers we have an obligation to give our voices to those who can't speak. We have to speak for the living who might not be able, and for the dead who can't."

"Exactly," Jane said. "Brava."

"Are you just browsing, or is there something we can help you find?" Catherine asked Antonia.

"Well, first, I was hoping to talk you into coming over for dinner tonight," she said. "Second, I really do want to talk to you sometime about Wyatt's novel. He was such a great writer."

"Is a great writer," Catherine said, anger edging her voice.

"Catherine," Jane said.

"No, she's right. He is a great writer," Antonia said. "I just want to tell you that your loss is the loss of everyone in the literary community. Wyatt was — is — a genius. I love *The Last Cigarette*."

"That's very gracious of you to say," Catherine responded, thinking the remark a little unctuous and ill timed. Still, just like that, Antonia had stolen another piece of her.

"So you'll come to dinner, then?" she asked.

Jane raised her eyes from the register, and said, "I thought we — "

"We are," she said, turning to Antonia. "I'm sorry. Another time?"

"Sure," she said sweetly, though her face held an unaccountable scowl. Something about the scowl, the suddenness of it, the way it darkened her face, reminded Catherine of her much younger self, the scowl she herself used whenever she didn't get her way. She doesn't take rejection well, Catherine thought, and for the first time this summer felt sorry for Antonia, whose loneliness emanated from her in unending waves. From a distance, one might not have noticed it, but up close, the girl throbbed with it. Why shouldn't she? A new place, a new life — Catherine understood it all too well.

She wondered whose idea it had been to invite her to dinner, Henry's or Antonia's, deciding finally on the latter. Then she wondered why it was so important to Antonia that she come. Was she misreading the girl's stab at friendship as mere politeness, or was she being her usually cool and restrained self? Wyatt sometimes accused her of having a cool restraint, a trait, he said, better suited to writers than to wives. Catherine knew that it took a great deal to get her involved, but once she was, she was utterly committed. So here was this girl, a stranger and yet not a stranger at all, reaching out to Catherine, and there was Catherine, inadvertently turning away from her. She thought again of the short story she'd read, and the novel she couldn't wait to read, the novel that had already been called wise and graceful, even though the girl who stood before her appeared to be neither. The scowl now gone, Antonia said, "I really think it'd behoove you, Catherine, to at least stop by for dessert."

Though she found Antonia's manner surprising, even aggressive, Catherine said, "I'll think about it. Thank you."

After reclaiming a smile, Antonia said, "Don't think. Do," then rattled off her address as if Catherine didn't already know it. With that she said good-bye to Jane and left the store, lighting up a cigarette the moment she stepped out on the sidewalk.

"She's kind of pushy," Jane said, after she'd left. "And hello? Wasn't I standing right here when she invited you to dinner?"

"I'm sure she meant nothing by it. I'm sure you'll be invited the next time," she said, and felt a sudden compulsion to tell her everything, about Linwood Lively and about the morning at Mead Hall, but didn't.

"You aren't thinking about going there for dessert, are you? I mean, it's bad enough you have to see Henry Swallow every — "

"Okay," she said. "I promise if I decide to go, I won't tell you about it."

"Catherine," she said, "if you decide to go, you have to call me the second you get home! Maybe then you can explain to me what she sees in him. You don't think he's serious about her, do you? She's about ten years old. A smart, precocious ten-year-old, but still."

"Ten is better than five," Catherine said, heading to the storeroom for two cups of ice for their warming sodas.

When she returned, Antonia was back and rummaging through the bin of used books. "I forgot I needed something to read," she said. "I just finished *Anna Karenina*. Do you think Tolstoy knew when he finished it that he'd just written the Great Russian Soap

Opera? Oblonsky, Vronsky, Dolly, and Anna. Is it cheesy of me to admit I was both laughing and crying by the last page?"

She pulled out *The Brothers Karamazov, Goodbye, Columbus,* and *Another Country,* replacing them when she discovered a copy of *The Last Cigarette,* which had apparently arrived without Catherine's noticing it. Antonia turned it over, gazing at Wyatt's photo, then flipped through the pages of the novel, reading silently to herself, emitting faint sighs. "I love it, just love it," she said. "Henry loves it, too. He thinks it's one of the best novels of the last thirty years."

"Excuse me?" Catherine said, shocked. Her face went bright hot, and she blushed against her will.

"People change their minds. Even Henry," Antonia said. "You should look through his new collection. He mentions it there. I'm not sure which page, but it's easy enough to find."

As Jane was helping a customer locate *How to Cook a Wolf* by M. F. K. Fisher, she rang up Antonia's purchase. "Come tonight," the girl said, more emphatic this time, as Catherine slid a bookmark into the book and the book into the bag. "See you later," she added, moving to the door.

Catherine remained at the register, still aghast. Had she heard Antonia right? Had Henry told her he thought Wyatt's novel was one of the best of the last thirty years? It seemed improbable, even impossible, that Henry could change his mind so radically, especially since he'd hated the novel with such vehemence. Still, Antonia's declaration stunned Catherine, and she left the register, moving toward the "New Arrivals" table. Here she searched for Henry's collection among the other titles, only to remember she'd sold the last copy yesterday. She pictured Henry's book still at home on the credenza, still untouched. She was happy not to have gotten rid of it, though at the same time she was terrified of what she might or might not find in its pages. What have you done, Henry? Catherine thought, going back to the register to finish out the rest of her shift.

A FEW DOORS down from the bookstore, Thai Palace III was still crowded when the three women were finally seated forty minutes after arriving. Louise, who occasionally reviewed new restaurants for the local paper, commented on the minimal decor, the posters of Thailand stuck on the walls, the small brass Buddhas perched on the tables, each Buddha holding a tiny daisy in his hands. "Plastic, of course," Louise said. No one wanted to say what each was thinking — that the Thai restaurant was located in what had once been the pet store, a place that held associations for all of them, a place that Catherine and Wyatt had often visited, looking at puppies but never buying one.

So here she was, thinking about Wyatt again, Catherine realized with chagrin. She willed her thoughts back to the table and her friends. Though the restaurant was long and dingy, absent of any charm or character, she was happy to be present for the grand opening. Happy to have at least one more option of places to dine, anything other than what had become a rather mundane experience at Maddox Cafe. Except for the food, she knew the experience here would be the same. She'd never tell her friends about this boredom of hers, because she loved them. Sometimes, like tonight, as the waiter took their order and served them complimentary glasses of plum wine, Catherine wanted to be somewhere, anywhere, else. As she glanced around her, she saw the same familiar faces she'd seen for years, the bookstore regulars, the college professors, her letter carrier and his girlfriend, her dry cleaner and his boyfriend, even the man who delivered her newspaper. All were in attendance and all smiled and nodded when they saw her.

For a moment, she looked around for Henry and Antonia, then recalled that they were dining together, without her. She even looked for Linwood Lively, oddly excited at the idea of seeing him again. She wasn't confrontational, but something in her wanted to challenge him, the same way she wanted to confront Henry. Silly men, she thought, sipping her wine, the taste of it far too sweet. Yet she drank on, the wine like an anesthetic, numbing her against the dread of Henry and his essays, against Antonia and what she'd told Catherine this afternoon. She was buoyant when she took her first bite of the pad thai, the delicious taste of noodles and peanuts, of bean sprouts, spices, and shrimp, exploding in her mouth.

"It's delicious," she said.

"Mine's fantastic," Jane said.

Louise remained unconvinced. "Dog food," she said, setting down her fork. "I suppose we can stop guessing what happened to all the animals."

"Louise," Catherine said, a little tipsy, "negativity isn't good for the digestion."

"Maybe not, but a healthy dose of realism is," she said. "You should try it, Catherine."

"Um, please," Jane said. "I'm leaving if you're going to bicker."

"We aren't bickering," Catherine and Louise said, in unison, which caused them to smile.

"I still don't understand why you haven't gotten rid of Henry yet," Louise said, "especially when I have someone far more suitable in mind."

"Who is that?" Catherine asked.

"My son, Chase, of course," she said. "Now, before you say no, just let me — "

"Absolutely not," she said. "Besides, you just want him out of the house."

"Well, I think it's a marvelous idea," Jane said.

"How much is Henry paying you?" Louise asked. "If you don't mind my prying, that is."

"Fourteen hundred a month," Catherine said with pride.

"I'll double it," she said. "Every young man my son's age needs his own place. You can believe me when I tell you that no one will paint words on the cottage as long as Chase is there."

"No, he'll just ransack the inside," she said. "No offense, Louise, but I'd just as soon leave it empty than hand it over to a twenty-one-year-old boy."

"Twenty-two-year-old man," Louise corrected. "Let me tell you something about my son: he's more of a man than that Henry Swallow will ever hope to be." And with that, she fell silent.

"Ready or not, I'm changing the subject," Jane said. "Let's talk about the man over there who keeps staring at Catherine." She motioned with her head to a table against the wall, where a handsome man in a blue suit sipped his water. "He's been eyeing Catherine since we got here," she said. "I think she should go talk to him."

"She will do no such thing," Louise said, without looking at the man. "This is a restaurant — yes, a bad one — but it's still a restaurant, not a singles bar."

While Louise spoke, Catherine stood, getting up on the pretense of using the bathroom. As she did, she eyed the gentleman — to her that's what he looked — who was neither old nor young, but ageless, his eyes blue, his face broad and open, carved with smile lines. To her he looked like a traveling salesman straight out of the 1940s, and she imagined he had a deep, resonating voice and that this voice would try to sell her a Bible, a magazine, or a vacuum cleaner. And she knew she'd buy or at least think about buying anything he was peddling.

As she passed him, she slowed her step and he nodded his head at her, said good evening. She nearly swooned at the sound of his voice, which was even deeper than she'd expected. "Sit with me," he said, but something else was in his voice, too, a sharp breathlessness and a hiss that caught her off guard, and then she was moving away from him, down the length of the restaurant, passing friends and acquaintances, his proposition still ringing in her ears. In the bathroom, she checked her face and hair, applied a fresh coat of lipstick, her fingers trembling. She'd never been much good at flirting and wasn't even sure she remembered how. Suddenly she wanted to flirt, and this admission sent further trembles through her. She understood that she wasn't beautiful, but she did have a compelling, unusual face, soft green eyes, and curly blond hair that fell to her shoulders. She tanned deeply in the summer. Most men found her interesting — that's what they always said — and she took this to mean that they didn't find her threatening. In addition, Wyatt was gone, and though she missed him, she reminded herself again that her grieving had to end and that what she was feeling now — excitement, anticipation — was okay. Sit with him, she thought, dropping the lipstick into her purse. She pushed out of the bathroom with newfound hope and purpose and headed for his table, but he wasn't there. Now slightly wilted, she joined her friends, who had already paid and were waiting for her at the door.

"How much do I owe?" she asked, digging through her purse for her wallet, unable to meet their eyes, shame rising in her throat like bile. She could tell that her voice was shaking, that her friends were staring at her. When she looked up at them, she asked, "What?"

As she said this, she glanced out the window to see the man standing in the shadows across the street, just standing there, a book in his hand. Her heart soared, even as Louise said, "You don't owe us a penny," and touched her hand. "You know, Catherine, that all of my fussing is merely a symptom."

"Of what?" Catherine asked, as the man moved deeper into the shadows of the park. When she lost sight of him, her heartbeat slowed, yet the shame lingered. Then she was filled with sadness and a strong need to get away from the restaurant and her friends.

"Of how much I love you," Louise said as they stood on the sidewalk.

A sultry night, the air was charged with rain, yet Catherine knew it wouldn't rain a drop. She wanted it to rain, wanted the skies to break open, to crackle with lightning and split with thunder, and she wanted the storm to ravage the town, uproot trees and tear shingles from homes — anything to upset the monotony that was her life, including her lovely but dead-end job, these dinners with her friends, the empty house. Another night alone with the radio — the dread of this was simply too much to bear. Bear it, though, she would.

After she got home, she turned on the radio, all the more frustrated with herself. It had been the first time in ages that she'd even considered flirting with a man, and then this man got up and left? Well, she thought, if it's meant to be, I'll run into him again. She curled up on the sofa and gazed absently at Henry's collection of essays lying on the credenza, surprised now that she felt no urge to read it. Why should she? Whatever I find in its pages won't bring Wyatt back, she thought.

"Here I am," she said aloud to the radio, to Wyatt. "Another night."

It wasn't just another night, however, because, like it or not, something had been set loose, and the storm wasn't outside but inside Catherine herself, and she sparked and tingled with longing. She jumped up and slipped back on her flats, not bothering to shut off the radio, not bothering to think about Henry and the lease, or Antonia and her strange invitation. After grabbing her purse, she fled the house and climbed into the car, heading for Tint, the bar at the Tweed & Twining Arms hotel. Halfway there, however, she lost momentum, picturing the place, the drunken, flirtatious college girls and the men who bought them pitchers of beer; the lonely, desperate women who gazed yearningly at these men, trying to catch their eyes; the college boys, who weren't at the bar to make meaningful connections, these inappropriate boys with just one thing on their minds, which wasn't love. Just like that, she turned the car around, the inner storm of lightning and thunder evaporating, leaving in its place a searing aridness.

At home, she paused in her yard while a group of drunken boys and girls paraded past her. She said hello, envying the girls and their voluptuous strides, the way they clung to the arms of the good-looking, muscular boys. It seemed to her that Antonia should have been among them, that one of these boys should have been at her side. Again, Catherine wondered what Antonia was doing with Henry, not because she couldn't imagine her with him but because it disturbed her to think that Henry was probably doing to Antonia what he'd done to so many other young women. Then, against her will, she was walking toward the green house down the block. It was a charming if shabby four-room house with a spacious wraparound veranda. The night air contained the smell of whiskey and cigarette smoke, and the throb of music, all of which was suspended in the membranous heat. The house was lit up, and inside Catherine could see the twosome at the dining-room table, Antonia on Henry's lap. They were playing Monopoly, she realized as Antonia's overloud voice floated through the air: "St. James Place is mine!"

Well, this is a sight, Catherine thought, remembering her own failed attempts to interest Henry in a simple game of cards. As she

neared the door and knocked, she saw herself again in his sumptuous office at NYU, the Scrabble set she'd bought him still on the
shelf, untouched. He'd thanked her for it yet never asked her to
play; only later did she learn how much he despised board games.
Hearing the knock, Antonia got off his lap and Henry appeared at
the door and greeted her distantly. Entering, she glanced at his face
for signs of a black eye or bloodied nose, but there was nothing, just
Henry and his thick, black-framed glasses, which, she conceded,
still made him look like Trotsky.

"I knew you'd come," Antonia said, giving her a quick squeeze.
"Didn't I tell you she'd come, Henry?" She was drunk, on both
whiskey and the glorious life she was living, it seemed to Catherine.
"He's such a doubting Thomas," she added, leading Catherine into
the room.

Henry said nothing. He just stood there, cleaning off the lenses
of his glasses with his shirt. Now it was Catherine's turn to feel
like an intruder, and she regretted coming. Antonia went to the
radio and flipped through songs, finally settling on "Addicted to
Love." She cranked up the volume and closed her eyes, mouthing
the words with her full, dark lips. Catherine was at once taken
back to her own college days, when love quickly soured with one
boy or another, and she swore never again, even as she listened to
familiar songs on the radio and wept.

"I'm addicted to you, Henry," Antonia sang, opening her eyes
wide and gazing at him from across the room. She motioned toward him with her fingers — "Come dance with me" — but Henry
continued to lean stoically against the fireplace's mantel. The room
was too close, the air ionized and hot, and Catherine couldn't help
feeling as if she'd disturbed the balance of the evening. The storm
is in here, with them, she thought as phantom jabs of lightning,
in the shape of harsh words, a lingering argument, sizzled around

them, and Antonia swayed and twirled, upsetting the molecules all the more, trying, it seemed to Catherine, to clear the room of discord.

Antonia reached for Catherine and drew her near, dancing her through the house as one song became another and the girl's scents — of whiskey, cigarettes, and sweat — mingled in Catherine's nose, enticing and repellent at once. The house was alive and hummed with their dancing, which echoed through the rooms. Catherine, who hadn't danced in ages, felt self-conscious, and she broke away from Antonia to join Henry, who had moved to the sofa. Then the song was over, and Antonia was back, saying, "Dancing's better than sex, right?" She laughed. "Well, maybe not better than sex, but it's definitely high on the list." With that she collapsed on the sofa between them, pressing her cheek against Henry's face.

Henry didn't nuzzle her back, though, but got up and went into the kitchen. As he left the room, Catherine thought she had a better sense of the couple and, she supposed, of the nature of love — how hard it was to get right, how much harder to maintain. Though she rarely counted herself among the lucky, she did count herself lucky enough to have run across Wyatt. Yes, at times, he had been difficult and selfish, but Catherine had always known where she stood with him. At least, it seemed that way, she thought as Henry returned and handed her a glass of red wine.

"If memory serves, you always liked a zinfandel," he said. She thanked him and took a sip, moving toward the window. She hoped for a breeze, but there was nothing, the air beyond the house thick and milky, like a cataract clouding the night's eyes.

Outside a car slowed down, stopping near the house, and in the faint dashboard light, Catherine thought she saw the outline of someone familiar, and she started to say, "Oh, look," but cut herself off. The car was already pulling away, and she was already being pulled back into the spell of the evening, putting on a smile as she sipped her wine, tired of what wasn't being talked about. She found herself drawing on the very last reserves of good humor and patience, and it tired her. I'm here to talk about the cottage with you, Henry, she wanted to say, but when Antonia appeared with a cake — a Henry Wallbanger, she called it — the moment of possibility passed away.

"It's my mother's recipe," Antonia said, her voice a little sad. She set the cake on the coffee table. "Henry, you do the honors."

While Henry cut the cake and placed the slices on the pale pink china plates, Catherine drank her wine and thought about Antonia's declaration this afternoon, wondering why she'd insisted that Catherine come over. The air was still full of music, and Antonia continued to spin around the room, downing the last of her whiskey. While Henry watched Antonia, Catherine watched him, his stare becoming odd and dark, as if he were seeing her for the first time and was truly puzzled by what he saw. Aren't we all just the constant reminder of who we were and never will be again? Catherine thought.

She took a bite of the cake, which she found dry. Keeping that thought to herself, she said, "Delicious. Tell your mother I'd love to steal her recipe."

"I would if I could," Antonia said. "She passed away."

"I'm so sorry," she said, then stood suddenly. "It's late. I must go."

Henry, who'd been silent and brooding since she'd arrived, rose as well. "I'm going to walk Catherine home, darling," he said.

Catherine was halfway out the door when Antonia grabbed her by the wrist and said, her tone abruptly sober and agitated, "Do you — don't you — think it's odd that he won't move in here with me?" She glared at Henry, but her eyes were mirthful. "I mean, don't you think he should?" Catherine didn't know what to say, though she wanted to say that, yes, she did find it strange, and that Antonia had every right to find it strange as well. What kind of man was Henry to turn down a chance to live with a girl who so obviously was infatuated with him? What kind of man was he to refuse such a welcoming offer, especially since he needed a home? She wanted to push the subject further, to bring all of her concerns out into the open, but Antonia cut her off before she could, saying, "Tell him he's being unreasonable. Tell him he's just being an unyielding old poop."

"Not now, Antonia," Henry said sharply, ushering Catherine out of the house. Though the night was still warm and humid, a slight wind gusted, picking up loose dirt and swirling it around. Catherine thought about that summer night when she'd mistaken Henry for the wind batting at the door. Again, she wished she'd pressed Wyatt into telling her why Henry had come and what he'd had to say, but she hadn't. Now, so many miles and years from that night, it seemed pointless to dredge it up. When they were beyond the hum of the music, Henry said, "I'm sorry about that. She's been after me all day."

"She's frightened, Henry," Catherine said, unable to control herself. "I'd be frightened, too. I came to see you this morning and learned about the scene in your office. Have you told her what her father did? Have you?"

Her candor apparently took him aback, and he shrank away from her, saying, "You have no idea what you're talking about, but I appreciate the concern."

"The spot of blood I found? Do you still believe I don't know what I'm talking about?"

"I get bloody noses," he said flatly. "The heat brings them on."

"You expect me to believe that? You expect me to believe Linwood Lively didn't —"

"At this point, I don't care what you believe. The man who barged into my office was not Linwood Lively," he said. "Not to hurt your feelings, but none of this has a thing to do with you. Besides, do you honestly expect me to believe your concern? I don't blame you for your contempt — I was expecting it — but please don't insult my intelligence with this show. You've never been able to lie well, Catherine. It hasn't changed."

You are the most incorrigible, infantile man I've ever met, she thought, even as she said, "You accuse me of an awful lot, Henry. You're living on my property as my tenant, and contrary to what you believe, I am concerned. I'm concerned for both you and Antonia."

"If this is about the cottage, then just give me fair warning, and I'll go," he said, their hands accidentally brushing.

Catherine looked at his fingers, which, at one time, had raced over her body, the same fingers that had written the pernicious review that had destroyed Wyatt's future, her future. She tried to fill herself with contempt, to loathe him as she had for years, yet at this moment she felt nothing but compassion, which shocked and appalled her.

"Please, Henry. Go back to Antonia," she said. "I'll be fine."

He stared at her. "Very well," he said finally, and turned back down the block.

Though the street was deserted as Catherine approached the house, the air still throbbed with laughter and music emanating from the neighbors' homes. It was eleven o'clock and the parties, she knew, were just gathering speed, would climax around two, and eventually peter out — but probably not without the help of the police. They'd arrive, as always, to break up the parties, haul in the underage drinkers, fine those who'd bought the kegs. Catherine never minded the rowdiness, but Wyatt had, and more than once he'd made the calls to the police himself. Sometimes she awakened to find him throwing on his clothes, shaking with fury. "Thoughtless little troglodytes," he'd say, and twenty minutes later he'd return, happier. "It'll take them hours to figure it out." When Catherine asked him what he meant, he made scissors out of his fingers and sliced the air. "Snip, snip, snip. No more speakers, no more stereo," he'd say with glee. "Wyatt, you just can't do that," she'd say, laughing, horrified. "Sleep is ours," he'd say, and pull her into him, snoring before she could scold him any further.

Climbing the steps and almost tripping in the darkness, Catherine cursed herself for not turning on the porch light before she left the house. Yet she felt uneasy, for somewhere in the back of her mind she remembered turning it on. It was not something she would have easily forgotten, something Wyatt would always remind her about. It was a habit she continued even after his death. I am not crazy, she thought, nearing the front door. She looked up at the bulb; it wasn't there. And then Catherine noticed tiny shards of glass scattered over the porch.

Suddenly, out of the corner of her eye, Catherine caught sight of a figure hovering behind the lilac bush. Unable to see much beyond the immediate periphery of the porch, she could just make out the buttons on his jacket, which glittered faintly. As the man shifted and took a step toward her, she screamed, the sound absorbed by the surrounding music and laughter. She took quick swallows of air as the figure took another step toward her, and she fumbled at the door, sliding the key into the lock and turning the knob, but it didn't budge. The door had been chained from the inside. Then she was overcome by the inky blackness, which in her mind was as bright and hot as the sun.

When she awoke a minute or an hour later — she couldn't tell the difference — she was looking up into a blurry, familiar face, and she gasped as this face came into focus, becoming Wyatt's. "Are you all right?" he asked, helping her up. His unblemished face was just as handsome as the day she'd met him. She reached up to kiss him, but before she could he pulled back and away. As he did, his face became Henry's face, and when she realized her mistake, she turned away. Memories of her first kiss with Henry soured the previous seconds of joy, when she had thought without a doubt that Wyatt had come home. She winced against the sight of Henry, remembering vividly that wintry afternoon at NYU when he'd stopped to kiss her under the library's portico, and how the affair had begun after that, the secreted rendezvous, the expensive dinners in out-of-the-way cafes, the lying. She shut her eyes as Henry fiddled with the door, managing to undo the chain. Then he was leading her into the house and settling her on the sofa. He went around turning on lights, and then everything rushed back at her and she said, "Henry?"

"Yes, Catherine, I'm here," he replied, returning with a glass of water, which he handed to her.

"Why are you here?" she asked, taking a sip of water.

She knew the answer, though, even as she asked the question. Of course, he'd been on his way to the cottage, where he was living. And then she thought about how stupid she was to have let all this happen, because Henry always brought trouble with him. Now this trouble was as much a part of the fabric of the summer as Henry was a part of her life again.

"Are you all right?" he asked. "Maybe you should see a doctor."

"I'm as fine as I can be for someone who was attacked on her own porch," she said, her pulse still pounding in her head. "Did you see him? Did you see Linwood Lively?"

"I didn't see anyone," he said, and she shuddered at what she thought was the condescension in his voice. "Do you want me to call the police?"

"You don't believe me?" she asked. "He was here. He smashed the porch light, Henry, and he was waiting for me — or for you and Antonia," she added.

"I never should have brought her here," he said, sighing. "This is not working out the way I planned."

"You didn't force her to come here," Catherine said, relenting. Though she liked blaming Henry for Linwood Lively's recklessness, she understood that Henry was not responsible for any of the things the other man had done, or would do. "She came on her own." Like me, she thought. For love, she thought.

"Circumstances," he said. "Hers and mine." And he left it at that. "Now, do you want me to stay with you for a while?"

"No, but thank you," she said. What I want, really want, she thought, is the last year and a half of my life back. She rose and headed for her bedroom, pausing briefly at the credenza, her back to him. She gazed at Henry's book and said, "Antonia told me what you said about Wyatt's novel. Is it true?"

When he didn't respond, she turned around, but he wasn't there. A moment later, she heard the sound of the back door shutting and then the bell on the gate jangled, and she was alone again. She didn't want to be alone, and the fear crept through her as she shut all the blinds, closing the house around her. A depressing Mendelssohn fugue played softly on the radio, and she switched to a different, livelier station, raising the volume on the last few seconds of "She Drives Me Crazy." It was midnight and she should have been tired, but she wasn't. Even over the music, she imagined she heard footsteps on the porch, fingers tapping at the windows, and the terror coalesced into a sharp, hard knot in her gut. As the adrenaline spilled through her, Catherine's thoughts formed and broke apart: Was the figure she'd seen Linwood Lively, and if so what had he wanted? Had Henry scared him away? She went to the kitchen window, wondering if Henry were still up, but the cottage was dark. She wondered about Antonia as well, if she'd gotten into her car and gone dancing. The will and determination of a young woman, she thought, remembering when she would have gotten into her own car and driven into the city, looking for excitement. She had none of that will and determination left, not tonight. As she wandered the rooms of her house, Henry's book called out to her, yet Catherine, however curious, had no desire to read whatever it was he'd written. She picked up the book and flipped through it, passing cursorily from page to page. Stop, she thought. Just stop. She dropped the book on the credenza, feeling nauseated, and retreated into the bathroom.

As she washed her face, Catherine thought about Antonia's story and the girl, Hazel Meeks. She thought about the army base in Georgia; the soldiers; the sergeant; the bar; the mattress; and the cabin in the woods. She thought about the engagement ring the girl had found, about the soldier who used this ring to pay for his safe passage to Vermont. Then she remembered something else: the silver lunette earring the man had in his ear. It was this particular detail that sent Catherine back to Antonia's story in *Modern Scrivener,* the copy sitting on the night table where she'd left it. She flipped hurriedly through the pages, until she found what she was looking for — the description of the girl, a mere couple of sentences. The earring, she thought, closing the magazine, picturing the evening at Maddox Cafe again: she and her friends, Antonia and Henry, and the man, Linwood Lively, at the window. She again saw the strain in his handsome face, the penetrating green eyes, and the silver lunette earring glinting in his ear. Had

Antonia written about her father? Was this why he'd come to the town? If so, why was he bothering Henry, and why had he defaced the cottage?

Unless the story isn't a story, thought Catherine, climbing into bed. Unless it isn't fiction at all. She recalled an interview in the *Times* she'd read about the recently debunked Holocaust memoir, *The Hunger Maiden*. According to the article, a man named Vernon Fried had actually written the book, although Fried claimed he had merely had it published at the request of the supposed author, Marlene Keyser, who, it was later discovered, had died years before. Fried was being sued by a man claiming to be the real Marlene Keyser's grandson. When the interviewer asked Fried why he hadn't just written a novel, he had said, "Because fiction fails whereas autobiography prevails. Look, I know what I did was wrong, but was I wrong to tell Marlene's story? I did know her, and I did appropriate her story. But this book has reached thousands of people who might never have heard about the heroics of one single woman. Is that such a crime?"

From Wyatt, Catherine had learned that writers stole all the time, that this was merely part of the profession. She'd also learned that a fiction writer's greatest asset was his ability to take the facts of any true story and bend them into fiction, obscuring if not erasing the original truth. "Good fiction lies to get at the truth," Wyatt used to say. "Good journalism tells the truth to get at the lies. It's only great literature that does both. It presents a world in which the two aren't just intertwined, they're inseparable." What differentiates a good writer from a great writer, then, Catherine thought, is the victory of his lies — the scope and determination of his imagination.

In bed, Catherine shut off the light, caring little if Antonia had stolen the story or not, because it was nothing less than a literary marvel. It wasn't just the sentences, which were polished to a high gloss, or the characters, which she felt as drawn and close to as any of her friends, but that the narrative itself dropped her into places she never quite imagined, upsetting her expectations. It seemed to Catherine, a voracious reader, that she always came across one or the other — the great stylist with a derivative story to tell, or the great storyteller with derivative style. Like Wyatt before her, Antonia possessed both strengths, a wicked sense of storytelling and style, which only deepened Catherine's respect for her. Still, she was apprehensive when she considered the girl's motivation for revealing her father's secret in this way, if that were the case. Moreover, she had to wonder if the real story weren't that Antonia had used her father's pain and suffering for her own benefit but that she'd turned him into a hapless monster, forever caught in print, having to carry out the same crime forever.

Harmful if Swallowed

It was yet another steamy Friday in Winslow, and Antonia sat at her small desk in the dark-paneled study, hunting and pecking on the old Underwood No. 5, a gift from her father when she'd gotten accepted to Columbia. She'd composed "Vitreous China" on it so felt compelled to keep using it. She'd also written the novel on it, and as Henry had promised, it had sold, for more money than she had ever dreamed. Although these were pleasant recollections, they were useless to her now. She pushed away from the desk, frustrated; the writing just wasn't coming.

Besides, it was already early afternoon, and she had dinner guests arriving in a few hours. It was time to tidy up the house. Of course, all she really wanted to do was to keep working on this new novel, to find a way through the block she had encountered this morning. Which she might have been able to do had the housecleaner — recommended by Henry — shown up, but she'd fallen ill the night before, and there was no one to get in her place on such short notice. She thought about enlisting Henry's help by summoning him from the college, yet she knew how much he hated to be disturbed.

After gathering up the dust rag and wood polish, she began on the dining room, thinking about her novel's imminent release and about the launch party in Manhattan. It was all happening in a few days! She refused to worry about the reviewers and critics, who might or might not like it. She also thought about her young hero, Hazel Meeks, remembering her uncle's description of the once-beautiful girl: the long black hair, the slender neck, the dainty ears, and then the opal blue eyes blackened and swollen, the broken cartilage of her nose, and the busted lips. Below the neck, where even her uncle had refused to let his imagination take him, Antonia could see the cracked ribs, the abraded belly, the spots of blood in the pubic hair, the bruised thighs, scuffed knees, and slender ankles that gave way to dirty feet and toes — the real Hazel Meeks, Sylvie Adams, a poor southern girl.

Yes, she'd imagined the rest because she'd had to. What it must have been like for Sylvie as she lay on the mattress, the blood leaking out of her onto the white sheet, and how the soldiers had left her there to die. Because that's what they were hoping, that's how the story had to end: in her death. Yet the story didn't end, not for Antonia, who'd taken what her uncle Royal had told her and wrote the short story, then the novel, never once looking back, never once abandoning the vision of her father, even as she toiled over the scenes and turned him into what she realized now he'd always been — a liar and a murderer and a fugitive from justice.

Yes, a murderer, she thought, remembering the afternoon her uncle had told her the story. At the time she'd laughed in disbelief, thinking he'd made it up, that there was just no way she'd been living under the same roof with a man like that. Impossible, she'd thought back then. No. Both the horror of the account he had given her and the need to prove him wrong had brought her to the New York Public Library, where she researched the facts as she knew them. She found articles about the military base, Fort Benedict, in southern Georgia, and about Command Sergeant Bennett Sturgeon, including his obituary. She even found a few words about the arrest of her uncle Royal, but nothing about her father, nothing to prove or disprove her uncle's accusations. More significant, she'd found nothing about the girl, Sylvie. So she let it go, refusing to give her uncle's story credibility, and she called her father, never once mentioning the story or how she'd come by it, even though she wanted to ask him, feeling it was her duty as his daughter to let him know what her uncle had told her. That her uncle had come to her to tell her his story kept her curious, kept her up late at night, wondering, pacing the floor of her tiny Harlem apartment.

Once she started writing, giving Sylvie a voice, she couldn't stop. She'd written the story over a couple of months, then made copies and handed these copies out to the members of her advanced-fiction workshop, bracing herself for the typically highly petty, highly insensitive criticism they'd lob at her. "Beautiful, but an unlikely plot," said the redhead with stubby teeth. "Nicely written in every way, though I felt at times the writer got in the way of the story," said the bombastic recent Harvard grad. "I loved it," Calvin, her best friend, had said. "Don't change a single word." "I'm not sure about that," his boyfriend, Ernest, had said. "It's a good period piece, but how many more stories do we need about the Vietnam War?" This last comment led to an argument among the class. Some of them defended Antonia for her ability to pull off a story set in the late sixties, while others felt she'd failed to include enough specific detail to bring the spirit of the time to life. Henry, her instructor, had said little, good or bad, but she took what he didn't say as utter disapproval.

His silence wasn't disapproval, though. "On the contrary," Henry said later, when he found Antonia outside, smoking deeply, trying to get rid of the workshop's bitter aftertaste.

"You didn't say much," she said.

"Did I really have to say anything?" he asked. "Superb writers don't need my approval or blessing." She remembered this conversation, remembered it well, because it had pulled her through that semester, through the long, arduous writing of the novel. "You seem to have a lot to say," Henry told her, as they made their way back into the building. "Keep saying it."

Now, hundreds of miles from that place and that moment, Antonia pushed the mop around the hardwood floors, dressed in one of Henry's button-downs, wondering what might have happened if he'd never handed the story over to *Modern Scrivener*. Back then, she'd hated and loved him for it, though even now she still couldn't quite believe the prestigious magazine had liked her story enough to publish it. More, that they included her in their "Debut Fiction" issue. She'd gotten attention for the story, much attention. She still suspected that a part of her early success was due to her age — twenty-one back then — and another part of it was merely luck, even after Henry reminded her that she deserved her success. Still, wasn't it luck that had landed her at Columbia, in Henry's class, luck that he'd loved the story and had passed it along? Unfortunately, this luck had cost her dearly in other ways.

She lit a cigarette and smoked it as the floor dried, the sun speeding the process along. Beyond the spotty windows lay another bright, hot day. Inside, the ceiling fans spun the smoky air around, and the air conditioners struggled against the humidity. Having finished cleaning most of the rooms, Antonia dressed and headed

out with the shopping list she'd made the night before. On her
way to the store, she stopped at Catherine's house. As she knocked
on the door, she remembered that Catherine usually worked on
Fridays. She turned to go, but then the door opened.

"You are home," Antonia said, surprised.

"I am," Catherine replied, unchaining the door and gazing out.
She looked unwell, her cheeks drawn. "I was just about to take a
swim."

"I don't mean to bother you, but I need a favor," she said. "I'm
throwing a little dinner party tonight and was wondering if you
could spare a couple of chairs? I haven't gotten around to furnish-
ing the house properly."

"Chairs," Catherine said, turning back into the house. "Let me
check the shed."

Through the door, Antonia glanced into the shuttered sitting room, remembering the afternoon when she'd first come to
this house. Though she hadn't been invited, she stepped from
the porch's ferocious heat into the cooler sitting room. She again
took in the room, which looked as it had before yet also remark-
ably different. She knew these things happened — that sometimes,
rooms, like people, became more of what they were the more you
visited and got to know them. She wanted to know this room,
this house, wanted to know Catherine better. She was alone in a
strange little town, and while she didn't mind relying on Henry
to fulfill most of her needs, she thought it would be fun to have a
girlfriend. Besides, she liked Catherine, and admired her fortitude.
Antonia wasn't sure she herself would have been able to handle
anything as horrible as the loss of a husband. Especially the loss of
a husband who'd died as tragically and mysteriously as Wyatt had.
She'd never dare tell Catherine this, but she'd followed the news
of his death with keen interest, always wondering what had sent

him out of the house that day. She'd meant what she said — that Catherine's loss was a loss for the entire literary community.

While she waited, Antonia wandered absently from room to room. When she came to the study — this had to be his study, she thought — she paused, feeling a heady rush, the same rush she'd felt after first meeting Catherine. This was the heart of the house, she knew, and she treaded carefully into the disordered room, an eruption of books and boxes, the floor barely visible for all the papers strewn across it. Antonia breathed in, imagining Wyatt at his desk, at his typewriter (she didn't know if he'd used one or not, but something told her he had). He was all around her, as Sylvie (and her father) had been during the days and weeks she'd worked on the short story, then the novel. She stood over one box — WYATT'S THINGS was marked in bold, black ink — and was about to reach inside it when the back door banged open. After shutting the study door behind her, Antonia retreated into the sitting room.

A moment later, Catherine appeared with two folding chairs. "Will these do?" she asked.

She was sweating, and the sweat dampened her poorly high-lighted blond hair, washing out the brightness. The sundress, Antonia noted, fit her poorly, a billowy drape down her slender frame. She wondered if Catherine knew just how unflattering the dress was on her. Still, she thought Catherine handsome despite the outfit, though handsome in a circumscribed kind of way, the kind of handsomeness you had to look for. Had Catherine been Wyatt's muse? She tried to see what the man must have seen in her, yet she felt guilty and mean for doing so. He married her, she thought, and that's what counts.

"Is that — was that — where Wyatt did his writing?" she asked, gesturing to the closed study door.

"Yes," Catherine said, her face darkening. "Until he moved

into the cottage. Then I almost never saw him." This was the first time Antonia had heard her speak of him, of her experience, and the revelation of this detail suddenly saddened her. "Living with a writer. It wasn't always easy," she added. "All of you have such particular habits." Then she smiled. "I've been meaning to tell you how much I loved your short story." For a moment, it looked as if Catherine might cry. Instead, she disappeared into her bedroom and returned with a frayed copy of *Modern Scrivener.* "Would you mind?" She handed the magazine to Antonia.

"I'm flattered," Antonia said, as she signed her name to the story.

"I have so many questions," Catherine said, "but you're in a hurry."

"Grocery shopping," she said. "I have a turkey to roast and potatoes to boil and stuffing to make and cranberries to soak and a pumpkin pie to bake."

"Thanksgiving in June!" Catherine said.

"You probably think I'm crazy to cook such a big meal in all this heat, but I'm doing it for Henry," she said.

At the door, Catherine smiled. "I'm sure your guests will appreciate it, especially Henry."

"Why 'especially Henry'?" Antonia asked.

"No particular reason," she said. "Don't most men go crazy for a big turkey dinner? All those delicious leftovers?"

"Henry doesn't know a thing about the menu," Antonia said. "I'm surprising him." Though she didn't know why, she felt the other woman holding on to a disturbing, unpleasant memory.

"Well, I'm sure he will be," she said, helping her with the chairs, settling them in the back of the car. Then Antonia was thanking her again and starting the car, as Catherine appeared at the driver's-side window, asking, "Would you mind — would it be all right if I bummed a cigarette?"

Reaching for the pack on the seat beside her, Antonia said, "I didn't know you smoke."

"Normally, I don't," she said, taking the cigarette. "I used to smoke a pack a day. Wyatt hated it. So I quit."

"Quitting for love," Antonia said. "That's very romantic."

"A cigarette every now and then won't kill me." Catherine smiled again and moved away from the car.

Antonia called out, "Hey, if you aren't doing anything tonight, why don't you join us?"

"I already have plans, but I'll see what I can do," she said.

"Then at least come by for an early cocktail, and you can tell me what a terrible cook I am. We can have mint juleps on the veranda and pretend we're in a William Styron novel."

Catherine laughed and waved good-bye, disappearing into the house. Yes, I like her, Antonia thought as she drove away. Don't get too attached though, she cautioned herself, because when she finds out what you're up to, she'll never talk to you again. You're going to lose her trust and her friendship for good. Yet, as she told herself this, she also told herself that this is what a writer did, this is who she was and she'd make no apologies for it, even if it meant the loss of trust and friendship, even if it meant hurting the people she loved most. She knew there was a story the moment she had set foot inside Catherine's house. It was the force that had drawn her here, to Winslow.

She told no one about her new novel, not even Henry. She didn't want to risk someone finding out. This story was hers and hers alone, and she would follow it to wherever it took her, just as she'd followed Sylvie and her father. She knew she was indebted to Henry, should be open with him. She'd left Manhattan for him, of course, yet she'd also come to Winslow in search of more. She owed her uncle Royal, too, perhaps even more than she owed

Henry. Without him, she'd had no story to tell, nothing beyond the stories she'd already written, those earlier failures of imagination. Perhaps her fellow students at Columbia had been right to say her earlier work lacked heart, what Henry called an emotional core. She'd taken the criticism badly; it was as if they'd just accused her of having no heart, no emotional core of her own. This deficit of heart had been, she now saw, merely a flaw in the design, a symptom of the disease and not the disease itself. It was difficult, she understood, to stumble upon the right story at the right moment. It was difficult to let it come to you, like love, she thought. The problem was personalizing the narrative without letting personality get in the way of it. "Vitreous China," which had garnered her an O. Henry Prize, was successful precisely because she'd managed to get out of her own way and allow the story a life of its own. It wasn't about her, yet she was on its every page. How could she not be? How could it be any different?

She parked her car and was soon cruising up and down the aisles of the IGA, the town's one supermarket. Twenty minutes later, she loaded the groceries into the trunk, picturing the evening ahead and how once upon a time she might have invited her father to join them. She'd only told Henry bits and pieces about him, though nothing of what she'd done or who he really was, or that part of her willingness to leave New York City had to do with hiding out from him. Still, her father had located her, though she wasn't exactly sure how, and Henry now realized her fear.

How dare he make such a scene, she thought with indignation. She knew if he found her he'd come to the town to try to talk her into changing her mind. He'd accuse her again of dishonesty and disloyalty, would try to persuade her to return the money. You had no right to this story, he'd say. There are other stories to tell. To Antonia, who'd always known a good story when she heard one, there were no other stories so worth the telling, none quite like this one. Besides, it felt more like the story had chosen her. No, she thought, imagining her angry, dejected father, stalking the streets of the town, relentless in his pursuit of her. He'd already found her once. She knew it was just a matter of time before he found her again.

At home, Antonia washed and prepped the vegetables, located the necessary spices, and went to work on the meal, all the while thinking about this new novel of hers, mapping it out in her head. She knew she had to write another page-turner, better than the first, because, as Henry liked to remind her, you're only as good as your last book. With Henry's support, though, she realized she couldn't fail. He'd already made sure she'd been well received at Chimera Books, an imprint of Beadle & Blau, one of the most reputable publishing houses in New York. He'd called his friends at the *New York Times,* peddling the novel as if he were its biggest and best fan. She thanked him repeatedly, yet she had no idea how to repay his generosity, except by loving him as best she could. And she did love Henry, as much as she'd loved anyone. One day she wanted to be his wife. Once, not that long ago, she and Henry had talked of marriage, but the subject hadn't come up again since her move to Winslow.

The turkey was in the oven, the pots simmering on the stove, and the atoms in the air were bumping furiously against one another, producing an incredible heat and aroma. The aroma of the holidays, she thought, looking past the hours of preparation to the evening's beautiful culmination — the five (or six, if Catherine showed up) of them seated around the table, drinking wine and laughing, while Henry carved the turkey. She was throwing this dinner in honor of him; a meal she trusted would launch the three-day rapprochement between him and his estranged son, Ezra. Just another thank-you among many: Thank you for your belief in me. Thank you for your support. Thank you for your love. She need not have thanked Henry, she knew, because her move to the town, he said, was thanks enough. Besides, how could she ever truly thank Henry, except by fulfilling her own promise to write another well-received book?

After she left the kitchen, Antonia unlocked the door to her study, heading immediately for the typewriter. She sat down, lit a cigarette, and stared at the few sentences she'd written this morning. Usually, she was able to sit for hours and work, as everything else fell away, and she filled one page after another. Five, ten pages later, she'd glance up to find the sun gone and the sky dark, realizing she'd been at the typewriter half the day. This novel — it balked and cried against her gentlest urgings. She was missing significant, indispensable details that would help shape the choppy, incongruous narrative and awaken her half-sleeping characters. She couldn't get at the heart of the story because she didn't have the body. She needed the body to get at the heart, plain and simple. Whereas the writing of her debut novel had been relatively easy — her uncle had supplied her with the blueprint, the body — the writing of this second novel was proving very difficult.

Not that fiction depends at all on truth, she thought, tapping a key, tapping another, trying to make connections where it seemed none existed. She knew they existed, because she still sensed them, had sensed them the minute she'd walked into the blue house, the minute she'd mentioned Henry, and Catherine went pale. There was more, so much more — Henry's refusal to talk about the accident; the girl's name, Wren, which he sometimes shouted out in sleep; the essay he'd written about Wyatt Strayed. Here were connections, however loose, and Antonia the writer was determined to get at them, while Antonia the friend and lover knew she should walk away from the entire endeavor. An hour later, after smoking several cigarettes and writing just one sentence, she pushed away from the desk, feeling defeated. In the small bedroom, she stretched out on the bed. With hours to go before anyone arrived, she shut her eyes. Sometimes all it took was a nap and she'd be able to find her way back into the narrative. She hoped when she opened her eyes that everything murky and unresolved would reveal itself to her. Yet when she awoke an hour later, the only thing that revealed itself to her was the darkening sky viewed through the window. Groggy and disoriented, she sat up, convinced that she was back in her old bedroom in Damascus, Vermont. For a moment, as she gazed out at the fleeting twilight, she had never left the safety of her father's house. Then, that familiar landscape blurred and dimmed into this one, and she rubbed her eyes, returning reluctantly to Winslow.

The air held a heavy, alarming suggestion of smoke, which filtered under the door. Sliding out of bed, she threw open the door and froze. Someone was in the kitchen rattling around. Henry, she thought, rushing out of the bedroom, the smell of smoke more pronounced the closer she came to the kitchen. Here, she paused in the threshold, startled to find Catherine and not Henry at the sink, scrubbing a pot. Antonia knew then that her oversleeping had cost her the meal, and she gazed at the stove, where the charred, awful remains of the bird still sat, belching up whispers of black smoke. Nearly hysterical, she asked Catherine if she were able to salvage any of the food.

"No," she said, drying the pot. "Nothing at all."

"Oh," Antonia said, wilting. "Now what am I going to do?"

"Don't worry," Catherine said, already picking up her pocketbook from the table and heading for the door. "I'll be back in a while. Set the table in the meantime."

Antonia glanced around the spotless kitchen, where Catherine had returned everything to its rightful place, from the knives, the cutting board, and the mixing bowl to the blender and grater. Everything shone, the counters and the porcelain sink, which the woman had scrubbed clean as well. Antonia leaned against the sink, glaring at the turkey's smoldering carcass, tears spilling down her cheeks. I'm an idiot, she thought, hating herself for the nap, the time when she should have been more vigilant. She approached the stove and gave it a good kick, hard enough to put a tiny dent in the door.

When Henry showed up a few minutes later, Antonia was on the sofa in the dark, sobbing for all that she'd ruined — the perfect dinner that was to christen the perfect weekend. Henry sat down next to her, saying nothing, and she sank into him, sobbing even harder. "I love you, Henry. I really, really love you," she said as he held her close, kissing the crown of her head. She shifted her body, and her lips found his, and then they were making their way into the bedroom and shutting the door, undressing in the low lamp light, his body still magnificent to her, all of him, his silver-haired chest, the constellation of minor scars that mapped the mishaps of his boyhood, the major scar on his thigh from the car accident. She traced a finger over this scar now, knowing enough not to mention it again, remembering how quickly and irrevocably he closed up when she did. "I don't want to talk about it," he'd say, and he wouldn't. Won't, she thought, as the slow rhythms of his hips met the rhythms of her own, and then he was inside her and this time it was he who was crying and she wondered why as she kissed the tears from his face. As she did, she thought she heard a car pull up to the house and footfalls on the porch and shuddered against this intrusion — was it her father? — but she didn't care at this moment who it was, because Henry was beneath her and she was above him, and they were one, an unlikely pairing that had always made sense to her. He knew her, the depths of her ambition, and she knew him, the depths of his own. We are royalty, she thought. The king and queen of letters.

After, Henry got up to take a shower, while Antonia smoked a cigarette, loving the sweat that glistened on her young body, her breasts achy from Henry's lips. She joined him in the shower, soaping his back, the wiry, taut muscles beneath the aging skin. How little she cared that he was fifty-nine and that she was twenty-three, that they were born of different times and generations, because they fit so well together. It still took her breath away, and when he said her name, his voice broke the surface of her daydream and awoke in her thoughts of the future, of marriage, of children, and of money. Privilege, she thought. We will get married, and I will have his children, and we will live in glamour high above the city. We will be the envy of our friends and enemies alike. We will grow old together, and I will dedicate all of my books to him, my husband. He will understand why I have done what I've done, and he will forgive me. Wren, she thought, but it wasn't a thought, because, without realizing it, she'd said the name aloud; and then Henry was shrinking away from her, already climbing out of the shower, cinching a towel around his waist and hurrying out of the bathroom.

AFTER SLIPPING INTO her favorite vintage baby-doll dress and sandals, Antonia wandered out of the bedroom to find the table set and the front door ajar. She heard the low murmur of voices on the veranda and paused. Henry was talking to Catherine about his son, Ezra, the weekend plans he'd arranged — the kayaking on the Mohawk River, the hikes in the mountains, the movies at the Mayfair. "I hope it all goes well," Catherine said, then she was saying good-bye, as Antonia headed into the kitchen. The bird was gone, a different, tin-foil-covered pan in its place. Through the open windows, a light breeze stirred the curtains, dispelling the last of the heavy stink of smoke. Now the room smelled as it had hours before, full of rich, savory odors emanating from the stove and the several brown paper bags lined up on the counter. Antonia peered into one of the bags, then another — mashed potatoes, cranberry sauce, candied yams, pumpkin pie, stuffing — everything necessary for a traditional Thanksgiving dinner.

Catherine, she thought, gratefully. She turned to the stove, lifting away the layers of foil that eventually revealed a modest-sized game hen, the drumsticks tied up and booted. It wasn't as large as the turkey, but it'd do. It has to, she figured, replacing the foil, just as Henry appeared in the doorway. "That was Catherine," he said coldly, not meeting her eyes. She suspected he'd remain like this all evening, punishing her in big ways and small for mentioning Wren. "She can't make it tonight, which is just as well," he said, turning his eyes to the clock on the wall. It was seven thirty; the guests would be arriving at eight. "You should have had the decency to tell me she was invited, Antonia." She went rigid, wanting to remind him that this was her house and her dinner party, which she was throwing for him. She didn't say any of this, because she finally understood his gruffness had nothing to do with her, that he was reacting (overreacting, overanalyzing, she thought) to the evening's indeterminate variations.

"Henry, everything's going to be fine," she said, moving toward him and kissing his cheek. "You look very handsome." More handsome than she had ever known him to be. In the three years since they'd met, she'd never seen him as vulnerable or exposed as he was at this very moment. Yes, three years of knowing him, during which there were the slow, sometimes painful baby steps of her seduction, coaxing him through the doors of his doubt and fear into the romantic rooms she'd decorated — all for him. This seduction took a far greater effort on her part, though she'd never thought about it as effort. Rather, she'd thought about it as nothing more than her right to him, to love a man like Henry Swallow. The love she had for him back then, which had been based partly on his illustrious reputation, bore little if no resemblance to the complex love she had for him now, which was based on moments like these. This was the Henry she idolized and cared about, not that other Henry, who clung to his ruthless prowess and even more ruthless, rigid ideals about literature. Look at what he did to Wyatt Strayed, she thought, and how he did it, which aren't half as terrible as his reasons for going through with the review at all. There was a story here as well, as old and bruised and buried as his dislike of Catherine and her dislike of him. Yes, Antonia saw the way Henry glowered through his smiles and Catherine scowled through hers every time they were in the same room together. They never seemed to notice that she noticed them, yet she did. What aren't you telling me, Henry?

Twenty minutes before the guests were due to arrive, she retired to the kitchen, organizing the food, tossing Henry's salad, which he'd brought with him: a bag of prewashed mixed greens and a bottle of salad dressing. When he came into the room, she poked fun at him for his domestic failing.

"I'm a critic, not a househusband," he said sulkily.

She laughed but resented the comment. Over the last few months, she'd done quite well at deflecting such offhand remarks, the insinuation that he'd never make a decent husband. He had been a decent husband at one time, but the accident had taken care of that. My wife left me, he'd told her, and that was all. That wasn't all, though, and she knew it. She yearned to get him talking about these past six years, why he no longer drove, why he called out the girl's name in his sleep. "Just tell me. Unburden yourself. There are ways out of this, Henry," she would say, wanting to add, "Write it down." Even as she thought it, she understood her own selfish impulses, her own greed, and she tamped them down; clearly, the story was too painful for him to relive. Yet she needed him to share this pain with her. It was the only way.

"I can't, Antonia," he'd say heatedly. "If I could tell you, I would." And that would be that.

Certainly, if it'd been up to Antonia, if she'd been the award-winning critic, she would have found something in the ordeal to lift the story out of tragedy and make it art. She'd come across one story and that story had resulted in a novel. Now she was ready for another, but she needed Henry to tell her. Yet she had other battles to fight (and win), like the one she'd raised again yesterday about his moving in with her. The explanations Henry gave against the move were flimsy: two writers, one office, he said. The house is far too cramped as it is, he said. The work on my house will be finished soon enough, he added, turning an indifferent eye to her protestations that she'd feel safer with him around, that she didn't see the point of living apart.

Tonight, as Antonia looked at Henry, she saw a glimmer of the man he once was and not the besieged man he had become. What she saw mostly was the accident, which was limned in his handsome face, in the etched lines around his mouth and in the dimmed brightness of his eyes. It was there every time he kissed her, made love to her, as if he were forcing all of his sadness and regret into her. Of course she wanted his sadness and regret, his suffering, because Henry was her second novel. Sometimes she'd watch him sleep, hoping that when he awoke he'd have forgotten in the night all that he'd lost. She'd forget as well, about all the secrets he kept close. She'd forget the novel altogether. How could

she possibly go through with it? Yet when she heard a car pull up
to the house, and she went to put on her makeup, knowledge of
the secrets he kept from her swirled through her, enlivening her
all over again.

From the other room came Nina Simone's gravelly voice tumbling through the cool air-conditioned house, while beyond them
lay motionless Winslow, this town she still didn't know or like.
When the car doors opened and closed, she wanted to meet her
friends on the walk and tell them, "Turn around. I have no idea
what I'm doing here. Let's go," joining them in their car and directing them back over the bridge and past Henry's house, which led
to the interstate, this four-hundred-mile ribbon of road that connected her to Manhattan.

When the doorbell rang, Antonia was applying her lipstick,
imagining a different night, her upcoming book party at Leland's,
the legendary restaurant and publishing haunt on Manhattan's
Upper East Side. "Everyone will know your name," Henry had
said. "I'll make sure of it." She believed and trusted him, even as he
seemed to blanch every time she told him her latest news: "They
want to send me on a twelve-city book tour," she said. "They're
taking out a full-page ad in the *Times*," she said. "I'll be inter-
viewed on Fresh Air by Terry Gross!" she said. She wasn't naive
enough to assume that these promotional tactics weren't often be-
grudged other writers who didn't have Henry Swallow as an ally,
who weren't sharing his bed. She relayed to Henry what her editor had told her, that she was the marketing department's darling.
"Well, of course," he said. "You're an easy sell: a young, beautiful,
and talented woman, who's written a deeply affecting, original
novel." Still, when he'd said this, she felt the words slice like a ra-
zor through her. She knew how he felt about originality, that he
despised disingenuousness of any kind. "If I can see the writer in

the work," he said on that first day of class, "then it's clear to me this writer is more involved with his own story than with imagining a fictional one." Then, cautioning them, he added, "This is a fiction class, where you will share and evaluate one another's stories. Notice the use of the word 'stories,' because that's what I expect from you — stories, not journal entries or personal essays or chapters from your Great American Novel that also double as your autobiography. Fiction is about character. Fiction is never ever about you." He flashed his eyes on the room. "Edith Wharton said that the writer must, above all, bear in mind at each step that his business is not to ask what the situation would be likely to make of his characters but what his characters, being what they are, would make of the situation. 'Characters, being what they are,'" he repeated, pausing to look at every individual face. "Most of you will never understand what I'm talking about. Most of you will never go on to publish. That's okay, because most of you couldn't write your way out of a paper bag. I'm only here for the one or two of you who do understand what I just said. I'm here for the one or two of you who know that the most interesting characters make the most interesting mistakes — they fall from grace and keep on falling until nothing is left of them. That, ladies and gentlemen, is what I like to read. The best stories do not have happy endings. If you write a happy ending in here, I will crucify you. Understand?"

She'd found these words of his harsh, rigid, and condescending, but he was Henry Swallow, after all. (She had been warned against him, precisely for these reasons.) She'd applied for his class, only because her top choice had taken a sabbatical. She'd never expected to get into his class, but there she was, one of eight. She took his advice to heart and struggled those first few weeks to leave herself out of the story, but she failed miserably at it; she found that everything she wrote was about her. Still, because it was her turn to workshop and she had nothing else to hand in, she distributed, in her opinion, one of the least offensive pieces, which Henry ended up slamming.

"This reads like a writing exercise," he wrote on the back of the story. "There's no emotional depth. Try again." Then, magically, miraculously, she stumbled across a story that had nothing (and everything) to do with her, and all of Henry's cautions suddenly made sense. Antonia was young and inexperienced in the ways of writing, the rules that governed fiction, yet she took to them with ease, clinging to and relying on her guide, Sylvie. Through the dead woman's eyes, she saw the world differently and her father differently, and she harnessed all of her imagination's power, which heated her words and seared away all trace of herself in the work. The process was mysterious and extraordinary, as close to the divine as she'd ever gotten. In the story, she was nowhere and everywhere, in every sentence and on every page, yet missing just the same.

Antonia Lively became Sylvie Adams, and Sylvie Adams became Hazel Meeks, both and neither, at once.

What would Henry say about how she'd come to find the story? What would he say about pillaging her father's past? In her mind, she defended the novel against him, even as she checked herself now in the full-length mirror. I'm his daughter, she would assert. By proxy, the story belongs to me as much as it does to him. Still, having read Henry's harsh reviews of such books — "egomaniacal claptrap," he called them — she knew that he despised writers who ravaged their own lives and the lives of others. Did it matter where the story came from as long as the writer did it justice, as she had?

Antonia liked to laugh at Henry when he railed against memoirs and memoirists, and, in particular, the ghostwriters they'd used to do the actual work. Tonight, however, there was no laughter when she thought about how she was nothing more than a ghost-writer herself, that the novel she'd written wasn't a novel at all. Still, hadn't Henry endorsed the writing of it? Would she have written it without his encouragement? Yes, she owed him a lot, but she didn't owe him any explanations. Besides, who cares what they call it as long as it sells, she thought. Hearing in the next room Calvin's and Ernest's hellos, then Ezra, who said, "I need a drink. That drive was bullshit," she wished suddenly for Catherine, an impartial, friendly buffer against the evening.

After switching off the bedroom light, Antonia took a deep, steadying breath and went out to greet the men, who beamed and clapped the moment she entered, as if she had just won the Pulitzer Prize.

TO HER SURPRISE and relief, the dinner was an undeniable success. She served Catherine's food as if it were her own, taking the compliments in stride, although the drunken Henry tried his best to expose her own domestic failing by alluding to the rickety plot of a short story he'd recently "read." "A young chanteuse throws a dinner party for the daughter she hasn't seen in years," he said. "Rather than keep an eye on the meal, she chooses to practice for an upcoming show and thus ruins everything." It was mean of him, but Antonia simply smiled. Henry's drunkenness, she knew, could go any number of ways. Tonight, unfortunately, it was leading him into the cruel.

Throughout the meal, Ezra kept getting up to smoke on the veranda. Antonia followed him on one of these trips while Calvin quizzed Henry on the last great novel he'd read. She found Ezra in the near dark, tapping out a cigarette from his pack.

"Do you have another?" she asked.

He lit two, then handed one to her. They stood in the hot

evening air and blew lines of smoke up to the starry sky. A tall, gaunt boy with slender, feline features, Ezra wasn't handsome like his father, but stately, more like his mother, she imagined. He wasn't that much younger than she, but young enough to have retained the soft, supple face of his boyhood. Though she tried, she didn't like him and supposed the feeling was mutual.

"This isn't such a bad place," Ezra said, gazing at the stars, then back at her. His eyes were irrefutably Henry's.

"I've only been here for a few weeks," she said, "but I think I'm getting used to the quiet."

"I love Manhattan. I couldn't live anywhere else," he said, smirking.

"I'm glad you're here," she said with cautionary warmth. "I'm also glad Calvin could give you a ride. Aren't my friends superb?"

"Ernest's really hot," he said.

"If you like shy, creative types from the Midwest," she said, "then, sure," though she herself couldn't quite see what Calvin saw in the Michigander, who Antonia believed was talentless.

"I met this one guy a few months ago at Duvet, that bar in the East Village," Ezra said. "We sort of hooked up."

She wondered if he were trying to be provocative but then realized that he must have felt just as uncomfortable and out of place as she did. She found his awkwardness sad yet endearing, and wondered if they might have been great friends under different circumstances.

"Sort of?" she asked.

"I fucked him," he said. "That was all he wanted because when I called him, he'd apparently given me the number to the time and weather."

"Ah, men," she said. "Most of them are such assholes."

"Men," he said, "have assholes and that's what I care about most." He smirked again. She laughed halfheartedly.

"Well, now that you know Calvin and Ernest, you should hang out with them," she said. "They throw fabulous parties, by the by."

"Thanks," he said, "but I'm way too busy for parties at the moment."

"You're only nineteen," she said. "You can't possibly be too busy for fun."

"I'm working at Granddad's magazine," he announced proudly, as if it were the greatest coup in the world: Dillard Bloom, Henry's erstwhile father-in-law, was the editor-in-chief of *Modern Scrivener.*

"That's wonderful," she said. "So you want to be a writer?" She thought how easy it would be for him to publish, with Henry as his father and Bloom as his grandfather. He's totally set, she realized with sudden jealousy. "Are you working on something now?" she asked.

"A memoir," he said. Then, lighting another cigarette, he added, "And wouldn't you like to read it?" Though he said it teasingly, she cringed, his announcement sending shivers up and down her back. "I'm calling it 'Harmful if Swallowed.' You like?"

No, she didn't like, but she was intrigued. It hadn't dawned on her until this moment that Ezra might be another way in. "It sounds juicy and promising," she said, feeling the need to say something. "You'll have to let me read it when you're done."

"You can read it when it comes out," he said, blowing a smoke ring, then immediately breaking it in half by dragging a finger through it. "He" — gesturing at Henry inside — "doesn't know anything about it. So if you tell him, I guess I'll just have to kill you."

Then Henry was through the door and on the veranda, saying, "Ezra, that isn't very nice." Antonia went rigid, wondering if he'd heard the first part of their conversation, but it seemed he hadn't, because he was smiling. "Apologize to Antonia, please," he said, still smiling as he wrapped an arm around her.

"Henry," she said, wrapping her own arm around his waist, "it's fine. We were just talking."

Had they really just been talking, or had she failed to read this tête-à-tête for what it was, less personal and more menacing? Because it seemed to her now that Ezra was implying an understanding of Henry that she herself would never be privy to. It also seemed that he'd simply been goading her for a reaction, which infuriated her.

Calvin appeared with two glasses of wine and handed one to Antonia, who took it and kissed him on the cheek. She'd met Calvin and Ernest in Henry's class, though Henry hadn't remembered either of them until she reminded him about their first workshop when Ernest unveiled his wretched story and Calvin supported it vociferously. She loved Calvin, every inch of him, from the top of his large, bald head to the bottom of his large feet. He was warm, charming, and southern. In his thirties, he still looked as young as Antonia herself. Ernest was Calvin's complete opposite in every way. In his midtwenties, he was tall and blond, with a decisive cruel streak that went against everything she'd ever heard about midwesterners. Still, because he and Calvin were together, Antonia had no choice but to tolerate him, which she thought she was doing a good job of tonight, even when Ernest, who was still in the house, shouted through the window, "You better not be smoking, Watts."

This was something else she disliked about Ernest, this tendency to call everyone by his or her last name, as if he were still in boarding school. "I wasn't going to until you reminded me," Calvin said softly, and turned to Ezra. "Would you mind?"

"I'm all out," he said, though Antonia knew differently.

"Oh, just give him a fucking cigarette," she said. She hadn't meant to say it quite the way she had, but there it was, her pent-up distaste for Ezra finally in the open.

Henry pulled away, though he said nothing, while Ezra just shrugged, which only further fueled her fury. She excused herself and went into the house for her own pack, which she thought she'd left in the kitchen. Here, she found Ernest, stacking the plates in the sink. It was a kind, surprising gesture, even for Ernest, and she warmed to him a bit. "You don't have to do that," she said.

"I don't have to do many things, Lively," he said, grinning.

"I'm glad you guys are here," she said. "Really. It's so great to see some familiar faces."

"We've been planning to visit," he said, and Antonia knew he meant that Calvin had been planning to visit. "Are you sure that this is the right weekend? I mean, you seem on tenterhooks."

"I'm fine," she said, but of course she wasn't. Before she could speak again, the kitchen window that faced the empty, black backyard suddenly shattered. Ernest yelled as Antonia tried to scream, her voice lost in her throat. She shut her eyes and felt a quick, rushing disturbance of air at her face, as if someone or something were exhaling a hot, angry breath. There was the quick rush of footsteps across the hardwood floor as everyone except Ezra converged in the kitchen. Ernest was kneeling on the floor, saying, "It's a typewriter." Sure enough, as Antonia opened her eyes, she saw what everyone else was seeing—a battered typewriter lying on its side, surrounded by broken glass. As she kneeled next to Ernest on the floor, she realized it wasn't just any old typewriter but her typewriter, the Underwood No. 5. All the keys were missing, and a single sheet of white typing paper was still spooled in the roller. Half of the sheet was gone, ripped away, but the other half, on which words had been typed, remained perfectly intact.

While Calvin swept up around her and Henry went to find Ezra, Antonia picked up the typewriter and placed it on the table. She sat down across from it, sighing, running a finger over the beautiful, eviscerated machine, angry tears running down her face. She ripped the paper from the carriage and read the words typed on the torn page in three single lines: *I know exactly what you are and who you are. You won't get away with this. You'll never write another word again, so help me God.* It was, of course, unsigned. Antonia didn't need to see a signature to verify the vandal, because it could have only been one person, this person who hadn't rushed into the kitchen along with everyone else: Ezra. She heard Henry calling out for him, then nothing, just the sound of the broom and the glass and the wind through the shattered window. She couldn't believe any of this was happening, though of course it was, all of it: the feeling that her life was being torn apart by vandals, a sense that the past was about to threaten her future, the fear that everyone despised her for being who she was. She wasn't a paranoid person, yet tonight, as she thanked Calvin for the help cleaning up, and floated into the study for a fresh pack of cigarettes, Antonia felt the world suddenly against her. All of it.

To her horror, the study door was unlocked, which was also a mystery, especially since she had the only key. The room was as she'd left it, except for the missing typewriter. She hurried to her desk, forgetting the cigarettes, far more worried about the pages of her new novel, which she always kept secured in one of the drawers. She used a different key, a small brass key, and opened the drawer, relieved to find the seventy or so pages still where she'd left them. The study window was open and the screen removed, and as she replaced the screen and closed and locked the window, she thought, Here is Exhibit A. She pictured Exhibit B on the kitchen table and Exhibit C, the note. What had those words meant? Hadn't she already gotten away with everything? Hadn't she already started work on something new?

As she left the study to look for Henry, to talk to him about

Ezra, everything about the night seemed to her all wrong. Doubt rippled through her. Not tonight, she thought. Not now. Now, she simply wanted to find Henry. Instead, she found Ezra lying on his back in the lawn, gazing up at the stars and smoking another ciga-rette. She stood over him and said, "Where's Henry?"

He blew a thick cloud of smoke toward her face, and said non-chalantly, "Am I my father's keeper?"

"That was a nasty thing you did," she said. "I've been nothing but kind to you. I invited you out here to have a wonderful week-end with Henry, and this is how you repay me."

He blinked at her, dumbfounded. His voice innocent, almost hurt, he said, "What . . . I don't . . . What are you talking about?"

"Don't play stupid with me," she said sharply.

"Where's my father?" he asked, rising.

"I just asked you that," she said. "Besides, Henry has nothing to do with this."

Then Ezra was laughing, saying, "He has everything to do with everything." He paused. "Do you know why I finally gave in and came out here this weekend?"

"Because it was time," she said. "Because Henry loves you and you love him, no matter your differences."

Again he laughed, but it was mechanical and hollow. "Hardly," he said. "I wanted to see this farce for myself. I wanted to see just how far the old man had fallen and what exactly he'd fallen for." He brushed a loose piece of grass from his arm. "I know who and what you are, Antonia. If my father can't see it, then he gets what he deserves."

So I am right about him, she thought, picturing the note, trem-bling with fury. "You little bastard," she said, her eyes white with rage.

"I wonder what it's like for you to kiss a man old enough to be your grandfather," he said with disgust, and when he said it, she slapped him hard across the face, knocking the cigarette out of his mouth.

The sound of the slap, like the sound of his laughter, went ricocheting through the air. Antonia dropped her hand, and Ezra stood there, a terrible, tight grin pulled across his face. She turned and rushed into the house, where she went into the bedroom and slammed the door. She couldn't stand the sight of him another second. Switching off the light, she shivered and burrowed her way under the blankets, although the room was warm. Five minutes later, she was asleep.

ANTONIA SLEPT FITFULLY and awoke with a start, her heart slamming in her chest. There was someone else in the room with her, a man, and for a split second she imagined this man her father and she shut her eyes against him. When she heard Henry say her name, however, she opened her eyes and sat up, waiting for his next words, for him to scold her. She knew already that in her own defense she would rebuff him, saying, "You should have heard the things he said to me. You should have heard what he said about us." Yet Henry said, "I'm sorry that took so long. I went to the cottage to get Ezra an extra blanket and pillow and ran into Catherine."

"Henry," Antonia said, her voice foreign even to her. "I'm sorry."

"About what?" he asked, sliding into the bed beside her. He was hot and sweaty and the feel of him brought her a surge of relief. She dug her face into the crook of his neck, and kissed him gently, thinking, Good, Ezra hasn't said a word, then.

"I was exhausted. I haven't been such a great host. I hope Calvin and Ernest are all right," she said.

"Sound asleep, as far as I can tell," he said. Then, "I'd say it was a successful evening, typewriters through windows aside." It angered her that he was making light of something as serious as what had happened, but then she knew Henry and that he'd do anything to leaven the moment, protecting her. "We can call the police in the morning," he said, drawing her closer.

"Let's just drop it," she said, because she knew how important this weekend was to him. "I'm sure it was just an awful prank, like — " She stopped herself. Now wasn't the time to bring up the words splashed across the cottage. "I hope it isn't too awkward with Calvin and Ernest here. They have to get back tomorrow anyway and then it'll just be you and Ezra."

"Me, Ezra, and you," he said, nuzzling her. "No, it isn't strange having them here. They're your friends, Antonia. They're important to you."

She kissed him again, then got up and went into the bathroom. She took a bath, because it always helped to calm her, and fifteen minutes later when she came out Henry was asleep, a copy of her novel open and resting on his chest. She removed it and switched off the small reading lamp. On the acknowledgments page, he was the first person she listed; it was his novel as much as hers. He'd gone through it with her, editing it and loving it, as if it were his own. Though she hadn't agreed with all of his suggestions, hadn't been willing to make some of the changes he'd wanted, she couldn't have done any of it without him.

Not long after the house fell into total quiet, Antonia awoke again with a start, thrust out of sleep by a terrible dream. Though she couldn't remember the particulars, neither where the dream had taken her nor why it had brought her there, she did remember that she'd been on a frantic search for her cigarettes, which she'd left in the pocket of a coat. In the dream, there were hundreds of coats, all exactly the same cut and color, and they were lined up side by side and she was shoving her hands into their pockets only to discover, to her horror, that the pockets were depthless, that she could never reach the bottom. No, in the dream, she hadn't recognized the coats, but now, awake, she saw them all too clearly: they were copies of her mother's coat, which was hanging in her closet.

Her heart still thudding wildly, she climbed out of bed and went to the closet, the dull light, when she slid open the door, pooling at her feet. There it was, waiting for her as usual, waiting for winter, a heather green wool coat with a high fur collar and pale, rose-colored buttons. Though the temperature of the room was mild, Antonia nonetheless was chilled, and she pulled the coat off the wooden hanger and wrapped herself in it: her mother's coat, which she'd been wearing for years; her mother's coat, which she could not part with. About to climb back into bed, coat and all, Antonia thought she heard voices coming from the veranda. They were muffled, indistinct, and she padded into the other room to find out whom they belonged to. The sofa bed, which was Ezra's that weekend, was empty, the front door slightly ajar. Through it, she smelled the whiff of cigarette smoke. She wondered whom he could be talking to at this late hour. Was it Calvin? Were they sharing a cigarette? Was Ezra telling him what a horrible person she was?

Quietly, she stepped out of the door and there was Ezra, leaning over the veranda's railing and speaking to someone down on the lawn. There were clouds, which blotted out the stars and moon, and she could not make out the features of the other person. When she heard the other voice above Ezra's, though, a deep, scratchy growl, she froze in place, her pulse beating heavily. It was her father, there under the moonless sky, though it could have just as easily been her uncle, the two often mistaken for one another. She wasn't sure whom she dreaded seeing more, skinny, shirtless Ezra in his camouflage shorts or her father, tall and imposing, this brutish man with his brutish love. The story rushed back at her, as she stood there, immobile, nailed in place as if by the spikes of memory itself. God, how she'd loved him, and God, how she wished he'd leave her alone.

Go away, she thought. Just go away, but he wasn't going away, not until he'd said what he'd come to tell her, she knew.

She took a step forward and the wood beneath her groaned. Ezra spun around, the tip of his cigarette an angry glowing eye in the dark. Then her father was saying her name and she hated her name, the way he said it, hated him all the more, saying her name as if she were still his, as if this were still their story. She wasn't his, not anymore, and she said, "Get out of here," but she spoke to Ezra, only to him, because she couldn't bear to look at her father. She hated him for what he'd done, for keeping the story from her, and she imagined, not for the first time, that her mother had known, that her father's secret had made her sick and put her in an early grave. Her father, who'd raised her and loved her, lived in quite a different story now. "You aren't welcome here," she said, wondering again how he'd found her.

"Just listen to what he has to say," Ezra said coldly. "You owe him that much."

"I owe him?" she asked, her voice quiet and hard, surprised by Ezra's butting in. "I owe him?" She was laughing, standing there in her mother's coat, as her father took a step onto the veranda, moving steadily until he was beside her, and Ezra was shaking his hand, then moving away, drifting into the yard.

She wondered, suddenly confused, why Ezra shook her father's hand like that. What could it mean?

She pulled the coat tighter around her, the wool scratchy against her bare skin. "What?" she demanded. "What do you want?"

He was standing close now, and for a moment she wanted to reach out to him and tell him why she'd done what she'd done, but she couldn't. She wouldn't. She'd disavowed him, swearing on Sylvie's grave that she'd never speak to him again. He'd murdered her. Her father had done that. This man who'd sung her lullabies and taken her to see the elephants in the zoo and ice skating on the frozen lake. He'd built her a castle for her eighth birthday and had inhabited it with miniature furniture, which he'd made by hand.

Now she stepped away and turned her back on him, shivering uncontrollably, feeling nauseated and feverish all of a sudden.

"Royal is here," he said. "I don't know how." He touched her shoulder gently. "You can't be here anymore." He paused. "Come back with me. We can leave tonight."

"Don't," she said, standing with her back to him, even as Henry appeared at the door.

"Antonia," Henry said, pulling her to him. "What are you doing here?" he asked of her father. "How on earth did you find her?"

"Life's nothing but a small town," her father said, casting a quick glance at Ezra, who was seated on the hood of Calvin's car. In this single glance of his, Antonia thought she understood.

"You," she said to Ezra. "You told him where I was." Ezra made no movement. He went on smoking, as if he hadn't heard her. "You conniving—"

"What in the world is this all about?" Henry asked.

"Then she hasn't told you about Royal," her father said. "No, I guess she wouldn't have." Then he was down the steps, adding, "Antonia, if you need me—and you will—I'm staying at that fancy hotel near the river."

She watched him leave, becoming just another shadow in the dark, and she wanted to go after him, to leave the house and the town behind. There was Henry, following her through the door,

Henry saying, "Who is Royal? What haven't you told me, Antonia?" He slumped down in a chair, his head in his hands. He kept his eyes on the floor and wouldn't look at her, although she longed for him to. She longed to tell him everything, yet Henry was a smart man, and she understood that he was quickly coming to his own conclusions. "Two brothers, both soldiers, and a cabin the woods. The short story, your novel — not a single word of it is fiction, is it? That's why your father's here, isn't it? Royal's your uncle, isn't he?"

"Yes," she said slowly. "He came to me with a story, Henry. An amazing story about my father . . ."

"He really murdered that girl, then?" he asked, with horror. "He raped and murdered her?"

"Yes," she said, her voice emotional. There were no tears, though. She'd expected to cry, but she couldn't. She went to him and sat at his feet, looking up into his face. "It is a novel, Henry. That's all it is. It's the only way it would work. Can't you see that? You told me to write it and that it'd sell and I wrote it and it sold, Henry. It is as much your novel as it is mine."

He shoved her away and stood, saying, "I want nothing more to do with it," and he left her seated on the floor and walked out of the house. She still wore her mother's coat, her knees tucked under her chin, and she rocked in place, her eyes shut. Even after all of this, she didn't shed a single tear. It's not my fault, she thought. I did a good thing. I wrote the truth. Besides, it's just a novel, and that's how everyone will read it. So what if I borrowed from real life, Henry. So what if it's based on people I trusted, who turned out later to be untrustworthy. I gave her a voice, Henry. I let the victim speak. Isn't that what matters? Isn't that the cardinal rule? Give a voice to those who can't speak, you said. Keep yourself out of the text, you said. That's just what I did. So, no, you can't hold this against me.

She thought back to her eighth birthday party — the vanilla cupcakes with buttercream frosting, the magician with his top hat and colorful handkerchiefs, her friends around the picnic table, her mother with the Hawaiian Punch, and her father with his camera, and her uncle Royal, who showed up that day with a beat-up porcelain doll. I like to call her Sylvie, her uncle had said. She remembered the smell of the doll, of mildew and ferment, like the beer her father drank alone in the basement. She remembered showing Uncle Royal her bedroom and the way he staggered and fell on the stairs. When it came time to take pictures, Antonia wished he'd just go away. Not only had he stepped on her favorite picture book and left his footprint on the cover, he'd also spilled his drink on her bedspread. She didn't know what to make of him, but he was her father's brother and he was amusing and he had brought her the doll, so she hugged him around the neck and said she couldn't wait to see him again. Then she dashed into the kitchen while her friends were out back with the magician, and she wrote her name and address on a scrap of paper.

When she gave it to him, he said, "I'll never lose my way again."

Her mother told her she needed to go play with her friends, yet before she went out back she lingered at the door, watching her father and her uncle. They were arguing, and Royal pushed her father so hard that he lost his balance. Her mother yelled at her to get outside, but Antonia stayed. Her father pulled out his wallet and handed his brother all the bills in it. Antonia knew this because he blew into the wallet, as if it were dusty, held it up and said, "See, that's it, Royal."

When she'd run into Royal on the subway that day in December, just six months after she'd moved to New York, she couldn't quite believe it. She'd heard about such random meetings from Calvin, who'd grown up there. It was as if the city's grid were more than an arrangement of streets but of destinies, too. She'd no idea hers would change so drastically that day, as she agreed to have coffee with her uncle, no idea he'd gone to such lengths to "accidentally" run into her. She had not seen him since her eighth birthday.

She realized then, as they went to the Hungarian on Amsterdam Avenue and had napoleons and coffee, with her paying for it all, that there was something terribly off about him. He didn't look like a transient in his dark blue serge suit and shiny black loafers, but when she asked him where he was staying, he gave her a vague address downtown on the Bowery. The way he stared at her, with his wet blue eyes, it was eerie how drawn she was to him, how her writer's mind went immediately to the details, trying to fill in the last thirteen years of his life.

It was when they were leaving the cafe and she told him she couldn't wait to call her father to let him know about their unexpected meeting that Royal became agitated. The tension had been there, just below the skin, and it erupted then: "I wouldn't like it if you did that," he said, suddenly angry.

She thought back on that chance reunion, thinking how it had both undone her past and created her future. She stood and went out onto the veranda. Henry was nowhere to be seen, but there was Ezra still on the hood of the car, still smoking. She hurried through the grass, which was sharp against her ankles, and when she approached him, she said, "You told my father exactly where to find me. You gave him this address."

This time, without any hesitation, he said matter-of-factly, "Yes, I did."

"Why would you do that?" she asked, her voice jagged.

"He came to the magazine offices a couple of weeks ago," Ezra said. "He was distraught."

"You did it out of spite," she said, "because you hate that I'm with Henry."

"My father's a fool," he said, flinging his cigarette to the curb and climbing off the hood. "Maybe I did it because it was the right thing to do." He paused. "I wish I had a father like yours, who'd come looking for me. You have no idea, do you?"

"No idea about what?" she asked.

"The kind of man my father is," he said. Then, "At least your father cares about you, despite what you've done."

"My father is a liar, plain and simple," she said.

"If you believe that, why are you crying?" he asked.

Sure enough, she touched her face, and there were tears. "I want you out of here," she said. "Right now."

"I think you need to take that up with Henry," he said.

"This is my house," she said. "My house and my yard and my trees and my town."

Ezra smirked at her, his eyes calm and unsurprised, looking almost pleased with himself. She felt suddenly as if she were an accomplice in his conspiracy to ruin the weekend, and she hated herself for playing along. Without another word, he wandered up the steps and through the door.

A few minutes later, on her way into the house, Antonia met Calvin on the veranda.

"You want him to go?" he asked sleepily.

"I can't bear having him here," she said.

"Antonia, you're being crazy and unreasonable," he said.

"He can stay at Henry's," she said. "He can stay at the cottage." She knew logistically that this would never work, however.

"He doesn't want to be here, either. He wants us to drive him back to the city," Calvin said. "I think Ernest is of the same mind."

She wanted to say, "Then let them go and you stay. I'll drive you back to the city on Sunday," but she didn't. Calvin was her best friend, yet Calvin's love for and allegiance to Ernest ran deeper than any other. If the situation had been reversed, she would have gladly sided with Henry and left as well.

"Calvin," she said as Ezra pushed past them with his duffel bag.

"I'm ready whenever you are," he said, heading for the car. He climbed in and slammed the door.

Moments later, Ernest shuffled past with their bags, saying nothing, and then Antonia was hugging Calvin good-bye, reminding him of the book party at Leland's the following week. "I'll try to make it," he said, taking a couple of steps down the walk. Then, turning, he added, "Congratulations, Antonia. I hope it was all worth it."

As they drove away, the headlights cutting through the darkness, she herself began to wonder if any of it — the writing, the money, the fame — was worth it. Still, she felt she'd done nothing wrong, nothing to evoke such hostility. She had to see Henry, to explain. Antonia dressed and headed to the cottage, passing Catherine's house, in which lights were still shining, as they were in the cottage. She called out his name and banged on the cottage door. "I'm sorry I didn't tell you, Henry," she said. "Please open the door." But he didn't open the door, and a few minutes later Antonia slumped down in one of the lawn chairs she'd bought for him. Just then Catherine appeared on the deck.

Gazing up at Catherine, Antonia now wondered what might have happened if she'd just had the sense to call her father the day Royal had confided in her, how different the story among the three of them might have been. As it was, her father was still out there and her insane uncle was on the loose, perhaps heading straight for her at this very moment, she thought, shuddering. She was afraid for herself, for her father, afraid of what would happen when her uncle caught up to him. Catherine called to her and Antonia stood, drawn to the warmth and concern in Catherine's voice, and pushed through the gate and up the steps.

On the deck, Antonia let Catherine hug her close and lead her into the house. "And I thought *I* had a bad night," she said. "Remind me never to go on a blind date again," and she laughed. As Antonia collapsed on the sofa, Catherine poured them wine and handed a glass to her. "Tell me everything," she said.

So Antonia related fragments of the evening, told her about the mangled typewriter (without mentioning that she now suspected it might have been her uncle's doing), and about her father, though she omitted any mention of Royal, who was, she imagined with a shiver, creeping through the town. She did not tell Catherine, however, about her real reason for moving to Winslow, or about this new trouble with Henry. Later, she thought. Later she'd tell Catherine about that afternoon when her uncle had found her, about the pastries they'd shared, and about the story that sifted off him, like the dust and dandruff on his tattered blue suit. She'd keep all of this for another night, when they were better acquainted, and she could trust Catherine with her secrets. She hoped that then Catherine, in turn, might feel more at ease and more inclined to share her own secrets with her, especially those that lived between her and Wyatt.

Before she went to bed, Catherine disappeared into the study and came out with a typewriter. "Wyatt's," she said. "You can borrow it. It's just sitting in there gathering dust. Sleep here tonight; you can take it home tomorrow."

"Oh, Catherine, I couldn't," she said, though the idea of using the same machine on which Wyatt had written his novel touched and thrilled her. "I'll take good care of it, promise."

"Just write something wonderful on it," she said.

Antonia lay awake for another hour, staring at the typewriter, running her fingers over the keys. She imagined all the novels he might have written on it if Henry hadn't come along. Poor Catherine, she thought, rising and going to the kitchen window. There was still a light on in the cottage, which meant Henry was still awake, too. I'm sorry, Henry, she thought, hating herself for ruining the weekend. She hoped he'd let her make it up to him. She hoped that in a couple days his resentment would have faded and he'd open the door to greet her as if nothing had changed.

A Revolver in the Room

———

Antonia was still asleep on the sofa when Catherine snuck out of the house the next morning. A solid sheet of low-slung clouds leached all color from the warm, humid day. Though the cloud cover was a welcome relief from the scorching sun, it worsened the quality of the air, trapping the heat and making it difficult to breathe. Everything is muted and washed out, the color of nothing, thought Catherine. It was, she realized, like her date the night before, full of dampened conversation and muffled desire. Still, she'd gone through with dinner, then dessert and coffee, because, though she didn't enjoy the man's company, she appreciated that she was not sitting at home, alone. It had kept her from having to socialize with Henry, yet in hindsight she would have given anything to see Ezra again. She'd met him only once, many years ago, when he was just a boy. He'd spent much of that afternoon at Central Park Zoo, holding her hand and leading her from animal to animal. At the end of the day, he'd cried, throwing a tantrum, not wanting Catherine to leave. "I'll see you again soon," she'd told him, though she hadn't.

Now, on the porch, Catherine stared out at the street, scanning in all directions. This had become her habit since that frightening night when she'd fainted after nearly being attacked. At least, that was how she imagined the gruesome moment — the figure hovering at the lilac bush, his eerie smile, a flash of menace. While the terror of the moment had subsided into a dull if persistent throb, the image of the figure remained vivid, and she'd taken to keeping the porch light on day and night.

All the years she'd lived in New York City, she never once felt scared or unsafe, but in the last week here in quiet Winslow she'd found herself more insecure and uneasy than ever before. Still, if pressed, she'd have to admit that the dread and anxiety she carried around was more than compensated for by the intrigue she'd experienced over the past several days. It was as if she were caught inside the plot of some mystery and that each day her role was being written more indelibly into it. The thing was, Catherine didn't want to be written out, not just yet, because, when she examined the last few days closely, she couldn't help but see just how silly and out of character she was behaving: there was no correlation between what was going on around her and what she imagined was going on around her. Furthermore, she had no clear evidence of any true malfeasance other than the defiled cottage, and this she could wholly dismiss, if she wanted to, as a fraternity prank, as the police officer had suggested.

Yet as she climbed into her car, Catherine thought about Antonia, the typewriter thrown through the window, the note. Was that also just another fraternity stunt? She didn't think so. It seemed all a part of a plot that was playing out, and like it or not, she was as much a character in the summer's drama as Henry and Antonia were. Perhaps even more so, since she'd had her own motives for telling Antonia about the house down the block and for arranging Henry's move into the cottage.

I lured them to me, she suddenly realized. A startling, upsetting revelation, it stayed with her throughout the day at the bookstore, lingering as the sky darkened and a strong wind bowed the tops of the trees. There'd been no talk of rain in the forecast — they'd just issued the first of many drought alerts — but sure enough the first fat drops fell around four o'clock, little welcome explosions against the sidewalk and windows. After rushing around, helping one customer even as another took his place, Catherine left Jane at the register and went out into the thunderstorm. Lightning flared and died in the green-black sky, the air electrifed and cooler. It was, she sensed, fall's first push against summer, a tease of what was to come, and she rejoiced in the downpour. She watched the air grow yellow and hail begin to fall, cracking against the sidewalk, ricocheting off the cars. She didn't care that the hail might split the branches of the ancient sycamore, put holes in the roof of her house, and damage the untrustworthy Corolla. Blow, winds, blow, she thought, but this time, blow us all away.

She stood under the awning and shut her eyes, imagining the falling ice crushing the spirits of Antonia's disavowed father, of Henry's disturbed Wren, of the terrible person who'd gutted Antonia's typewriter. She wanted it to fall and to keep falling, not only obliterating the spirits of those people, but their presences in the town as well, because the things they were doing and had done made no sense to her. She wondered as she stepped back into the store if it were high time that she stopped looking at them as people and thought about them more like characters in a book, because, as she reminded herself, you can never know anyone completely, but you can imagine a character indefinitely.

It was something Wyatt used to say, and she thought about him now, wondering what he'd make of her situation. She still missed him, but the missing felt different to her today, less keen. Her memory of him was breaking down, which upset her because

Wyatt wasn't a character, he was a man, and she didn't want to have to imagine him indefinitely.

The store was crowded now with people who had come in from the rain, and she busied herself with helping them. The hour flew by, and then she was saying good-bye to Jane and walking out into the cool evening. The sky was clearing, and everything around her seemed washed clean. She stepped around the puddles on her way to her car and marveled at the heavy, curling mist rising off the asphalt. How fast things can change, she thought. If only it would last. Once she got to her car, she checked it for hail damage but found only the same usual dings and dents and spots of rust. After rolling down her window, she released the stale, hot air trapped inside and, with it, her own sense of worry. I am involved, she thought. I am not a woman of cool restraint.

Yet with this thought came another — in letting herself get involved, she'd also allowed herself to hope, to dream of a great, long-lasting friendship with Antonia, and of forgiving Henry. By the time she arrived home, though, Catherine had concluded that there would never be a real detente with Henry since she could never truly forgive him, and he could never truly make enough amends. He will have to go sooner than later, she thought as she stepped through the mud and muck on her way to the cottage. She called out Henry's name, and when he appeared at the door, unshaven and unkempt, wearing yesterday's clothes, she didn't know what to make of him.

"Henry, you and I have to talk," she said.

"Is this necessary? Important? Because I'm a little busy right now," he said curtly.

Catherine wasn't sure what to say or how to go on, stunned that her heart was beating heavily, not with anger, but with excitement. "Yes, Henry, it's very important," she said, trying not to sound shrill. She kept expecting him to invite her in, but he didn't. You rude, insufferable man, she thought, flashing back some ten years to the last time she'd shared his bed.

As she'd left his spacious Upper West Side apartment that last time, he'd presented her with a gift — *Liars in Love* — because she was as fond of Richard Yates as he was. On the subway ride downtown, she pulled the book out of her bag, flipping through it. A used copy, it was full of underlined passages and notes in the margins. She skimmed through a few of the jottings, then turned to the first page, where Henry had inscribed a message. She read what he'd written, then shut the book, dumbfounded, struggling to breathe. *We are liars in love. I cannot go on with this.*

The following day, in class, he treated her coolly, and later, when she went to his office, she found the door locked, although she knew he was inside. With no further explanation other than this tattered book and two hurriedly scrawled sentences, he'd ended their affair.

Now, today, remembering that hurt, Catherine nearly pushed past Henry, smelling cigarette smoke and whiskey, in the air and on his breath. Who was smoking — he or Antonia? Was she in there?

"You aren't smoking, are you?" she asked as pleasantly as she could, though it was impossible to keep the scold from her words. "We had an agreement."

"Our agreement," he said, laughing. "God, but you haven't changed a bit." Then he slammed the door in her face.

Suddenly losing control, Catherine banged on the door, screaming, "Henry Swallow." After a minute, realizing that he was not going to respond, she turned to go but first called out, "Fran, Laurel, Rachel, Wren — are you doing to Antonia what you did to them?" (To me as well, she wanted to add but didn't.) "Is that it, Henry?" But even this outburst did not provoke a response.

The clouds had gathered again, and it was beginning to rain as she gave up and went into the house. She changed clothes, then poured herself a glass of wine. For a moment she considered storming over to the cottage again, considered demanding that Henry join her in a glass of wine because they had business to discuss. Hadn't she made herself perfectly clear? Hadn't she expressly forbidden cigarettes? While nothing about Henry should have surprised her, everything about him did. Still, the most surprising to her of all was her own odd, unsettling feelings upon seeing him at the door, the surge of affectionate concern that had come over her. What's wrong, Henry? she wanted to ask. Let me help.

For years, long after their affair was over, she'd followed his career, poring over his writings, many times disagreeing fervently with his take on a novel she herself had loved, though always amazed at his style, the way he skinned the fruit of the prose to get at the pith of the story. It didn't matter if the writer had one book or several, if he were unknown or famously read, Henry went after each one with the same bloodthirsty abandon. He'd told Catherine once that he was lucky he didn't write fiction, because if he did, he didn't think he'd be able to take even one negative review. Certainly that had not kept him from going after Wyatt or from understanding how his horrible attack might change their world.

Now Wyatt lay buried in a small cemetery not far from the house, but Catherine did not visit him because she knew he was not there. He was here, in these rooms, piled in the untouched boxes and hidden among the pages of books. He was in the cottage. He was beside her on the sofa, in the bed, on her skin. He was everywhere and nowhere, inside of her and beyond. "I'll be back soon," he'd said that day. Soon became hours, though, and hours became the first snow of the year, and the world outside was white and thick with drifts by the time she answered the knock at the door.

The officer had called her Mrs. Wyatt Strayed, which she'd found absurdly formal. It made her feel leashed, his name snug around her throat.

"Yes," she'd said, uncertain why the man was there.

"I'm so sorry to have to tell you this, but your husband . . . We found his car . . . in the river."

The leash around her throat loosened, then evaporated, and she no longer belonged to anyone.

"Yes, I understand," she'd said, but what was there to understand?

"Would you come with me, please," he'd said.

"Did you find the groceries?" she asked. "We needed things, you see."

"Ma'am," the officer said, "we didn't find any groceries in the vehicle."

Then she was grabbing her purse and pushing past the officer on her way to her car. "We needed things," she said again. "He was supposed to do the grocery shopping."

"Ma'am, please," the officer said. They were at the Corolla and the snow was falling, blanketing the windshield, which Catherine cleared with a swipe of her hand. "Ma'am, it's too dangerous to drive," he said.

"We needed things," she'd repeated, climbing into the car.

She'd gotten halfway down the block before the car skidded into the curb. The attempt, she remembered, gave the day meaning. She was going to get the groceries, because they were married, and she loved him, and they needed things. Isn't that what wives of absentminded, brilliant writers did?

Now it was summer and there was rain instead of snow, and here was Catherine going to the credenza and taking Henry's latest book with her to the sofa, a collection of his essays, signed by him, of course. She flipped to the table of contents, looking for what she didn't know. Most of the essays' titles looked familiar, as she'd read them all before in various magazines and journals. She dragged a finger down the page, until she came to the second-to-last title and she paused, her heart galloping — "My Crime and Punishment: New Notes on *The Last Cigarette*."

She read the title, saying each word aloud. She turned to Henry's handwritten inscription: *Even this is not enough.* No, nothing was enough to bring Wyatt back. Nothing was enough to erase what Henry had done.

She thought about last night and Antonia, standing at the cottage door, trying to get through to Henry. She thought about this evening, her own unsuccessful, frustrating attempt to break through his stubbornness. She rose and looked out the window at the rain, increasing now, the storm building.

Catherine stood at the window, the abrupt darkness of the room overtaking her as the lights flickered and went out. She hunted for candles and lit the three she found, returning to the sofa. Against her better judgment, she picked up Henry's book and turned to the essay, straining to read in the quivering light. Though she'd imagined herself struggling through the essay, incapable of separating the critic from his work, her impartiality shocked her, though it was Henry himself who shocked her all the more. She read slowly, unsure what to expect. When she finished, Catherine was stunned. Henry had not only retracted and recanted what he had previously written, but he also went on to attack his own earlier arrogance and myopia, turning on his own sentences — the reviewer becoming the reviewed. "I was wrong," he concluded, "so very wrong about Wyatt Strayed and what he attempted and ultimately succeeded in doing in his debut (and, sadly, only) novel, *The Last Cigarette*.

Over my career, I have laid siege to many outstanding novels, and though some of them deserved excoriation, others, like *The Last Cigarette,* did not. If I had been a better man, I would have kept my grievances with the writer to myself. I was not a better man, and in this case I will always regret what I wrote. Wyatt Strayed was a great writer with great potential, and his was an outstanding novel."

Unbelievable, she thought. Also despicable. She shut the book, despising Henry again. She shouted into the dark, empty house, "It's a little late, isn't it, Henry?" After getting up, she walked slowly toward the kitchen to drop the book in the trash — she wanted it gone, out of the house. She carried a candle in one hand, the book in the other. She was almost in the kitchen, when the candle sputtered and went out, but not before she saw Henry seated at the kitchen table. Startled, she dropped the candle and the book just as lightning flashed across his rough cheeks and glinted off his glasses. A cigarette hung in his lips.

"Yes, you're right," he said, dropping the cigarette. "A little late for anyone, really." He leaned over and lifted the book from the floor, then stood and went to the back door. After opening the door, he threw the book out into the rainy darkness. "The irrelevance. The . . ." He didn't go on.

He's drunk, Catherine thought, wondering why he had come, what he was doing in her kitchen. He wobbled and stuffed a hand deep into his pocket. She noticed, in the intermittent flashes of lightning, that he wasn't wearing any shoes. From his pocket, Henry produced the lease, which he set on the table, and a check, which he held out to her. "Take it," he said, and thrust it at her. "You deserve it, Cathy." The abbreviated version of her name, which she hadn't heard in years, sounded more like a taunt than an endearment.

"I don't want it."

"You might not want it," he said, "but it belongs to you. So take it."

Glancing down at the check, which he'd placed on the table, she saw the zeroes — were there three of them? — and the lease beside it, signed at last.

"I've really taken to the place. I'm getting some work done," he said. "Besides, I have nowhere else to go."

"Henry," she said, "this was only meant to be temporary," and she shuddered, remembering what Jane had said, that temporary had a way of becoming forever. "Antonia has many rooms. You should have gone there to begin with. I never understood — "

"You aren't supposed to understand," he said, as lightning flashed again, lighting his face. It was no longer the face that love had preserved, the face she'd suspended in memory, but the face of a fifty-nine-year-old man falling into old age. There was little left of Henry Swallow in this face; the varnish of the critic and scholar had been wiped away. "I can't do it anymore, Catherine. I can't believe . . . I can't see her again. I'm done with her," he said, his face sagging. He repeated what he said, as if she hadn't heard him. She had heard him, though, and the shock of this news left her distressed. She knew about the failure of love. Her own marriage had been dying for years before Wyatt died, but in an odd way his death had undone the damage.

Then suddenly, Henry was crying hysterically. He dropped his arms and head onto the table and he sobbed, letting out extraordinary animal cries, his body wracked with the effort. Even though she found him pathetic, the sight of him still managed to arouse a swelling of feelings in Catherine. She'd been looking forward to this moment, she realized, this moment when Henry sat across from her and wept. Yet she'd always imagined it differently, for other reasons — his sincerest, most genuine apology for taking away Wyatt's success, for taking him from her. She'd expected a shift in the dynamic between them when this finally happened, but tonight there was no satisfaction, no triumph. If anything, she felt the pangs of her own buried regret. She'd never seen him as vulnerable, and she wanted to console him. She reached out a hand, but Henry leaned back in his seat, out of reach.

Catherine turned away, then forced herself up, until she was standing right behind him. She placed her hands on his shoulders and whispered into his ear, "I'm sorry." She wanted to comfort him yet also needed to be honest. How could she tell him what she'd known all along, that Antonia was and would be always be far too quick and nimble for him to keep? "Think about Antonia like this: you found her, you discovered her, but she's as unpredictable as a revolver with an endless supply of ammunition," she said. "Even if she didn't mean to, she would have shot up every room of your life."

By now, Henry's sobbing had abated, and he picked up his head, wiping his eyes. "That's one of the most awful metaphors I've ever heard," he said.

"That's why I left the writing to Wyatt," she replied as the lights in the house flamed on and their eyes adjusted to the sudden glare.

"He was a good writer," Henry said. "A great prose stylist and storyteller. It's very rare to find both in one person." Of course, without having to mention her, she knew quite well that he was also referring to Antonia.

"Yes, he was," she said. "Underappreciated and underrated."

"I hope the essay helps change that," he said, rising, his eyes more alert now, his voice more sober.

She watched his eyes as he looked about the room, taking in the shoddy countertops and avocado green appliances, the ringed stains on the table. Yes, see what you have done, she thought, but instead said, "Even so, Henry, it still doesn't change a thing. The summer term's nearly over, which means properties open up and become available." She paused, thinking, Tell him he can't stay. Tell him he has to go. But she couldn't say it, not now. "What about your house? Isn't it finished yet?" she asked tentatively.

"My house," he said, "is structurally unsound. The foundation has cracks. It'll be months."

"Months," she said, startled, finding this news nearly as shocking as his news about Antonia. "You must have other options, Henry. What about going back to the hotel?"

"Catherine, you ought to be a little more grateful," he said, standing. There was nothing left of the watery, unsteady voice. It was cool once again and officious, scolding. "I signed your lease, and I've paid you your rent. Do you think you'll find another tenant like me here?"

"That isn't the point and you know it," she said. They were very close, as close physically as they'd been in several years, and she smelled the whiskey on his breath again, and she could see the silver hairs in his beard, and the wiry muscles of his chest through his shirt. A momentary flash of desire shot through her, then was gone.

"Just another couple of months," he said. "That should be plenty of time," but he didn't elaborate at all about what "plenty of time" meant. Still, she suspected he was no longer talking about a place to live but something else entirely. She wondered what it was, if Henry himself even knew, because he already seemed far away, beyond this summer night.

"I can only give you another few days," she said, wishing she could lie. My sister's going through a terrible divorce and needs a place to stay, she might have said, or even better, She's very sick and I told her she could come stay with me. Of course, there was no sister, and no lie she could tell that Henry would not have seen through immediately.

Ignoring her remark, he turned toward the door. As he did, she surprised herself and reached out to hug him. Her hands sliced the air where Henry had just been, and she pulled back.

"I'm sorry about you and Antonia," she said.

"That makes two of us," he responded, and then he was gone, drifting across the slick deck.

The rain eased into a gentle drizzle, the wind relaxing, as Catherine cleaned up the kitchen, wiping away Henry's muddy footprints. Then, collecting the lease, and Henry's check from the table, she returned to the sitting room, where she glanced out the window, the silence falling through the house. She settled on the sofa as a thought, persistent and nagging, hung in the still air. It was a thought she'd had for days, a terrible realization that in wanting an end to her loneliness, she herself had brought Henry back into her life. Henry is more than just your tenant, she thought, as he's always been.

She looked over the lease, then the check, letting out a laugh as she read the amount — ten thousand dollars — finding it utterly absurd. It was far too much, insulting in its implication. First the review, then the essay rescinding the review, and now this? She couldn't help but wonder what Henry was up to.

Taking the last sip of wine, Catherine returned to the kitchen and set the glass in the sink. Then, from the table, she grabbed the cigarette and the matches he'd left behind. Outside, on the deck, where a cool breeze had replaced the rain, Catherine smoked the cigarette, imagining the many ways she would spend Henry's money. She allowed herself this reverie, because, like most spells woven at night, this one, too, would lift, and come morning, she knew she'd have no other choice than to rip up the check, which she should have done to begin with.

All You Do Is Sit
at a Typewriter and Bleed

———

Just before dusk the next day, Henry got on his bike, passing
Antonia's house, wanting to stop, since he hadn't seen her for a
couple days, not since she'd come by the cottage. The house was
dark; her car was not in the drive. As he rode past, he thought
about Ezra and the ruined weekend. The boy had called him once
he'd got back into the city. It had been the middle of the night.
"Why are you with her?" he'd shouted, fuming.

Henry had wondered this himself, though he'd also wondered
how he could ever live without her. He rode over the Kissing Swans
Bridge, so like the bridge he had to cross to get to his house on
Osprey Point. So many bridges, he thought, remembering another
bridge, this one in Vermont, one of those covered bridges, and he'd
just found out he'd won the Pulitzer Prize again and the future
yawned bright and sparkling ahead of him. Joyce, his wife, had
handed Ezra to him, and he had held the baby in his arms, cradling
him as the summer afternoon cradled them. It was love, it had to
be, he thought now, as he hurried across the bridge, his thoughts

traveling from that bridge in Vermont to this one in Winslow, and Wyatt Strayed suddenly reared up in his memory.

The rain hadn't stopped until the late afternoon, keeping him indoors, but now the sun was out again, the day steamy and choked with humidity. He went speeding down Old Devil Moon Road; ahead, his house, the yellow Italianate, rose up through the evergreens. Around him, the light was still bright, though he knew that it would soon fade. He could not stay long; besides, he had work to do. Even then, he suspected that he would find himself at Antonia's door later, his desire for her reawakened. He wondered if she missed him as much as he missed her.

He knew that he'd behaved badly, and his accusations, he suspected, had been a part of his own fears. When she'd come to the cottage, wanting in, he'd refused her. How could he have seen her, knowing what she'd done? It was a violation that ran deep, yet even Henry, who disliked Antonia's father, Linwood, felt sorry for him. She should have known better than to keep the story and novel a secret from him. Her vague past had finally caught up to her, to them. With horror, Henry again thought, Oh, Antonia, what have you done to us?

His house lay in disrepair, and he took it in, sighing. Behind him, a car crept past, slowing as Henry turned to watch it. Then the car stopped abruptly, headlights slicing through the dusk. As it did, Henry tried to make out the driver. He couldn't, however. Then it was going again, sending up gravel in its wake. Henry watched until it was gone, then went into the house to find the key. There were hanging plastic sheets and white coats of dust everywhere. Poor house, he thought as he crossed to the secretary that was also covered in plastic. He kept the key hidden here because he had to, because not even Antonia could know about it.

A thirty-six-year age difference between them, and it hadn't mattered. He had trusted her — would trust her again, he thought, he hoped — though he would also have to watch her more closely. He thought back to that first time three years ago, the pure alchemy of it, her nakedness under him, the moment when he entered her and she was no longer his student and he was no longer her professor. Skin and nothing more; everything else burned away on his damp, wrinkled sheets. He felt this burn still, even now, as he grabbed the key, then went out the back door, following the last of the light into the underbrush, the path that led into the heart of his property, which sat at the base of the mountains.

Around him, the frogs bellowed and the crickets chirped, the wood a living, breathing thing. The walk seemed endless, the density of flora unyielding. The wood swallowed the light and there was darkness now on all sides of him, but he remembered, he had to remember — and then he took a right and then a left and came to a small clearing and there it was again, hidden under the tarp — his late father's 1958 Porsche Cabriolet. Once a month, he'd been coming out here to check on the car. He never drove it — he wasn't supposed to drive — though tonight, out of some desire to know that he could go at any time, he got behind the wheel. More, though, he wanted to show the car to Antonia, to regain what had been lost between them, to restore her sense of faith in him and his own faith in himself. Trust her, he thought. Trust her. He started the car's engine and drove out of the wood down a path that he himself had cleared and around the house to the road. Then he was crossing the bridge again and finally pulling up to Antonia's house. There were lights on inside. Outside, though, it was dark and no one would see him.

As he got out of the car, he thought again, Trust her. Let her know that what she has done is not irrevocable. There is a way through it. I can fix it. On the veranda, Henry found one of her cigarettes still burning, and he heard music spilling out the open windows. He knocked on the door, but she didn't answer, so he used his key. "Antonia," he called out. "Where are you?"

He wandered through the house, the air pungent, full of the scent of Chinese peonies, which he'd had a local florist deliver to her this morning. The vase sat on the kitchen table, the card beside it unopened. She had sent his son away in the middle of the night, and that was wrong, though Ezra had had no right to tell Linwood Lively where to find her. No right at all.

As he sniffed the peonies, he had a sudden flash of fear. Had her father come back here? Or was it Royal, this uncle of hers? This man, he now realized, who had burst into his office, wanting to know where Antonia was living. The violence in him sent Henry running out of the office. He'd brought her to Winslow, but he apparently couldn't protect her, and this thought saddened him greatly. Though she hated Winslow, she stayed for him. She'd set herself up in this house and had thrown herself into her second novel. He knew that the writing kept her focused and happy and that her happiness was his.

He went to the study door and knocked, saying her name, because he thought he heard some movement behind the door. He tried the knob and turned it, feeling suddenly that he was making a huge mistake. This was her world, her sanctuary, and how many times had he scolded her for coming into his study without permission? He would just open the door to see if she were all right, that's all, though when he did so he found the room empty. He took a step into the room, then another, until he was at her desk, staring down at the Olivetti typewriter, Wyatt's typewriter. On the desk, he was surprised to see a snapshot of his house at Osprey Point. Above the desk on the wall was a quotation from Hemingway: "There is nothing to writing. All you do is sit at a typewriter and bleed."

He wasn't going to read the page that was rolled into the

typewriter, though a word caught his eye and then he was looking down at it, winded. He saw his name and he saw Catherine's name and Wyatt's name and as he read the sentences to himself, he understood what she was doing and he left the room, nauseated. Oh, Antonia, he thought. Oh, God. He removed his glasses and ran his head under the faucet in the kitchen, then walked over to the vase of peonies. He wanted to rip them apart, to tear the delicate heads off each blossom until nothing of them remained. He searched inside himself for the original urge to see her again, to trust her again, but it was gone, erased. She'd taken from him before, and if he let her, he knew she'd take from him forever.

Henry got back into the Porsche and pulled away, the lights of Antonia's house fading behind him, just as he prayed his fury might fade as well. It didn't. In fact, the farther and faster he drove, the more it came at him. He gripped the wheel, white-knuckled, and drove with a recklessness he hadn't experienced in ages, not since he'd been on that beach road. After returning the car to the wood, he jumped back on his bike and pedaled hurriedly to the cottage. Once inside, he wandered around the space, confused and hurt, going over what he'd just discovered. How could she? The story of Catherine and Wyatt and him? It seemed impossible to him that he hadn't been able to sense it, that all this time she'd been excavating that story. Yet it was hard for him not to understand her desire to know all of him, especially since he would tell her nothing about his past, which of course only made her more curious. It was, he saw at last, his own fault. Yet he also saw that if she really loved him, she would let it all go. She wouldn't. She couldn't. Trust her with it, he thought. Then he laughed at himself for even indulging the thought. He would not abet her in her ruin of him or of Catherine. He would not stand by and watch her trespass. He wasn't sure what to do, so he went into the study and sat down in the chair and waited for her to come to him, as he suspected she would.

WHEN ANTONIA CAME to the cottage later, it had started to rain again. He let her in as she reached into her pocket and pulled out his glasses. "I thought you might need these," she said sweetly. "You must have left them the last time you came over."

He had another flash of fear — the glasses that he'd left on her kitchen counter tonight. Then she has to know, he thought, shuddering. "Do you want me to stay?" she asked, kissing him, and for the moment, he felt himself spared. He kissed her back, though it was without fire or tenderness, and the sex they had then was just the friction of two bodies, two strangers, a passionless rutting in the black. If she felt any of this, as Henry felt it, he didn't know, since he realized he had no idea what she was feeling, if he'd ever known at all. As they lay side by side, he thought about the night he'd gone to talk to Wyatt, how they'd sat on the deck until morning, until Henry had nothing left to tell him.

"I can't write it," Henry had said, "but you can."

To his knowledge, though, Wyatt had never written it, which meant the story still belonged to Henry and Henry alone.

It would never belong to Antonia, not as long as he was still alive.

"I forgot to thank you for the flowers," she said, resting a hand on his chest. She kissed him again and then she was slipping into sleep. As he listened to her breathe, he wondered what it would be like if she never woke again. How this second novel of hers would go unwritten and unpublished and how he could mourn the girl he'd known, not the girl he'd come across tonight.

He had to find out if Wyatt had written what he'd told him. And since only Catherine would know for sure that's whom he would ask.

What's a Ring
Without a Finger?

——————

The rain fell for the next two days. A cold, harsh rain with colder, harsher winds, it overturned, Catherine thought, all the wickedness that had come before it — the blazing trapped heat of the air and the blazing trapped heat of her anger. Every time she stepped out of the house, she pushed her face into the wet wind, breathing in the chillier air. On the third day, the rain slowed and the wind subsided, the quality of the light rapidly changing until the bruised clouds parted and the sun reappeared.

As Catherine made coffee this morning, she thought of the lightning and thunder, the great sheets of water that flooded the streets and her yard. Now, as if by magic, nothing of the storm remained, no sign except that everything looked as if it had been scrubbed clean. Standing at the kitchen window, she imagined the chill in the air and, excited, threw on a lightweight cardigan before stepping out on the deck. Yet the moment she opened the door and breathed in the soupy, turgid air, she understood that the storm had done nothing more than renew summer's hateful promise. Everything around her oozed with sweat, and looked jaundiced under the pulverizing sun. She took a sip of the hot coffee, and it was as though she were swallowing summer itself. Disgusted, she dumped the coffee out, imagining the skin of the entire town drenched not in sweat, as she suddenly was, but in an oily combustible mist. She shut her eyes, imagining lighting a match and torching the town. Her nose filled with the imagined smoke of this imagined conflagration, the fire eating its way through the present and the past. She watched as the life she might have led went up in black curls of ash. She let the flames come, to take the house, the cottage, and the town, savoring the delicious scene with a small smile.

Then, all of a sudden, she opened her eyes because she did smell smoke, and she sniffed the air, alarmed. Yet when she saw the rings of smoke rising from the bottom of the stairs, she understood that it was only Antonia, lighting a cigarette. The sight of her in the big flouncy sunhat, the sunglasses, the sandals, and the neon pink bikini made her look to Catherine much younger, an eager girl ready to spend the day at the beach. Even when she had been in far better shape, Catherine wasn't sure she would have had the sense to go around dressed like this, her whole body on display. We women do such extraordinary things in the face of calamity, she thought. A little jealous of her, she applauded Antonia's pluck anyway and called down to her.

A moment later, the girl was beside her, saying, "I just came by to see how you were doing."

"To see how I'm doing?" Catherine asked, surprised. "I should ask you the same question."

"Luckily, the sun changes everything," she said, flicking ash into the air. "I guess you haven't heard, but Henry and I made up." She glanced at the cottage. No, Catherine hadn't heard, the news of this just as shocking as Henry's own had been. Antonia released one last thin line of smoke, stubbed the cigarette out in the ashtray, then went rummaging through her tote bag. "Henry was supposed to come with me to meet some friends of mine at Asbury Park, but he's developed a spontaneous cold."

From the tote, she extracted a fresh pack of cigarettes. She handed a cigarette to Catherine, who took it and slid the filter tip between her lips, thinking nothing about Wyatt, who would have been horrified, but only about her days when she had been a serious, driven student, who had endowed cigarettes with the magic ability to write her papers for her. For a moment, as Antonia struck a match and lit her cigarette, Catherine was that student again, inhaling the burning tobacco deep into her lungs and, with the tobacco, time itself. Exhaling, she remembered a line from *To the Lighthouse* in which Mrs. Ramsey said, "Life stand still here." Unlike Mrs. Ramsey, Catherine didn't want life to stand still here. Not this life. No, she wanted this life to rush on and away, past this moment on the deck. She wanted life to offer up new summers, new falls, new springs, and new winters. She wanted this for herself, but she also wanted this for Antonia. She wanted to offer her some comforting words, yet nothing about Antonia suggested that she needed any. Success is an armor against unhappiness, Catherine mused. Perhaps she's wearing hers, after all. Well, I'm glad for her.

They chatted briefly about the heat — "I love the heat. I love summer," Antonia said — and then it was on to her novel and her upcoming book tour. "Twelve cities in six weeks! I don't know how I'm going to do it," she said, her voice transfigured with both excitement and fear. After reaching into her tote again, she brought up a copy of her novel. "This is for you, Catherine," she said humbly. "I've been carrying it around with me, but I've been, well, I've been reluctant to give it to you. What if you hate it?"

"How could I possibly hate it?" Catherine asked, laughing, and thanked her for the copy.

"My agent doesn't like the cover," she said. "The fights we had about it! Between you and me, I almost fired him, but I think he's finally coming around. It's weird how proprietary he can be about me and my novel."

Catherine ran a finger over the dust jacket, the deep red letters of the title, *The Death of Her,* curved delicately inside a gauzy crescent moon that hung above a ramshackle cabin. Yet this was no ordinary moon — it was in the shape of a silver lunette — and Catherine shuddered against the memory of Antonia's father. Yes, the dust jacket was beautiful, but it was also shocking because it served as another reminder of what Catherine now believed Antonia to have done. The image on the dust jacket tied all of it together and told a further tale. Opening up the novel now, the spine tight and unyielding, she traced a finger down the unblemished, deckled pages, loving the feel of the imperceptibly raised words against her skin. "I can't wait to read it," she said, though she wondered if her experience of it had already been tainted by knowing too much and becoming a player herself in the larger, more sordid story.

Antonia said, "Well, I should get going. I have a lot to do." Catherine hugged the book to her chest and gazed past the girl to the cottage. Look, she wanted to say, you will never understand him, so I wouldn't even bother trying. Before she said good-bye, Antonia added, "You are coming to my party tomorrow night, aren't you? I think Henry's up to something, but I don't know what. I can see it in his eyes. It's like he wants to ask me — well, he's been acting very strange the last couple of days. He wrote a speech to introduce me, and I just wonder if . . . I mean, we've been together long enough, and I know how much he loves me . . . Do you think — oh, wouldn't it just be so perfect if he asked me to marry him? He hasn't mentioned anything to you, has he?" Catherine told her that he hadn't. "Well, don't tell him that I'm onto him, okay. He certainly knows how to keep a secret. It's just eating me alive." And with that, she hugged Catherine and drifted down the steps.

The bell on the gate tinkled, and then she was gone, though not all of her. For in her wake, she'd left Catherine with some strange, unsettling news. That she and Henry had reconciled did not surprise her but that he was even contemplating marriage certainly did. Hadn't he sat at her kitchen table not a few days earlier and announced that he was done with Antonia? Fickle, fickle man, she thought, cringing at her own experience of him.

"Marriage," she said aloud, scoffing, and went back into the house. As she dressed, she found herself talking to Wyatt, who'd asked her to marry him just a week after Henry had ended his affair with her. It was as if he had held back asking her to marry him, until he was dead certain she was free to say yes. At the time, she had found it utterly distressing to have to grieve the loss of Henry while simultaneously giving into the idea of becoming Mrs. Wyatt Strayed. She'd had to work overtime at dismantling her love for Henry, refusing, she had told herself, to believe that his leaving her had been anything other than cowardly and spiteful. Yet the more she'd tried to rid herself of her love for him, the more this love held tight. Then one day she just woke up and realized she was sick with it and of it, worrying that it had putrified inside of her. Lying beside Wyatt in the early morning hours, she worried further that she stank of it and that if he kissed her he'd smell it on her breath.

Now, on her way to the bookstore, Catherine recalled how awful it had been to abandon Wyatt and his engagement ring — a small star sapphire set in an antique platinum band — on the nightstand and sneak out of his apartment. She knew he would find her excuse — "I just can't" — inexplicable and cruel, but she also knew how much crueler it would have been to marry him. I am not a cruel woman, she had wanted to tell him as she wandered through the city and ran into the specter of him everywhere. He did not call her. After three long weeks of silence, though, she called him. She was planning to tell him everything—the whys and the why-nots—yet the second she heard his voice, she hung up, appalled at herself. There was a time and a place for honesty, but this wasn't it, she knew. She had to purify herself first, before she could even think about sleeping beside him again, think of taking his name.

Back then, it seemed that her heart was in a constant state of breaking, and it was breaking again now as she thought about Wyatt, who had wanted to marry her, and Henry, who had left her. The more she had tried to reason it all out, to make sense of her wounded heart, the more she felt the ongoing strain that she was placing on it and the more she realized that in Henry she was idealizing a man whom she never should have idealized at all. She wished she had had more self-control when it came to Henry, and then later when it came to Wyatt—and then she was quickly backing out of the drive, because she couldn't stand the sight of the cottage. She had given Wyatt the cottage out of what she had thought was her deep, steady love, although it had come at the cost of something she had held precious and dear—her mother's diamond engagement ring, a family heirloom, which Catherine had inherited and hoped one day to pass on to a daughter of her own.

Catherine had worn the ring for years and had cherished it as she had cherished the occasional compliments people gave her. Though not garish by any means, the ring did call attention to itself, the antique oval stone large and perfectly cut, the rose gold band encrusted with pavé rubies. She had worn it so constantly that Catherine forgot she even had the ring on until someone, like Jane or Louise, took her hand to examine it.

On her way to the bookstore, Catherine remembered those three weeks after she'd left Wyatt, and after Henry had left her, and how she'd wandered around the city wearing the ring, although it felt to her as if the ring were wearing her, as if it knew far more than she did — about love, about marriage, about how to find and to keep them both, not separate but a single thing. She remembered sitting in the same cafes in which she and Wyatt used to go, taking the same paths through Washington Square Park that she and Henry used to travel — in the hope of "accidentally" running into one of them. But she never did.

During one of her marches around the island — she took to calling her walks "marches," as she stomped through the sludgy snow in her boots — she kept thinking about her parents, specifically about her father, who was only a few years older than Henry, though without any of Henry's spirit, and certainly with none of Wyatt's compassion, which she craved more than anything. As she marched, her thoughts marched with her, always circling back to Henry, which inevitably led her back to Wyatt. She wanted to talk to one of them and went to use a pay phone, then realized that Henry would be at home, with his wife, and that Wyatt was at his job at the law firm. She bought a pack of cigarettes and smoked as she marched, wondering if anything was worth the effort when it left you unhappy in the end. She focused her thoughts on Henry, because had it not been for him, she would not have undertaken such a rigorous dissertation topic. Would he still keep the promises he'd made, to help her to get her articles published and to land a good job at a good university? Probably not, she realized, flinging the cigarette into the gutter and ducking into a diner to get warm.

As she sat down on a stool at the counter and ordered a cup of coffee, she removed her thin gloves and gazed at her chafed, red hands and her mother's ring, which sparkled in the diner's fluorescent light. She took the ring off, admiring its weight and beauty again, recalling her mother, who, before her death, had handed her daughter the ring and said, "Rings are nothing without fingers. Don't let this sit in a drawer, Catherine. Find someone to love."

And I did, she now thought. I found someone to love — Wyatt with his great big talent and his great big heart, Wyatt who initially slid the ring onto her finger, then, years later, without exactly saying it, wanted her to take it off again, which she did eventually, because she knew it was the only way to make him happy and, more than this, to keep herself happy, too.

We were happy, weren't we, Wyatt? she asked herself now, as she sat at a stoplight, absently staring down at her finger, at where the ring ought to have been but wasn't. She pictured the ring where she'd left it — at Louise's house, in Louise's possession. After Catherine parked the car on Main Street, she sat for a few moments, remembering the afternoon she'd gone to see Louise, the ring tucked in her pocket. She had already been to the bank, which had refused her a loan, and to the town's sole pawnshop, which had made a ridiculously low offer, and so there was Louise left, only Louise who could help her.

They sat in Louise's vast kitchen, at her vast kitchen table, in her vast ten-room home, and after a lull in the conversation, Catherine brought up the cottage and the renovation. "I want to do this for him," she said, pulling the ring out of her pocket and setting it on the table.

"Just let me lend you the money, then," Louise said. "You don't have to — "

"If I have to sell it — and I do — then I want it to go to someone I trust," she said. She thought there'd be tears after Louise had written her a check, and tears when she deposited the check in the bank, and then when the workmen arrived the following week. She thought there'd be tears when she looked down at her empty finger and when she went to remove the ring at night only to remember that she no longer owned it. But there weren't any tears, only a kind of sickness in her gut, which vanished the moment she climbed into bed beside Wyatt and curled up against him.

Now, in the bookstore, as Catherine went to help a customer, she knew that, contrary to what Louise had said — that she'd act as Catherine's pawnbroker but not forever — that she'd never have enough money to buy the ring back and that even if she did she wasn't sure she'd want it. Like memories of Wyatt, the ring belonged to a more promising time, when the price of love hadn't been so steep and what had been lost could always be found again. She thought they had found each other again, she and Wyatt, after the hardwood floors had been laid, the paint had dried, and Wyatt had moved into the cottage. And for a time, it seemed to her they had, as he disappeared into the cottage every morning only to reemerge at night, cheerier, it appeared, than he had been before. Catherine thought that everything would be okay at last, the cottage a beacon to vanquish the dark, shadowy doubts she still had.

But standing in the bookstore this morning, as she had stood in it for the last nine years, Catherine understood again just how fleeting and weak that light had been and, beyond this, just how much she had grown to rely on it, as she had grown to rely on Wyatt to write his way past his early disappointments and failures and in this way to secure for them what he had promised so long ago — a bright and golden future full of bright and golden dreams.

A Few Remarks on a
Rainy Night in Manhattan

———

On the morning of her book party, Antonia woke before the sun, made coffee, and took a cup of it on the terrace. Below her, the park fanned out in a dark green swath while the avenue unspooled in a quiet, empty ribbon. This yellow-lined street, she knew, connected her to Henry, whose apartment was twenty blocks north. As she lit a cigarette, she glanced uptown, thinking about him in Winslow, if he was indeed there. Yesterday evening, she'd shown up at his apartment around dinnertime only to be told by the doorman that he hadn't seen Mr. Swallow. She might have used her key and stayed there anyway, but staying in Henry's apartment without Henry in it seemed wrong. She left him a note, telling him she'd be at Calvin's, yet he still hadn't called or come by.

The sun peeked over the tops of the east-side buildings and rouged the cloudless sky. The air was already muggy and full of grit. A fleet of off-duty taxis headed downtown in an undulating yellow wave. The city hummed around her, arousing in her the fierce longing to work. Writing was the only way through. It was the only thing that could sustain her.

Back in Calvin's small guest room that he had done up in damask, she took her place at the desk. She'd brought along Wyatt's typewriter, which Catherine had so generously lent her, and ran a finger over the keys, staring at the blank sheet of paper. She typed a few sentences while she thought about Henry's accident again, her conscience working on her. How could she possibly write this novel? Then again, how could she not? Without Henry, she wouldn't be sitting here as the writer she was, whose debut novel he had helped launch into the world. How could she think about Henry without also thinking about her uncle Royal? Without him, she never would have had a story to tell. How could she ever thank either of them for such a Pyrrhic victory? Because she understood that's all it was, just as surely as she suspected Henry of knowing more than he was letting on. She recalled that night when she'd come home from Catherine's to find his glasses on the kitchen counter. Had he misplaced them, as he'd said? She shivered again at the idea that he'd been in her house, worse, in her study.

As the sun bled across her fingers and the typewriter and the empty page, it revealed her most disturbing thought yet: the story of Henry's accident was getting away from her, which also meant that Henry was getting away from her as well, didn't it? To keep him near, she set aside her fear and plunged again into his past, hauling up the accident, Wren, all the things that she knew and thought she knew. As she wrote, she renewed her own vows to this shapeless, nascent narrative. I will capture it all, no matter how ugly, no matter how awful, she thought, because the truth has to win out. Again, as she often had, she felt as if she were this new novel's guardian. It told her where to go, to use the gift of her situation as honestly as she could. The world will go on turning, it said, and in no time at all people won't care a fig about Henry or what he did. Yet even as she made some headway, her mind kept drifting back to her father, to the trouble she'd caused him. So how could she go on like this? How could she tell Henry's story when she knew how much trouble it would create for him?

I can't, she thought, lifting her fingers off the keys. I won't, and she pushed away from the desk, disgusted at the sight of the paragraph she'd written, which was not about Henry at all but about Catherine. She said the name aloud, said it again, picturing another way into this story, perhaps an even better way in, because Antonia did not have the same regard for Catherine that she had for Henry. She liked Catherine, sure, but she didn't love her. She valued her friendship with the older woman, yes, but not as much as Catherine apparently did. Besides, just whom did Catherine think she was fooling anyway?

Over the last couple of weeks, it had become more than obvious to Antonia that the docile, unassuming Catherine had feelings for Henry. Why else had she rented him the cottage, especially after the way he'd treated her husband? Though she'd suspected as much from the start, it wasn't until she'd learned about Catherine's doctoral work when something leapt out into the open, as if from behind a giant black cloud. She knew Henry would never confirm it, but it seemed to make sense: he'd always had a penchant for young, driven women. It wasn't hard to imagine Catherine as she once had been, young and ambitious (she was still young, thought Antonia, though now utterly unambitious), or Henry as he'd once been, too, even more handsome and at the top of his literary game. It also wasn't hard to imagine the romance the two might have shared, or the way it had ended — with Catherine leaving Henry to marry Wyatt. No, perhaps Antonia was coming at it from the wrong angle. Perhaps it was Catherine, and not Henry, whom she should have been looking at more closely.

As she wrote for another couple of hours, morning turned into afternoon, and her attention flagged. It was frustrating for her to keep writing in circles, the heart of the story like a target that kept moving out of range. What tied everything together? How could she braid the loose strands of Henry's story into a cohesive narrative when all the strands kept unraveling? Wren was one strand, Catherine and Wyatt Strayed another. How were the two intertwined, if indeed they were? Lacking precision, her story, she knew, lacked credibility. Her uncle had given her the story for the first novel by way of an insane letter. She wondered who would give her this story, and how it would be delivered.

Right in the middle of a sentence, she heard voices in the next room. Hello, she wanted to call out. I'm working in here. Instead, she opened the door, and there was Ezra Swallow, perched on the sofa. He was smoking a cigarette.

"Ezra, Ezra, Ezra," she said, "what a surprise," the words breaking apart like the rings of smoke he blew into the air.

"Hello, Ms. Lively," he said coolly, without looking at her.

Calvin appeared and offered her a glass of champagne, which she took, appreciating his show of good cheer. The cheer, however, turned out not to be for her, because he was saying, "Ezra just got some awesome news. One of the most respected lit agents in the land wants to represent him."

"That's wonderful," she said, hiding her irritation by taking a sip of champagne. "Who is it?"

"George Marceau," Ezra said, beaming, knowing how Antonia must feel to learn he had landed her agent. "I'm not even finished with the memoir yet," he added triumphantly. "George swears he can sell it based on the first chapter. He thinks it's going to be *huge*."

"It happened so fast," Calvin said. "Tell her the story. Go on."

"Well, it was like this: George came to the magazine to visit my grandfather, and my grandfather told him what I was writing . . . Hmm. It doesn't sound like much of a story after all."

"It is. It is," Calvin said, encouraging him.

"Yes, it most certainly is," she agreed, despising Ezra all the more. Who was he to upstage her like this, and on today of all days?

Though she smiled to herself when she remembered how easily and how well her own novel had sold, there was just no palliative against the trouble she'd had to endure, the trouble, she knew, that she'd continue to endure as long as her uncle was still out there. She shivered against the memory of him and took a big gulp of champagne. "Slow down, huh," Calvin said with a laugh. "We have an entire night of boozing ahead of us."

"Ezra, if you ever need any advice or another pair of eyes. Anything at all," she said, trying a new tack. "You can always come to me."

"Antonia, that's very sweet of you, but you're the bloody enemy," he said matter-of-factly, dazing her. It was so hurtful that it took her a few moments to recompose herself.

"Me? The enemy?" she said at last. "Oh, I see. You mean that unfortunate night at my house. Look, I'm sorry about that. It was a terrible night for me all around."

Though not as insincere as it sounded, the apology still managed to rankle Calvin, who whispered in her ear, "You shouldn't feel threatened, Antonia," which was the truth.

Why should she feel threatened by the nothing Ezra Swallow? It might take him years to write his memoir, or he might lose interest in it and abandon it, or once it sold, his editor might get fired, orphaning the book. So many things might happen to derail him. So many things could go wrong. Still, if she knew anything at all about Ezra, she knew that he possessed his father's same ferocious drive.

Slipping away, she went back into the guest room while Ezra talked endlessly about his memoir and Calvin needlessly cheered him on. Although perhaps not so needlessly, she realized, since her friend could now make better use of the boy. Most writers she knew, even the nicest of them, like Calvin, cultivated connections with other, more famous writers, not for the friendships themselves, but for what these friendships could do for them. Though ambitious, she refused to put herself in the same category, refused to believe that she was using Henry to further her career — though, of course, she suspected that everyone thought this about her anyway. Let them think it, Henry had said. She hated to be hated, she had told him. If other writers hate you, then you're doing something right, he had said.

When she was a girl, she had often imagined what it was going to be like to be a successful writer, how the world would embrace her and love her for it, as she embraced and loved the books it produced. She had imagined moving to New York City and sitting in cafes, surrounded by others like her. She had imagined publishing run by those whose only concerns were the printing of great literature. Henry had opened her eyes to her mistakes, to the pitfalls and traps of the publishing industry, a business, he said ruefully, that runs on the fumes of tastelessness and profit. I have no reason to complain, she thought, and struck a key. The moment she did, however, she faltered. What she needed was to hear the reassuring voice of someone who had always loved her despite whom she had become. What she needed was to hear the voice of the man who'd raised her. "Daddy," she said into the room, though no sooner had she spoken it than she deflated, the word having no meaning to her whatsoever. He was not her daddy, and how could he be? He was a monster. Yet if he were a monster, what did this make her?

Rising, she grabbed a baseball cap and her big sunglasses and put them on. Tentatively, she again opened the door and glanced out, though Ezra and Calvin were nowhere to be seen. Once she was out on the sidewalk, she headed north under an impolite, sweltering sky. She didn't mind. She'd take a miserably hot day in the city over a thousand beautiful days in that wretched little town. I don't dislike Winslow as much as all that, she thought, correcting herself. Henry is there and I still love him, even if he's been acting so bizarre lately. He came to my house that night and left his glasses — but no, she wouldn't allow herself to think about it now on her way to see him. Whether he wanted to believe it or not, he would come to understand, she hoped, that she was writing this second novel for him. For them. In the writing of it, Antonia knew she'd find her way into the literary pantheon, and in the reading of it she prayed that Henry would find his peace.

THE LUCERNE SAT on the northwestern corner of Eighty-fifth Street and Central Park West. The facade of the prewar building was made of white limestone and jutting cornices, roosting gargoyles and lead casements. It smelled of old money and old New York, and whenever Antonia passed into the mirrored lobby she felt herself instantly at home. Unlike yesterday, she cruised through the lobby in silence and headed for the elevators. She was determined to talk to Henry, who, she thought, had to be in the city by now. The rickety old elevator slowed on the tenth floor, and then she was standing outside his door. Excited to see him, she got out her key, then wilted when she realized how this sudden appearance might to look to Henry, who valued his privacy as much as she did. Leave, she told herself. Now.

Yet she couldn't leave. She was too keyed up, too nervous not to see him. As she stuck the key in the lock, the door swung open on its own, surprising her. Calling out his name, she stepped into the

short, dark hallway. It alarmed her that Henry had left the door
unlocked, or perhaps his housekeeper had forgotten to lock it on
her way out. Today there were no signs she'd been in the apartment; the shutters were closed, the air hot and stale. It seemed to
her as if no one had been in the apartment in ages. She switched
on a lamp, a gentle pink glow lighting the unadorned walls. For
a moment, she felt as if she were trespassing and nearly did leave.

From the street below, the sounds of incessant traffic filled up
the quiet while she crept from room to room, each one shuttered
and empty. When she came to the door to his bedroom, she rapped
lightly, in case he were napping. She breathed out his name, a whis-
per, then opened the door, and there he lay, his hands folded on
his chest as if in effigy. Fully dressed, his body looked longer and
larger to her, his loafers dangling off the edge of the bed. The sight
of him suddenly filled her with desire, and with sadness. Silently,
she made her way to the bed and, looking down at him, she let out
a gasp, because the man on the bed wasn't Henry at all.

"Antonia," her uncle Royal said, his eyes blinking up at her. She
wanted to run, yet couldn't move, and she wanted to scream, yet
her voice was trapped in her throat. He sat up, and in his face she
recognized traces of her father, though this man was nothing like
him. His smell hung in the room, unpleasant and appalling. She
was shocked to see him, yet even more shocked at herself for har-
nessing her fear and rising up to combat whatever demands he had
of her.

"If you've hurt Henry," she said, "I'm going to — "

"Hurt Henry?" he said. "Now why would I do a stupid thing
like that? Seems to me that of the two of us, you're the one who's
hurt him. My, my, the stories I'm sure you told him, Antonia. The
stories you told him . . ."

"How did you get in here?" she asked, as her eyes finally adjusted to the gloom. She twisted her head this way and that, searching for Henry.

"Young Polish housekeepers with three children cannot be trusted," he said. "Twenty dollars was all it took. As for Henry, I've been expecting him all day. We have a lot to discuss, me and him."

She stiffened, saying, "You have no business bothering Henry and you have nothing to discuss with him." Then she turned toward the door and ran into the hallway, rushing for the elevators. It had been nearly two years since she'd invited her uncle up to her apartment in Harlem. Back then, she wasn't sure which had been more traumatizing — his very presence or the story he'd relayed to her. Afterward she'd gone to stay with Calvin, returning a few days later to her own place where she found an envelope under her door. That envelope contained a long letter from her uncle in which he had detailed his time in Georgia. Reading it had confirmed for her that she had to write his story. She had not seen him since, not until now. Her uncle trailed her to the elevator. "Enough of this. You leave us alone," she said, her voice a tangle of anger and disgust.

They stepped into the elevator together, this man who would not stop hounding her and this girl who would never be rid of him. This is no longer destiny, she thought, staring at the red alarm switch. This is something far worse. As she reached for the switch, Royal grabbed her hand and held it in his firm grip. "I could get out my knife right now and slice off every one of your fingers. What's a writer without her fingers, huh? Maybe even better is that tongue of yours. I cut it out, and then you won't tell so many stories, so many lies."

Then, suddenly, he let her arm go as the doors opened on the ground floor, and he walked away, drifting through the lobby, the city drawing him out and away from her. Trembling, Antonia moved slowly through the lobby, too, past the tenants, who took no notice of her, past a hall of mirrors that reflected her own startled eyes. Great drops of cold sweat ran down her back as she pushed out into the heat of the afternoon. After stepping off the curb, she hailed a taxi, though not before her uncle was beside her again. "So how is my favorite writer and niece doing these days?" he asked sweetly now, his words gentle and beguiling, as if he were interested to hear what she had to say.

"You hurt me," she said, wiggling her fingers. "I could have you arrested."

"You won't," he said. In her novel, she hadn't had to change much about him, because he was as fixed in her memory as the words she'd put down on the page. To her, he would always be the same, in print as in life. The sun caught the stains on his thread-bare suit, one of the buttons of his jacket loose, hanging limply, and she laughed at herself for her sudden compassion, wanting to mend it for him, to offer him a shower, shelter, some food. "I always told your father you were going to be a force to reckon with," he said. "You won't have me arrested because, you see, my darling niece, I could just as easily return the favor and have you arrested for thievery."

He grinned at her, and she saw the dried bits of food in his ratty beard and wondered if he weren't living on the streets. "Thievery?" she said. "Why did you leave that letter if you didn't want me to read it? You had to know this might happen, Uncle Royal. You knew that I was a writer."

He laughed a mean, boiling laugh that shook the air around her. "I had come to seek your advice," he said. "As for the 'letter,' did you see any 'Dear Antonia' on it? That was no letter, my darling niece, but a chapter from my Bildungsroman." From his pocket he produced the rumpled pages of "Vitreous China" that he'd obviously ripped from the magazine. "I have read this a dozen times, and every time I do, I find it more fascinating than the last. You do have an imagination. I have to wonder where you got it, since your father is about as imaginative as an old shoe."

"Look, I have a lot money now, Uncle Royal. We can go to a bank, and I get you all the money you want," she said. "Consider it a thank-you."

"Money," he said, laughing again. "No, I'm afraid I'm not here about any money."

"Then what?" she asked, as the city roared around them, oblivious. As the light changed and the traffic eased, Antonia thought about how easy it would be to sprint into the park, and lose him for good. Yet her curiosity kept her from it.

"You are most certainly your father's daughter, utterly remorseless and utterly unwilling to take responsibility, I see. Well, I'm sorry for you," he said. "I'm here because you took that story of mine away from me," he went on, gripping her by the nape of her neck. "Still, I do think it's unfortunate that you got so much of it wrong."

She thought about shouting for help but stopped herself, realizing she wanted to hear the rest of what he had to say. "Uncle Royal, you're hurting me again," she said, and he released his hold on her. "Look," she said, "I made up what I needed to make up. There is no right or wrong when you're writing fiction. There is no truth. It's all lies."

"Lying for the greater good," he said, laughing. "Twisting the truth does not make it a lie. It just makes it into nothing." He wiped the sweat from his eyes and continued, "You got the most important details wrong. Don't you think a novel based on fact ought at least to get those facts right? You have cheated the reader out of the real story, the true one, my darling niece, and you have cheated me out of my due. Stories belong to the people who live them, not the people who type them."

"Cheat? How did I cheat them?" she asked. "Are you trying to tell me that the story you left for me happened differently? That my father — "

"I thought writers, good, dedicated writers, did their research," he said. "You should have gone to Georgia to find out for yourself. Firsthand knowledge is your only defense against attack."

"Find out what?" she asked. "That my father raped an innocent girl, who eventually died, and then he went AWOL? What more is there? You told me everything, I thought. Those pages you left for me — I had to embellish on them. It's what I do. If I told it differently from how it happened, it's because you didn't make yourself clear. It's because you willingly — "

"No," he said. "I must stop you right there. You got it wrong because you wanted it to be the way you imagined it, not the way it happened. I'm afraid that even your imagination couldn't come close to seeing the truth for what it is. I spent — "

"You came to me — "

"I spent thirteen years of my life in prison, writing hundreds of pages of that story, and you have the gall to think you know all of it better than I do? I killed a man because of it, because of that girl. She did die but not because of the rape, as you imagined. That was only the beginning. All of it happened, just not the way you wrote it. My brother had nothing to do with that girl's death. Nothing at all."

"Oh, God," she said, suddenly more frightened than she'd ever been before. "But you told me — "

"That he murdered her? No, my darling niece, you forced that connection yourself. I said that he never took responsibility for what he did. He ran off and left me to clean up the mess," he said. "What inside of you wanted it to be the way you wrote it? That's what I want to know." He took out a dirty handkerchief and wiped his brow. "I killed that girl, and then you came along to kill her again. You might have given her a voice, but you didn't let her have her final say. You wrapped the story up in a pink-ribboned ending, but you wrapped it up way too quickly." As he continued to change the story on her, she no longer knew what to believe and felt a sickening tightness in her gut. Her face dripped with sweat, yet she felt chilled. "I paid for my sins. Now your father's got to pay for his. He's got to hold up his end of our agreement." He put his hand on her arm. "You need me, and here is why: to finish the story you started and bungled."

It was all too horrible, and she staggered away, leaving him with his crazy grin and deranged talk. He was insane, she finally realized, and probably went around telling this story to anyone who'd listen. But who would believe him? In her memory, he was always showing up at the house drunk, and her father was always slipping him money. Wasn't this proof of her father's guilt and even more proof that silence about Sylvie had been their agreement? She sprinted into the park and all the way to Sheep Meadow, where she joined the mass of sunbathers, Frisbee throwers, and everyone else out on this broiling summer afternoon.

As Antonia caught her breath, her mind kept returning to her uncle. What would Henry say when she told him about her terrible run-in with him? What worried her more, though, was not knowing what her uncle had needed to discuss with him. A Frisbee landed right at her feet and broke her trance. Then she gazed around her at the young men and women either engaged in conversation, or playing games. She took the most interest, though, in the ones reading books and silently applauded these solitary figures going about their solitary pursuits. Maybe at this very second one of them is halfway through my novel, she thought, and was

filled with a moment of joy. She picked up the Frisbee and sent
it flying back to the young man who'd lost it. He shouted out a
thanks, then flipped it back to her, but she let it sail past. I don't
have time for this, she thought, though she wanted more than anything to spend the rest of the afternoon there in the park, being a
young girl again, if only for an hour. Shrugging, the young man
headed over to collect the Frisbee, as Antonia headed out of the
park, already picturing the evening ahead at Leland's, when Henry
would introduce her, then ask her to be his wife.

Back at Calvin's, the midafternoon sun poured through the
windows, tossing sinister shadows up and down the walls. After
collapsing on the sofa, Antonia shut her eyes, but was unable to get
her uncle out of her mind. She hurried into the guest room, replay-
ing what he had said. You have to get this one right, Antonia, she
told herself as she sat down at the desk. The writing would save her,
and she turned back to it now, pushing through her doubt, each
sentence better than the last. She wrote for about twenty minutes,
happy to be back in this place, feeling her center connected to the
story again. She felt the muse close, nearly upon her, but then, suddenly, it went running off again, taking her inspiration with it. She
needed Henry, needed his reassurance now more than ever, and
went into the kitchen to call him.

When she finally heard his hello, Antonia let out a muffled sob.
"Henry," she said, "oh, Henry, you're there. Please come over. Please."

"Antonia," he said. "I'm right in the middle — "

"Henry, please. Now," she said, imploring him.

Twenty minutes later, Henry was standing at the door. The moment she saw him, she threw herself at him, trembling, her body
pressed as tightly against his as possible. Rather than calming her,
though, his presence, she discovered, seemed to have the opposite
effect and brought on an even more violent panic. There was just

too much to tell him, and she knew no way to begin it. She hated herself for all that she'd done, and for all that she would do. He was her lover, soon to be her fiancé, and she didn't understand how she could go on deceiving him when her love was as honest as she was dishonest.

"Has something happened?" he asked, drawing a soothing hand down her back.

He is here, and everything is going to be fine, she told herself. He is here, and there's no reason to scold him for standing me up the night before. He's been preoccupied with the party and with his speech. I can't fault him for wanting to give me the perfect evening. "N-no. Nothing," she said at last. "You aren't — " But she stopped herself from finishing the thought — you aren't angry at me, are you? — because he was here. After tonight, we'll get away, she thought. All we need is a few days' rest. We'll go someplace where no one knows us. Yes, a trip, she thought, softening against him. There were so many roads to take into this story, but Henry was her road and her destination, and she clung to him in the waning afternoon light, whispering, "Thank you so much for being here, Henry. Thank you so much for everything."

BACK AT HIS apartment, Henry had ordered them a lavish dinner, which they ate out on the terrace as the sky clouded over, and the wind flipped the leaves of the trees below. When the phone rang, Antonia went to answer it. It was Calvin, who told her that he'd see her later. When she returned to the table, Henry was pouring wine into two crystal goblets. She expected a toast, but when he didn't raise his glass, she raised hers, and said, "To you, my king of letters. To you, my love." And even through all of this, she couldn't stop thinking about her uncle and finding him here and what it meant—to both of them. She wanted to tell him, oh, how she wanted to tell him, but how? To tell him would ruin this moment, would ruin everything, all of their plans, so she didn't.

Henry smiled up at her, his big eyes shining with the love she knew he still had for her. "You did all the work," he said. "To your future fame."

It was odd to hear that word leave his lips, since it had always seemed to her that he was embarrassed by his own celebrity. He shunned it and once said that, in retrospect, he would have been happier with obscurity than a life in the limelight, even something so insignificant as the literary limelight, he'd added with a scoff. Antonia knew he had worked hard to get where he'd gotten, toiling and striving to carve out his name. After thirty years of the same old thing, he looked exhausted to her, and more than that, he seemed bored. Had writing criticism taken the life out of him? A little drunk on wine and confident in her assessment, she now said, "In my experience, critics have always made the best storytellers. You've written your reviews and your essays. Now, I think it's time for you to put everything you know about the written word down in a book. Write about your life, Henry. Write about what happened to you. Just get in there and — "

"In your experience?" he said coolly. Then, "Just leave it alone, Antonia." This is what he usually said whenever she brought up the subject of a memoir.

All at once, she felt something new gaining traction inside her, a freedom she had not experienced before, the potential to see Henry in a whole different way. She realized now it wasn't that he wouldn't tell her about the accident but that he couldn't, because he had not taken any steps to distance himself from it. He's still living it every day, she thought, and this both saddened and infuriated her. As it appeared to her, he had let the past dictate his present. Rather than exorcise the story by talking about it, Henry chose silence. For now, though, she would let it all go, because this evening was as much his as it was hers. She got up and drew her arms around him, kissing his ears and his neck, tasting the salt of him. Then he was out of his chair and undressing her while the city watched them from its many lighted windows. She didn't care. She cared only about this moment, before they were swept up in the evening. And when he entered her, his body was strong and decisive, and when the first drops of rain fell, he shuddered against her. As the rain came down in torrents, they raced into the apartment, stripping and laughing on the way to the shower. Under the water, however, Antonia felt Henry withdraw as she lathered up his back. He did not return the favor but reached for a towel instead. You vexing man, she thought, yet then he was telling her about all the writers, editors, and publishers who would be at the party, people she hadn't met and had always dreamed of meeting. "Everyone will be there," he said. She imagined them all shaking her hand and how she'd blush at their praise, forgetting about her father and her uncle, about Henry who remained mute at her side, and they'd ask her about the novel and want to know where her inspiration had come from, and she'd respond to them as candidly as she could and she'd say, "To answer the dead — isn't this fiction's greatest virtue?"

IN THE TAXI, they drove east through the park, the water on the drive reflecting the park lights. The town homes and apartment buildings along Fifth Avenue gleamed through the misty rain, the windows sparkling just as Antonia sparkled in her long-sleeved black dress, pearl earrings, and lace choker, her hair wild and loose. She felt wild and loose herself, seated beside Henry, her heart beating with anticipation. Henry kept fiddling with his breast pocket, where, she knew, he had put the pages of his speech. Why was he fiddling? Why wouldn't he look at her? She was about to ask him if something was wrong, when they pulled up to Leland's restaurant, and the moment was lost.

Leland's at last, she thought as she stepped out of the taxi. Leland's — where book deals were made over plates of steaming squid-ink pasta, and writers huddled at the bar, lamenting poor reviews and plotting revenge, where editors came to gloat about their latest best sellers, and publishers called one another out on poaching writers. In his day, Henry had often frequented Leland's, he'd told her, though he didn't understand her desire to have a party there when the city offered so many more interesting venues.

"That place is as pretentious as the stuffed shirts who patronize it," he'd said. How could he say such a horrible thing about it? "Because those stuffed shirts are my friends and colleagues," he'd said, "and I've earned that right."

She took Henry's hand, and together they walked through the doors, but then he let go of her hand to say his hellos, moving away from her, leaving her awkward and discomfited. Yet here she was, among Henry's people, his friends, allies, and enemies. Here she was, in Leland's at last, where she'd been only once before, with Calvin, when they'd sat at the bar and ogled the famous (and infamous) writers and editors. Here she was, losing her awkwardness and her discomfort, taking in the tables set with flickering candles, and there was her novel, propped up on a big table in the center of the room. Some of the servers, dressed in black shirts, black slacks, and white bow ties, carried trays of hot and cold hors d'oeuvres while others circulated with trays of champagne. Then, she was swept up in the smiling congratulations, the handshakes and the hugs. Everywhere she turned, she met another face, a fellow writer, an editor, a publisher, all of them with such kind things to say. She spotted her own agent and editor speaking animatedly at the bar, and she looked for Henry among them but didn't find him.

She did find Calvin, however.

"You made it," she said, throwing her arms around his neck, kissing him.

"I made it," he said, kissing her back. "Ernest should be — " But then a short, porcine man interrupted him.

"Antonia Lively," the stranger said, his big red face made all the bigger behind his black horn-rimmed glasses.

" 'Tis I," she said.

"Leland Dubois," he said, extending a big fat hand. Of course, who else could this be but the owner himself? Who else would show up to her party in a red satin tuxedo? She thought back to what Henry had told her about the sixty-something-year-old Leland, about his novels — all southern Gothic — which had failed to sell, and how he'd given up writing three decades ago to open his own restaurant. ("Better to serve the cats than wind up as their kibble," Leland had told Henry.)

"Mr. Dubois," she said, "I'd like to introduce you to my good friend, Calvin Blanchard."

Turning a flirtatious eye to him, Leland looked Calvin up and down, then said, "And you, are you also one of this young woman's ilk?"

"Aspiring to be," he said, smiling. "Before you ask, no, you've never heard of me."

"I'm sure I could change that," Leland said, turning to Antonia. "You were about to ask me if have seen Henry. Well, I haven't, but if I know him, he's off on some remote island collecting his thoughts." He looped an arm through Calvin's and dragged him to meet, as he said, the rest of his ilk.

While lighting a cigarette, Antonia watched them go, then she, too, was swept up in the crowd, everyone wanting to talk to her, as she had hoped and had secretly expected.

HENRY, THOUGH, WASN'T on some remote island collecting his thoughts. He wasn't even in the restaurant. Having stepped out for some air, which had done nothing to relieve his headache, he was now gazing through the windows at all the faces he'd come to know and to love and to hate. He spotted Antonia at the bar, her back to him, speaking animatedly with Leland, who tilted his head up and laughed. How he still loved her in that moment, remembering her face staring back at him on that first day of class, strong and demure at once. Now he wished that he could walk back into Leland's, grab her by the wrist, and lead her away. Away from this, from all of it, he thought, turning from the window, because he couldn't bear another second of it, and he hurried across the avenue. There had to be an ending to this, a release of all the emotions that welled up inside him. She was killing him, this thing with her far too unfathomable, and it had drained him.

He fiddled again with his breast pocket and knew he should go over the pages of his speech. How could he deliver it, knowing what he had learned, knowing that she was betraying him even tonight? He had been so excited by the prospect of introducing her, so proud of what he had helped to create. And though the excitement was still a part of him, there was something else to it now — the thrill of exposing her for what she was, the need to punish her for what she had done, and would do. He looked back at the restaurant, and watched her, his resolve crumbling further, as the rain came down, spotting his glasses. He had just taken them off to clean them, when he heard his name, a woman's familiar voice. It was Catherine.

"Henry, what in the world are you doing out here?" she asked from under her umbrella, which she positioned over his head as he put the glasses back on. Happy to see her, he nearly grabbed her by the arm, wanting to say, "Come with me. Let's get out of here." He wanted to tell her that he couldn't go through with it, that his love for the girl had done him in, just as she predicted it would. He thought back to that afternoon when Catherine had shown up at his office and had accused him of sending Antonia to her house. He'd done no such thing, of course, and why would he? "It's a pity that it's raining. I hope it doesn't spoil Antonia's night," Catherine said, but Henry wasn't listening. There was this thing churning inside him, this nameless, mean-spirited thing, and he wanted to be rid of it. He wanted the evening to end, so that he could return to Winslow, to the dry comfort of the cottage.

After resigning himself to what he had started and to what he, too, had become, he finally said, "Let's get out of this damnable rain," and led her across the street and into the restaurant.

EVERYONE HAD ALREADY taken his seat around the tables, as Henry and Catherine stepped into Leland's. When Antonia spotted them, she waved, her face bright and warm, but inside, where no one could see, she was seething. Why was he holding Catherine's arm like that? The gesture seemed too intimate to her, too telling. Then she laughed at herself, realizing how silly she was being. As he took his place beside her and dried his face with a napkin, Catherine came up to say hello. "I'm so glad you're here," Antonia said. "It wouldn't have been the same without you."

"If only I had the power to make this rain go away," she said.

"You just did," Antonia said, squeezing her hand.

"Congratulations. I'm so proud of you," she said, turning to gaze at all the occupied tables, trying to decide where to sit. She spotted Wyatt's former agent, George Marceau, and his former editor, Lacey Blount, neither of whom acknowledged her, which was just as well, because if they had, she wasn't sure she would have been able to control her tongue. She had a few things to say to them, none of it pleasant. For a moment, she felt as if she were caught in the middle of a terrible, raging sea and that the reminders of a painful past were about to wash over her, to drag her down and under. Her chest tightened, and she turned back to Antonia, who seemed to understand and patted the empty seat beside her. "Sit with us," she said, her words to Catherine a sudden reprieve.

"Thank you," she said, grateful to have been spared the awkwardness of saying hello to George and Lacey.

As Catherine settled into her seat, Antonia glanced at Henry, who had a stricken look about him, and she wondered if she'd done wrong by offering Catherine a seat. What harm could it do, though? Still, his strange reaction — if he were indeed reacting to this, she thought — made her wonder again what had gone on between the two. But she quickly pushed the thought away. There would be time for that later. Still, Antonia wasn't exactly sure how to feel about this longed-for night now that it had arrived. It was hard for her not to think about her father, wishing that he could have celebrated it with her. It was even harder not to think about her uncle, whom she looked for among the faces that passed by the windows. Was he out there, biding his time? But no, this thought, too, had to be banished for now. Instead, she turned to Henry and said, "You're going to be fine," because he was fidgeting nervously with his breast pocket again.

Then Lacey Blount, her middle-aged, southern-born, auburn-haired editor, rose and asked the room for quiet. She clinked a fork against her wineglass as the room finally hushed. "Friends," she said with a slight lisp, "I want to thank y'all for braving the inclement weather and coming out to help me celebrate with Antonia." She picked Antonia's novel off the table and held it up. "Once in a great while, I find a novel that instantly speaks to me. This novel didn't just speak to me, though. Oh, no, this novel called to me in my sleep." Everyone laughed, including Henry, which buoyed Antonia.

"It never once said, 'I promise I'll make you a ton of cash.' It never once said, 'I will be an instant *New York Times* best seller,' though I have a feeling this is exactly what it will become. I cannot tell the future, but I can tell y'all this much: the success of this novel is already written in the reception it has received in *Kirkus* and *PW,* both of which gave it starred reviews." Lacey took a sip of her wine before continuing. "Here's another juicy little surprise. Just this afternoon, I received word that *The Death of Her* will be featured on the front page of the *New York Times Book Review.*" She set the novel back on the table. "I love this novel, I really do, and I love it all the more because of the young woman who wrote it. She's an incredible talent, she really is, and her novel's just as complicated and beautiful and breathtaking as Antonia Lively herself." She held her eyes on Antonia and smiled, then turned to Henry. "I told him I wasn't going to do this, but we do have another outstanding writer with us tonight. Wait. I take that back — there are many of you in here, aren't there?" The room burst into laughter. "I've edited Henry Swallow for years and have enjoyed every second of it. Tonight, I want to thank you, Henry, because if it hadn't been for you, I never would have heard of Antonia, and I wouldn't be here now to honor her. Thank you for having such good taste, in books and in women." And with that, she took her seat to a flourish of applause.

There was nothing left for Henry to do but to rise, which he did. He breathed in deeply to fight back the dread, and as he thanked Lacey and looked out over the room, he realized just how ill prepared he was to meet this moment. He took a sip of wine, then removed the speech from his pocket. Unfolding the pages, he looked down at the words he'd written, these alien words, no longer his own. When he went to speak, the words caught in his throat, and he took another sip of wine, sensing Antonia's restlessness, her irritation. She was waiting, as everyone was waiting, but waiting

for what? He knew what they all wanted to hear — how he'd discovered Antonia, how he'd passed her short story on to Dillard
Bloom, and how, later, he'd passed her novel on to Lacey Blount.
Handed down through the publishing ages, he knew — they all
knew — that the story of Antonia Lively was mythical and un-
changing. He also knew that they wanted to see him as the savior
of letters he had always made himself out to be, though, in reality,
he knew all too well that he was nothing more than a man who'd
gone to bed with one of his writing students. Most of all, he knew
they wanted him to confirm the good they'd done, by him, by Antonia, and by literature itself, just by being there tonight.

Yet something was happening inside him again, a cramp of will,
he thought, because the longer he stood there, the clearer his own
complicity in all of this became. Antonia's ambition, her success,
her betrayal — they were his, too. So what could he possibly tell
them? He glanced down at Antonia, experiencing her beauty, her
youth, and yes, her arrogance yet again. Her eyes were aglitter, as
they had been all through his class. Tell them, he thought. Just tell
them what they want to hear.

When Henry finally opened his mouth to speak, he was surprised by the ease with which the words tumbled out, surprised
all the more because they were not the words he'd written. This
was a different speech, something he'd been writing in his head
long before this evening, begun, he thought, on that beach road
on Osprey Point, and finished on the night he'd read portions of
Antonia's second novel. He knew what he was about to say — to
do — was unforgivable, that once said it could not be taken back,
but could his disloyalty compare to what Antonia had done, and
would continue to do? And while a piece of him understood that
it had to happen like this, another piece of him — the piece that
still loved and adored her for who she was, a young woman blessed

with a rare talent — wanted to reach down, lift her into his arms, and carry her away. He had loved her and had wanted nothing more for her than a long, splendid career, yet now all he wanted was to hurt her, to ruin this evening, to make her understand the price of disloyalty.

"You've all come out tonight because you want me to tell you about Antonia," he said. "You want me to tell you that she's everything a writer ought to be — genuinely talented, with a dozen novels inside her. Of course, if I know any of you at all, I know that you won't rest until her face is everywhere, on the cover of every magazine, in the subways, and on radio and TV. I want to ask you something, however: Do you honestly believe she deserves this much attention?" A sudden and dissenting murmur rose up through the room, yet Henry would not be deterred, not now. "It wasn't always like this, if you recall," he went on, galvanized by the wine and his insistent awakening. "You used to buy good books. This business of ours used to be the business of real ladies and real gentlemen. Now it's just brutish and ugly. Literature is art. Remember? Literature exists despite us. You good people, you're killing it. You find 'beauty' in cheap stories told by opportunists, given legitimacy through your complicity. You pay ridiculous sums of money to celebrities and politicians who don't need it. Yet you're stingy with the real writers who can't make ends meet. Writers like Wyatt Strayed — " He glanced quickly down at Catherine, who appeared startled at the mention of her husband. "Look, I know that publishing isn't fair, that it's as random as a slot machine, but when you give an advance of four hundred thousand dollars to a girl of twenty-three, can't you see what you're doing? Can't you see that you're not only undermining publishing's very foundation, but you're also creating the very monsters who work against it? You can't possibly let them fail because then the failure would be yours and mine. You have done much good, too, of course you have, and you should be congratulated for it, though you should not congratulate yourselves, as you so often do. Creating an overnight literary sensation isn't easy, but let's face it — it doesn't take a rocket scientist to figure out the formula. You and I both know that the books you launch into the stratosphere aren't traveling to brave new worlds. They're traveling the same orbits they always have, which means their trajectories are equally predictable — they are pushed into every display window in every bookstore, although the prose is mediocre, and the story never quite rises to the claims made by those who should know better — like me. The names of the writers might change, but the books remain the same: some better than others but few of them good enough." He paused and took a deep breath before going on. "Generally, I believe over the years you've done far more harm than good. Generally, I believe that you don't have any taste, my friends, and tonight I wonder if you ever really did." He reached for his glass and took another large gulp of wine, draining it. All the while, Henry expected someone to stop him, to heave him from the restaurant, for Antonia to drive a fork into his throat, though when he looked down at her, she remained as still as a tree on a windless, cloudy day. No one stopped him or heaved him out of the restaurant, and Antonia didn't move or say a word. On everyone's face he saw an expression of anger and disbelief.

"It's time for you to look at what you've done, and you can start with Antonia's novel, because I'm here to tell you that despite its carefully crafted prose, it is a fake, a hollow, heartless story stolen from the lives of innocents." He paused, swaying on his feet, the wine taking hold of him. He held up Antonia's novel and spoke directly to her: "This book will launch your career, but it will also be the end of it. You aren't a god, though I think you believe you are. You're just a writer, but you seem to have forgotten that you're also a daughter, a friend, and a lover." He fell silent, then turned toward the door and the street beyond, just as Antonia stood up and, much to Catherine's amazement, began to applaud.

I myself wasn't at Leland's to hear Henry's denunciation, nor was I there to see Antonia applaud him. I heard all about it later from Catherine, who watched Henry stagger to the door, as Antonia kept clapping, swinging her small hands out in front of her, clapping against her abject humiliation, against the sadness that suddenly hung in her face. Catherine didn't remember if there were any tears, only that the girl kept on clapping long after Henry had gone, clapping lightly, then again ferociously, an unending applause that echoed in the hushed, awestruck room. Then, all of a sudden, Antonia stopped clapping and rushed out of the restaurant. She stood on the sidewalk, shouting Henry's name, until Catherine got up from the table and went after her. No, I wasn't there, but I could imagine the scene — the rain-soaked, inconsolable girl, and Catherine trying to draw her back into the dry warmth of the restaurant, the murmurs and accusations that rose from the tables as coats were donned and umbrellas gathered, the evening shattered. Many, of course, did not leave, loathe to pass up the promise of music, hors d'oeuvres, and drink — all gratis, thanks to Leland.

According to Catherine, Antonia returned to the restaurant, though she kept glancing out the windows, her eyes wild and dark. The girl shook hands with her guests, and she moved around the room as before, yet it was now with a slow, halting step, as if she'd sliced her foot open on a shard of broken glass and were exulting in the pain.

"If it had been me," Catherine said, "I'm not sure how I would have gone on."

Yet Antonia did go on. She had to go on. There was nothing left for her to do but to stitch the two halves of the disjointed evening together into a single seamless one and to save herself in the process. This she accomplished with Catherine's help — Catherine who was always within sight, always within reach, working to undo the damage Henry had done, unwittingly helping to seal her own fate.

HAVING LEFT THE restaurant, Henry hurried along Third Avenue, then cut west toward the park. From somewhere behind him, he heard his name and slowed down. One of his friends had come to find him after all, and his heart expanded at the thought. His words had reached one of them at least! He imagined that he and this friend would climb into a taxi and go to a cafe, where they would sit and laugh at the evening's absurdities. It took real guts to say what was in your heart, his friend would say. Yet when Henry eventually did turn around, he didn't immediately recognize the man rising up and out of the watery gloom, even though he looked familiar, like Antonia's father, like the intruder who'd barged into his office. As this stranger, full of the same brutish anger, closed in on him, Henry saw at last exactly who he was, and who he wasn't — not Antonia's poor, naive father but the other Lively, her unpredictable, unhinged uncle.

The sight of him sobered the literary critic, who took off as fast as he could, thinking how this thing with Antonia would never end. Though he did not regret loving her, he did regret being drawn so unsuspectingly into her family's struggles. Henry ran, his loafers sliding on the slick sidewalks. He slipped once and fell, scraping his palms, then righted himself. He ran. Then he ran some more, and he did not look back, because he knew that if he did, he would stumble, and then her uncle would be on him. As he ran, turning corners, the bones of his feet ached and cried, and then Henry himself was crying. The pain was amazing, and he let it come, all of it, and he realized that he was no longer running to get away from Antonia's uncle but to put as much distance as possible between him and her. He might run the whole night, up the length of the island, though he suspected that he'd never be able to run far enough or long enough to burn her out of him.

As Henry rounded the corner onto Park Avenue, his legs quivered and gave out at last, and when he fell this time, he did not get up. He sat on the sidewalk as the traffic along the avenue splashed by him, and he craned his face up to the sky, breathing in the rain, wondering what it might be like to drown. He had given her everything, had loved her as fiercely and as steadily as he could. How could she have done this to him? How could he have been so foolish? As he sat there, he massaged his battered feet through the ruined socks, and wept. From the breast pocket of his jacket, he removed the wrinkled pages of the speech and read them again as the rain moistened the black ink, which bled through the paper and stained his fingers. These lovely words of his were melting, one by one, just as everything around him was melting. None of his friends were looking for him. No one was going to find him. Then he suddenly felt the touch of a hand, and he jumped, because he just knew. Oh, no, he thought, resigned to whatever was coming, understanding at last that he had invited this violence the moment he had kissed Antonia for the first time. There was a voice now in his ear, a gentle voice, asking him if he were hurt. He looked up at this stranger, who extended his hand, and taking it, Henry pushed himself up. "I was having dinner. I saw you fall," the stranger said, and glanced at the windows of the brightly lit diner behind them. "Do you need an ambulance?"

"No," Henry said, "unfortunately, I'm going to live," though his whole body hurt, his feet blistered and destroyed.

"Let's get you out of this rain," the man said.

"I'd like a taxi," Henry said. "Do you think you could call me a taxi?" The man left him on the sidewalk and went into the street. Once a taxi was at the curb, Henry limped over to it. "I appreciate your kindness," he said. It was then he noticed the book that the man was holding out to him.

"You dropped this," he said as Henry looked down in dismay at the dust jacket.

"Keep it," he said, having little recollection of how he'd come to have Antonia's novel. He did have a dim, foggy image, however, of picking it up as he'd spoken, but there was nothing much after that, only the memory of being chased. He was still being chased, he realized, as he leaned back in the taxi seat, allowing the gravity of what he'd done to settle over him. Not that he cared. The ears of publishing might ring for a day or two, but then it all would go on as deafly as before. Buying up the trash that sold and neglecting the books that didn't, like Wyatt's, he thought sullenly. He shut his eyes again, recalling the afternoon he'd found *The Last Cigarette* in his mailbox at Columbia. An accident — at least this was what he'd assumed at the time. Yet now he understood that it could not have been an accident at all. He recalled gobbling the book down in a single sitting, compelled he knew not why, but the story had opened up to him in new, exciting ways just as he had opened up to the story in new, exciting ways. How had it been possible that he'd gotten it so utterly wrong?

Now, as he hobbled into his apartment, peeling off his clothes on the way to his bedroom, he imagined that Antonia had left the book in his mailbox — Antonia with her wicked plans for it, and for him. He had no idea how she could have known that by rereading it he'd recant his review. He had no idea how she'd stumbled upon his past with Catherine, either, though clearly she had. All of this would be written, he suspected, in those terrible pages of her wretched follow-up. Once he was in bed, Henry burrowed under the sheets, the room as black as the ink stains on his fingers. The night was his solace, and the darkness his final escape.

PART TWO

————

After the King Died, the Queen Died of Grief

A Matter of Infinite Hope

‒‒‒‒‒

After sitting through his rude, infantile stunt at Antonia's lovely book party — "Saved in large part by our host, Leland Dubois," she had told Jane — Catherine had nothing good to say about Henry and wondered if she ever would again. A smart move to leave the restaurant when he did, or else, she suspected, she would have told him to get out of the cottage and not come back. Pack up your stuff and leave, she would have told him. She never had a chance to say anything, though, because he'd scuttled away, like the detestable creature he is, she thought. Though his screed had not shocked her, his wanton disregard for Antonia had. It reeked of sabotage, though no one should have been surprised. It was Henry's way. No excuse for what he'd done, she knew that he'd conjure excuses anyway. This, too, was Henry's way. Reaching into the past to haul out a litany of grievances against the people who had not only supported him, but who had helped him succeed. She guessed that he'd simply felt himself justified.

This was the story that Catherine relayed to the girls over dinner tonight, although Jane had heard most of it already. It was for

Louise's sake that she repeated herself. In the hashing and rehashing of it, she hoped she could close this sordid tale, and move on to cheerier subjects.

"His timing couldn't have been worse," Jane said, keeping the story alive.

"I should say not," Louise said. "I do have to wonder, though, if the girl didn't deserve it."

"Louise," Jane said, "you can't mean that!"

"I most certainly do," she said. "It was the most inappropriate time to come out with it all, but I think he was in his right to say what he did. The man may be many things, but he's no fool where that girl is concerned." The idea that Louise was now defending Henry galled Catherine, who took a bite of salmon, swallowing it along with her resentment. "What if she'd written about Jane or me or even you, Catherine? Cannibalizing other people's lives is . . . It's, well, it's indecent." It might have been indecent, but had Henry the right to humiliate the girl publicly? Catherine asked. "People need to know who they're dealing with. You of all people should appreciate that at least," Louise countered, and rested her eyes on Catherine. "Well, now at least you now have good reason to evict him and reconsider my son," she added.

But Catherine didn't want to reconsider Louise's son, much less talk about the cottage, Henry, or Antonia. She just wanted to enjoy this evening with her friends, to talk about their planned trip to Vermont in October — an annual weekend getaway, when they stayed in a small inn and took in the colorful fall foliage. She was about to mention the trip when she glanced out the window and thought she saw Henry meandering down the sidewalk. She went rigid, dropping her eyes to her plate. When she looked up again, he was gone, though the vision of him persisted long after she'd said good night to her friends, long after she'd climbed into bed to read.

At work the next day, however, Catherine thought little about him as her time was taken up by a string of customers. In between helping them, she also had to sort through the latest arrival of books and find a place in the storeroom for the new box of bookmarks. They had dedicated the summer bookmarks to Kafka: *We ought to read only books that bite and sting us.* Fall's was Fitzgerald: *Reserving judgments is a matter of infinite hope* — except that instead of the word *hope,* the printers had goofed and the word *nope* glared up at her.

Incensed, she lugged the box into the storeroom, where she called the printers. As she held the line, she thought about how she'd been reserving judgment for weeks on end and how it was less a matter of infinite hope and more like the misprint — a matter of infinite nope. If I hadn't ever invited Antonia into the house, if I hadn't gone to see Henry at Mead Hall, if I hadn't rented him the cottage. . . . The opportunistic, pontificating prick, she thought, remembering how much she'd been looking forward to spending a few hours in the city. For the party, she'd splurged on a new dress and shoes. She'd had her hair lightened to almost the same blond as Jane's. She'd even dabbed a few drops of Evening in Paris (Wyatt's favorite) on her pulse points — and for what? To be snubbed by Lacey Blount and George Marceau yet again, to have to witness Henry make a dreadful mockery of himself and the evening? In Leland's, Catherine had sat back, aghast, as Henry had stolen the air from the room. She'd watched Antonia's countenance fall, the caustic effect of his words palpable in her every smile and movement. After his speech, she smiled and moved differently, wandering through the restaurant on the feet of a revenant. Then, not more than half an hour after Henry had gone, she disappeared into the rain. Catherine had not seen her since.

She'd been meaning to stop by Antonia's to check up on her. Yes, the girl may have been callow in the way she apparently stole the truth of her father's life, but she was young and needed time to grow into her talent. Surely she didn't deserve Henry's denouncement. Yet whenever she thought about how much money the girl had, she felt the same old twinge of jealousy and realized that she just couldn't face her. Besides, she had enough on her hands in having to deal with her house. Thanks to the storm back in June, the house needed extensive repairs. The storm had damaged her already fragile roof and had sent rivers of water leaking into the study and flooding the basement. Already, she'd wasted hours obtaining overpriced estimates. She might have used Henry's rent check to pay for it all, yet this check went instead to pay her late property taxes. As for the other check of ten thousand dollars, Catherine still hadn't decided what to do with it yet. Yesterday she'd gone to the bank with the intention of depositing it, yet when she got to the teller window, she turned and walked away. The money would have changed her situation completely, yet to cash Henry's check, she knew, meant that she was on the verge of forgiving him. And how could she possibly forgive him now after what he had done to Antonia?

Dirty man, dirty money, she thought as she waited impatiently for the printer to pick up the phone. She was about to redial when she heard Harold's big booming laugh through the storeroom door and withered. Leave it to him to visit today of all days, she thought, gazing in despair at the bookmarks. As she climbed the stool ladder to make some space for the large, heavy box, Harold wandered into the room, saying, "And a good afternoon to you, Catherine."

"Good afternoon," she said, climbing down off the ladder. She lifted up the box, which was clearly too heavy for her, and waited for Harold to assist her. Instead, he just stood back and watched, sucking on a toothpick.

"I'd like to offer my help," he finally said, "but you know I'm hypertensive."

Yes, she knew all about his hypertension, his hyperthyroid, and his hyperawareness of his employees' performances, hers, it seemed, most of all. Having nearly got the box above her head and into the empty space, she sneezed and lost her balance, the box spilling to the floor with a crash. The noise startled Harold, who clutched his chest, while the bookmarks scattered at his feet. After he realized that he was going to live, he leaned down and picked up one of them, his red face slackening the more he stared at it. "'Nope,'" he said, spitting out the toothpick. "*'Nope'?*" In this one mistake, which wasn't even hers, she knew she had left herself vulnerable. "All you had to do," he said, glaring at her, "was to make sure these were done properly," and he leaned down again to pluck up a fistful of the bookmarks. "That's all you had to do."

She might have defended herself, though any defense, she realized, would have only sounded like an excuse to him. "You're right," she said, suddenly ablaze with anger. "That's all I had to do, besides ordering and receiving your books, designing your window displays, and coming in on my days off to manage your inventory. You're right. All I had to do was make sure your lousy bookmarks were done properly. I'm a complete failure." And then she was crying, which surprised her, because she hadn't cried since she'd buried Wyatt.

"Now, now, come on. It's not as bad as all that," he said, letting the bookmark fall to the floor. "We'll just have more printed up. It's not that big of a deal, really," but of course it was that big of a deal. When it came to the bookstore, she knew everything was a big deal to him. "Catherine, you've been . . . Are you happy here, because it seems to me . . ."

"Yes," she said, drying her eyes. "It's just . . . I needed those extra hours."

"Maybe you should think about switching careers. Get back to your dissertation," he said, as if he hadn't heard her, or maybe as if he had, she thought bitterly.

"This is all I have," she said. Then, "Are you unhappy with me?"

"In all honesty, yes, I am," he said, digging into his pocket for his vial of toothpicks. "You used to be my top earner. You used to bring such energy to this place, but you haven't been like that for a long time." Since Wyatt's death, you mean, she thought. Today, right now, she finally understood the trap she'd set for herself by taking the dead-end job, which she'd only accepted to give Wyatt his hours of uninterrupted writing time. Temporary has a way of becoming forever, Jane had warned, and here it was, forever, and here Catherine was, crying again. "If you need some time off, take it," he said, sucking on a fresh toothpick. "Maybe when you come back, you'll bring some of that old Catherine with you. See, I need you because you want to be here, not because you have to be here. If selling books isn't your thing anymore, then cut your losses and move on. That's all I'm saying." Move on where? Move on how? Catherine wanted to ask as they gathered up the bookmarks and replaced them in the box. "Jane has to run an errand," he said, "and I have to go to a meeting. We'll talk soon, okay? In the meantime, I want you to think seriously about our little tête-à-tête."

THE AFTERNOON DRAGGED on, with only a handful of customers to break the monotony. Around four o'clock, Catherine slipped out to the deli to quickly buy a soda and a bag of peanuts. Under the awning, she sipped the soda and nibbled on the peanuts, thinking not about what Harold had said but about Antonia, whom she thought she saw in the gazebo across the way. She went to wave, then realized it wasn't her at all and felt silly. Back in the bookstore, she had just taken her place at the register when Linwood Lively walked past the windows, then slowed. He hadn't shown up at the party, though Catherine had looked for him. She wondered how he would have taken Henry's awful stunt. Knowing his penchant for scenes, she imagined that he probably would have bloodied Henry and maybe even sent him to the hospital, a thought that was not unpleasant to her. Linwood had stopped just beyond the windows and stood under the awning, the glare of the sun making it hard for her to see his face clearly. He wore a dark blue suit and a black fedora, so out of place, she thought, in all this heat. To get a better look, she took a step closer to the window, just as he removed the hat to wipe his brow. She realized, then, it wasn't Linwood at all but a man closely resembling him — they had the same drooping eyes, the same oddly shaped head — a man who could have only been his brother. Could he have been the man at her house that terrible night? Could he have been the man who had nearly attacked her?

Royal gazed with fiery intensity into the bookstore window, the display filled with Antonia's novel. He pressed a hand to the glass, as if he thought he could reach right through. There was ire in his round face and, beyond this, an unassuming, childish sweetness that took Catherine aback. He was not unattractive and had a conical, muscular neck and, she suspected, a taut fighter's build beneath his suit. Taller than Linwood, though not by much, what she most noticed was his smile, because it was Antonia's; he had her mouth, full of the same cramped gray teeth. His smile, though eerie, was also strangely placid, even friendly, she thought.

In a different world, Catherine might have invited him in to discuss the latest books. She might have even been attracted to him as, she hated to admit, she'd been attracted to Linwood. Yet this was not a different world. It was the world the Lively brothers had created and that Antonia had written about and that she, Catherine, now found herself inhabiting. In this world, she knew enough not to befriend or trust Royal Lively. When he tapped on the glass and called out her name, smiling, she involuntarily reached under the register and grabbed the handgun. She'd never handled the gun in all the years she'd worked for Harold, and it felt much lighter than she'd imagined it would. Rather than wait to find out what Royal wanted with her, she hurried through the store and locked herself in the bathroom, her breathing suddenly shallow and irregular. She hadn't had a spell since that awful night on her porch and didn't want to have another. Sitting down on the closed lid of the toilet, she put her head between her legs, trying to control her breathing. The tiled floor spun in circles as she shut her eyes, though this only worsened her dizziness. She remained like this for what seemed like hours, waiting for the approach of footsteps; the small gun rested in her lap. Then, suddenly, there were footsteps, and he was at the door, banging on it, and she jumped.

"Leave me alone," she said, though she might have merely thought it because she could only hear the pounding of her heart. As the banging grew louder, she raised the gun, and when she finally fired — her finger shook so much that she accidentally pulled the trigger — the kickback both deafened her and knocked her to the floor. The air smelled of cordite and of pine disinfectant, a plastic bottle of which she'd spilled. Her fingers ached as she pushed herself up and went to the door. She looked through the hole the bullet had made in it, though she saw only the far wall with its shelves of overstock. Now she put an ear against the door, though could only hear the ringing in her head. There was, however, a sudden and faint shrill cry that filled the space, intensifying moment by moment. It did not belong to a man, she noted with fear, but to a woman. Please, God, she thought, shaking. Cautiously, she unlocked the door, giving it a gentle shove, and there was Jane, slumped in one of the fat leather chairs, tears running down her stunned pale face.

They looked at each other without really looking at each other, saying nothing; then Jane got up and raced out of the room. When Catherine saw the silver-dollar-size hole immediately to the left of where Jane had been sitting, she shuddered, realizing what might have been and understanding that she had let the mayhem and savagery of the summer spill over into her own psyche. She hurried after Jane, wanting desperately to explain, to tell her about Royal and about his smile. She wanted to tell her about how she still spoke to Wyatt, to tell her about the affair she'd had with Henry, and why she'd rented him the cottage. Catherine wanted her to know how important she was to her and what their friendship meant. When she called out her name, however, Jane refused to turn around. She simply got into her car and sped away. As Catherine watched her go, she felt her hand heavy with the weight of an object and looked down, horrified to find that she was still holding the gun. She quickly slid it into her pocket, then went back to the deli, where she bought a pack of cigarettes, smoking one after another until the sky turned to gold and it was time to close up for the evening.

Wyatt's Big Revenge Book

Back in the bookstore, Catherine straightened the shelves. Absently, she kept glancing out the windows, scanning the faces to make sure none of them was Royal. As she rushed around, she cursed him. She hated how she'd reacted, how she'd reached for the gun, as if guided to it by the same force that had brought this man to the town. She was not a violent woman, but she was a frightened one, and this fright had driven her to do something terrible. Oh, Jane, she thought glumly, what have I done? She knew that, come morning, every business up and down Broad Street would have heard the story, which meant that Harold would have heard the story, too. "You've jeopardized the reputation of this store," he would say. "I'm afraid you've left me no choice but to let you go, permanently."

Now she not only cursed Royal but Harold as well. She also cursed Wyatt for dying, Henry for being Henry, and even Antonia, blaming her, too, for the malevolence that swirled through the summer air like a virulent pollen.

As she collected her purse and went to the shop door, she

wondered what Royal Lively had wanted with her and how he had known her name. He's been watching us, all of us, she thought, unlocking the door and peering out at the darkening street. He could be waiting for me anywhere, waiting for me to step outside, for me to pull into my drive, for me to go out on the deck with a glass of wine and a cigarette. After taking a deep, fortifying breath, she locked the door behind her, then walked quickly to her car, checking all around her. Once in the car, she locked the doors, breathing easier, yet the moment she pulled up to her house and saw the black windows that gave onto the blacker rooms, she turned the car around. She felt a need to tell someone about the afternoon, about Royal and the gun and Jane. Though she guessed that Jane had already called Louise and told her everything, she didn't care; she wanted to tell Louise her version of things. Because she will understand, she thought, turning onto Louise's street, dismayed to find Jane's car at the curb. Catherine might have been able to face Louise by herself, but she couldn't possibly face Jane, not tonight, and certainly not both of them together. They must think I've gone crazy, she thought.

As she drove off, she considered taking in a movie, then decided against it. Instead, she drove around aimlessly, up one deserted street and down another, then suddenly wound up at Tint, where she sat several minutes in her car, telling herself there were far worse things for her to do than to go into a bar and order a drink. Still, she couldn't find the necessary gumption to get out of her car. People talked, she knew they did, and she had absolutely no desire to have to explain herself to anyone, least of all her friends, who would reprimand her for it. So turning the car around again, Catherine headed to the one house where she knew she would be welcome, and, she reasoned, where she should have gone first, if for no other reason than to warn the girl that her uncle was afoot in Winslow.

THIS TIME, CATHERINE did not waste any time sitting in the car. After getting out, she hurried up the steps to the veranda and knocked, even though the windows were dark and Antonia's car was nowhere in sight. As she knocked again to no avail, Catherine felt ashamed for having cursed her earlier. You might deserve many things, but you don't deserve my scorn, she thought. I hope you're safe. She left the veranda, the evening breeze rustling the trees around her and conjuring up all kinds of shifting shadows. After pulling the car into her drive, she stared through the deepening blue dark at her house and cottage, whose windows flickered faintly with light. The sight of these familiar, solid structures eased her fear, though she still wanted to barricade herself in her bedroom. Before she did, however, she had to tell Henry that it was time for him to go. Though she knew it would pain her to have to say good-bye to his rent money, she would gladly rip up his check if it meant she never had to see him again. She would rent the cottage to someone else. Yes, even a stranger, she thought, tapping on the cottage door.

"Henry, unlock the door, please," she said. The door, however, was already unlocked. Apprehensively, Catherine stepped into the cottage, calling out, "Henry, are you here?"

She didn't see him as she entered, although he was in evidence everywhere she looked — from the still-burning candles that sat on the low-slung mosaic table to the bottles, newspapers, and cigarette butts that littered the floor. She blew out the candles, then turned to the study. She knew he was in there, because a dim light spilled under the door. Pressing an ear against it, she heard nothing but the hum of the wind and the beat of her own angry, disappointed heart. "I'm not mad, Henry, but I really have to talk to you," she said, lying, keeping the fury out of her voice. "What went on between you and Antonia is none of my business. I'm not here about that anyway. I'm here because we had an arrangement, remember? I just don't want this to become forever. Look, if you don't come out, I'm going to have come in, and I'd rather not." Even as she said this, she reached in her pocket for her keys.

After fitting the key into the lock, she turned the knob, dreading what she might find. Opening the door, she said, "Henry," though he was not in the room. The light came from the street outside, and from the full moon, which shone brightly through the windows. She was relieved to find that nothing had changed. Wyatt's cherrywood desk still sat under the windows, Henry's typewriter resting on top of it, the demure stained-glass lamp beside it. He'd spooled a single sheet of paper into the typewriter's roller, but the page was blank, as blank and unused, she thought, as the room itself. Then, really, what has he been doing?

Suddenly, Catherine looked out the window, where she thought she saw a figure streaking past. She let out a gasp and stumbled backward against the wall, which caused a small avalanche of what felt like soft bricks. She reached down, grabbed one of the bricks, and held it up. No, she thought, not a brick at all, but a stack of what looked like newly minted dollar bills, bound with rubber bands. "Dollar bills? What in the world, Henry?" she said aloud, replacing the stacks as neatly as she could. She counted forty-three of them, guessing that each stack contained one hundred bills. If Henry were planning some kind of escape — though from what she couldn't imagine — forty-three hundred dollars wouldn't get him far or last him long. Clearly, he was up to something. Clearly, he'd been using the cottage for no good.

BACK IN HER house, Catherine went around locking all the windows. When the phone rang she stared at it, hesitant to pick it up. From the kitchen, the answering machine clicked on,

filling the house with a whistling echo and a terrible laugh. It was
Royal, she knew it was Royal, and she went to the front window,
peering out into the dark. After this, the night unfolded in a series
of endless scratches and groans that arose from everywhere and nowhere. Again, she checked the front and back doors and windows,
to make sure everything was secure. No one was getting in, she
understood, but then she wasn't getting out, either.

After pouring a glass of wine, she took it to the sofa. Deciding
then that she wanted to talk to someone, anyone, she got up to use
the phone, just as it rang again. This time, she answered it, only to
hear what sounded like someone typing — and she slammed down
the phone. When she had been a girl and afraid of the night, she
had always read a book to distract herself. She looked for Antonia's
novel, though after a few minutes remembered she'd left it out on
the deck. There were other novels to choose from, however, and
she rummaged the shelves, yet nothing grabbed her eye.

"Wyatt, what should I read?" she said aloud as she entered the
study, where she was met with a mildewy, decaying scent. She'd
been back inside it only once since the rainstorm, and in that time
it seemed to have rotted even further. A cluster of what looked like
small toadstools had pushed up through the spaces between the
planks in the hardwood floor. The walls were graying, and black
mold clung to the window frames. When she tried to move one
of the cardboard boxes, it came apart in her fingers, spilling out
her incomplete dissertation — "The Deconstructing Williams: Es-
chatological Anticipation in the Novels of Gass and Gaddis" — a
couple of frayed scholarly journals she'd published in, her diploma
from Stanford, the acceptance letter to NYU. There was also the
first edition of *Poor Folk,* an anniversary present she'd planned to
give to Wyatt, which was still wrapped in the same blue tissue paper, the card with his name still stuck under the red-satin ribbon.

It was a nasty surprise — she'd forgotten about the book — and it sent a ripple of sorrow through her. She tried another box, which also fell apart, letting go Wyatt's magazines and papers, which hadn't gotten wet, and his manuscript, which had. She set the damp pages aside, then climbed over the odds and ends of the life she'd stored in the room to get at the box marked BOOKS. Over the last year and a half since Wyatt's death, she'd intended to go through all the boxes but hadn't found the courage.

Now she opened the box and gazed down into a world that had once belonged to both of them. Every book she pulled out reminded her of Wyatt, every title a different memory. She began to weep.

"I can't do this without you anymore, Wyatt," she said. "I don't want to do any of this without you. I-I hate you for leaving and for taking Henry's review to heart. I hate you for giving in."

Though she had imagined saying this before, hoping it might make her feel better, she'd never let herself. Having done it, she was sad to feel as she always did, and even sadder because she missed Wyatt all the more. Abandoning the books, she was about to leave the room when she stopped and looked down at the manuscript. She remembered wanting to read it the day she'd brought it home from his office, though it turned out she hadn't had the courage for this, either. She also remembered telling Jane about the manuscript and how Jane had asked her, "Do you really want Wyatt in your head right now? Give yourself a few months, Catherine, then maybe you'll be ready." Tonight, she still didn't know if she was ready, but she knew it was time.

She had always taken a keen interest in Wyatt's writing, yet when his novel had met with such an unkind reception, she stopped asking him about it. She trained herself not to pry. Then, one mild, sunny winter morning, she had awoken from a dream in which Wyatt had won the Pulitzer Prize. A wonderful dream, she had wanted to share it with him. Without thinking, she had turned to him in bed and described it to him. He had said nothing, the look on his face telling her everything. She had gotten up to shower while Wyatt had gone into the kitchen to make coffee. Yet when she had walked into the kitchen, there had not been any coffee, just Wyatt at the sink, gazing out the half-open window. Just as she had been about to say his name, he slammed the window shut. The birds, he had said. The damn birds and their damn singing.

Now, after Catherine undressed and put on her nightgown, she went into her bedroom and locked the door. Then she climbed under the covers with Wyatt's manuscript—*The Girl in the Road*—knowing this was what he had intended for her to read all along.

WYATT HAD NOT dedicated the book to her, as she had hoped, but to Jim, whoever he was. The epigraph was a quotation from Richard Yates: "Dying for love might be pitiable, but it wasn't much different, finally, from any other kind of dying." He had broken the novel up into three parts—1956, 1982, and 1988. She read through the first part, 1956, which followed the narrator, Walter Schell, from his childhood in Connecticut through his graduation from NYU, ending just before he sold his debut novel. He had based Walter on himself, which startled her, since he detested romans à clef. "It's cheating," he used to tell his students. "Yes, of course, we all write about ourselves, we're always a part of our creations, but writing fiction is about leaving ourselves out of our work. If you want to write autobiographically, don't call it fiction and don't expect me to read it."

The first part of the novel exposed all of his family's secrets, some of which she knew, others he'd either made up or hadn't told her. She'd no idea, for instance, that he'd ever felt such animosity toward his mother; his depiction of her, she found incredibly unjust, especially since he'd always spoken so highly of her. As she finished this first part, her heart began to beat faster, worrying about what she would find in the second. If he could depict his mother like that . . .

She began to read and didn't stop until she had come to the end of the section. She had to admit that he had done what he did best — he had presented an honest portrait of her and their marriage. He didn't describe her as a bad or incompetent person, only as the woman she was, and it stung. She had loved him and trusted him to do the same, trusted him to forgive her mistakes as she forgave his. She had forgiven him for making her leave Manhattan, for moving them to Winslow. She had forgiven him for needing a space of his own. She had even forgiven him for his daydreams of big advances and book royalties that would see them into the future. But how could she now forgive him for this, for exposing her flaws and secrets to the world, for telling the story of the ring?

"No," she said, shucking back the covers and sending the pages of the manuscript tumbling to the floor, her mind swirling with what she'd just read — how Wyatt the writer had used Walter the narrator to reveal his truest feelings about her, how he'd wanted to leave her, how he nearly had, how he'd found touching her repulsive after he'd learned about her past involvement with the renowned literary critic, Hiram Simonov. She wondered how Wyatt could have possibly found out about them when she'd never told him. Then, with horror, she remembered the night Henry had shown up at the house, asking to see Wyatt. While the two had talked on the deck, Catherine had sat up in bed, trying to read. Henry, you unbelievable bastard, she thought.

After getting up, she unlocked the door and went to the small secretary in the sitting room where she rummaged through the drawers until she found the date book she had kept at the time. Flipping through it, she came to June, trailing a finger down the page, until she paused on this entry: *June 8, 1988 — H at house to talk to W. WHY???* She shut the diary, reeling. Clearly, Henry had come over that night to unburden himself, to confess. It made no sense to her, though. Why would he do such a thing? Hadn't he caused her and Wyatt enough pain already?

Back in her bedroom, Catherine collected the scattered pages from the floor, wondering how Wyatt could have kept this knowledge from her, wondering what other secrets he had brought to light in the third part of the novel. She thought she'd been ready to learn all this, that there had been enough distance between what had been and what was, yet she'd been wrong. She couldn't help feeling that instead of turning his revenge upon the world, Wyatt had turned it on her, because this novel, as far as she could tell, was nothing more than a retelling of their lives. Wyatt's betrayal was an unbearable weight, and she wanted the manuscript out of her life. She could not bring herself to read the last part. She thought about dumping it in the trash. She thought about setting it on fire. In the end, however, she couldn't bring herself to do either and simply returned it to the study to molder along with everything else.

Then, as she should have done an hour ago, Catherine quickly stole onto the deck, grabbed Antonia's novel, and hurried back into the house. She returned to her bedroom and again locked the door. After climbing back into bed, she turned to the first page, and began to read.

Champagne for
My Real Friends

—————

The first couple days after the fiasco in New York were the worst for Antonia, who spent them on the sofa, breathing in the hot, fetid air, feeling as if she deserved to die. Having used up the last of her energy driving back to Winslow, she had none left, not even enough to turn on the window air-conditioning unit. Instead, she denied herself every available comfort she had — food, drink, even cigarettes — because she knew that it was only in Henry that she'd find any comfort at all. He had said what he had said, and it had nearly killed her, and as she lay there, she went over those ten minutes again, turning each word over to make some sense of them, of him. He had been angry at her before, yet his anger that night had been different, made of something even she hadn't recognized. Oh, how she'd wished he'd have keeled over dead, that someone in the room had shut him up. They had let him go on, though, as she had let him go on, because he was Henry Swallow.

Antonia had no recollection of finally rising to take a shower, her first in days, yet when she found herself under the water, she began to cry, remembering the shower she'd taken with Henry and how she hadn't wanted to ruin the moment by asking him what was wrong. She cried as she toweled her body and as she dressed and as she went into the kitchen to fix some dinner. She cried as she ate and as she rinsed the plate and set it in the rack to dry. She wandered the rooms of the house, avoiding the study altogether, crying all the while. She talked to Henry, asking, "Baby, why did you do this to me, to us?" Though she knew his reasons why, she took no comfort in this, either. Henry was gone for good, that much she understood, and wasn't coming back, although she still went to the window and drew back the curtain to watch the street, just in case.

No one called or came to see how she was faring, which she found unusual and cruel. This was Winslow, after all, and people often dropped by unexpectedly, so where were her friends? Where was Jane? Where was Catherine? Neither the phone nor the doorbell ever rang.

On the fifth day, Antonia opened the study door, though she did not go into the room. The hot, stale air seeping around her, she hung back in the threshold and lost her nerve. On the sixth day, she tried again, and this time she made it as far as the desk before retreating. Gradually, she felt the sadness giving way to a more useful anger, though she just wasn't ready for it yet. After lying down on the sofa again, she tried to find a way back to the story she had begun, but her imagination wouldn't take her there, no matter how much she pleaded. She felt both physically and spiritually exhausted, her body and heart reacting adversely to the privation she was putting them through, intentionally and unintentionally. No Henry, no coffee, no cigarettes, no writing — the dissolution of her habits, her happiness. She suspected that if she didn't come around soon, she really would die.

Then, on the seventh day, Antonia rose before the sun and went out to her car, humming. The first time in days that she'd breathed the morning air, she relished all the country smells — the honey-suckle, the roses, the fresh-mown grass, even the hints of baking manure the wind sometimes brought her way. After grabbing the pack of cigarettes she'd bought in the city, she went back into the house and made a pot of coffee. She hummed to herself as she poured the strong, medicinal coffee into the thermos, hummed as she took down a mug, then went into the study, crossing easily into the room. She hummed as she took her place at the desk and as she lit a cigarette, realizing only after dragging on it that she'd had the same tune in her head all morning — "The Merry Widow Waltz."

WHILE SHE SMOKED another cigarette, Antonia stared at the words on the half-filled page. A heated slant of sunlight shone through the aperture in the curtains. Like her own personal sun-dial, she thought, guessing that it was late afternoon, because of the sunlight's position on the floor. She hadn't left the airless room all day, feeling bound to the desk, to the story that had finally returned to her. Without Henry around, there was no one and nothing to interrupt her. I will not let anyone or anything interrupt me again, she thought, reading over what she'd written. As she did, she found some of it good, though most of it bad, and, taking the lit end of the cigarette, she singed a hole in the center of the paper, then ripped it out of the roller, wadded it up, and tossed it over her shoulder.

"Tell me about Catherine, Henry," she said into the air. "Tell me about Wren."

As Henry had damned her at Leland's, she'd felt the story moving through her, writhing like a worm in her gut. Once she'd rolled another a sheet of paper into the typewriter, she struck a key, will-ing herself back into the novel, but it was no use — the characters had fled. Whenever this happened, she had to leave them be for a while. She got up and went to the room's spacious closet and parted the doors. After tugging on the light, she stepped under the wooden rod toward the empty cardboard boxes, and stood staring at the wall of index cards she'd tacked up.

Having found it relatively easy to track the course of Sylvie's story, because she'd had most of the elements of it handed to her, she was finding the opposite true of Henry's elusive story. The few index cards only told her what she already knew.

At Calvin's, Antonia had come up with the brilliant idea of using Wyatt to find her way through the narrative, though now, as she studied the index cards, she didn't see how this was possible. She had also thought about Catherine, who might be her ticket, yet without more of the facts she just couldn't be sure, and she needed to be sure, absolutely, positively sure. So she read the index cards and, finding them unhelpful, pulled them all down, then flipped them over, sat down, and began to write on them. *Okay, different premise,* she wrote on one. *Henry's job at college only an excuse. Came to Winslow not because of it, but because of— Catherine? Rented cottage to be closer to her? Maybe fire at his house wasn't accidental.* This last idea stopped her cold. She wondered why he would do such a thing. Why would he try to take his own life? If I believe, which I do, she thought, that he had come here for Catherine and that they had been lovers, don't I also have to believe that patterns repeat themselves and that someone at NYU must have found out about them, and that's how he got fired? What if Catherine hadn't broken it off with Henry at all, but the other way around, and what if sweet, docile Catherine made sure that someone found out?

Antonia liked where this trajectory was heading, and she scribbled all of it down as fast as her fingers would let her. Let's start again, she told herself: Henry and Catherine had an affair. After Henry broke up with her, she got him fired out of anger, then married Wyatt and they moved to Winslow. A galley of Wyatt's novel managed to find its way into Henry's hands, and he, unable to help himself, negatively reviewed it. All this was logical and made the most sense to Antonia, who began to tack the index cards back up on the wall. Okay, so this explained how Henry wound up living in a mediocre town teaching at a mediocre college, but it did not explain his motivation for starting a fire or renting Catherine's cottage. It also didn't explain Catherine's reason for renting it to him. Unless she'd never intended to rent the cottage to anyone, and my showing up that afternoon changed her mind, she thought. What if it were just about convenience, and money? Henry had money; Catherine didn't. "Et voilà," she said, tacking up another card. Yet she knew that all this would continue to be speculation until she found out for herself.

Even so, Antonia went to her desk, smiling happily, and was lighting a cigarette when the doorbell rang. Peeking out through the curtain, she saw Catherine, and a sudden, glorious idea came to her. As she closed and locked the study behind her, she took slow steps to the door, thinking about Henry, how much she'd loved him, and what he'd done to her, and by the time she opened the door, she was softly crying again.

"Oh, you poor thing. You look so bereft," Catherine said. "Is there anything I can do?"

You can tell me what you know about Wren, she thought, yet said, "You haven't spoken to Henry, have you? Is he . . . all right?"

"Oh, that contemptible man," Catherine said. "You mustn't think about him. You have to think about yourself now." She pulled out a pack of cigarettes from her purse and lit one. "Though nowhere near as unforgivable as what he did to you, the old so-and-so wrecked my cottage top to bottom. I have a good mind to toss his things out on the street and change the lock."

"He's not a terrible man, Catherine," she said. "He's just had so much on his mind. First my crazy father and then my crazier uncle — "

"Speaking of," she said, then told Antonia about what had happened at the bookstore.

"Oh, Catherine," she said. "Oh, I'm so sorry."

"It's not your fault," she said. "That uncle of yours needs to be locked up. He can't go around menacing people like that."

Antonia gazed past Catherine to the gathering dusk, the shadows coming to life. She shuddered, imagining her uncle hidden among them. "It's cooler inside," she said, as Catherine stubbed her cigarette out and followed her into the house. "See, so much better," she said as she bolted the door. "As I was saying, Henry's just had so much on his mind, as we all have. Did you ever find out who Wren was, by the way?" When Catherine looked at her blankly, Antonia added, " 'Wren was here,' on your cottage. Remember?"

"Oh, that," she said. "I'm almost certain she's just another of Henry's affairs gone awry."

"Yes, you're probably right," she said, though she wanted to add, "No, Catherine. Think harder. Henry must have mentioned Wren to you."

"I know this might not be the right time or place for this, but I didn't want to bother you at the . . . the other night," she said, pulling from her purse the copy of the novel that Antonia had given her.

Antonia could tell that Catherine wanted to talk about that awful night, though she also knew that Catherine was too shrewd to mention it. After all, she, too, had lived with a writer whom Henry had attacked. Antonia wrote a little note, then autographed the novel and handed it back to Catherine.

"It's a beautiful read," Catherine said, "just as I knew it would be. Now I can't wait to read your next one!"

"It means a lot to hear you say that, and it means a lot that you're here," she said. "It seems everyone's abandoned me, including my editor."

"Not everyone," Catherine said, smiling. It seemed to Antonia then that the woman was holding back from telling her something important, though what this was Antonia couldn't fathom. She thought she saw it in Catherine's face, which seemed to have aged ten years since she'd last seen her. The tiny lines around her mouth had deepened and her usually clear eyes were bloodshot. It looked to Antonia as if she'd been up all night drinking. "I don't know how to ask this, so I'll just come out with it," she said. "Why is your uncle here? What does he want with you?"

"I just don't know," Antonia said, the tears returning. "I guess he thinks he feels entitled to a share of my money."

"Then give him some and be done with him," she said.

"You're probably right," she said.

"Well, I'll let you get back to whatever you were doing. I don't want to take up any more of your time," Catherine said, turning to leave.

"Are you hungry?" Antonia asked. "I haven't eaten all day and I thought we could have dinner together. Maybe take a little dip in your pool before."

"It needs cleaning, but if you don't mind a few dead wasps and some leaves — "

" 'Live in the sunshine, swim in the sea, drink the wild air,' " she said.

"Oh, I love Thoreau," Catherine said.

"So do I," she said, even though she'd quoted Emerson.

"Are you sure you want to do this?" she asked while Antonia went into her bedroom to put on her bikini. "What if Henry — "

"We can't avoid each other forever," she called, reappearing a minute later. As she reached for her bag, she added, "I hope I do run into him, because I want him to see what he's missing."

ANTONIA HADN'T BEEN back to Catherine's house for a while but remembered as they crossed the ugly yard just how unsightly it was. Patches of the blue paint had peeled away, and the roof was missing many of its shingles. The few plants on the porch were wilted or dead. The lilac bush sagged, in need of water, and the sycamore looked like it was about to fall over.

Poor Catherine, she thought, following her into the shuttered sitting room.

"Wine," Catherine said, heading for the kitchen, as Antonia again took in the shabby furniture and bookcases, which, she now noted, leaned at precarious angles. The floors sloped, as if the house were sliding off its foundation. The air held an odd, vegetative smell of mold and dust and broccoli gone bad. The whole house, it seemed to her, echoed with unhappy memories, which made her curious about what had happened there. What exactly had driven Wyatt out on that winter morning?

After handing a glass of wine to Antonia, Catherine said, "I'd fix us some dinner, but I'm out of everything. You make yourself comfortable, while I run up to the store. I'll only be a minute," and then she was gone.

Antonia almost went out on the deck, but instead sat down on the sofa, observing the room differently, with eyes that now saw more than they had on that first afternoon back in June. The circumstances surrounding Wyatt Strayed's death had always intrigued her, mostly because she had been such a huge fan of his novel. She had come to the house to see where Wyatt had lived. The spontaneous lie she'd told Catherine about Henry sending her had been just that — a lie. Still, the moment she'd uttered

Henry's name and had seen Catherine stiffen, she had surmised that something more was going on. Just a tiny moment between them, it had sparked Antonia's imagination. She had never agreed with Henry's review of *The Last Cigarette* and knew that if he just read the novel again, he'd change his mind about it. She'd left the novel for him anonymously in his mailbox at Columbia, never once alluding to it. She'd had no idea then that he'd not only change his mind but also recant all the negative things he'd said. Henry's essay had deepened her curiosity about Wyatt. Had it really been a suicide, as the papers reported, or something more sinister?

After leaving the sitting room, Antonia went to pour herself another glass of wine, when she noticed a part of a sheet of paper lying under the door to what she knew was Wyatt's study. She kneeled down, picked up the yellowing page, and flipped it over gently to find this:

> "Okay, so now you've told me everything," I said. The sun was just beginning to climb into the sky, the starlings just beginning their operatic tunes in the trees. "What do you expect me to do with it?"
>
> The literary critic slowly rose from his chair, went to the railing, and looked down at the pool. "If you write the story exactly as I told it to you, it will make your name," he said. "Then maybe you'll be able to buy yourself a real pool, one that sits in the ground." He grinned. "Maybe you'll even get away from this town and move back to the city. I know I would if I could."
>
> I laughed, although I found nothing amusing in Hiram's proposal. "You want the world to know what you did, and you want me to write it," he said. "You want me to —"
>
> "I want you to write it because I can't," he said, turning

around. "I'm giving you this story, Walter. If you don't want it, I'm sure I can find someone else who does."

I looked at the sky curving into brightness as the sun continued to journey over the horizon. From the trees, the starlings sang a deafening, unbearable tune with cheery abandon. I had never liked the birds, this town, or this house. Though I still loved Cecelia, I had never much liked my life with her. "If it doesn't sell, I'm coming after you," I finally said.

"If it doesn't sell, you only have yourself to blame," Hiram said.

The man is right, I thought, and I burned suddenly with the story I would tell.

Even after Antonia had finished reading this last page, the scene between Wyatt and Henry — who else could Walter and Hiram be but them? — continued to tumble through her head. She wanted more, to find out what came before. She took a step toward the door, her fingers already reaching for the knob, when she heard Catherine's car. Quickly, she laid the page back where she'd found it and hurried out on the deck with her wine. A few minutes later, Catherine appeared, saying, "I hope you don't mind, but I just don't feel like cooking. I bought one of those premade gourmet lasagnas. I'm heating it up," and she sat down in the lounge chair beside Antonia. The air was sticky and full of gnats and the crickets sang in the brittle grass. A string of bats kited above them as Antonia's head filled with questions she didn't dare ask. Oddly silent, Catherine shifted on her lounge chair, then all of a sudden turned to her, and said, "Henry will be out of here by the end of the week. I promise."

"Oh, Catherine," she said, "I appreciate that, but he doesn't have anywhere else to go. You don't have to take sides." Yet, of course, she had to take sides, and they both knew it.

"I'm, well, I'm glad you're handling all of this so well. If it were me, I'm not sure I wouldn't have fallen completely apart."

"Oh, I did that already," she said, laughing. "I'm sure I'll fall apart again, too, but for right now, I'm just enjoying what I have." She glanced absently at the cottage, remembering the first time she'd laid eyes on Henry, how excited and overwhelmed with desire she'd been. She felt the pull of the story again, the worm in her gut. "Bad things happen. It's why I write, to make sense of it all. Like what happened to your husband," she said. "He was such a talent." Catherine said nothing. "I often wonder what else he might have written if he hadn't taken his own life," she said, worrying that she was overreaching. "I'm sorry. You don't want to talk about him."

"No, I'd rather not," she said, falling silent again. Then, "Look, Wyatt might have been my husband, but I don't — well, I don't think he liked me very much. I mean, it happens sometimes, I know it does, but to find out the — " She stopped herself from continuing. "Sometimes there are things you just never want to know, Antonia." Turning to the young woman, her eyes were wide when she added, "My suggestion to you is that you leave Winslow. Get away from here and don't come back. You have the means. If I had the money, I'd probably leave, too."

"We could go on a trip together. My treat," Antonia said, smiling. "Where would you like to go?"

"Some place far away, where there aren't any writers — no offense — or literary critics," she said. "Someplace cool, like the Himalayas, or Iceland, just for a couple of months until summer's over."

Catherine smiled, which warmed Antonia's heart. She wanted

to do her a kindness, because she liked her, but also because she knew that it would further cement the woman's trust in her. So when Catherine brought up the bookstore and Harold's troubles with her, telling her that her job was in total jeopardy, Antonia said, "How can I help?"

"I think if I could show him how dedicated I still was — because I am — if I could bring in a big name to give a reading, then he might trust me again and — "

"Then why don't I give a reading?"

"Oh my God," Catherine said, giggling. "I didn't know how I was going to ask you. I mean, I thought it was probably the last thing you'd want to do. You have no idea what a relief it is to hear you say you'll do it."

"Anything for you," she said, glancing behind her into the house. She still longed to satisfy her one true desire — to read everything that came before page 298 of Wyatt's manuscript — though she knew that she would have to wait for another day.

"I think the lasagna's probably ready," Catherine said, rising.

Yet as she followed her into the kitchen, Antonia's appetite vanished, and she felt her stomach churning. She was unaccountably nauseated and wanted suddenly to lie down. Lie down and never get up again, she thought. "Hey, would you mind if I took a rain check on dinner?"

Catherine looked at her with disappointment. "I understand," she said. "If you're feeling better later, come back over. We can talk about your reading. I was thinking midweek, so I have a few days to prepare."

At the door, Antonia reached out and hugged Catherine tightly, as though she never wanted to let her go. All at once, she didn't care anymore about the woman's past with Henry, about Henry's past with Wren, about Henry's past at all. All at once, she no longer wanted to be the writer she was but the girl she used to be, who knew nothing about anything. All at once, she craved nothing more than to have walked right past Catherine's house that June afternoon, walked right past it without ever stopping. She had never meant for any of this to happen. She had never meant to hurt anyone.

"Thank you again, Catherine," she said, her eyes filling with tears.

"Oh, now don't start crying again, or you're going to make me cry, too," she said. "Do you want me to walk you home?"

"No, I think I'll be fine," she said.

As she crossed the yard, though, Antonia imagined her uncle Royal leaping out from the bushes, waiting for her on the veranda, even already in the house. From across the street, she studied the house's dark windows, the motionless curtains, the stillness that had settled over it. Nothing moved, though she knew everything was alive, beating as her heart beat. She flew to the front door, and then she was in her house, locking the deadbolt, the gray, stale air full of the traces of grayer, staler cigarette smoke. Once safely inside, the wave of nausea passed, her stomach settling as she unlocked the study door, and went into the room, though she stayed only long enough to make certain that nothing had been tampered with.

In the kitchen, she pulled out the expensive champagne that she and Henry were to have shared a week ago tonight. As she slid her hands down the cold, curved bottle, she imagined that it was her body and that her hands were Henry's. Then she was crying again, even as she popped the cork, which ought to have sounded like the auspicious beginning to her new life — the pop of the paparazzi's cameras, the pop of her success. Instead, it sounded like what it was, just a cork going off in an empty room.

After pouring champagne into a glass, she sat at the kitchen table, the sky beyond the windows as black as she'd ever seen it. She
raised her glass into the air and recited, "Champagne for my real
friends, real pain for sham friends." The critics had already praised
her as being the voice of her generation, though the words rang hollow in her ears now. Still, she repeated the words aloud and slowly
gave in to the idea, as she gave in to the idea of the future. Someday,
several years from now, long after she'd moved away, she imagined
returning to Winslow and going to the bookstore to see Catherine,
who would no doubt still be working there. She thought about
the unlikely conversation they might have over an unlikely dinner.
"How can you sit across from me and tell me that you were ever my
friend?" Catherine would ask as Antonia dragged on her cigarette.
"Friends don't act the way you do. They don't vandalize cottages,
writing messages on walls just to see how someone will react. What
kind of person are you?"

I'm the kind of person who won't stop until I get the whole story.
That's the kind of person I am, Antonia thought. People keep far
too many secrets from one another, hurtful, terrible secrets, but
I'm glad they do, because without them I wouldn't have a career.
Without them, I wouldn't have a thing to write about.

IT WAS WELL after midnight when Antonia awoke from a
dream in which she'd just won the National Book Award. She had
given her speech, thanking her mother and father who were in the
audience. Though she hadn't seen her own face in the dream, she
knew she was middle-aged and turning gray. Suddenly she sensed
that older self in the bedroom with her, leaning over her, judging her. Yet the moment she turned on the lamp by her bed, the
woman vanished and took the last of the beautiful dream with her.

A Tale of Two Soldiers

———

Linwood, in his bed at the motel, had been dreaming, too. Now he was awake and stood at the balcony railing, staring at the liver-shaped pool below, thinking about her, always about her, Antonia, and about his brother, the idiot, and the agreement they'd made. Property, he thought, that's what all this nonsense has been about. What belonged to Royal, and what he thought Linwood had stolen from him. The moon came out from behind a cloud and transported him back to 1968, and Sturgeon was putting his pistol away, saying, "Breathe a word of this, boys," and Linwood knew then he'd have no trouble killing them. Daybreak and they were heading back to Fort Benedict, the sun hot, the air rotten. He still tasted the brandy on his lips, and when he looked down, he saw the dried blood on his fingers, her blood, and he tried to wipe it on his fatigues but it wouldn't wipe away. Royal was in the backseat, passed out.

Linwood thought about how he'd joined the army to see the world, to get out from under their old man and the piss of poverty. He'd wound up at Fort Benedict, near Savannah, on the heels of his brother. Only seventeen years old, he'd cried secretly into his pillow. He had been skinny, frail. He had gotten into fights, but Royal had been bigger and fearless. No more fights. No more tears. Suddenly he had become a man. Off base, the girls had flirted with him, and he had flirted back. One night, they'd gone to a bar and there was Sturgeon, his command sergeant, talking to this young blond thing, such a sweet little face, though barely any breasts. Thirteen years old if she were a day, though she talked older, moved older, too. The four of them had driven out to some abandoned farm. In the cabin, she lay down so willingly on the mattress, too willingly, Linwood had thought. Sturgeon had watched. Didn't even touch himself, just stood and watched from the shadows. Royal fucked her a few times; then it was Linwood's go. "Your turn," Sturgeon had said. The girl was already bleeding when he kneeled over her and Royal was handing him the brandy. "Courage, my brother," he said. "Do it," the girl said, her eyes vacant. He rolled her over, so as not to see her eyes, and he did it because that's what he'd been brought there to do. They watched him and Royal cheered him on, even as he watched the tiny constellation of moles on the girl's back. When he'd finished, he rolled off her and vomited.

Halfway back to the base, Linwood had leapt out of the jeep and run.

Now, years later, that night still haunted him, always had. The interstate curved past the motel, and tomorrow Linwood hoped to join it. If he made it through tonight, that is. The pool shimmered, the black water beckoning. No, he thought. No. Back in the room, he put on the TV, a distraction against calling Antonia and telling her what he should have told her when he'd had the chance. Now he only had what was left of her, her stinking novel. After settling on the bed, he flipped to the dedication: *To all the men in my life who pushed me and to the others who caught me on the way down.*

Which was he? There was a quote from Virginia Woolf, whoever she was: *For the truth is (let her ignore it) that human beings have neither kindness, nor faith, nor charity beyond what serves to increase the pleasure of the moment. They hunt in packs. Their packs scour the desert and vanish screaming into the wilderness.* Amen, he thought. Amen. He flipped the book over to her picture and there she was, his little girl. He read the first page, and Sylvie was back and he saw her vividly again. He'd built a room around her and visited this room from time to time, just to make sure she never escaped. Yet thanks to his brother, she had, and Antonia had gotten it all wrong. I should have told you sooner, he thought, reaching for a pen. Your mother knew. Now you should know, and he removed the book jacket, flipped it over, and began to write on the white space. The words didn't come easily, but they came, and the Linwood of tonight kept trying to quiet the Linwood of then, who jabbered away in his head: *It was you who raped and killed her. Now, out there is the water, and you can save yourself. Forget the truth. No one cares about it.* Before he sank to the bottom, however, he would put it all down. He wrote it the way he'd lived it. He filled the white space, and had to find more, some paper in the room's desk drawer. He wrote until the pen ran dry, and he had to get another. He wrote until his fingers ached, until he filled every inch of available space. Then he started writing in the novel itself, in the margins. Outside, the sky lightened. He got up, went to the window, and looked down at the pool, the sun reflecting on the surface of the water. From his pocket, he pulled out the earring and pushed it through the hole, wincing from the familiar, excruciating pain. His fingers were bloody and trembling, and he washed them clean before reading over what he'd written.

This story was the last thing he would ever give her.

Another Fan
in the Graveyard

A hot, muggy morning a couple of days later, Catherine got into her car and tried to start it, but the engine just kept turning over without catching. While she pumped the gas, she stared at the cottage, willing Henry to walk out the door with his suitcases. She had left him a note: *Dear Henry, This is your last warning. You have one more day to find another place to live, or I will have you forcibly removed.* Today was Saturday; she'd left him the note the previous night. So far he showed no sign of honoring her wishes. Yet did she really want to get the police involved? Maybe that's just what I should do, she thought, imagining the cottage empty and putting Antonia inside it, as she should have from the start.

The car backfired a couple times, but then Catherine was reversing out of the drive. She parked in her usual spot on Broad Street, then, approaching the bookstore, got out her keys only to find Jane already standing at the register. The sight of her chilled Catherine's blood. Though she'd phoned her a dozen times, Jane had not bothered to answer or to return a single call. Now she entered the bookstore, walked right up to Jane, and said, "Good morning," not expecting her friend to reply. Not only didn't she reply, she didn't even look up, and Catherine, deflated, took this as a further sign. So this is how it's going to be, she thought as a customer wandered through the door, and she went to help him, all the while wanting to explain herself to Jane. She wanted to tell her about Royal, though in telling her about Royal she would have to tell her everything. Well, maybe it's time for that, she told herself as the sun rose over the park and turned the day to fire.

By late morning, Catherine had taken all she could and so during a lull in customers went up to Jane again, more determined. "Tell me what to do. How can I make this up to you? You're my best friend, my dearest friend. You can't possibly believe that I meant for this to happen." Yet Jane just kept on restacking the books, as if she hadn't heard her. "Jane, I'm sorry, you know I'm sorry. It just went off. You can't think I — "

"I don't know what to think anymore," Jane said at last, though she still refused to look at her. "You could have killed me. All I really want to know is what you were doing with Harold's gun?"

Tell her everything, Catherine told herself. She's your best friend and deserves to know. Yet there were even some things, she knew, that she couldn't possibly tell even her best friend, that she couldn't possibly tell anyone. Like about Wyatt's novel, she thought.

"If you ever want me to talk to you again, you will tell me exactly what happened."

So, sighing, Catherine broke down and told her about Royal, about the night in front of her house, everything.

"Oh, my heavens!" Jane said. "Catherine, what do you think he wanted? Why didn't you call the police? Do you think he'll come back?"

The questions dazed Catherine, not because Jane had asked them but because she simply didn't know the answers.

"And you thought I was her uncle," Jane said, laughing a nervous laugh. "I just needed to use the bathroom!" As Jane laughed, Catherine began to cry, the tears running down her face. "Oh, no, don't do that," she added. "It's okay. You didn't know it was me."

"But I could have killed you," Catherine said, sobbing bitterly now, though she was also sobbing because of what she'd read about herself in Wyatt's manuscript. Sobbing also for what Henry had done to Antonia and what Antonia had done to her father and what Royal was going to do to Antonia once he found her. She sobbed for Wyatt, who would never write another book, and for her terrifying future without him. "You could have died, and it would have been my fault," she said.

"I didn't die," Jane said, drawing Catherine to her. "I'm here. I forgive you." And they stood like this, holding each other, although Catherine could still feel the tension in Jane's body and didn't quite believe she'd been forgiven.

AROUND NOON, SHE said good-bye to Jane and went to meet Louise, who was leaving on a family vacation to Italy for the rest of July. As she made her way through Danvers Park, she pictured Louise's Tuscan villa, the vineyards, the brown-eyed men and women taking their evening strolls, the sweet country air, the cheeses, the bread, the wine. Except for her one disappointing night in Manhattan, Catherine hadn't been out of Winslow in ages. They were meeting in Maddox Cafe, which was closing down for a week. Like the cafe, the town, too, was closing down, as it did around this time every summer, which Catherine never understood, since it was the height of the tourist season. Though the unusual heat this summer lingered on, it had no effect on the glut of vacationers. She remembered how much Wyatt had disliked Winslow in the summer, citing the litter in the park, the lines at the grocery store and the movies, the general chaos and noise.

She found Louise sitting at a table near the window, buttering a piece of bread. The air was cool and dry. Thank God, Catherine thought, taking a seat across from her. She looked into her friend's face and found nothing in it to indicate that she'd even heard about the incident at the bookstore. Maybe Jane never told her, she thought. Or maybe she just wants to ignore it.

"I can't believe you're really leaving us," Catherine said after she'd ordered.

"Oh, I'll be back sooner than you think," she said. "I'll send you a dozen postcards."

"Just send me a handsome Italian man to do my bidding," she said, and they laughed.

They ate and talked, and when the check came, Louise took care of it. Then they were strolling through the park and past the gazebo, where a band of kids was smoking cigarettes and listening to music.

"Ugh, these ragamuffins," Louise said, scoffing.

"Teenagers," Catherine said.

"I never wasted my time like that," she said.

"Oh, Louise," she said. "I really am going to miss you."

A skinny girl with frizzy blond hair looked up at Catherine as they passed. In her face, she couldn't help but see Antonia. Was this how she'd spent her young summers in Vermont? No, Catherine mentally put Antonia in the library, devouring book after book, like a voracious little shark, darting through the waters of literature. She also saw herself in the girl's face, the taunted girl who'd had no friends and had been forced to eat lunch alone in the library. Every day, she strolled passed the elderly, nearsighted librarian who never acknowledged her. Now there was no school, just work, and she was no longer the skinny, tormented girl she'd been. Now she had friends, like Jane and Louise and Antonia, and she was miles and years from those awful days. Yet sometimes she felt that girl rising up and out of her again. She didn't like her and wished her gone, as she did today, thinking jealously of Louise's trip and wishing she were the one going to Italy. *I can't afford to go anywhere, though,* she thought as Louise asked her when she wanted the movers to come.

"I'm sorry," Catherine said. "The movers?"

"Now don't be angry with me, but I did you a favor and hired a moving company to haul that man's things away," she said.

"Louise!" she said. "I can't believe you. It's a thoughtful gesture but completely unnecessary and utterly inappropriate. I can handle Henry myself. But thank you very much."

They were on Broad Street, the sun beating down upon them. From her bag, Louise produced a compact umbrella and opened it, further darkening her already darkened face. "Look, I wasn't going to say anything — I was hoping you would have taken care of this before I left — but now I see I have no choice," she said, leaning into Catherine and lowering her voice. "People are talking. I won't repeat what they're saying, but it isn't flattering."

"What people?" she asked.

"I've defended you from the moment you let that man into your cottage," she said, "but I can't keep protecting you from three thousand miles away."

"Protect me?" she said. "Louise, what are you talking about?"

"I'm talking about the affair you've been having with him. Deny it all you want, but I know you; you haven't been acting like yourself for weeks. Besides, someone saw him sneaking out of your house in the middle of the night. There, I've said it," she finished, and adjusted the umbrella in her hand. Catherine didn't know what to say in response, and glanced away so that Louise couldn't see the hurt in her face. "I'm just repeating what I was told," she said. "I just thought you'd have better sense. From what you've said, you and that girl have become quite friendly."

"We have," Catherine said softly.

"Then why on earth would you do such a thing to her?" she asked. "I told you it would all come to grief if you rented him the cottage."

"Well, if I had a husband who owned a successful business, which gave me the freedom to lunch all day long," she said, exploding into anger, "and I got to have my hair and nails done whenever I wanted, I wouldn't have been forced to rent the cottage to anyone. Maybe, if my husband were still alive — "

If my husband were alive, she thought, I wouldn't have been able to rent the cottage to Henry. I wouldn't have gone up to see him at the college, because there wouldn't have been a reason. I wouldn't have let Antonia into the house that afternoon, which meant I never would have met her and in not meeting her, I never would have heard Henry's name again.

"I see," Louise said. "Just forget I said anything, then."

Catherine couldn't forget it, however. "You're going to cancel those movers, Louise," she said, "and you are never to mention any of this again. There is nothing remotely sexual between Henry and me, and you and the gossips have it wrong."

Then Louise was walking away from her without saying good-bye and another part of Catherine's life had come undone.

THE MOMENT CATHERINE returned to the bookstore, she told Jane what Louise had said and done. "She was only trying to help," Jane said.

"You don't need to defend her, and I don't need her help," she said.

"So you aren't having an affair with Henry?" she asked innocently.

"Jane," she said, "I can still shoot you, you know."

• • •

WHEN CATHERINE GOT home that night, she was surprised to see Antonia on the porch, smoking while turning the pages of a book. When she heard Catherine say hello, she lifted up her head and said, "We're going to a party."

"No, not tonight," Catherine said, gazing at the cottage and thinking about her quarrel with Louise. I just want today to end, she thought, sitting down beside the girl and taking a drag off her cigarette.

"We could both get lucky and meet the next loves of our life," she said energetically.

But beneath Antonia's bravura, Catherine could sense the same shattered little girl who'd sat and listened to Henry disown her. You're so young, she thought. Go to your party and find your next love without me.

"If it's boring, we'll leave. I promise."

Catherine gazed at the dark house, imagining the evening ahead, when night fell and she went around locking all the windows and doors again and then locking herself in her bedroom with a book. Suddenly the idea of spending some time away from the ghost of Wyatt and his festering novel seemed like a good idea. "Okay," she finally said. "An hour, that's all." Antonia laughed. Then they were in the house and Catherine was saying, "Help yourself to a drink," as she slipped into her bedroom to change. She put on a black sundress and black heels, then brushed her hair and put on some lipstick.

"Oh, that's a beautiful shade on you," Antonia said, eyeing her lips.

"Well, that's a beautiful dress on you," she said.

"Vintage, naturally," she said, showing off the yellow baby-doll dress. She wore pearl studs in her ears, and her hair fell in bouncy corkscrews around her face, which made her seem coquettish. Even adorable, Catherine admitted, as they climbed into her car, which stalled three times before they'd even made it out of the drive. "It's a hundred degrees out. How much warmer does the car have to be?" she asked, laughing.

Yet as they drove and Catherine told her about the movers Louise had hired — omitting the part about her alleged affair with Henry — the girl's face took on a new gravitas, which made her wonder if she weren't mulling over the last week, if she weren't thinking about Henry. Stop it, she wanted to say. Just stop it, but then Antonia was directing them across the railroad tracks into Winslow's gloomier east side.

"Take a right here," Antonia said, as Catherine turned down a sinuous street, the yards neglected and the curbs crumbling. "It should be up ahead." And there it was, a big, dingy pink yet dignified-looking Victorian house that seemed to Catherine to bow as the land bowed under it. In the front yard, a lone juniper tree sagged like the unsightly tangle of telephone lines that hung above it. At the house next door, a rusty car carcass sat on cinder blocks.

Before they got to the door, Antonia turned to her and squeezed her arm. "I'm glad you're here. I really didn't want to come alone."

Catherine, too, was glad, though she couldn't help recalling that other party, the one in Manhattan and Henry's undeserved attack on her. She thought about how the girl had suffered through it and about her novel, the resolve and determination it had taken to dig so deeply into her father's past and to write so honestly about it. How painful it must have been for her, she thought. How painful it must have been for Wyatt, too, to learn about her involvement with Henry. Oh, Wyatt, she thought, feeling again the sadness rising through her even as she'd felt it rising off the pages of his manuscript. Oh, Wyatt, please forgive me, she thought as they stepped through the door and into the strange house.

ONCE INSIDE, CATHERINE followed Antonia through the wide, high-ceilinged rooms to the kitchen. The open door led to a Juliet balcony and into a spacious backyard dotted with tombstones. "Don't be creeped out," Antonia said. "Daniel has made peace with the residents. Apparently, they told him they like his parties." Then, they were a part of the gregarious chatter and music, as Daniel, the host, came up to greet them. A good-looking, disheveled man in his midtwenties, his face was all angles and sharp lines. He wore a pair of sawed-off khaki shorts, which sat loose on his narrow hips, and a faded green T-shirt. He had a fresh daisy tucked behind his ear, a mane of curly, black hair holding it in place. From his pocket, he produced a pipe, which he lit, the sweet-smelling tobacco reminding Catherine of the air in her dissertation adviser's office at NYU. She was gripped again with regret, though the moment Daniel said, "I know you. You work at that groovy bookstore on Broad Street," the sorrow lifted.

"So tell us, Daniel: what are the dead drinking tonight?" Antonia asked, laughing.

"Rum punch, sangria, beer, whatever you want," he said. "There's iced tea for the teetotalers, but I don't think any are making an appearance tonight." Tall and lean, he had a blunt nose, white teeth, and a gentle, deep voice. He'd done some modeling, Antonia whispered to her, and had lived in Paris for a while. "Now don't be telling any tales out of school. I never would have done it, but this old girlfriend of mine worked for an agency." He shook his head as if ashamed to be so attractive. "She wouldn't let it go till I agreed to do it. Then, the second I took the bait, she left me for her boss. Years later, we ran into each other, and she finally confessed that she just couldn't be with a guy with better bone structure than she had." His brown eyes shined in the firelight of the tiki torches.

"Now, if you don't mind, I will inspect the drinks table," Antonia said, wandering off.

Over the noise, Catherine thought she heard the rush of water and suspected that if she walked to the edge of the property, she'd come to a bend of the Mohawk River. Beyond the dilapidated cemetery, the land sloped and ran on endlessly. Lying in the weeds, the decapitated heads of cherubs stared up at her, marble wings in ruin beside them. No one else seemed to mind that they were all standing in a cemetery, though to her it was a strange, unsettling place for a party.

As Daniel wandered off to say hello to a new batch of arrivals, Catherine wondered what it might be like to kiss him. Yet the second she imagined it, her face blushed hot with embarrassment. Besides being far too beautiful, he's far too young for you, she thought. He isn't too young for Antonia, though, and she looked for her in the chattering crowd. She found her smoking a cigarette and speaking animatedly with a girl who had shocking pink hair and blue eyebrows. As she watched, Antonia stomped her feet angrily, then raised a hand into the air, as if she were going to strike the girl.

The moon came out from behind the clouds, silvering the land, and reminding Catherine that Wyatt also lay in a cemetery, one not far from there. She hadn't been to visit him at all and felt terribly guilty. Meandering through the party, she said hello to people, then found herself at the edge of the cemetery, reading the eroded names and the dates on the stones. A natural hem of trees separated the cemetery and the house from the rest of the land, and through the trees she could just make out the glowing white-marbled facade of a mausoleum. Taking a step into the brush to get a better look, she tried to make out the family name above the door, thinking it looked familiar, though in the darkness she could only see the first couple of letters. She took another step and then another, until she was standing directly in front of the mausoleum, surprised by the name above the door — Leggett, her mother's maiden name. As far as she could remember, her mother had never mentioned having any ties to or family in Winslow, so there probably was no connection.

A single tree stump sat in the vast flat meadow behind the mausoleum, the dense wood picking up beyond it and rolling down to the river, which she now heard clearly. As the moon vanished again and everything went black, she heard footsteps and froze. Yet it was only Daniel. "Apparently, they used to hang people from right over there," he said, pointing to the stump. "Adulterers, mostly, and 'witches.' A few blacks, I'm sure. Same old story."

In the dim light, Catherine imagined the limbs of the tree and the bodies swinging in midair. She shuddered and turned to him, saying, "This is all yours, isn't it? You're a Leggett."

"I'm a Katz, actually," he said. "This is my uncle's property. I'm house-sitting for him for a few days."

"Antonia tells me you're a poet," she said.

"I write sometimes, but am I a poet? Not really. I'm in law school. If you ever need some legal advice, I'm your man," he offered as they wandered through the brambles and the bracken and back to the party, where they met Antonia.

"I've been looking for you," she said. "I thought you'd been kidnapped, but I see you're in safe hands."

"No safer hands than mine," Daniel said.

"You're all out of beer," Antonia said. "I'm going into the house to get some."

"You must be very proud of her," he said as Antonia ducked inside.

"I am proud of her," she said, though was confused by his non sequitur.

"Do you think her success will affect your relationship? I mean,
I've heard about sisters — "

"Oh, Antonia's not my — "

Someone suddenly leapt between them and handed Daniel a
joint. He took a puff, then offered it to Catherine. In the spirit of
the evening, she brought it to her lips and inhaled deeply, filling her
lungs, then handed it back to him. They shared the joint, passing it
back and forth, and then he excused himself, moving through the
party, shaking hands, laughing. Her body began to loosen as the
marijuana coursed through her, and she giggled to herself when
she thought about his mistake. Sisters, she thought. Maybe distant
cousins but certainly not sisters, and she giggled again, because she
could see now how Daniel had made the leap — they shared the
same color hair, the same olive skin, the same athletic frames. They
were even almost the same height.

When Antonia returned, she was still giggling. "What's so
funny?" she asked, and Catherine told her what Daniel had said.
"Sisters in spirit, for sure," she added.

"Don't look now, but the pink-haired girl is back," Catherine
said, gesturing at the Juliet balcony where the girl was standing,
gazing down at Antonia.

"Her," Antonia said glumly. "She's one of Henry's former students, if you can believe it. She just finished reading my novel. She
hated it, of course. She said she couldn't believe anyone had published it."

"Do people really say that kind of stuff?" Catherine asked.

"Jealous writers do," she said just as Daniel reappeared.

"Hey, there's some guy looking for you," he said. "He's around
here somewhere. He really wants to talk to you."

"Oh, great," Antonia said, gazing around. "Another fan in the
graveyard."

"Yeah, he told me that he's your biggest and oldest fan," he said. "He said he knew you when you were a little girl. He was passing around a Polaroid of you on your eighth birthday."

When Antonia heard this, Catherine noticed that the muscles of her face constricted, and she lost the last of her smile. Suddenly she was rushing through the graveyard on her way to the balcony, as Catherine followed her, knowing already that Royal had found them. Yet every step Catherine took was labored and worse, she couldn't stop laughing. She tried to follow Antonia up the stairs and into the house, though the house looked miles and miles away and the ground kept shifting under her feet and she kept laughing, tears spilling down her face. She saw Antonia disappear into the house and then she thought she heard screaming, though it could have simply been in her head, yet it wasn't in her head, it was Antonia's scream, and this sobered her long enough for her to make it up the stairs and into the house, just in time to see Royal dragging Antonia by the hair out the front door while everyone looked on. Help her, she wanted to shout, though her tongue wasn't working. Finally, she was through the front door and out in the night, but there was no Antonia, no Royal. She called out for Antonia and took a few steps into the yard, looking and looking, as people passed her on the way into the party. Catherine staggered through the yard and looked down to see a copy of Antonia's novel in the grass, and then she was at her car and looking through the windows, and that's where she finally found her — curled up in the backseat, her face pressed into the vinyl, and Catherine saw that she was shaking and sobbing. Daniel was suddenly behind her, asking what the hell that was all about and she hushed him and sent him back into the house. Climbing into the backseat, she held the girl, who trembled and sobbed. She sat with Antonia as the men and women arrived with cases of beer because this was a party, and they were all so young, and Catherine was stoned and she looked down at the girl and thought about how she'd now lost everything and how Catherine could do nothing to help her but stroke her hair and tell her everything was going to be fine, although they both knew she was lying.

She sat with Antonia on that wretched, hot night as all the beautiful, young people swarmed across the yard, floating in and out of the house that to Catherine also seemed to float. She shut her eyes against the dizziness and the sorrow of what she, too, had lost, and for one brief moment she felt herself the receptor of an unearthly message, and the message said that things were going to end miserably. The sensation came quickly and went just as quickly, yet it would stay with her that night and for many nights after. Finally she spoke to Antonia and asked if she were hurt, yet the girl said nothing, curling further into herself as Catherine felt her own body growing heavy and knew that within minutes she'd be fast asleep.

THEY WERE STILL in the backseat of Catherine's car when dawn broke. Catherine woke first and let Antonia sleep; she climbed out to stretch her arms and legs. Her back ached, and she leaned over to touch her toes, and as she rose, she gazed around the littered yard, full of discarded plastic cups and cigarette butts and even a lampshade, which sat beside Antonia's novel. She wandered through the grass, her head swimming with the night's images, the stricken look that had come into Antonia's face. She gazed up and down the street, feeling suddenly as if she were being watched, though the street was empty. She picked up the novel, its spine broken, the jacket ripped, returned to the car, and drove them back to her house. There, she woke Antonia and led her into the bedroom, the girl saying nothing as she lay down and curled into the same fetal position she had been in the backseat. "Sleep as long as you can," Catherine said, shutting the door behind her.

Then, she went into the bathroom to remove her makeup, shocked to see the face staring back at her, which did not seem to belong to her at all but to someone else entirely. Her eyes were big and sunken, her cheeks smudged black, as if she, too, had been crying, though she had no recollection of crying at all. The lines around her mouth were more pronounced, her lips oddly swollen, the whole of her face distorted, which made her wonder if she still might be stoned. She knew she wouldn't be able to sleep, so she went into the kitchen to make coffee. Through the window, she gazed at the dark cottage, knowing that Henry probably hadn't moved out of it yet.

Outside, the birds chirped obliviously; she just wanted them to stop. Right now she hated them, though not as much as she hated Royal, and Henry. Everything led back to him, it seemed to her, and she realized that she wouldn't have been surprised to learn that Henry had some part in Royal's scheme, in his terrorizing Antonia. What have you done, Henry, she thought, and what are you up to now? She suspected she had only one way of finding out for sure, and upset with herself for what she about to do, she grudgingly went into the study and grabbed Wyatt's manuscript. After pouring a cup of coffee, she went out on the deck and began to read the third and final part of his novel, hoping to find a connection between Henry and Royal.

The Bats Under the Bridge

———

A couple of hours later, Catherine finished reading the last page, then set the whole manuscript in her lap, sighing. The late morning spun around her in a bonanza of colors, the sun glinting off the pool's oily surface and reflecting prismatically in the trees. The stultifying heat lay thick in the air. Though she was sweating, her skin was cold as she thought about Wyatt, and all at once it was a different morning, a winter morning, and he was getting into his car again and driving away. The image was still just as vivid to her as the chiaroscuro of alternating sunlight and shadow that passed over the cottage, which became Henry's beach house the more she looked at it. Now she knew everything about him and why he'd come to see Wyatt that night. Now she knew everything about Wren, the girl in the road, and about those dollar bills. Now she not only had the complete story of Henry's life but also the complete story of her life with Wyatt, one version of it at least. His version.

You poor man, she thought, though not knowing if she meant Henry or Wyatt or Royal or Linwood. Maybe all of them. Maybe none of them. She only knew that each of them had done terrible things, wittingly and unwittingly, and that they were all paying for it.

Catherine went back into the house and set the manuscript on the counter, then went to check on Antonia. The girl was still curled into a tight ball, asleep, sucking one of her fingers. The sight of her brought Catherine such sadness that she quickly shut the door just as the phone rang. It was Harold. "I know it's your day off, but I need to see you right away," he said.

"I can't leave the house right now," she said, wanting to be around when Antonia woke up.

"It should only take a few minutes," he said. "If you value your job, you'll make the right decision."

"Are you threatening me?" she asked.

"I wouldn't dream of it," he said. "After all, it seems you have quite an itchy trigger finger."

"That's not the least bit amusing," she said.

"No, it isn't," he said, and hung up on her.

She didn't want to have to argue with Harold or to defend herself, not today, when she'd had only a couple hours sleep, Antonia was languishing in the next room, and she had to figure out what to do about Henry. You can start by tearing up his check, she thought, going to get her purse, which she always left hanging on a hook next to the door. Yet the purse wasn't there. "Oh, Jesus," she said, hurrying to the car, but it wasn't in there, either. "Where in the — " Then, she remembered bringing the purse into the party with her, just in case she wanted to touch up her makeup. She had no recollection, though, of where she might have set it.

So she left Antonia to sleep and locked up the house, driving back across the railroad tracks to the east side of town. She walked through the door of the old house, which still sat open, and called out Daniel's name, yet the house remained silent. She went out

back into the cemetery, which, to her, seemed just as forlorn in
the daylight, stepping around the trash on her way toward the tree
line, because, she suspected, that's where it must have slipped off
her shoulder as she and Daniel had shared the joint. She found the
purse lying in the weeds and, relieved, made her way back into the
house. No sooner had she pulled the front door closed behind her,
however, than she saw Royal Lively leaning on the hood of her car.
She turned to go back into the house, but the door had locked itself
behind her. "You have something of mine," Royal called to her. For
a moment, Catherine thought he meant the novel that he'd clearly
left in the grass and that she'd picked up, though, it turned out,
this wasn't it at all. "Where is she, Catherine?"

"You leave her alone," she said, her voice sounding weak and
stringy even to her. "She doesn't want to see you."

"Oh, I know she doesn't want to see me, but she has to see me,"
he said, making his way toward her. "I need her to make my intro-
ductions to that literary critic of hers. Unless you'd like to do the
honors," he added, grinning at her.

"Henry Swallow is gone," she said. "I kicked him out. I have no
idea where he is, and neither does Antonia, so you're just wasting
your time here, Mr. Lively."

"Call me Royal, please," he said, glancing down at the lampshade still in the grass, his face oddly youthful and bemused. "How
is my niece doing this morning anyway? Talking up a storm, I
imagine. She was always so very chatty."

Catherine was no longer listening to him. She knew her only
chance was to get to her car and, though exhausted, she leapt down
the stairs, and ran. Royal lunged at her, yet she managed to get past
him by slicing his cheek with her car key. He let out a loud curse
as she climbed into her car and sped away, not daring to look back
until she reached the end of the block. Yet when she checked for

him in the mirror, she saw no sign of him at all. It's like I imagined it, she thought, blinking her eyes, her whole body shaking, except of course she hadn't imagined it, because, when she got to Broad Street and parked, she found his blood on the key.

Before Catherine could face Harold, she needed a cigarette, so she took a seat on a park bench to smoke. The act had no stimulating effect at all, however, instead leaving her all the more drained and sluggish. She only finished half of it, then dragged herself across the street and walked into the empty bookstore, the cooler air fortifying her just as the sight of Jane fortified her. Even before Catherine could say her hello, Jane said, "He's expecting you. In the back," her voice sounding cool and flat to Catherine, who made her way toward the storeroom.

In the room, she found Harold sitting in the same chair in which she'd found Jane a couple days before. He was staring intently at the bathroom door, rolling a toothpick in his fingers. "Do you know how much a new door costs?" he asked, spinning around to meet her. "A lot, that's how much."

"You can take it out of my next paycheck," she said.

"Oh, that's already a fait accompli," he said, rising. "I won't even tell you how much a new leather chair goes for these days."

As he spoke, Catherine folded in on herself, but then she was telling him about running into Royal this morning and about the party and about Antonia. When Jane appeared at the door, she pivoted in her direction and said, "Jane forgave me, so why can't you?"

"This has nothing to do with forgiveness. You should have called me immediately and told me what you did, Catherine. I had to hear about it from Jane? Unacceptable," Harold said. "This is more than just a safety matter. This is about how you damaged my property and endangered the life of one of my employees."

"What about my safety?" she asked. "The gun was there, I was terrified, and I used it. How many times do I have to explain myself?"

"That's my point exactly," Harold said. "You don't use guns. You fought against even having the gun in the store, remember?" She did remember. "If there really was an intruder — and I'm not saying there wasn't — why didn't you just call the police?" he asked.

"There wasn't enough time, and I just wasn't thinking," she said.

"Well, Jane and I have been talking it over, and we both think —"

"You've been talking about me?" she said.

"Yes, and we both think it would do you good to see to someone," he said. "Professionally, that is."

Now Catherine turned to Jane. "You didn't believe me?" she asked. "You think I made the whole thing up? Why would I do that?"

Harold stared down at the floor, as Jane said, "Why does anyone make stuff up? Maybe it's because they're under too much stress, or they aren't getting the kind of attention they feel they deserve."

Then Catherine was getting out her keys saying, "Look" — she held the long, grooved car key up to the light — "that's his blood, right there. Royal Lively's blood." Yet she knew even then that she might as well have been holding up his still-beating heart for all they believed her. "You told me you forgave me," she said, turning to Jane, who took a step away from her.

"You shot at me. You could have killed me," she said as coolly and as flatly as before.

"Speaking of which, where is the gun?" Harold asked.

"I thought I'd returned it."

"No, because it's not under the register. You need to find it. Today. It's my gun and I'm liable. Jesus." Catherine said she'd go home and look for it. "You know something, you're just lucky Jane doesn't want to press charges."

"Press charges?" she said, stupefied. "I made a mistake. So shoot me." And then she was laughing, laughing so hard that she thought she might never be able to stop. She laughed at the way Harold and Jane were looking at her now and at the utter absurdity of it all, a deep, furious, sorrowful laugh that brought tears to her eyes. She laughed at the summer itself, at the girl lying curled up in her bed, at Henry and his dollar bills locked away in her cottage, and at Wyatt — she laughed at him, too, for keeping his secrets and for writing them all down. She laughed even as she said, "Antonia's giving a reading here next Wednesday, so you'd better let the world know." She laughed as she walked out of the storeroom and into the afternoon heat, laughing all the way to her car and all the way home, laughing even as she climbed the porch steps and went into the house. Then she abruptly stopped laughing because there was Antonia on the sofa reading Wyatt's manuscript.

The girl did not look up when Catherine said, "What do you think you're doing?" She did not look up when Catherine went over to her and reached for the stack of pages. She had luckily only read a few of them, she noticed, but even a few was a few too many. She tried to wrest the page out of the girl's hands, yet the girl clung to it and wouldn't let go. "Antonia, really," she said gently now. "Let me have it."

"It's so good," she said, finally looking up at Catherine and reluctantly releasing the page. "It's so . . . compelling."

Catherine took the page from her and added it to the others, then wrapped her arms around the stack and pressed it to her chest as if protecting it. "Yes," she said, "but you really had no right to read it."

"It was just sitting there," Antonia said.

"Yes, well, I'm sure you wouldn't like it much if I went rummaging around your house," she said.

"It was just sitting there," she repeated. Then, "I don't have anything to hide."

"What makes you think I have something to hide?" she asked.

"Oh, I've upset you," she said, and climbed off the sofa.

Catherine sighed. "No, it's not you," she said, then told her about running into her uncle and about Harold and Jane. "You need to call the police, Antonia" she said. "If you don't, I will. This has got to stop."

"It will stop," she said, though she didn't explain how or why. Then she was drifting toward the front door and opening it, mumbling incoherently to herself as she went. She stepped out into the twilight, down the steps and into the yard, drifting away, even as Catherine went out to watch her. She didn't call her back, she didn't go after her, just let her go. She watched the girl float down the sidewalk on bare feet, her hair a tangle of knotted curls, and she looked to Catherine like someone who'd just escaped from an asylum. She watched until the girl disappeared around the curve in the street, then went back into the house, where she locked and chained the door.

For what felt like the first time in weeks, Catherine was relieved to be alone. She poured a glass of wine and took it out on the deck, lighting the citronella candles and savoring the final moments of sunshine. This was supposed to have been her day off, and she had wanted nothing more than to spend it with a good book, a few laps in the pool. After finishing the wine, she disrobed and lowered herself into the dirty, lukewarm water, caring nothing about the dead insects floating around her. She swam back and forth, the water on her skin caressing and gentle. Then she was on her back, the heat hanging tautly above her, and she breathed easier, knowing that in less than a month, the air would cool down and she would have to cover the pool. Like a great rolling tide, the town would sweep away the vacationers only to draw back the faculty and students. The students would arrive in an onslaught of shiny new cars ("Get ready for the assault vehicles," Wyatt would say every year), running red lights and drag racing down Broad Street. Her quiet neighborhood of West Campus would again become home to raucous fraternity boys and sorority girls, the evenings erupting in house parties that stretched well into the night. From the porch, she and Wyatt used to watch the parade of students return with their clear and simple desires — fun at any cost. We used to have such fun, she thought as she kicked at the water. The neighbors' dogs barked at the bats that suddenly appeared, as they did every evening.

Winslow had few actual tourist attractions, but the bats happened to be one of them. Thousands of them spent their days under the Kissing Swans Bridge. As she swam, she remembered all the times that she and Wyatt had gathered on the bridge at dusk to watch the bats' swirling exodus. She avoided the bridge and hadn't been back on it since his death, since a lone backpacker braving the snow had discovered his car and his body in the ravine. She drifted for a while on her back under the darkening sky, imagining her poor Wyatt in all that cold water. The police had ruled it an accident, though even now Catherine still wasn't so sure. Others clearly thought it was suicide.

Suddenly she stopped floating and stood up. Someone was knocking on the cottage door. Was it Royal, who'd finally come for Henry? She climbed out of the pool as quietly as she could and hurried up the stairs to the deck. She gathered her clothes and was heading for the door, when she glanced down to see Antonia, still wearing the same dress and still barefoot. Catherine wondered what she was doing there, since it seemed to her that Henry was the last person she should have wanted to see. It's always like this, she thought. We go back to the ones who hurt us most because it's comforting and familiar.

Antonia knocked on the door again while Catherine remained motionless, not wanting the girl to know that she was watching her. She looked to Catherine now as if she were sleepwalking, her face in the gloaming drawn as blank as, Catherine imagined, her own face had been when she'd stepped back into Mead Hall in June. Yes, she had loved Henry once, and that love had been all-consuming, so passionate, at least in her memory, that she had been terrified to lose it, because she had suspected that she'd never love like that again. His age had not mattered to her, though his reputation and the fact that he was already married should have. When they were with each other, though, nothing mattered. They were not equals, of course, but when they were alone together, the distance between them disappeared. That is, until she held the Yates in her hand and read what he'd written to her, and then she saw the deep chasm that had come between them, and that's when she'd written the anonymous letter to her dean, detailing the affair — this letter that had ultimately gotten him fired. She'd gone to see him at the college to find out about Antonia, but she had ended up finding out about someone else entirely — about him again, the Henry she had once known but also a new and different Henry, who needed her as he had never needed her in the past. It had been this need, this awful, beautiful need of his that had drawn her back. That night at Leland's, she had finally seen what the years had done to him and though she had hated his every word, she had also hated how the world had taken the magic from him. Brilliance like his was singular and rare. He had wasted his life on the folly of fiction, on trying to show the world why it should care about this sentence, that paragraph. He'd disgraced himself that night, disgraced Antonia, and had lost as much as Catherine had, perhaps even more.

When Antonia looked up at Catherine, her eyes were huge and stunned. Then she glanced away, as though she'd just heard her name, and she lifted her eyes to the sycamore, her face as pale as the moonlight falling through the branches. Catherine stepped out of the shadows to follow Antonia's gaze, and there were the bats, hundreds of them, whirling and diving through the air. As Antonia watched them, Catherine watched her, thinking about all the things that came out after dark, all the things that people did when they thought no one was looking. In less than a minute, the bats were gone, and Antonia dropped her eyes, then rushed at the door, kicking it, dragging her long nails down it, saying, "Wren was here," repeatedly, until the words faded away.

After Antonia had gone, Catherine went down to the cottage and almost knocked on the door herself, though she stopped, because she was in no mood to deal with Henry. The windows were open, and through them, she thought she caught the whiff of burning tobacco. She had promised Antonia that he'd be gone by the end of the week, and here it was the final moments of Sunday. The night was upon her again, and there were noises from everywhere and nowhere. Beyond the house and the cottage, the town was settling in for the evening. And while Antonia slipped silently away, Henry inhaled and exhaled his cigarette smoke, and Catherine stood at the door, thinking about the future. Perhaps it's time to put the house on the market, she thought. A new job in a new town. Maybe go back to school and finish my dissertation, as Harold had suggested, although it had been so long, too long, she thought — but who knew what the fall might bring?

In the house, Catherine poured another glass of wine, feeling the full effect of the day at last. She took a seat on the sofa, sipping her wine, her eyes burning with every blink. She thought about Louise and about Jane, and how it sometimes only took one misplaced word, one simple mistake, to end a friendship. She thought about Henry and Antonia, their complicated love, and about her own complicated love for Wyatt, and his love for her. She had loved him, though not like she had loved Henry. Her love for Wyatt had been less patient, and it had not made her a better woman, she realized sadly. It had made her competitive and needy; worse, it had made her obsequious and shrill. It had left her feeling diminished, when it ought to have raised her up. She did not blame Wyatt for any of this, however. She blamed it on circumstance and on the fundamental discrepancies of love itself.

After placing the empty wineglass in the sink, Catherine went into the bathroom to brush her teeth and comb her hair. Then she went around switching off the lights. In her bedroom, she closed and locked the door behind her and, turning on the lamp, let out a gasp when she saw Antonia, who was sound asleep in her bed. She had no idea how the girl had gotten past her and into the house, but she had. She thought about waking her, then thought against it, as the girl had been through so much and would go through so much more in the coming days and weeks and months. Instead, she pulled the covers over her and wished her a good night's sleep. Then she went into the other room and lay down on the sofa as outside the wind picked up and shook the windows and the doors, though Catherine was oblivious to it all, because she had already fallen asleep.

A Few Remarks on a Sunny
Afternoon in Winslow

———

Antonia awoke in the early afternoon in the small, airless bedroom, and sat up, disoriented, having no memory of how she'd
gotten here. She was covered in sweat, her skin itching and burning, as if someone had come along in the night and taken a wire
brush to her. As she climbed out of bed, everything hurt, her feet
most of all. She looked down at them, noticing the scratches and
the bruises, and then she simply didn't want to know. Everything
was coming apart, and she shut her eyes, picturing the girl she had
once been, the girl celebrating her eighth birthday, and there had
been vanilla cupcakes with buttercream frosting and the magician
and her friends and her mother and father. There had also been
her uncle, yet now she imagined her father turning him away and
slamming the door in his face. What if I'd had the same strength,
she thought, to shut the door on Henry? Yet she knew she never
would have shut the door on him, because she had loved him so
completely. With his love, nothing had been impossible. Now,
alone, she saw just how impossible all of it was, though even as she
realized this she also realized that she no longer needed Henry to

make the story hers. She only needed Catherine. She only needed to talk the woman into letting her see the rest of the manuscript and then she could be done with Henry Swallow forever.

After lighting a cigarette, Antonia wandered around Catherine's empty house, though her searching turned up nothing. She hadn't thought she'd be so lucky to find the manuscript on the counter as she had before. No, Catherine was too wise to leave it sitting out in the open again. Catherine's reaction to finding her reading it had told Antonia everything she had needed to know and proved what she had always suspected — that Catherine did have something to hide. Why else had she wrenched the pages away from her like that?

She'd only managed to get through part of the first section — 1956 — when Catherine had come home. She wished she'd had the wherewithal to have made a copy of the book, and now she cursed herself for that missed opportunity, knowing that it might not ever come again. Though she was sure Catherine had no inkling about the subject matter of her second novel, she was also sure that she would never let her see those pages again. Whatever was inside them was just too precious for her to part with.

Antonia rummaged frustratingly through some drawers, then headed for the study, but of course the door was locked. She banged one time on it, sighing heatedly. Wyatt's novel held the key to the mysteries Antonia had been struggling to unlock, and without it she would never know the truth of their story. The truth of what had really happened to Wyatt. How could she possibly abandon this story when she was so close to unraveling it? What was she without her desk, her cups of coffee, her typewriter? What was anyone without his habits, his loves?

After slipping on a pair of Catherine's sandals, Antonia headed out into the heat of the day. She hurried back to her own house,

looking over her shoulder as she went, just in case her uncle was
hiding in the bushes. Inside, she kicked off the sandals and went to
take a much-needed shower, staying under the water longer than
she usually did, trying to rinse away the last couple of days, and the
memory of what Royal had whispered into her ear. She shook as
she dried herself off, shook as she dressed, shook as she went into
the study and sat down at the desk. She was shaking when she lit a
cigarette and brought her fingers to the keys, shaking far too much
to type a single word. The fear and dread of what Royal had whispered filled the space inside her, overpowering her will to work and
sending her running out of the study.

"Where exactly is your proof?" she screamed into the air. Then,
"If it isn't true, though, why am I so terrified?"

And she was terrified, though she was also angry. Stomping
through the house, she went around drawing back the drapes and
throwing open the windows. She unlocked and threw open the
front door, then grabbed her purse from the bedroom and took a
seat on the sofa in the living room. In the purse, she fingered the
tiny handgun that she'd taken from Catherine's — she'd found it
lying on the nightstand, just sitting there so small and so delicate,
silver and ivory — fingering it even as she stared out the door to the
street beyond. "Let him come," she whispered as she thought about
her uncle and how he'd made her his habit and his love, concocting
yet another impossible, untrue version of the story, to hold her near
and to fill her with even more doubt. Yet the more she pushed this
new version away, the more she came to see that it really could have
happened the way Royal had said it had, which meant that she really had gotten everything wrong and had sacrificed her father for
nothing. She could not raise Sylvie from the dead to speak to her
any more than she could take back what she'd written. Just how

reliable was Royal's memory anyway? Just how much of what he'd whispered to her could she trust?

After he'd found her that night and had told her what he'd come to tell her — what he'd been meaning to tell her for years and years, apparently — she'd left him in the middle of the yard and had crawled into the first car she'd seen. She'd curled up in the backseat, sobbing, unable to think past what she'd just heard and unable to see anything but the engulfing, obliterating darkness. She had been happy for the darkness, because in it she had let herself disappear, and she was no longer a writer but a little girl in the backseat of a car waiting for her daddy.

The afternoon turned into dusk and still Antonia remained on the sofa, keeping a vigil, her eyes on the street. On occasion, she glanced into the study at the Olivetti, imagining Wyatt's fingers tapping out "The Girl in the Road," the same keys she would use again to tap out her own second effort. As the light left the sky, Antonia continued to sit on the sofa, waiting for her uncle, because she knew he would come. She knew it just as she knew that what he'd told her had to be another lie. It could not have happened like that, she thought, and prayed that he would come through the door, because she was ready for him this time, ready to shut him up, to take back the story, all of it, every word and sentence, every image, every truth and falsehood, everything that made this novel of hers into what it was — a tour de force, and an instant best seller.

YET ROYAL NEVER came into the house, or if he did, Antonia didn't know, because she'd fallen asleep. When she woke, the stars were out and the black oozed into the house through the open door and windows. There was no moon, no light at all, and she stood, groggy. She was about to close and lock the door when she saw Henry. He was standing at the edge of the walk, his hands thrust into the pockets of his pants, rocking gently back and forth on his heels. He was staring at the house, just staring at it. She came out onto the veranda, the purse still in her hands, and they just looked at each other. She said nothing, he said nothing, yet she felt a communication with him. He was so handsome, as always, she thought as the first tear spilled down her cheek. Henry. His name was on her lips and in her head and on her body, which longed for him, even now, even after all that he'd done. Henry. There, in the darkness, Henry, her Henry, tall and lean, her Henry taking a step toward her, even as she took a step toward him. Her Henry, who would never walk this path again to her house, who would never again say her name as he once had, never again smile when she entered a room. Please don't leave, she thought as she took another step toward him even as he took a step away. Please don't go, she thought as she watched him turn, and then he was gone, and she followed the lines of his back until he was nothing more than an impression, nothing more than a thought.

Wren Was Here

———

Unbeknown to Antonia, Catherine had gone to the police herself to warn them about Royal Lively. As she'd written down her statement, she'd felt certain she was doing the right thing. I'm sure Royal Lively vandalized my cottage, she told them. He's a menace. She knew that it would be a battle to convince the police without having any hard proof, so she lied. "Yes, I remember seeing him that afternoon," she'd said. "He painted those words on my cottage. I want him arrested."

Two days later, an officer had come into the bookstore to tell her that they'd apprehended the suspect who had been loitering in Danvers Park. "He's a long way from home," he said. "Looks like he'll be going back to Georgia to serve out the rest of his time, having violated parole. He won't be harassing you or anyone else again for a while, ma'am." And Catherine was finally able to let out her breath.

She had done it for Antonia, who, for whatever reason, had not been able to do it for herself. Her loyalty aside, the girl's inability to defend herself against her father and her uncle had never made much sense to her. Though she chalked it up to youthful loyalty and naïveté, she still wondered about it anyway, even as she continued to prepare for the girl's reading that evening. She called Maddox Cafe to remind them about the platters of food and bottles of wine they were to deliver in the late afternoon — all this on a budget of two hundred dollars. "A drop in the bucket," Harold said to her this morning on the phone. "We should sell ten times that in books, although let me rephrase that: you better hope we sell ten times that in books."

"Harold, please," she said. "I'm doing my best. I can't make anyone buy a book."

"Your best," he said, "has not been able to find my gun, though." It was true. Catherine remembered putting it in her pocket, though after that she had no memory of the gun at all. It wasn't in the house, because she'd turned over everything looking for it. It wasn't in her purse, either, the only other place it could have been. The one thing in her purse, besides a compact and a lipstick, was Wyatt's manuscript, which she'd been carrying around with her. "The last thing I wanted to do was to have to report it stolen," he said. "Well, you'll have to reimburse me the five hundred dollars I spent on it."

Oh, you insufferable oaf, she thought, hanging up, though it was hard to be angry at him, since it was her fault the gun had gone missing. While she called the printers again to remind them about the bookmarks, Jane went onto the floor to help the customers. Catherine refused to speak to her, though Jane had tried her best to apologize. "I didn't tell Harold anything he didn't already know," she had said.

"You told him enough, apparently," she had said. "Just let me have my anger. It will pass eventually."

Though now, a couple hours later, Catherine was still nowhere nearer to forgiving her. During an afternoon lull, she slipped away and drove home, wanting to deal with Henry once and for all. If I can go to the police about Royal Lively, I can certainly go to the police about you, she thought, banging on the cottage door. "Henry Swallow, open up," she said. "I have given you every chance to find another place. Now you've left me no choice. I'm going to the police . . ."

Frustrated at his refusal to respond, she turned to leave just as the door creaked open and there was Henry, or what was left of him, she thought. He was thinner and grayer and paler, less the Henry she'd known and more like the Henry he was quickly becoming — a man tumbling into old age. His face was a bag of wrinkles, his eyes bloodshot and set deep in the sockets. He looked absolutely awful. "Catherine," he said, "I was just coming to find you."

"Oh, don't give me that," she said. "Look, I want you to pack up your things, and I want you out of here by nightfall. Do you hear me? Have I made myself perfectly clear?"

"Yes," he said meekly. "Perfectly. I understand."

"I know everything about you, Henry," she said, as if she hadn't heard him. "I know what you did to Wren. I know about the settlement. I know everything there is to know. The only thing I don't know is why, out of everyone in the world, you chose to tell Wyatt."

"Then he did write it," Henry said earnestly.

"Yes, he wrote it. It's right here," she said, patting her purse.

"May I see it?" he asked.

After reaching into her purse, she pulled out the rolled-up manuscript, though before handing it to him she said, "Don't think for a second that this changes anything between us."

"Oh, I don't," he said, taking the manuscript and removing the rubber band. "I never thought it would." Then he was reading the title and the dedication and the first page to himself, smiling as he did. "This is good," he said. "Very, very good. He took my advice. He took the story and ran with it." Catherine didn't know what to say. She could feel the tears in her eyes and turned away. He grasped her arm. "Now you must listen to me closely: I want you to find a way to publish this."

"You must be out of your mind," she said, spinning back around. "No one is ever going to see this book. Ever. Not while I'm alive anyway."

"Catherine, whatever you want to believe about me, you must believe this: I gave him this story — for you." She thought about Wyatt, who had abandoned his side of the bed to sleep here, in the cottage, and she thought about Henry, who'd made the cottage his home for several weeks. She thought about how she'd imagined having to pile all his things into the car and drop them at his house. She thought about how she'd imagined meeting him at the door and the polite small talk they'd make, how he'd eventually say, "It was good seeing you." She'd imagined standing on his porch on that afternoon in late September. She'd always remember it, because it had been on a similar afternoon many years earlier that she'd first imagined what it would be like to be with him. A fall afternoon and a quick glance out the window at Washington Square Park while Henry had lectured. A fall afternoon before she'd ever met Wyatt. She had just been a grad student and Henry had just been her professor and the future had not yet become what it would be. She had been making a name for herself and she'd had such lofty plans and the world had still been within her reach. "Now there's something else you need to know. It's about Antonia," he said. "You must never let her see this, Catherine. Do you understand me?"

She didn't understand, not fully, though it was slowly coming to her, as slowly as the day revolving around them. "She's writing about us," she said at last. "She's writing about you and me and Wyatt, isn't she? That's what you were saying at the book party."

"Yes," he said. "You can't let her have this story, and I'm afraid the only way to stop her is to make sure it gets into print." Then Catherine sat down in one of the plastic chairs, winded. She thought she should feel betrayed, though she didn't, because she knew that this was an inevitability, that it had to happen like this. There was just no way to be around a writer and not have it happen. Still, that Antonia had befriended her merely to get to this story — hers, Wyatt's, theirs — did gall her. "You're going to have to make a decision," he said.

"I can just . . . I can just get rid of it," she said, thinking that, since Wyatt didn't like making copies, this had to be the only one. A guarded man, with a touch of the paranoiac running through him, she recalled, he had been an even more guarded, paranoiac writer, who never showed his works-in-progress to anyone, especially not other writers, because, as he said, there was nothing like seeing his ideas show up in someone else's prose.

"No, you can't," Henry said. "She'll just find another way into it. She's very crafty. She'll speak to your friends, and they won't even figure out what she's doing until it's too late."

"I'll warn them," she said, though when she thought about Louise and Jane she couldn't help but shudder.

"Your only option is to publish," he said, handing the manuscript back to her.

"Thank you for telling me about Antonia," she said as he turned to go back into the cottage and she thought, for some reason, that this would be last time she ever saw him. "Henry, wait. Where will you go?"

"Back to wonderful," he said cryptically, then shut the door.

Catherine stood at the cottage for another minute. As she herself turned to go, she thought she heard typing, and paused, wondering, as she drifted to her car, how she'd ever been able to stand the sound of it.

The Rose and the Milkweed

———

Henry sat at Wyatt's desk and typed. He wanted to record some of it at least, if for no one other than himself. He thought about the boy he'd been who'd started reading at the age of three and hadn't stopped since. He thought about all the stories he wrote when he was a teenager and then when he was an undergrad at Yale. His handicap as a fiction writer was well documented in the rejections he'd amassed over the years. Perhaps if he'd found a way into his own pain these stories might have succeeded. He had no way of accessing the pain, however, because he had been born without an imagination. He knew this, though he'd pressed on anyway. Even his marriage to Joyce hadn't helped him get published in her father's magazine, *Modern Scrivener,* which rejected him every time. Still, he never gave up, because what kind of writer would that make him? He kept revising, paring down, and resubmitting. In the meantime, he wrote the occasional book review for the magazine; he was good at that at least.

He enjoyed writing these reviews, because it was much easier to judge someone else's work than to create something of his own.

In reviewing, he thought he might eventually come to some better understanding of the craft, what made a good sentence, a good story, a good novel.

Henry typed. He wanted to record some of it before he went.

One editor who rejected him said that his story lacked an emotional core, as he called it. "Here, at the *Armadale Review,* we only publish stories with tenacity." Such words of encouragement! He thought about the last and final story he sent to Dillard Bloom nearly thirty years ago, and the usual rejection that followed. "You know my father has particular tastes," Joyce had reminded him. Yes, he knew. Still, why was it that some writers roll sixes, while others, like Henry, rolled twos? The numbers, it seemed, were against him.

In his youth, he'd also tried his hand at a novel, yet like the rest of his fiction, it had never found a home, either. He'd written the story of his life — a roman à clef — yet apparently the story of his life wasn't all that compelling. Well, no matter. It was his life, and it had been good, better than good — until six years ago, of course.

Henry got up — he couldn't sit still for long these days — and surveyed the study, then looked through the other rooms. He'd made this town his home for three years, and it had been kind to him, accepting him readily, as one of its own, even though he wasn't, and could never be. Mostly, though, it left him alone, and he was grateful to it. His celebrity did not matter here at all, and the townspeople had not bothered with him — until recently. Now it was different, and they looked at him differently as well. Someone at the local paper had written an article about the fire at his house, speculating on its cause. Though the police had ruled it an accident, Henry had known better. He'd meant to die in the fire while Antonia had been off in Manhattan. Six years of his life spent reliving that awful night on Osprey Point. He wondered even now how he'd managed it for as long as he had. Wren was always with him, just as surely as that other girl had to have been a constant companion to Linwood Lively. It was strange for him to think how much they had in common, yet how little — one girl dead on purpose, the other dead by chance. A single second, a turn of his head, and there she'd been in the middle of the road.

Henry folded and taped the boxes he'd bought and started on the main room, dropping things into them without thought or care. Then he started on the study, dumping his books willy-nilly into one box, the folders that contained all his reviews into another. He knew that somewhere inside one of the folders was the review of Wyatt's novel, which was, and always would be, the most perfidious review he'd ever written. He'd written it in half an hour, with a bottle of bourbon at his elbow, drinking it for clarity, he'd thought, not for courage.

He grabbed a trash bag and filled it with his students' stories, happy to be done with that part of his life as well. They were far too young to have anything to say, far too self-obsessed to leave themselves out of their work. Antonia had been one of the only exceptions in a lifetime of rules. And at twenty years old, she'd done what it took most writers a lifetime to do — regret nothing. In the beginning, he'd admired her for it, and at the end he hated her for it. Yet he suspected now that, like him, her young life would be spent regretting and regretting.

The facts of his story, their story, were unchangeable. Fiction went where facts could not go, he thought. He'd never told anyone the story about Wren, other than Wyatt, of course. (Why couldn't the agency of destruction also serve as the agency of mercy?) Now Catherine knew it as well, and he was glad about this. She knew about Dolores and Wren Novak, his neighbors on Osprey Point, and how Ezra and Wren used to play together in the summers. She knew how much he and Joyce adored Dolores, single working woman and mother, even though their lives were as different as the rose and the milkweed, despite living in the same garden. Like her mother, Wren had clear blue eyes and black hair, and she was precocious, reading by the time she was four. Ezra didn't read until he turned six, and even then it was with reluctance, which infuriated Henry. Secretly, he compared Ezra to Wren, and not so secretly Joyce to Dolores. Dolores took a keen interest in everything he said and everything he published, unlike his wife, who never quite listened to him and never read his essays or reviews. Catherine also now knew about why Henry had come to Winslow College and how he had kept waiting to run into her, how horrible it was to have to see Wyatt in the hall day after day. Wyatt who never spoke a single word to Henry, which had been fine, because he felt he deserved the silence. Antonia had found Henry, as Catherine had found him years before, and although utterly different in shape and size, they shared certain qualities of spirit: ambition, intelligence, perseverance. Antonia, however, was not nearly as kind or as malleable as Catherine. So Catherine now also knew how Henry saw her, and how, if she'd only believed in herself more, he might have been able to go on being with her.

I simply couldn't bear the weight of her selflessness, her need for me to anoint her, Henry had told Wyatt. She needed a man like you to tend to, to mold. I was already molded, hardened, and set. With every passing summer, he began to see the same fawning tendency in Wren. She belonged to Ezra, who bossed her around, and she let him, as if she were less than him, when, in truth, she was so much more. Henry loved her like she were his own, because she had a way with words from a very young age. She'll be a writer, he told Ezra. Wait and see. Now Catherine knew about how Henry had been at the beach house and how he had been in a mad dash to get back into the city, how he'd forgotten the review he'd been working on and how he'd gone speeding back to the house for it.

He'd been drinking, not heavily but enough, and the road

unwound before him like a black tongue. He'd been drinking, and he'd been tired, and he'd fallen asleep, just for a second.

At first, Henry thought he hit a deer. In all that blackness, this seemed the most logical thing, the most hopeful. It was winter and the houses along the road were dark, the stinging wind ripping across the dunes. Wren had been thrown into the reeds, and when he looked down at her, her eyes were still open, though there was not a part of her that wasn't broken. He sprinted to Dolores's and pounded on the door until she appeared in a nightgown and slippers, and Henry fell into her, sobbing. Wren died on the way to the hospital, and though it had been an accident, Dolores was out for blood. She didn't want his money. All she wanted, she told the lawyers, was that he should suffer the way she suffered every day. What she wanted was that he never forget — so every week, he was to sign the girl's name on a dollar bill and he had to have these bills ready to mail to Dolores without fail, anytime she might so request. Otherwise he would face prosecution for manslaughter. Knowing himself and that he wouldn't last a day in jail, he signed the settlement willingly. He didn't care about the other stipulations — that he was never to profit from the tragedy or that his driver's license had been revoked indefinitely. He had no desire to tell this story or to put it down on paper, and he had never liked to drive anyway.

Every week for six years, Henry had signed the single dollar bill, adding them to the stacks that had become like a chain around his neck, something to drag around with him wherever he went. Once again he packed the bundled bills into boxes and stacked them by the door. He would have them collected later. For now, he just wanted to leave, to be as far away from here as possible, to be so far away he would no longer feel the urge to turn around and go back for Antonia. He would leave, and he wouldn't stop until he found a place free of any bookstores and freer still of any fiction writers.

Chekhov's Smoking Gun

——————

After talking to Henry, Catherine made her way slowly through
the gate and up the stairs to the deck, where she sank down in
a lounge chair. *After all I've done for her,* she thought, stunned
at the realization of Antonia's betrayal. She gazed down at the
withered backyard, at the shriveled leaves and the lifeless bodies
of insects floating across the green-tinted, still water. That summer, she realized, was not unlike the pool, a shimmering watery
grave. Until Antonia had arrived on the porch, called out her
name, and stepped into her house, Catherine had pictured her life
in Winslow as one of these dead and dying things. Then, suddenly,
she'd found the strength to let go of the mourning, so buoyed was
she by the girl's spirited friendliness and disarming flattery. How
extraordinary it had been to sit with her and to hear how much
Wyatt's novel meant to her. How fabulous it had been to feel the
air charged again with hope. For a writer, Antonia had none of
Wyatt's penchant for melancholy, Catherine had noticed, none of
his debilitating professional jealousies. Antonia had not seemed
tormented in the least, and this, too, helped to fix her star brightly

in Catherine's heavens. She had genuinely liked the girl, she sensed she might even have loved her, not only because they shared a past with Henry but because the girl reminded her so much of herself.

Now this, too, was finished. Now she knew there would be no bonding trips together, no more cigarettes to share as they talked about future plans, no more glasses of wine or dinners or parties. It amazed her that she could end up here, exactly where she'd started, even after all they'd been through. There were no tears when she finally got up and went into the house, and no tears when she opened the bedroom door, peering nervously down at the bed, relieved not to find Antonia in it. After tonight, I am done with her, she thought, wandering into the kitchen. She drank a glass of wine to steady herself, though it did nothing more than make her incredibly sleepy.

As she lay down on the sofa, Catherine pictured the evening ahead and all that could go wrong with the bookstore event. The cheap sound system Harold had installed might act up, the attendance might be poor — although she'd taken steps to make sure it wouldn't be by placing last-minute announcements in the paper as well as posting flyers all over town — and who knew if another crazy member of Antonia's family might turn up and cause a scene: so many possibilities for failure. Yes, failure, she thought glumly, her mind returning to Wyatt's manuscript. She had failed him as his wife, or so she had read in his novel, yet hadn't he failed her as well? Instead of confronting her with his grievances, he'd let her go on as if all had been well. Instead of letting her explain, he had filled the pages with every ounce of his animus and resentment he had for her. She had gone on believing that Henry's review had led to his death, though now she had to wonder if she herself weren't to blame. How unhappy he'd been. "Oh, Wyatt," she said. "You should have come to me. I was your wife, not your enemy. I never meant to hurt you." Yet hurt him she had. Worse, though, than this was that she had wasted a year and a half of her life indulging her grief, crying over a man who had apparently never even liked her very much. She wondered if this made them even. And then she was shutting her eyes, even as she shut out these thoughts, knowing that she needed a nap if she were ever going to face Antonia and the evening ahead.

CATHERINE AWOKE TO dusk out the windows and the incessant ringing of the phone. Groggily, she stood up and went into the kitchen to find Harold screaming down the line. "Where the hell are you?" he said. "Do you know what time it is?" When she didn't answer, he said, "Time for you to get up here, Catherine. Everything — the folding chairs, the platters of food, the boxes of wine — was all just delivered right now. Tonight is your deal, remember? Do not let me down."

She'd been asleep for three hours, and in that time she'd done something awful to her back, which ached terribly, so much she could barely stand up straight. Not now, she thought bitterly, and reached over to touch her toes, just as she heard a knock at the door and Antonia calling out her name. She wasn't ready, not for any of this, and wanted nothing more than to crawl into bed and never leave it. She willed the pain in her back gone, though even thinking about it made it hurt more. There was nothing to do but live with it, she thought, because Harold was right — tonight was her deal.

She moved slowly to the door and opened it, and there was Antonia, smoking a cigarette, looking as she did all those weeks ago, perhaps a little less young, a little less vibrant, but still Antonia Lively, still the girl that Catherine had come to know, to like, to trust. "I thought we could go up to the store together," Antonia said, stepping past Catherine into the sitting room. In one hand, she held her purse and in the other, her novel. "I still haven't figured out what I'm going to read. Maybe you can suggest something. Tell me your favorite scene and that's what I'll read," she said.

"Oh, I don't know," Catherine said, wincing as her entire back spasmed and she leaned over to stretch the muscles. Then, "You see what you have to look forward to when you're my age?"

"Just stop it. You aren't old," Antonia said. "I used to get backaches all the time until I met — " She paused. "I've been told that lower backaches are a sign of financial stress. Is it your lower back?" Catherine said that it was and went to sit on the sofa, unable to bear standing, unable also, she conceded, to bear Antonia's presence. She wondered then if the backache was a manifestation of the betrayal she was feeling. Please get out of here and never come back, she thought. "Look, you should let me help you out, Catherine. I have so much money now, and I'm your friend, and that's what friends do."

"In exchange for what?" she asked sharply, too sharply, she thought, and regretted it instantly.

"I'm sorry?" Antonia said. "What do you mean by that?"

"Nothing," she said. "I didn't mean anything by it." She sensed, though, that the current in the room had shifted, the air around them seeming to darken.

"Yes, you did," Antonia said. "I've gotten to know you, and I know that you don't say anything you don't mean. So I'm going to ask you again: what did you mean by that?"

"We really should be getting to the store," Catherine said and tried to rise, but couldn't. "I'm going to need your — "

"We'll go, but not until you tell me what you meant," Antonia said firmly. She took a step forward, and paused. "I'm doing you a favor by giving this reading, remember, so the least you could do is be honest with me."

Catherine stared at her, and it was as if the girl she had known — had imagined, she thought with displeasure — was fading to become the girl she had always been. In the last of the light, she could just make out Antonia's face, the severity in it, and noticed again just how unattractive she was. "Henry told me everything," she said at last. "He told me what you've been doing in that house. He told me all about your second novel."

Antonia took another step forward, then paused again. "You'd really believe anything that came out of that man's mouth?" she asked. "I'm surprised at you, Catherine. I didn't take you for an idiot."

I am an idiot, she thought sadly. She had just wanted a friend, a new friend, and here is what she had gotten instead. "Has it all been one big lie, or just most of it?" she asked.

"Oh, you people," Antonia said, stomping her feet in frustration. "Where is it written that certain stories are forbidden to tell? Look at the world we live in, Catherine. I am a part of the world we live in, whereas you've always just been a visitor in it. I ask too many questions and I'm way too nosy and sometimes I hate myself for it, but it's always with one purpose in mind — to get to the truth, because the truth is what I do."

"The truth is what you do," Catherine said, trying to rise again. "You're twenty-three years old. I'm not sure you'd recognize the truth even if it bit you on the leg. There is a vast difference between what we know and what we think we know, and some stories, I'm sorry to say, just aren't meant to be told, no matter how badly we'd like to tell them." Henry was right about her, she thought. She does think she's above it all.

"Do you know why I write fiction?" she asked. "Because I get to write about what I know, and learn about what I don't. I get to discover the story as I go along. It's never static, it's always in flux, but you have to have the facts before you can begin to alter them. That's why you're going to let me see Wyatt's manuscript." And she turned her eyes from Catherine to the room, searchingly. "I didn't come all this way for nothing, and you can't honestly believe I'd let this story go because it's going to hurt your feelings. No one cares where the story came from, only that it was told. I'll tell it well, Catherine. Why can't anyone ever see that I love my characters as much as I love the people they're based on? Why isn't that ever mentioned? I'm not just some selfish girl sitting at a desk. I'm a selfless writer trying to understand why we do the things we do and why we hurt the people we most love. What else is there, Catherine?"

Catherine didn't know. She didn't have an answer, and she didn't want to think about the question. She didn't know why anyone wrote. It seemed to her suddenly like the most ignoble profession anyone could have. Ignoble, ugly, self-indulgent, irrelevant — and just plain mean. She struggled off the sofa at last and moved painfully, slowly, past Antonia to the door. "There is propriety. There is privacy. Certain stories remain hidden because certain stories cause too much pain. I didn't see it until this very moment, but you feed off the pain and suffering of others," she said, opening the door, knowing that the moment Antonia left, the night and her job would be lost for good. "Now, if you don't mind, I'd like you to leave." Yet even as she held the door open and Antonia gazed through it, she understood that she would have to go on with her life as she had had to go on after Wyatt's death. Antonia had been right about one thing at least — for the last year and a half, perhaps even farther back than this, Catherine had been a visitor in the world. She had clung fiercely to what little remained in the hopes of spinning the flimsy gray threads of her days into something more durable, something with value and weight. Tonight she finally saw that she had only managed to fray the threads until they had fallen apart in her fingers, as thin and as light as cobwebs.

When Antonia took a step toward her, Catherine braced herself by shutting her eyes. She felt the whoosh of air as Antonia hurried past her and onto the porch, where she stopped and said, "Like certain people, we stumble upon a story by accident and only when we're ready, Catherine. You might not be ready to let the story go, but I'm certainly ready to take it from you."

Catherine opened her eyes, angry now, and slammed the door. Then she hobbled over to the counter and grabbed her purse, because she had to face Harold; she owed him this much, she thought. Though she'd hoped and expected to have seen the last of Antonia, the girl still had not left the property. Now she was banging on the cottage door, shouting Henry's name. When she heard Catherine approach, she spun around and asked, "He's in there, isn't he?" Yet Catherine simply shrugged. As Antonia returned to her assault on the door, Catherine turned to see a figure standing across the street. In the dark, she had a hard time making him out. It can't be, she told herself, as she felt a flash of fear, and her back spasmed again. She had no idea what Royal Lively was doing across the street, when she'd been told that he had been arrested. He was not wearing his suit or his hat, like he had the last time she'd seen him, though she would have recognized his imposing posture anywhere.

Catherine was just about to warn Antonia about him when she lifted up her foot to take a step, and her back gave out. As she stumbled, she lost her grip on the purse, which tumbled out of her hands, the compact, lipstick, and manuscript spilling out. The girl looked down and without a moment's hesitation reached for the manuscript. Then she sat down in one of the chairs, Henry forgotten for now. Catherine watched her unroll the rubber band and flip through the pages with an avidity she had never seen before. As she massaged the small of her back, the pain radiating up and down her spine, she wished she could do something to stop her. All the while, she kept wondering about Royal, and turning her head, she glanced at the spot where he had been standing; he was no longer there. His presence continued to baffle and appall her, just as Antonia's behavior continued to distress her. When I get hold of the manuscript again, I'm burning it to ashes, she thought, trying to rise but falling back, again.

Then, suddenly, Catherine heard him behind her, a mere rustle coming from the lilac bush, nothing more, and she called out to Antonia. Later, after it was all over and they were rolling Catherine away on a stretcher, she could recall only the merest of fragments — Royal rushing out of the bush and Antonia dropping the manuscript, the pages being scattered by the wind, the horror on her face as Antonia watched them go, then turning her eyes on Royal, even as she went rummaging through her purse and rising from the chair and closing her eyes and Catherine saw the shiny flash of the gun in her fingers, which she was pointing directly above Catherine's head. The air sounded with an enormous, explosive echo, as Royal Lively crumpled to the ground. When Catherine opened her eyes again and picked herself up from the ground where she, too, had fallen, she looked at the man sprawled behind her. She let out a cry, because it was not Royal Lively lying there but his brother, Linwood, Antonia's father, who lay bleeding from a wound in his throat. She would recall how Antonia was again in the dirt gathering up the loose pages and how Catherine made her way over to her, wanting to comfort her, which shocked her, as it had been the last thing on her mind — to comfort this child who had just murdered her father.

"Antonia," she said, but the girl was frantic now, grasping for this page and that page, seemingly unaffected by what she'd just done, by any of it, the gun now lying discarded in the earth. Unable to bend, Catherine had no way of getting the gun, no way of getting the pages, though she tried her best anyway, even as the girl ferociously swatted her away. "Antonia," Catherine repeated, and pointed to the man lying in the dark behind her. The girl, though, didn't seem to hear her, focused as she was on the pages, which the wind kept blowing away. Antonia was about to go after them but then stopped abruptly and stood up, as if what had happened had just registered. She gazed past Catherine, then took a step toward her father. When at last she realized what she'd done, every part of the girl drooped, her bones seeming to liquefy, and before Catherine could stop her, she had picked up the gun, and had brought it to her mouth. At least this was what Catherine thought she'd seen her do, but she couldn't be sure. She couldn't be sure of anything. She was only certain that she'd found the strength to rush at Antonia, knocking the gun out of the girl's hand, though not before she'd already pulled the trigger and the pages went flying from her hand, the wind scattering them once more, all the pages of that godawful book, and the breath was leaving Catherine's body, the ground rising up to her as her legs gave out again. The last thing she remembered before she collapsed was the blackness of the night rushing over her, and the earth under her, dampening from the blood that escaped from the hole in her chest.

Buzzards above the Bed

———————

After that, the night seemed to Catherine to be a constant surge of police officers and doctors and nurses, who came and went from her hospital room. To the police officers, she tried her best to explain what had happened, and to the doctors and nurses, she tried her best to convince them that she was fine to go home. She wasn't fine, they told her. You've been shot, they told her. Rest now. They gave her morphine for the pain, and she sank into happy oblivion for a while. When she woke, the room was empty, though not entirely, because Wyatt was sitting in the chair beside the bed. "Oh, Wyatt, you're here," she said. "I just had the craziest dream . . . We'd rented the cottage to Henry. Why would we do that?"

"Henry's gone. Hush now," he said, and she did.

When she woke for the second time, Linwood Lively was sitting in the chair where Wyatt had been. "Oh, Linwood, you came back for her. She thought you were her uncle . . ."

"You have to tell her now," he said.

"Tell her what?" she asked.

"The novel," he said, and that was all.

When she woke up for the third time, it was morning, and no one was sitting in the chair.

They kept her for two days, then released her. The bullet had entered and exited without consequence, passing through her and leaving a deep flesh wound that would heal in time. She wore a bandage. "

You're lucky," the doctor told her.

She didn't feel lucky.

JANE HAD SENT her jonquils, her favorite, but she did not take them home with her. She dropped the card in the trash, the card on which she'd written *I'm still your friend. Love, Jane.* She had not visited. No one had.

WHEN THE TAXI approached the house, Catherine shuddered, gazing out the dusty window at her quiet, tree-lined block, at the familiar sights, the familiar cars in the familiar driveways. Everything looked exactly as it always had, except that nothing was exactly as it had been. The painkillers worked marvelously, giving her a buffer against the chilling reality. She paid the driver, then she was standing at the edge of her yard. It was a hot, stuffy day, no wind, no sound, not even birds singing in the trees, which she found odd. It was as if someone had come along and vacuumed up every sound, she thought, remembering that she'd had the same thought on the afternoon she'd gone to see Henry. She moved slowly toward the cottage, knowing that he wasn't inside it anymore, wishing suddenly that he was. Wishing that she'd never written that letter to her dean, wishing that he'd never been ousted from NYU, wishing that she'd chosen a different course of study than comparative literature.

In the house, Catherine disrobed, then took a shower, careful to keep the bandage dry. The muscles of her shoulder and chest were stiff, but that was about the extent of it. There were other pains, hidden and deep, that surfaced and sank again, as she moved about the rooms. She thought about Antonia and the gun, and about her father. The police had taken Catherine's statement, then asked her if she wanted to press charges, but she told them she wanted to forget it, so no charges were drawn up.

We're looking into the other matter, they told her, and asked her to explain again how Antonia had gotten hold of the gun.

"I lent it to her," Catherine said, surprised at herself. "For protection."

"The gun is registered to a Harold Brody," they said. "He reported it stolen."

"Not stolen," she said. "I borrowed it. I told him that. He just didn't remember. Antonia was unsafe," she went on. "Her uncle . . ."

"The one we apprehended," they said.

"Yes, him," she said. "It was dark. Neither one of us knew. We thought it was him."

"Then you thought you were both in imminent danger," they said.

"Yes," she said. "Imminent and horrible danger."

"So it really was self-defense and an accident. Is that what you're telling us?" they asked.

"Yes," she said. "What else could it have been but an accident?"

Catherine dressed, then pulled the small suitcase down from the attic, and filled it up with clothes. She grabbed her purse and her keys and headed out to her car. She needed to be somewhere, anywhere that was away from here, and she was about to get into her car when she looked down to see a book — a battered copy of Antonia's novel — sticking out from under her car. She picked it up and tossed it in the passenger's seat, then threw the suitcase in back. She was leaving. As she reversed out of the drive, she gazed at the cottage, at the spot where she'd fallen in the dirt, still stained with her blood. She looked also at the spot where Linwood Lively had died. She sighed. Nothing was right or would ever be right again, she knew, and Catherine felt the summer expand and contract around her. She thought about the day Antonia had shown up at her door, called out her name, and stepped into the house, drawing Catherine away from the chaos of grieving. Moments like these came out of nowhere, the announcement of a stranger. But who had been the real stranger, Antonia or her?

Life sends us people all the time, she thought, and we either invite them in or send them on their way. On that afternoon in June, she had invited Antonia into her house and felt the passing of something between them.

Catherine took the road that led over the Kissing Swans Bridge and crossed the sparkling water, thinking about Wyatt. She hadn't been back to the bridge in ages. In a few hours, the bats would awaken and take flight, filling the night. The further she drove, the more her thoughts returned to Henry, but she was going, heading into the mountains and beyond them to the interstate. The Corolla shuddered the higher she climbed, and she wondered if she'd make it. The engine groaned, the gears cranked, and the radio came in and out, broken lyrics and sharp crackles of static. She gazed down at Antonia's novel, at the girl's face staring up at her. In it she saw her own face, or at least a resemblance. In the photo, Antonia was smiling, looking out from clear blue eyes that hadn't yet seen the sights of this summer.

Finally the car stalled. It was an old, unreliable car, but she loved it and talked to it now, saying, "You can do it," saying, "Don't let me down." When it started again, she turned it around and headed back into Winslow, to the garage, where she dropped the car off, knowing that she had no money to pay for whatever the mechanics would find wrong with it. Then, reluctantly, she called Jane, who was there in fifteen minutes, happy to see her, overjoyed that she'd called. Jane, her friend, and when Catherine saw her she began to cry, and began to tell her the story about Antonia Lively, and about all that was, and all that was not, and about all that would never be.

The House at
the End of the Block

————

Catherine spent a week with Jane, who nursed her and changed her bandages. She got her tea and scones from Maddox Cafe and brought home a different movie for them to watch every night. To Catherine, it was almost like being back at college, with only the best parts of it. They were girls again, and they went swimming in Jane's tidy, well-kept pool and had dinner on the sunporch, under swirling ceiling fans. Catherine was pleased that Jane did not mention what had happened, or encourage her again to bring up Antonia or Henry.

One afternoon, Catherine was headed out for a walk, when she saw Jane pull up in the Corolla. It was dusk and the distant mountains were gilded under the last of the sun. "No more stalling," Jane said, handing Catherine the car key. "It should run for another hundred years, or so they tell me."

Jane had had the car detailed, and she'd put in a new stereo. "I'll repay you," Catherine said, getting into the car and closing the door. She was surprised by how much she'd missed having the car around.

"No, you won't," Jane said. "I can't believe you didn't get the car checked out sooner, though. They told me that it was completely unsafe to drive."

Catherine thanked her, then pulled out of the driveway, not knowing where she was going, simply wanting to drive. As she did, she thought about Wyatt and the day they'd bought the car and how he'd told her that it was only temporary. "Until I sell my next novel and make a bundle, and then I'll buy you whatever you want," he'd said. He had not made a bundle, and he had not been able to buy Catherine whatever she wanted, yet she had never cared about any of that. Not really. She had only cared that they were together, that she would wake up beside him every morning and go to bed with him every night. She had only cared that he was in the next room, working, that he would always be around. She missed him more than ever and knew then that she always would. She would go on missing him even after the summer was over, and the winter came, and then the spring and the summer again. She would miss him, even though he'd written such horrible things about her. Despite everything, he had loved her, and she had loved him — of that she was certain — and the story of their lives together was as much about that love as it was about their mutual grievances. Wasn't every marriage like this?

The pages of his novel had blown away that day; as they had carried her to the ambulance, she'd watched them go, watched the wind scatter them up and down the block, into the yards and the gutters and the trees. She had watched it all go, and it was as if the wind had taken her away as well. She drove into town, until she came to Broad Street, where she passed slowly by Page Turners. She had spoken to Harold briefly on the phone, and he had told her that she could come back, if she wanted, but she didn't want to come back. "Not now," she'd said, "maybe later," though she knew, as she hung up the phone, that later would never come. She had spent nine years of her life behind the register, helping customers, shelving and reshelving books, ordering the bookmarks, designing the display window, which, she now saw, still held Antonia's novel. She had heard that it was still selling well, even better than expected, and that someone, a big producer in Hollywood, had optioned it for film. Good for her, she thought as she left Broad Street and made her way to her own. She passed her house and the cottage, both of which were dark and empty, though tomorrow, when she came back, she would clean out the cottage and then put an ad in the weekly looking for a new tenant. A woman, she thought. A woman with a real job. She would run a credit check on her. She would charge her seven hundred dollars a month.

She hadn't known it until she'd arrived at the house down the block that this had been her intention all along. It's not that she wanted to talk to Antonia or share a cigarette with her again; it's only that she wanted to make sure the girl was all right. Yes, even after all of that, Catherine still felt partially responsible for her. Still felt that she had, in some way, been taken advantage of. It was naive of her to think about Antonia in such a light, she knew, yet she liked being naive, she liked being the least bit gullible. It softened the edges of the world.

As she stood on the veranda and knocked, she thought about Antonia's father, about her own, about the men who came into their lives and pushed their way through, about the detritus they left in their wake. She knocked again, but Antonia never came to the door. It was just as well, she thought, wandering back down the sidewalk and turning to look at the house. And there she was, a cigarette in her fingers, the smoke curling into the air. Though they'd become friendly, they'd never become friends, not in the way Catherine had wanted. She spoke Antonia's name, feeling

grateful for the first time that there were years and a distance between them, that Antonia was there and she was here, that their
lives had briefly touched and that she'd gotten to taste what it
might be like to be this girl. No, she'd never need what Antonia
needed, never move through the world the way she did, and she
was happy for this, happier now than she'd been. Though she'd
lost a lot of her grounding that summer, she knew she'd given up
much less than Antonia had. Catherine also knew that years from
now, she could look back and say, Yes, I didn't have everything, but
what I had was more than enough.

She had also gone to Antonia's house to get Wyatt's typewriter
back, but she saw that she'd leave without it. Because a typewriter
without the ambitious man who used it, she realized, is just another typewriter. Ambition, she now thought, took hold of everyone, and kept everyone in a constant state of yearning, even if
what they yearned for was the success that came at the expense of
someone else's failure.

Then, without saying a word, Antonia turned and disappeared
into the house. As Catherine watched, the wind picked up and
the cicadas went noisy in the trees, the moon shining down from a
clear sky. There, while standing at the edge of the yard, she heard
the sound of the typewriter, this familiar, energetic music. She listened for a minute, a minute out of a lifetime, and in this sound
she heard the voices of the summer. She heard Antonia's industry
and, yes, even her love, and as she turned away from it and took a
step toward her car, the typing faded into other sounds — the birds
in the trees, the barking dogs — and was eventually lost for good.

The Redemptive Power
of Fiction

———

We come to stories only when we're ready for them, Antonia once told me, though I'm not sure I was ever ready for this one. It was never mine and belonged to others, to Wyatt and Catherine, to Henry and Antonia, to Linwood and Royal. Wyatt and Linwood were dead, though, Henry and Royal gone, and I knew Catherine didn't have the stomach to tell it — not many people would. As for Antonia — let's just say I got there first.

Henry had been right when he'd said that Antonia would make a name for herself. She did. No publisher, however, would touch her second attempt, as Henry had also predicted (and perhaps made sure of). Even I, a complete novice when it came to writing fiction, knew enough not to slander my characters. How she made such a silly, amateurish mistake, given her talents and her smarts, still astounds me, as it must have astounded anyone who read about it. The publishing industry, like love, I have learned, has a punishing memory. To this day, I have never seen a single indication that it ever forgot or forgave Antonia her mistakes.

All this happened many years ago, however, and I'm not the

same woman I was when I first sat down to write this story. I'm older now, thirty-nine, the same age Catherine was when she first set eyes on Antonia. Perhaps you knew this already, but here's something you might not know — after Wyatt had finished writing his second novel, he uncharacteristically made a copy of it and had given that copy to me, because he loved me and because I loved him and because he wanted me to know everything. He might have still loved Catherine, yet his life with her, as he told it to me, had turned unbearable. "She's cold," he'd said. "She's nothing like she used to be."

Our affair began the way most affairs do — with an unhappy spouse turning to his wife's best friend for support, to help him figure out what to do. I knew Catherine, better than Wyatt apparently did, and so naturally he came to me.

His death was shocking. I still like to imagine that he wasn't on his way to my house that morning. Of course, I felt guilty. Who wouldn't, after sleeping with her best friend's husband?

Yet tonight, as I get ready for my reading, I have to remind myself that this is not about Catherine anymore. This is about my enduring love for Wyatt, who gave me a copy of his manuscript, a gift, because I knew he never showed his work to anyone. Ever. Such intimacy between us, such sweetness.

I knew everything, and all it took was the will to write it.

Stumbling upon Linwood's confession that he'd written down in a copy of Antonia's novel, however, was a coup. I'd found it when I'd picked up Catherine's car from the garage. The novel was just sitting there, on the seat, which I found odd, given what she had been through. Clearly, Catherine hadn't bothered to look at it, because if she had, everything might have gone differently.

Perhaps the most terrible thing isn't that Antonia took the story from her uncle and made it her own, or that she agreed with it so willingly and thus incriminated her father in a brutal, senseless crime, but that she omitted the most important, most exonerating details that would have helped to clear his name.

Fiction is always pressed up against some truth, Wyatt used to say. I couldn't imagine the sort of burdensome truth that Antonia had had to carry around, after running into a man who knew more about her than she knew about herself. To the best of my knowledge, this is how it happened: Poor Linwood had returned that night to deliver the novel to Antonia. He had wanted her to know the truth, as I had finally known it — that he had gone back to that cabin in the woods later and had carried that girl to her sister's house. That she hadn't bled to death on the mattress, as Antonia had written, but nine months later, during childbirth. Sylvie was her mother, and Sylvie's sister, poor, single, and alone, had given the child to Linwood. The product of a rape, the daughter of the men who'd killed her mother. It didn't matter to Linwood if he or his brother were the father. The only thing that mattered was that he would do right by Sylvie.

Yet Royal believed that he was Antonia's rightful father, even though he had no proof of this, even though Linwood had raised her. She looked more like Royal and that was enough for him. This was the story Royal told Antonia that night at the party, before Catherine had found her in the backseat of her car. Antonia was their agreement. Linwood never wanted her to know about her origins.

Tonight I am in Manhattan, and tomorrow I will be in another city. I leave the hotel and get into my car, place my novel on the seat beside me, my picture facedown, because I cannot bear to see myself, the fine lines of my face airbrushed out, my hair highlighted and sprayed into perfection, the thin lips, the black cashmere cardigan hanging loosely open, revealingly. The publishing house hired a famous photographer to take the picture. He was twenty years old, if a day, and kept telling me to "think young, think sexy." But I could not think young, I could not think sexy, I could only think about Wyatt and Catherine, and the way this story smashed our summer to smithereens.

These pages, I hope, are as much a testament to my friendship with her as they are an honest rendition of its loss.

It was a trade-off, it always is, I think, the lives of others for one's own. Yet hadn't I suffered, too? Hadn't I nearly been shot and killed by her hand?

I never really got over it, I suppose, my anger festering over the years while I taught myself how to write. I didn't know until I started this story, though, how much that anger had been feeding my need for revenge. Such an ugly thing, revenge, yet look at what it produced.

Sometimes I wake up in the middle of the night and I sense that Royal Lively is standing over me, or it's Wyatt or it's Catherine. Sometimes it's Antonia, wielding the gun. I know she's never that far behind me. I know one day we'll just happen to run into each other. I bought a handgun, just in case.

I get to the bookstore — Three Lives & Company — on West Tenth Street. The bookstore is packed, I assume, because of the laudatory review I got in *Modern Scrivener:* "[Jane Iris Miller] could just be the greatest fiction writer of her generation, and Ms. Miller's novel, *Antonia Lively Breaks the Silence,* is nothing short of ingenious and nothing less than a page-turner."

I clipped the review out and stuck it on the fridge next to Henry's yellowing review of Wyatt's novel. I kept it to remind myself just how cruel and random the publishing world could be. Henry remained hateful, sad, complicated, misunderstood — though without him would I have had the teeth for this story?

Some of the faces in the bookstore look familiar; most of them, though, are not. Even as I shake hands with my fans, I am taken back to Page Turners, feeling the pull to straighten the shelves, to ask someone if he needs my help locating a book. Odd, isn't it, how things stay with us.

When Catherine steps forward, I almost don't recognize her. Under the dim lights, she looks much older, the last youthful traces finally gone. She looks old now, I think, yet she is still the same Catherine I remember, attractive in an unassuming, unthreatening kind of way, her manner cool and reserved, as Wyatt had often complained. I did not expect to see her again, especially not after having sent her a galley of my novel. I included a short note with it, because I thought I owed her as much: *You will recognize yourself in these pages. I am truly sorry about that. I have changed your name to protect you, though, as I have changed every name, including Winslow, which is and is not our town, just as you are and are not Catherine Strayed. I hope you take some comfort in this.*

Though I do not believe in spirits, I suddenly feel Antonia in the room, too, as if she followed Catherine into the bookstore. I never knew her well and feel tonight like I know her even less. If I had known her better, might I have been able to change the course of that summer? Perhaps the real tragedy isn't the friendship I lost in Catherine but the friendship I never made in Antonia.

Catherine says nothing, doesn't even look at me, as she takes her seat in back, and I think about Wyatt, the months I grieved for him in secret, even as I kept showing up at Catherine's house with playing cards, board games, anything to distract her. I never once let myself cry in front of her, yet every time I stepped into that house, I was meeting Wyatt again, his smell lingering in the air, his voice. In one irrevocable moment, Wyatt had gone from the man whom Catherine and I had shared into an ugly secret that would turn us into enemies.

Here, then, is my enemy, who was once my friend, and, oh, how I want to tell her how good it is to see her, but I know enough not to.

After I am introduced, and the room finishes clapping, I go to the podium and look out over the faces. Young and old, men and women, white and black — these people who have come out on this freezing winter night because my novel has touched them in some way. I thank them for coming. I tell them I hope they won't be disappointed, that I'm not a very good reader. I take a sip of water. Then I clear my throat, open up the book, and begin.

"We thought ourselves good people who lived good lives."

Acknowledgments

A gigantic thank-you to Emma Sweeney, who worked her agent mojo and made all of this possible; to Chuck Adams, good friend and editor rolled into one—how lucky I am; to Kelly Bowen, publicist extraordinaire, and to the rest of the amazing crew at Algonquin Books—the first time I met all of you I knew I'd found the right home.

To my awesome copy editor, Jude Grant—there will be a special place in heaven for you.

Shout-outs and much love to the following people: Angela Sinclair, Kimberly Elkins, Sarah Goodyear, Aaron Hamburger, Emily Stone, Michael Thomas, Naomi Schegloff, Jane South, Sean and Jennalie Lyons, Brian Sloan, Joel Childress, Catherine Curan, Lisa Dierbeck, Laurel Cohen-Pfister, Steven Stern, Martin Kley, Gabrielle Danchick, Yvète Morales, Kate Christensen, Beena Kamlani, and Fred Morris. Without friendships and support like yours, I probably would have hung it up ages ago.

To the lovely folks at Jentel, Yaddo, Ledig House, the Carson McCullers Center, and Gettysburg College, who gave me shelter during some of the writing of this book.

And an enduring thanks to Bret Easton Ellis and to Dale Peck, whose generosities know no limits, as well as to Gerrit Jackson, who lugged an unwieldy, unedited version of this book with him from place to place and who made my life more wonderful and more full than it has ever been. Bitte das Klischee verzeihen, denn ich werde dich immer lieben und vermissen.